KIRSTY SCOTT

Between You & Me

HODDER

First published in Great Britain in 2007 by Hodder & Stoughton
An Hachette Livre UK company

First published in paperback in 2008

I

A CIP catalogue record for this title is available from the British Library

ISBN 978 0 340 89555 9 (B format)
ISBN 978 0 340 93327 5 (A format)

Typeset in Plantin Light by Palimpsest Book Production
Grangemouth, Stirlingshire

Printed and bound by Clays Ltd, St Ives plc

Hodder & Stoughton Ltd
338 Euston Road
London NW1 3BH

www.hodder.co.uk

For Mum and Dad, with love and thanks.

Acknowledgements

A big thank you as ever to Annette Green, my agent, for all her help and support, and to Sara Kinsella, my wonderful editor, for her expertise and encouragement. Also the rest of the Hodder team, particularly Isobel Akenhead, Emma Knight and Bob McDevitt.

To Claire and Murray McMillan, for casting a critical eye, and Sandra Lewis, Sue Parsons, Lorraine Ferguson and Christine Jardine, for their interest and support.

And finally, to Homer, Christina and Keir, for everything.

Prologue

Margie Holland sat on the loo and looked at the white plastic wand that was balanced on the sink, pointing towards her like a pale, accusing finger. It had a squareish spongy tip like the flattened butt of one of her mum's cigarettes, and she had been careful not to place it in the soapy slick from the bar of Camay leaking onto the avocado-green ceramic. She reached out with a shaky hand and repositioned the small plastic well beside the wand, memorising the instructions from the sharply folded piece of paper that had come in the box. Hold in urine stream and place in vial. Opposite her, on the windowsill, the plastic doll whose capacious crochet skirt hid a new toilet roll stared down with wide-eyed disapproval. Margie felt her throat constrict with rising panic.

Hold in urine stream. Place in vial. Die a death.

'Have you done it yet?' The voice outside the door was a half-whisper, but she jumped as if it had been a shout.

'Fuck, Cate. No!'

There was a muttered apology and then a pause. 'Do you want a hand?'

It was such a ridiculous thing to ask that Margie felt a snigger bubble instinctively within her. 'No!'

'Okay.' Cate was still whispering. 'And you're absolutely sure your mum's not coming back?'

'Yeah,' said Margie. 'Bingo finishes at ten, then they go round to Aunty Betty's to drown their sorrows. I told you.'

They had heard the front door shut as they lay across Margie's bed, trying to distract themselves from what was to come with revision for the English exam, as if Alfred Lord Tennyson could help. Margie had levered herself up and walked over to the window, pulling the net curtain to one side. Her mum was halfway down the path, clutching her coat closed with one hand in the odd way she always did as if she didn't want the world to see her. There had been no goodbye, but then there never was. Margie had blown a contemptuous kiss into the empty air and had let the net curtain drop slowly through her fingers, feeling the scratch of cheap nylon, unwilling to let go.

Cate had looked at her questioningly and Margie had nodded and said, 'Fuck,' very quietly, and Cate had said, 'It'll be fine,' which was mad because she didn't know if it would.

'But you're going to do it now, though.' Cate's voice had grown a little louder through the door. 'I've got the other stuff all set. Just . . . when you're ready.'

'Okay.'

'Okay.'

Margie heard Cate move away and she reached out for the applicator, gripping it firmly and angling herself on the seat. She felt the warm rush of urine and held the stick into it, suddenly wanting to giggle, realising as she did that the tears had come, hot and stinging in her eyes.

She bit her lip and tried not to mind the splashes on her hand, tried not to think of the look on his face when he came out of her, the boy with the razor rash and the Suzuki GSX. The condom, limp in his hand. 'It came off a bit,' he had said, and smiled feebly as her world fractured.

She wondered what her mum would say if she knew what Margie was doing right now. Jesus, Mary and Joseph would probably come into it.

How long was that? Enough? She counted to ten and

lifted the stick out, stabbing it into the small well with panicked precision and laying it back on the sink's edge as she pulled up her pants and flushed and washed, prising the Camay from the sink and scrubbing her hands as if she were Lady Macbeth.

Cate had set the other small vial on the dressing-table top with the instruction leaflet smoothed out neatly beside it. Two red patches had appeared on her cheeks. Cate always went scarlet if she was anxious. Or really scared.

'Did you rinse the end after it had been in the first one for two minutes?' she asked.

Margie nodded, holding the wand awkwardly like a toddler grasping a spoon.

'Well it needs to go in this one now.' Cate watched as Margie placed the wand in the second vial. 'All we need's a Bunsen burner,' she added, forcing a laugh. 'It's kind of like being in Mr McCulloch's class, isn't it?'

'Yeah,' said Margie, flatly. Only it wasn't.

'So.' Cate sat back on her heels. 'Half an hour and then we look to see if the end's . . .'

'Blue,' said Margie.

'It's not going to be.' Cate reached over and grabbed her hand. 'It's really not.'

Margie held on tight. Seventeen and pregnant. Five weeks away from leaving school.

'Fuck,' she said quietly again. 'Fuck.'

The cassette deck clicked noisily to the end of the tape and Cate leant over the bed and rifled through the neat stack of tapes piled in two rows on Margie's desk.

'What do you want next?'

'No more Bon Jovi,' said Margie.

Cate picked out *Now That's What I Call Music 9* and slotted it into the machine. The urgent beat of Europe's 'The Final Countdown' filled the room.

'Maybe not.' Margie pulled a face, and Cate quickly pressed fast-forward until she came in three songs on, at the Pretenders' 'Hymn to Her'.

They sat side by side on the end of the bed.

'If it is . . . if I am,' said Margie, twisting her fingers together, 'I'm getting rid of it.' She looked down at her stomach, flat under grey gabardine. The thought of something growing there made her feel sick.

'I know. But it won't be.' Cate reached for her hand again and Margie noticed Cate's bitten nails. She'd only started biting them since her dad had died. Just last November. When her perfect ordinary life was dismantled in an instant. What a shitty, shitty year.

'Where's the Kahlua?' asked Margie, noticing the sweet hint of liqueur on Cate's breath.

'Under the bed.'

'Why is it under the bed?'

'In case your mum came in.' Cate fished below the covers and pulled out the brown bottle with the yellow label. She handed it over.

'You know she doesn't,' said Margie, unscrewing the lid and filling her mouth with the thick creamy liquid.

It was why they only drank here, because Cate's mum *did* come in. 'You girls!' she would laugh when she found them singing or mucking about. Maybe if her mum was more like Cate's she'd be in the room now, waiting with her. Cate could tell her mum if it happened to her. Cate's mum would want to know. Cate's mum would care. Margie passed the bottle back.

'I'll need to borrow your toothbrush before I go home,' said Cate, taking another gulp and handing it back. 'My brother kept sniffing at me last time, like a dog or something.'

Margie nodded and sat holding the bottle between her legs. Cate reached for it again and took another long draught.

4

'Steady on,' said Margie.

'I could do your hair,' said Cate suddenly.

'Okay.' Margie knew Cate was trying to distract her, but she couldn't think of anything else that might work better. She lifted herself off the bed and went to sit at the dressing-table.

'How do you want it?'

'Straight,' said Margie.

'No, really.'

'Different.' She bent her head and felt Cate's hands, soft and tugging in her curls. Cate took her time combing it, then she eased a hairband over Margie's crown, and pulled a thin, sprung curl from under the elastic at one side.

'There,' said Cate. 'Kind of . . . Bananarama.' She sat back and took another swig from the bottle.

Margie looked up and into the mirror. 'Bananarama? I look more like fucking John McEnroe.' She raised her hand and pulled at the loose curl, now twisting around her ear. 'What's this?'

'A tendril,' said Cate. 'It looks cute.'

'It looks like a giant pube, that's what it looks like.' Margie tore the band from her head and pinged it across the room. She looked back at her reflection and gave a mock wail. 'I hate my fucking hair.'

'Maybe you could iron it,' offered Cate. 'My mum saw a programme on telly where the woman ironed her hair.'

'That would look nice,' said Margie. 'Big scabby burns all over your head. You're a nutter, Cate Wishart.'

'You don't put the iron on your head, dipstick,' said Cate. 'You put your hair on the ironing-board.'

Her laugh was forced, though, and they both went quiet.

Cate must have seen her try to glance at the bedside clock because she said, 'It's only been about ten minutes.'

'I know.'

5

Cate nodded numbly. 'Do you want to go for a walk or something?'

Margie shook her head. The tape had ended again and Cate crossed the room and switched it for another one, then sank down against Margie's narrow single bed.

Margie joined her, noticing as she did that she couldn't see the clock or the desk or the wand from the position Cate had chosen.

'When you're in Manhattan, magazine editor or something, I'll come over 'cos I've got an exhibition.' Cate stetched out her legs and studied the thin ladder in her tan tights.

'We could get a flat,' said Margie. She tried to think of two women, grown and poised.

'Yeah. Like in *St Elmo's Fire* or something.' Cate motioned for the Kahlua and took another drink.

'I love that film,' said Margie.

'Yeah.' Cate pressed her head back against the covers, closing her eyes and swaying slightly to the music. 'I really love this,' she said, starting to hum. 'I'm going to play it at my wedding.'

Margie burst out laughing. 'You can't play this at your wedding, you divot. It's "Like a Virgin".'

'Oh.' Cate gave a spluttering snigger.

'Although I suppose you might be.'

'No I won't,' said Cate. 'I'll have done it by then.'

Margie watched her. 'I can't believe you want all that,' she said, 'being Mrs Wifey to some bloke.' Cate had talked about it a lot since her dad had died, about the man she would marry, the family she would have. Although maybe that was something you needed to do. When all your certainties were gone.

Cate smiled without looking back at her. 'You're gonna be my bridesmaid. I'll make you wear yellow. You'll look like a canary.'

'You do that and you're dead,' said Margie. It had started to rain quite heavily and she watched the little slashes of water spatter onto the window above the net curtain. Maybe it was the Kahlua, but she suddenly felt warm and secure, safe in the small room with Cate, not having to know.

Cate had gone quiet and when Margie glanced across at her, she saw that her face was scrunched into a silent sob.

She sat forward with a jerk. 'What is it? Cate?'

'I miss Dad.' Cate opened her eyes. 'I really miss him, Margie. The stuff came from college last week and Mum had to fill it in and . . . he's not going to see anything. Not that and not if I get married and he won't be there, and . . .'

She dropped her head onto Margie's shoulder and gave in to the tears and Margie hated herself for having said the word. Dead. Hated herself for reminding Cate of what she'd lost; the man who called her 'love' as if he meant it.

She hooked her arm around Cate's shoulder and spoke softly to her like she had so often in the last six months until Cate sniffed noisily and wiped her nose on the sleeve of her shirt.

'I wish you could come to art college with me.'

'Like they give degrees for stick figures,' said Margie gently.

'But we'll see each other. Lots.'

'Yeah,' said Margie. 'All the time.'

Cate nodded. 'All the time.'

Margie wasn't sure how long they sat like that but the songs changed one into the other and the rain stopped. There wasn't much Kahlua left when she lifted the bottle again and Cate was sitting so still she might have fallen asleep.

Margie pulled herself up and looked at the clock. Her hand reached instinctively for Cate, who opened her eyes and leapt, a little unsteadily, to her feet.

'Is it time?'

Margie started to nod then shook her head. 'I can't do it. You'll have to.'

'Okay.' Cate nodded frantically. 'Okay.' She walked over to the desk and Margie watched from the corner of her eye, digging her nails into her palms. Fuck. Please. Fuuuck.

Cate's voice, when it came, sounded almost disbelieving. 'It's not blue.'

Margie wheeled round. Cate was holding the wand above her head, up to the light, wobbling like an unstable Statue of Liberty. 'It's not blue! White. Look. It's not blue.' She held it out. 'You're fine! I knew you were! You're fine.'

Margie grabbed the stick from Cate's hand and stared at the little absorbent square. Not blue, not even remotely. She burst into sudden noisy tears and fell against Cate.

'You're fine.'

'Oh, God. Fuck.' Margie stood back. She looked again at the stick. 'You won't tell anyone?'

'No,' said Cate, shaking her head.

'Promise?'

Cate flung her arms back round Margie's neck. 'I promise,' she said, her words a little slurry now. 'You're my best friend.'

'You're my best friend.' She could tell Cate was crying too, with joy and relief and too much liqueur. She smelled of coffee and Anaïs Anaïs.

'We always will be, won't we?' Cate's voice was muffled against her shoulder.

'Always, yeah.' Margie let go of the little white wand and it landed at their feet.

'Promise?' said Cate.

'Yeah,' said Margie, and she had never meant anything more. 'I promise.'

I

'You've been sleeping on the buttons again.'

Dan stretched across and pressed his fingers, briefly, to the side of Cate's face. It was more of a poke than a stroke, and his hand was gone before she reached up to feel the round indentation in her right cheek.

'Remind me why you got pillowslips with buttons on them?' yawned Dan, standing with his back to her to stretch.

'Because they're gorgeous, and they complement the rest of the bed linen and the buttons are far enough at the side, that, technically, you shouldn't end up sleeping on them.' Cate rubbed her cheek. God, she'd look like she had the pox. There was no way this was going to be gone before the school run, and it was too big to fill in with eye pencil and pass off as a beauty spot. They were big buttons. Mother-of-pearl, with the name Dolti stamped into them in bold, italicised script. She'd sourced the pillowslips in a little shop in Glasgow. They were in a set of four with two matching tasselled cushions, too lovely to pass up. A dense purple silk and linen mix, the colour of a sultry night. And she loved purple. She moved her index finger lightly across the mark, hoping she hadn't pressed hard enough for the print to have taken as well. Branded by her penchant for interior design.

'You crack me up, Catriona Beane,' said Dan, smiling at her.

He'd been saying that a lot recently. He'd been smiling at her a lot recently, too. Benevolently. Like he sometimes did at his Great Aunt Gert when she farted at Christmas dinner. Cate wanted to say, 'And you make me go weak at the knees. Still.' But she didn't. He'd probably laugh at her for that as well. She watched him rummage in the chest of drawers for fresh boxers, tall and rangy, with the easy grace of someone supremely comfortable in their skin. It must be the Dutch heritage in him. Dutch men were beautiful. And Dan was beautiful. Even two generations on, with a hint of paunch and a good mix of Scottish blood. She felt her throat constrict. There had been a day when he wouldn't have had to stretch across the bed to reach her when they woke. There had been a day when the look in his eyes would have been lust and not just laughter. She would kill for a little bit of lust.

She slipped out of bed and padded over to the large, vaulted oak mirror above the dresser. She looked surprisingly fresh. Maybe the liposomes or amino peptides or sheep's innards in the face-cream she had bought last week were actually working – although they hadn't worked on the button mark, still furiously red. She looked closer, just able to make out the letters curved in the centre of the circle. Actually, it was only the first four letters that had imprinted themselves. D. O. L. T. Oh, crap.

'Hey, princess.' Dan planted a noisy kiss on Emma's head as she curled herself into him.

'Hey, Dads,' she said, blinking in the light of her parents' room. Cate watched them, wondering if it was awful to feel envious of your daughter, jealous of a father's fierce, unconditional love. She smiled at her drowsy girl. Only if you didn't feel it, too, she thought.

'Hey, angel, where are your sisters?'

'Stevie's running around starkers again,' said Emma, 'and Jo's snoring like a pig.'

'Emma!'

'Well she does, Mum. We need our own rooms.'

'You're only eleven,' said Cate. 'I only got my own room because I had a brother.'

'I know, I know,' muttered Emma. 'Blah, blah, blah. Anyway, did you remember to fill in the form for the school trip? I've only got four days till it's got to be in. And if we don't, then there's . . .'

'Done and by the door,' said Cate. 'Four days early.'

'What's that on your face?' Emma peered at her.

'She slept on the buttons,' said Dan, disappearing into the en suite. 'Again.'

'Muum!' Emma started to giggle. 'You look like you've got carbolic plague or something.'

'Bubonic,' said Cate. 'Not carbolic. Carbolic is to do with soap.'

'Whatever.' Emma shrugged. 'It looks like a giant zit. Can Dad take us to school?'

'No.' Cate yawned deeply and reached for her robe. 'Freddy Krueger can.'

She loved to listen to the girls in the back of the car, the inane, intimate chatter. For all that they could pretend to loathe one another, they were as close as only sisters can be. It was a blessing that the twins weren't identical, though. Jo had Dan's thick, straight dark hair, but Emma's was a shade or two lighter with some of Cate's kinks and waves. Twins came from Dan's side, and though they had talked of three children, they stopped after two. The possibility of four just seemed too much.

Until six years later, they got careless and got lucky, and Stevie came, on her own. But there had been many times since then that Cate had dreamed of a tiny boy with Dan's dark eyes, tucked into the warmth of her neck.

'Did I tell you?' Emma prattled on. 'Paul's getting to go to T in the Park, with his brothers.'

'You did,' said Jo. 'And it's crap.'

'Jo!' said Cate.

Stevie, whose booster seat was strategically placed between her sisters, started to giggle.

'It's not crap!' Emma reached across to aim a slap at Jo. '*He* is.'

'Of course he's not,' said Jo. 'There's no way he'd get to go. You're just trying to make your boyfriend sound good.'

Emma's voice rose into a whine. 'He's not my boyfriend. Muum! Tell her she's not to call him my boyfriend.'

Jo whispered something in Stevie's ear and Stevie started to sing lustily, 'Emma loves Paul, Emma luuuuves Paul!'

Cate sighed and twisted herself round to reverse park into the only available space she could see near the school gates. 'Stevie, shoosh, and Jo, stop it. Paul is not Emma's boyfriend, Jo. He's just a friend. He may or may not be going to T in the Park with his brothers. Without calling his parents to check, we don't really know. And I'm not planning on phoning them to find out. And Emma, don't get so wound up over something so trivial.' She pulled tightly on the handbrake and cut the engine. 'Now, all of you, out of the car.'

'Why are you parking?' Emma paused, suddenly suspicious. 'Aren't you just going straight to the gym?'

'Not today. I need to hand in the forms for the trip. And I've got to sort out the new sweatshirts that came in for the netball team.'

'Do you have to?' Jo was outside the car now and looking like she was getting ready to run.

'I have to.'

'Well, can you stick your hand over your face, or pull your hair across or something?'

'It's not that bad,' lied Cate, knowing that it was.

'Muum!' the girls chorused.

They abandoned her halfway across the playground, with just the quickest of kisses on her unbuttoned cheek. She left Stevie outside the primary one classroom with an admonition not to bite anyone – even in fun – as she had the previous day, and went to hand the forms in to the school office, managing fairly deftly, she thought, to keep her face in profile. She found the netball sweatshirts waiting for her, still in their cardboard box, in the small cubicle that acted as the school's swap shop. She was only meant to be the parents' rep for the twins' year, but she'd ended up doing more: chaperone for the netball team and parent liaison for P1. If a list went up at school for parental involvement, it was a given that one of the first names on it would be Catriona Beane. It was the story of her life, really. Cate'll do it. She's happy to. She doesn't work, after all. Cate'll fix it. Ask Cate. Good old Cate.

She'd almost finished sorting the sweatshirts into their class piles when she was startled by a small, polite cough. She turned to find the school secretary behind her.

'I'm sorry, Mrs Beane. I didn't mean to sneak up on you.' She stood, watching Cate and twisting her hands nervously.

'Do you need me to get out of here?'

'No, no, that's fine.' The secretary took a deep breath. 'I just saw you down in the office.' She paused again. 'Mrs Beane, I don't mean to be indelicate, but we got word there was a bit of an outbreak down at St Salvator's Primary last month, and with you going with the girls to the match at Craigmount tomorrow, we'd prefer to be safe than sorry.'

Cate looked at her, confused. 'Yes?'

'That thing on your face. It's not ringworm, is it?'

The mark had gone but not the mortification by the time she got home. She lugged the shopping onto the kitchen counter, rubbing the scythe marks on her palms where the bag handles had cut in, and draped Dan's newly dry-cleaned dinner suit over the ottoman. He'd only told her about the Ear, Nose and Throat benefit yesterday. Too late to arrange a babysitter so she could go too, but enough time for her to have his suit cleaned. Not that she relished another 'orifice outing' as she secretly called them. She'd been bored rigid at too many hospital fundraisers over the years, and Dan didn't really need her to play doctor's wife now that he was a consultant.

She'd enjoyed them at first, even looked forward to them. It was a chance to dress up, to watch Dan schmooze with his easy charm. It was only over time that she had realised how indiscernible she became at these events, a translucent creature, faint and unimportant, no matter how animated her conversation or vibrant her smile. Each time she went she felt as if she faded a little more.

In the girls' bedroom she deposited a pile of clean, folded clothes onto Emma's bed and scooped up the tangle of skinny jeans and bright T-shirts on the floor near their laundry bin. Emma was right, they really ought to have their own rooms. They'd both started asking recently and it would be easy enough to convert the spare room. Cate wasn't sure why she was resisting. Perhaps because it was proof that they were growing up, that they needed their own space a little more, that they needed her a little less.

She tilted the window to let in some of the sharp March air and then perched on the chair by Josie's desk. The room was a study in opposites. Jo's wall was filled with animal posters and her own drawings, most of them studies of Hamish the hamster, currently asleep in his nest of newspaper. All Cate could make out of the family pet was a small, fat golden bottom gently rising and falling to the rhythm of his breathing.

Emma's desk was crowded with tiny bottles and vials of

pre-teen make-up, and hung about with a confusion of bangles and belts and necklaces. She still had a few animal posters up, but Orlando Bloom had appeared above her bed in the last few weeks to join Avril Lavigne, and the cast of *Black Hole High*. Cate tried to remember when she had first thought about boys as anything other than odorous and obnoxious pests. It must have been about this age. Egged on by Margie Holland. Cate found herself smiling at the sudden image of a scrawny girl with mad frizz and a raucous laugh. God, Margie. Long time no see.

The hamster stirred and turned to poke a small nose out of his shredded newsprint. A Sunday broadsheet had been used to line his cage and Cate found it fitting that a small pile of hamster droppings was now obscuring the face of a junior foreign minister who had been caught screwing one of his advisers on a Cabinet Office table. It must be a mark of motherhood that the first thing she had wondered was whether they had wiped it afterwards. With an antibacterial spray. She smiled and tapped her fingers on the bars. Hamish emerged and stretched a little stiffly. He was getting old but neither of the twins had mentioned replacing him when he died, as they had with previous pets. Another milestone reached. They didn't tell you this at parentcraft classes or in the baby books. That one day pets would become passé and the opposite sex a little more diverting. That one day, long before you expected it, they reached an age when you could see their future so clearly, with all its chance and promise, and your own not at all, just an expanse of time with a great void where children used to be.

She watched the hamster climb onto his wheel, and left him spinning sedately to go and load the washing machine, reschedule Stevie's dentist's appointment so it didn't clash with the twins' netball fixture, and retrieve Dan's dress shoes from the back of the airing cupboard. It was close to noon when she finally opened the door to the study. Compared to everywhere else, the little room at the far end of the upper hall was chaotic, the walls a riot of images torn from magazines, of Post-its with scribbled contact numbers and smears of paint samples.

Cate switched on the computer and eased a heavy tome from a pile of textbooks on the desk. She had two more days to finish her essay on Venetian glass before it had to be sent off. When she might finish the course was anyone's guess. She'd been at it two years already. Two years of draughtsmanship and limewashing, of textiles and lighting, squeezed in between the school run and the swimming lessons and the Saturday sleepovers. As she waited for the computer to fire up she pulled a thick manila folder from the bookcase and flicked through the cuttings of villas for sale. Umbria, the Dordogne, Castilla La Mancha, Languedoc, scores of different dwellings clipped from magazines and adverts, some rustic and ramshackle, some pillared and marbled, all bathed in deep, golden light.

One day, when she'd finished, if they had the time and the money, she and Dan could go and see about buying somewhere that she could do up and sell on. He'd said as much when she'd started. She traced her fingers across the stuccoed exterior of a Tuscan steading and closed her eyes for a second, imagining the steady heat of a bright sun. They'd travelled a lot before the children came. Not just holidays. Real travel. The week in Guatemala, deep into the rainforest, watching a red-bottomed tarantula amble across their path, lying in the scraped-out hollow left, the night before, by a jaguar. The big bugs in Tanzania that they'd christened the B52s because they flew, blindly, into your face. The night-time horse ride in the Sonoran desert with just the coyotes for company. Dan running, helpless with laughter, from the small herd of angry javelina pigs.

Or the lovely medieval inn, near San Gimignano, before the Blairs went and spoiled it, when they ate orange cake for breakfast and the swallows dived around their heads and a dog barked distantly on another sunny hillside. When Dan might have laughed at her, but he also sat close and held her hand and told her, every so often, not that she cracked him up, but that he loved her. Really, truly loved her.

2

In the third cubicle from the left, Susann Lingenfelder was reaching a crescendo: 'You go girl. You go. You go GIRL. You GO! YOU. GO. GIRL! YOU GOOOO!!!'

Marg Holland stood by the sinks and studied her reflection in the broad, darkly silvered mirror, flicking an imaginary speck of dust from the lapel of her black jacket. She stifled a yawn and checked her watch: 5.53 a.m. Two minutes of yodelling to go.

She remembered how surprised she'd been on her first day at Global News Corp's European bureau when she'd learned of Susann Lingenfelder's little morning ritual. 'She goes for a pee at 5.50 a.m.,' the PA had explained. 'Then she likes to psych herself up.'

Marg had looked at her blankly. 'Psych herself up?'

'It's just thigh slapping really,' the girl said. 'Like the haka, you know the thing the rugby guys do? But she likes someone there when she does it. Validation, I suppose. Last producer liked to join in.'

'Oh yeah?' Marg had wondered if it wasn't too late to withdraw her application for the post of senior news producer and editor. But it was a dream of a job, even if it meant indulging the anchor's peculiar little foibles. Marg understood foibles. And Susann Lingenfelder was good at what she did, Newscaster of the Year for the last two years running. If it took some thigh slapping to keep her on form, then so be it.

18

Now she almost didn't hear the commotion in the cubicle and spent the time checking herself in the mirror. Straightened, shortish, warm blonde hair tucked sharply behind her ears, white blouse opened a little further down than it should be, the man's watch, chunky, and slightly loose on a slim wrist still tanned from the Mogadishu trip. She stood back and smiled. Pretty damn hot. Her. Not Mogadishu.

A runner popped her head round the door with a frantic grin. 'How we doin'?'

'Susann,' Marg leant towards the cubicle. 'Are we good to go?'

Susann emerged and smoothed down the front of her sleek tweed trousers. 'Good to go,' she said confidently and strode from the loo. Marg went to follow but stopped as she caught the door. She could hear dripping. A tap wasn't off. She turned back quickly, located the offending faucet and jerked it hard to the right. Then again. Off. Absolutely off. She double-checked from the door.

In the control booth above the studio, she slung her jacket over the seat back and slipped into her chair. She felt like a pilot. Beside her, the assistant producer was fixated on the red hand of the clock, sliding steadily towards 6 a.m. Susann was in her seat, scanning her computer screen, mouth moving soundlessly as she tested out awkward words in their phonetic spellings. Fron swa meeter ond. Keer giz stan. Marg clicked the earpiece mike to 'on' and bent forward. 'Susann. On in ten. Lipstick smear. Front tooth. Right.'

She watched her anchor swipe her tongue across her teeth. Above Marg's head, the images on the TV screens flashed and flickered like demons. Stand-off on the Kashmiri border. Small explosion in Sadr City. Bridge collapse in Austria.

Gas prices on the up. She checked that the package on the new Tate installation was in from the arts correspondent. The dozy cow had been leaving everything until the last minute. The package was there. All set. All her ducks in a row. And how dull was that? She hoped something happened. Something big. Breaking news. And then the backscreen would flood blood red and the panic would swell all around her and she would stay cold and controlled. Like she always did. Like she could take all the chaos the world could create and hold it in the palm of her hand.

'Three. Two. One. And live on air.' The light went to green and Susann steadied her head with its helmet of glossy immovable hair and lit her veneered smile like a beacon. 'Hi. I'm Susann Lingenfelder, and this is Morning Report. Rise and shine.'

High in the booth, Marg Holland bent over her display for her own daily ritual. 'Lies and shite,' she said, as she did every morning, low under her breath, in a very un-Susann-like kind of way.

The world hadn't ended by 8.45 a.m., but the wires were reporting that students in Iran had gathered for their third demonstration in as many days. The news alert bar appeared, and Susann Lingenfelder gave a brief summary of the development, then swivelled to address the big screen behind her as it filled with an image of Rick Rutner. 'Richard Rutner, our chief foreign correspondent, is in Tehran and joins us now. So, Rick, it looks like the protests are really gathering pace. Are we witnessing the first waves of a new revolution?'

Beneath his flak jacket he was wearing the shirt Marg had given him at Christmas, the sky-blue cotton, smooth as silk, which drew out his dark, grey eyes. He'd insisted on going with her to Ozwald Boateng to choose it.

The blue shirt was the uniform of the foreign corre-spondent. White said you were normally desk-bound, khaki said you were a wannabe, a T-shirt said your kit had been confiscated or you'd lost the plot completely. Marg had even known Rick to delay his segment for a precious few seconds while the collar of his favourite blue shirt was being pressed. She wondered if the viewers knew that behind most great foreign correspondents was some poor sod of a fixer running around with a bottle of Dab-It-Off and a travel iron. Did they never wonder how you get a knife-edge crease and stain-free armpits in the middle of a coup?

Rick Rutner nodded emphatically at the question. 'It looks very much like it, Susann. This is the third day of political dissent that Tehran has seen this week . . .'

Marg watched his mouth as he talked. He had a marvellous mouth, thin-lipped, utterly masculine and bloody great to kiss. She'd once dumped a business journalist because his big soft lips reminded her of a baby's bottom. Not that she'd ever kissed a baby's bottom. Or was likely to do so.

It's not that she actively disliked children, she just had no desire, no need, to make one of her own. There was a reason she was an only child. And her mum had said as much one raging night. That she'd never meant to get pregnant. Not then. And not with her. Marg had known already. Her Aunty Betty had informed her two years before that she was not only An Accident but also The Reason He Left. But even at age eleven, it had made sense. No point in getting upset. Call a spade a spade. Call your mother a sour, vindictive old bitch. If that's what she was.

It all suited Rick fine, too. She knew he loved that she wasn't so naive as to think she was his one and only, that she wasn't angling for anything more than great company and good, if sporadic, sex. She loved that he was only around for part of the year, but could make her laugh when he was.

Marg eyed the clock. Enough of the revolting students. Time for the Tate.

'Wrap it up, Susann,' she said and Susann dutifully brought the two-way to a close, signing Rick off with her trademark 'stay safe'. Rick nodded abruptly and stood still and unsmiling until his face was replaced by Tracey Emin's giant wheelie bin upended in the foyer of the former Bankside Power Station.

Marg adjusted her headset. 'Thanks, Rick. Slick and succinct. Just how I like it.'

'Hey, babe, how's my favourite girl?'

'Not a clue.' Marg laughed. 'Give me her number and I'll ask her.'

'Very droll,' said Rick. 'So why are you not out here producing and why have I been lumbered with some Roedean alumnus with thick ankles and an attitude problem?'

'Poor baby, so she doesn't fancy you? But she needs the experience and Tehran this time of year makes my hair curl.'

'I'll make your hair curl.'

'God, you're so cheesy.' Marg smiled indulgently. From the corner of her eye, she saw a flicker of panic cross Susann Lingenfelder's face. 'Gotta go. Autocue's on the blink. See you when I see you.'

'Big smacker,' said Rick. 'Go save us from an ad-libbing anchor.'

There was nothing quite like the first Bloody Mary of the day. Marg raised her glass to a good day's work and to the man with the mullet. He had a magnificent mullet, whoever he was, a mane of golden hair that bobbed as energetically as he did inside his giant hamster ball.

'All muscle groups get a great workout in the Rolovater,' the man beamed at the camera. 'Just six payments of thirty-nine ninety-nine and the Rolovater can be yours. Spin your way to a better body and a better life!' He rattled off across the TV screen, a blur of bleached teeth and outrageous pecs.

Marg surveyed her apartment. As beautifully positioned as it was in Chelsea Bridge Wharf, even the most creative estate agent would be hard-pushed to describe it as anything other than bijou. She would have to pass on mullet man and his Rolovater. And anyway she was paying enough for Roy, the grievously expensive personal trainer, to whip her into shape. She flicked idly on through the shopping channels, past the spray-on hair remover that could epilate a yak and the control pants that reached from ankles to armpits squeezing as they went.

She stopped when she came to the jewellery channel. Now that was quite nice. Draped across a manicured female hand was an amethyst bracelet, the stones unusually big and round like the eggs of a small exotic bird. She liked the way the bracelet sparkled under the lights. And she loved purple. Every shade of it. Lilac, aubergine, violet. Especially violet, the colour of her first ever lipstick, the one she'd bought from Boots with the money from her Saturday job and worn, liberally applied, to school discos. What was it again? 'Lick of Passion'. Frosted and vibrant. The one that Cate Wishart said made her look like she'd been punched in the gob. Marg found herself smiling. God, Cate.

The lady with the bracelet interrupted her thoughts: 'If you're thinking of buying this beautiful piece, you need to be quick.'

Marg peered at the price along the bottom of the screen. Only £59.99. A bargain, really, and just sixteen left. Now fifteen. Going fast. She drained her glass and reached for the phone, flicking one of her credit cards from her opened wallet with a practised hand. If she didn't like it, she could give it to Susann or her PA for Christmas, although it was a little like the fake jewelled cuff she had given someone in the office last year. She couldn't quite remember whom.

By the end of her third vodka and tomato juice she had almost been tempted by a grater that gave you carrots like miniature palm trees, but went, instead, for the scarf of crinkled silk that you could knot in one hundred different ways. If you carried around the book that showed you how. She closed her wallet and switched off the TV, suddenly feeling exhausted. Time for her nap. She'd tried lasting without a siesta until her bedtime at 9 p.m., but the 3 a.m. starts had taken their toll. So when everyone else was thinking afternoon tea, she was often tucked up in bed, dead to the world.

She stood up a little unsteadily and walked to the window. The street was quiet, just a handful of people with places to go. She watched two women meet at the café on the corner, heads bending in for a kiss on each cheek, smiles broad and intimate. They sat down at a table and slung their bags over the back of the seats, chattering constantly as they did so. Whatever they were talking about must have been funny, because one of them threw back her head in laughter and laid her hand on the other one's arm.

Marg felt a sudden pang of regret. She didn't have many female friends. The job made familiarity difficult and weekday routine virtually impossible, and news tended to kill off normal conversations. I'm getting my hair coloured at that new salon in Clerkenwell. Really? I'm interviewing a gangmaster about people trafficking from China.

She pulled the blinds shut and headed for the hall, past the Peter Howson print from Bosnia that Rick had given her. Jesus, she was feeling a little ropey, she needed to cut back on the Bloody Marys. It's not exactly what Roy had in mind when he'd told her to drink nothing but vegetable juice before lunch.

In the kitchen, she took a slow breath and started from the doorway. Toaster, kettle, juicer. All off. Oven. Off. She swung the tap and pressed her fingers to its tip. No drips. She flicked the light switch, then felt it with her hand on the way out. It was the best way because when you feel a switch you know by its position that it's off. Eyes can play tricks and Marg liked to be sure. She moved through the flat, flicking, ensuring, double-checking. Sometimes she got annoyed at herself for having to do it, most times the ritual passed almost without her noticing.

She reached the bedroom and shut the door. Everything checked and sorted. Everything perfect. She lay back on the bed with its soft, expensive sheets. And it was perfect, wasn't it? This life she had crafted. Everything she'd ever hoped for. Back when she was a girl, back when she was Margie.

3

It was close to 2 a.m. when Dan got home from the Ear, Nose and Throat do. Cate listened to him stumbling around the hall, tripping over the jumble of school bags and shoes at the bottom of the stairs. Stevie had woken at midnight with a squiffy bottom and Cate hadn't been able to get back to sleep afterwards. Her essay was bothering her. She knew she was rushing it, but she didn't want to ask for yet another extension. If she did, that would be the fourth time this year. She felt a sudden flash of annoyance. She'd heard from the tutor that two other students had made it down to the exhibition of Venetian glass at the Victoria and Albert. And all she was asking was for Dan to be around for a whole evening so she could have got a good couple of hours done. Instead of spending her time trying to find two sets of non-identical images of Antarctica on the Internet for the twins' class project, and then extracting Stevie's favourite Bratz doll from the letterbox and repairing its coltish limbs with wholly inadequate Sellotape splints.

She let him tiptoe into the bedroom before she said, 'Hey,' quite loudly.

'God. I thought you would be ashleep.' He sounded slurry and not unlike Sean Connery. Only Dan could sound good pissed.

'Dr Drunk,' said Cate. 'I hope you didn't drive home?'

'Taxi,' he mumbled. 'Run me in tomorrow to pick up the car?'

'Depends.' Cate wasn't feeling very charitable.

'On what?' He steadied himself against the wall to pull off his socks.

'On what I'm doing.'

'What are you doing?' She watched through the gloom as he shrugged off his shirt and dropped his bow-tie on the dresser.

'The essay that I still haven't finished and the gym.'

'Well that should be okay, shouldn't it?' He wobbled in the direction of the en suite, then stopped. 'What's that noise?'

'Hamish. On his wheel. He's always on it this time of night.'

'How can they sleep through that?' asked Dan. 'We should oil it.'

'I like it,' said Cate. 'It's kind of comforting. And the girls don't mind.'

Dan yawned. 'Good night tonight. Lots of dosh. The trustees gave a guarantee to pay the balance for the new thoracic scanner.'

'Really,' said Cate. 'Stevie had diarrhoea.'

'How loose?' Dan switched on the bathroom light and Cate blinked in the sharp glare.

'How loose what?'

'The stool.'

'Dan, you don't need to diagnose. It's dealt with. I was just telling you, that's all.'

'Cate's in a mood.' He moved unsteadily across to the bed, and stooped to kiss her hard on the mouth. He tasted warm and sour.

'And you're inebriated,' she said as he pulled away. He laughed as he shut the bathroom door. Cate turned over in the darkness. She knew he would never have kissed her like that had he not been.

★

It took three flights of stairs to reach the entrance to Tif's Tone and Trim. Cate stopped at the bottom step and held her breath. The hallway always smelled of wee, and not always cats'. On the peeling green paint, just above the wheelie bins, a laminated notice had been stuck for as long as Cate had been going there. *Your New Body Starts Here!* With an arrow to point the way.

There were other gyms, of course, including a spanking new one by the out-of-town cinema complex which Cate had heard sprayed aromatherapy oils through the air conditioning and offered Indian head massage. But her friend Orla went here and Tif was here and it wouldn't have felt right to quit, as so many other customers had. Dan laughed at her. He said you should never frequent an establishment with alliteration in the title, especially not a hairdresser, and definitely not a gym. He used the gym at the hospital. Not often, but enough to maintain muscle for his beloved cycling. Dr Dan, Action Man.

He had been suffering a little at breakfast and had snapped at the girls when they got into an argument over who was going to use the bathroom first. Cate had given him an Alka-Seltzer and a warning look and had run him to the Caledonian Hotel to retrieve his car after they had deposited the girls at school. He had kissed her when he got out, but it was chaste compared to his drunken embrace of the night before.

Now she was late for her Salsercise class. She dropped her gym bag at her feet and leant on the counter to sign herself in. Tif appeared from her office and flashed her gorgeous smile. 'You running behind today?'

Cate nodded. 'Fractious kids to be dropped off. Husband to be chauffered. Car to be picked up. You know how it is.'

'Oh, I know.' Tif handed her a locker key. 'You're okay.

They've just started warming up.' Cate smiled at her gratefully. This is why she loved coming here. Tif must have been
fifty-eight if she was a day, but she had the body of a thirty-
something – lithe, proportioned and toned. She'd been a
dance teacher in a previous life but had caught the aero-
bics bug and had opened her own place fifteen years ago.
She didn't often take classes any more, though, not since
the arthritis had tightened its grip. Cate sometimes found
it hard to look at Tif's hands, the lovely long fingers starting
to claw involuntarily. Tif never mentioned it but it seemed
unusually cruel that a woman who had cherished her body
so carefully all her life should have it turn on her now.

Cate changed quickly into her kit and scraped her hair
back into a small ponytail. She loved her hair. A little wavy
and a little fair, and cut so it swung just above her jawline.
She'd always worn it long, and had insisted that she always
would, but there came an age when it seemed a little sad
to have hair longer than your daughters. There were few
people who could pull off tumbling tresses as they
approached forty. As Orla said, you might think you resembled Elle MacPherson but it was far more likely you looked
like Princess Anne.

Cate slipped into the back of the class, nodding at the
instructor who was up on the small dais swinging her arms
and legs to and fro, the two rows of women in front of her
copying her moves like a troupe of trained monkeys.

Cate joined in the swaying, enjoying the heavy, syncopated beat. Orla spotted her in the mirror and turned to
grin. A thin sheen of sweat was already coating her face.
She made a motion with her hand and mouthed 'Coffee?'

Cate grinned back and nodded. Coffee meant coffee and
doughnuts. Their new bodies may start at Tif's but they
always ended up in the café next door.

★

'So how's the lovely Danny?' Orla slung her gym bag under the table and collapsed into the seat, her face still pink with exertion.

'Hungover,' said Cate, doing the same.

'Where were you?'

'Well, he was out at a hospital fundraiser and I was at home doing nothing much.'

'If my husband looked like Dan I wouldn't let him out on his own,' laughed Orla. 'What are you after? The usual?'

Cate nodded and while Orla was at the counter fished into her bag and pulled out the mail. She'd grabbed it from the floor as she was leaving the house and had deposited it on Dan's lap in the car, but he'd said it was all for her and had stuck it in her bag unread. She flicked through the bundle. There was a postcard from her mum and stepdad from Portofino, one of the stops on their latest cruise. Their postcards were always late – they'd actually got back last week – but Cate read it anyway. It was Ed who had written it, and it was full of his warm humour. Her mum had married him four years after Cate's real dad had died. He was a lovely man, good and kind, and he made a great dad and a much-loved grampa. Cate adored him.

There were two bills, phone and gas, and a large white envelope with an illegible stamp. Cate scanned the single piece of foolscap inside. She gave a hollow laugh.

'God.'

'What is it?' Orla deposited a tray with two cups of coffee and two doughnuts in the middle of the table.

'The council are knocking down my old school. Jesus, I didn't think it was that old. I didn't think *I* was that old.'

'Why are they writing to you to tell you they're knocking it down?' Orla looked confused.

'They're not,' said Cate. 'Some kind of school society is holding a fundraising do to try and save it. Look.' She turned the letter round.

'The Wrecker's Ball,' read Orla. 'Join the fight to save Abbeyhill High. Forty pounds a head for a buffet and a tribute band for every era.'

'Era!' said Cate. 'I have an era.'

'Course you do,' laughed Orla. 'One of the ones that taste forgot.' She took a noisy slurp of coffee. 'Are you going to go?'

'I don't know. I didn't even know they were doing this. I didn't know the school was under threat.' Cate studied the letter again. Planners would decide in the autumn whether the building was to come down. The ball was at the Sheraton in less than a month.

Orla nudged the plate of doughnuts towards her. 'Could be a laugh. Do you keep in touch with anyone?'

'Not really. Well, Margie Holland, maybe. She was my best friend. But we just do Christmas cards now. She's something in TV news in London.'

'When did you last see her?'

'God, years ago,' said Cate. 'She worked in Glasgow for a while but then she moved down south. The BBC in Bristol. And I met Dan . . .' She tailed off.

'Weird how that happens, isn't it?' said Orla. 'You're best pals with someone and then you end up complete strangers.'

'I was sure we'd stay close,' said Cate. 'Some people manage to hang on to their best friends from school, don't they?'

'Not many,' said Orla. 'She famous?'

'Not yet,' said Cate. 'But if anyone was going to be it was Margie.' She thought of the last Christmas card she'd received, addressed, as always, to Cate Wishart. It had been a grand affair, glossy and embossed and printed with a personal message by a company that did such things for people too busy to bother. Margie never sent any other kind, although Cate wasn't sure why she kept using them because for the last five years they had misspelled her name as Marg. Cate's own Christmas card had been a more homespun effort, handmade from some lovely parchment paper she'd found at the Leith market and painstakingly penned in her best calligraphy.

'You should go,' said Orla, through a mouthful of doughnut. 'You look fantastic. And they're all bound to be fat and bald.'

'Including the women?'

'Maybe.' Orla laughed.

'But what have I done?' asked Cate. 'Six years at an ad agency after art college doesn't really constitute a career. Aren't these things all about self-aggrandisement?'

'What have you done?' Orla put down her mug. 'You've had three gorgeous kids, and found yourself the sexiest husband this side of the Solway, who's a doctor to boot, and you've got the best sense of style of anyone I know. Perfect life, Cate. Picture bloody perfect.'

'But what have I done?' Cate persisted.

Orla shook her head. 'Will that Margie go?'

'Doubt it,' said Cate. 'She hated school.'

'You sound very different.'

'We were.' Cate placed the letter on the table and picked up her coffee. 'But in a really good way.'

'What, you were the swot and she was the party girl?' asked Orla.

Cate pulled a face. 'She was both actually. Really bright and a bit . . . off the wall. Direct as anything. God, she didn't hold back in telling you what she thought.'

'And here's you, Mrs Amenable,' said Orla. 'How on earth did you hook up?'

'She was sick on my gym shoes.' Cate smiled. They were brand-new gym shoes, clean and black and smelling richly of rubber with a little panel of tight elastic to keep them snug. She'd felt the warm splash as they changed in the corridor for gym and had looked down and then up at the riotous light brown curls and brown eyes sparkling with surprise and a flash of mirth. 'Oopsie,' said the girl, as the teacher hurried her away to be doused and changed.

'Please tell me that wasn't secondary school,' laughed Orla.

'No,' said Cate. 'Primary one and day one, actually no, day two. On day one I sat beside a girl who peed herself because she was too scared to ask where the loos were.'

'Jesus,' giggled Orla. 'Where were you? St Margaret's College for the Blessedly Incontinent?'

Cate glanced again at the sheet of paper. She and Margie had been so excited when they moved up to Abbeyhill together. It had seemed so huge compared to their small primary. No prefab huts, just a massive stone edifice with endless corridors and cold, cold classrooms and stern if redundant etchings above the two entrances. Boys. Girls. And Margie hadn't been fazed by it at all, giving the pupils and teachers all nicknames which made them seem far less terrifying. There were the fuckers, the senior boys and girls whom Margie had decided would be doing it without a shadow of a doubt, because she was obsessed with sex. And the girls who played hockey, stout with too much hair, were Chewbaccas. And the teacher with the dark pageboy was Dingo after Lindy Chamberlain, and even now Cate couldn't remember her real name.

She and Margie had fitted in somewhere between the in-crowd and the desperados, another Margie moniker for the awkward few who hadn't learned to fake the social graces as they had done, practising bored insouciance in front of the mirror, knotting their ties to suitable thickness. And then they had settled into a group of friends, a loose clique who never quite managed to understand or alter the bond between them.

Cate took a sip of her coffee. Margie Holland. God, it would be great to see her again.

Marg eyed the large dollop of dog shit on the sole of her new Brooks trainers and swore vehemently under her breath.

'Just block it, Marg,' barked Roy, jogging on the spot behind her. 'It's crap. It's just crap. Now lean. And hold. Hoooooolllld.'

Marg stretched her foot forward on the park bench trying to ignore the smell rising from her shoe. She felt her gluteus maximus extend to what felt like breaking point.

'Jesus, Roy, I want to be limber, not in bloody traction.'

'Stick with it, love.' Roy didn't sound out of breath even though they'd been running around Battersea Park for forty minutes, although that's maybe what fifteen years as a fireman did for you. 'A year of these and you'll have an ass like Paris Hilton.'

Marg twisted sharply to eyeball him. 'Who says I don't already?'

Roy smiled ruefully. 'I've seen the video, love, and I get paid to watch you bend over. You got a ways to go there.'

'Yeah,' muttered Marg. 'Two decades and a whole new DNA double helix. Hey, talking of decades, guess what I got in the mail this morning?'

Roy threw her a towel as she switched legs on the bench. He grinned. 'Dentures? A conscience? Subscription to *Reader's Digest*?'

'Not far off on the last one,' she said. 'An invitation to my school reunion. Well, not a reunion as such. They're planning on knocking the place down and some bright spark wants former pupils to rally round and save it. There's a big do up in Edinburgh.'

Roy whistled. 'Actually, you're not in bad shape for an old bird. You going to go?'

'Christ no!' Marg did her stretch then perched on the edge of the bench and removed her trainer to scrape off the dog mess. 'I honestly can't imagine anything more dismal. I'm quite glad they're demolishing it. It was just a bog standard comprehensive in an old stone building with some twirly bits on the top. Nothing special.'

'Dunno,' said Roy. 'You might meet up with your old boyfriend, reignite that first love. It's happening all over with Friends Reunited, you know.'

'No first love,' laughed Marg. 'No loves at all. Just some frantic fumblings at school discos with boys with sweaty pits and a snog like sucking warm melon.' She gave a little shudder.

'Slutty Marg.' Roy grinned at her.

'Not slutty,' said Marg, 'so much as curious.'

Roy raised his eyebrows and gestured behind her. 'We've got company.'

It was a girl, possibly about six years old, with long brown hair and a dully curious expression. She was standing a little way off on the grass watching them both.

'Yes?' said Marg flatly.

The girl bit her lip. 'Is that your dog?' She gestured towards a miniature Schnauzer ferreting in the bushes behind the bench.

Marg shook her head. 'Don't like dogs. Shouldn't you be in school?'

'I've got conjunctivitis,' said the girl proudly.

'Congratulations,' said Marg. 'Where's your mum?'

The girl didn't move. 'Why do you not like dogs?'

'They smell.' Marg held up a trainer still smeared with dog mess. 'And they get shit on your shoes.'

The girl slapped her hand over her mouth to stifle a hysterical giggle, then turned and ran off.

Roy shook his head. 'You shouldn't speak to kids like that, you know.'

'Why not?' Marg turned to face him once she had seen the girl reach a woman with a pushchair strung about with carrier bags. 'I think they appreciate it.'

'Because now she's going to tell her mum that the nice lady over there taught her the word "shit".'

'Well, Roy, sweetie,' Marg slapped him on the back and stood to go. 'Better she learns it from me than from life.'

The waiter placed an espresso and a bottle of Badoit on the table in front of Marg, flashing her the briefest of smiles. She folded the *International Herald Tribune* and sat back in her chair. The table was covered in newspapers and magazines, some still unread, others folded at inside pages and scored with red pen. She knew she shouldn't be doing this, given that it was one of her days off, but she hated to feel she had missed something. It was her job not only to know what was happening, but also what might be about to. There was no greater sin than coming second on a story and Marg rarely had.

The café was quiet at this time of the morning, just a handful of customers and the battery of waiters in their bow-ties and long white aprons, waiting for the high-tipping lunch crowd. Marg took a sip from her espresso, twisted the top from the water and turned to the *Financial Times*. Her legs were still sore from the session with Roy so she stretched them gingerly under the table as she read.

It was only a tiny piece, tucked at the bottom of a column on page 11, little more than a digest paragraph.

REUTERS. NDJAMENA: Aid agencies working in the Abeche region of Chad say it is facing its worst food shortages in a decade. Three successive years of drought and an influx of refugees from the neighbouring Darfur region of Sudan have put intolerable strain on local communities and officials have warned there is little aid stockpiled in the country. A United Nations spokesman said they were monitoring developments.

Marg ringed the story with her pen. She'd been looking for something to highlight the continued failings of the G8 nations ahead of their latest summit in a few months' time. This could be it. Stuff Edinburgh and Abbeyhill High. If she focused on anywhere in the next few weeks it would be somewhere below the Sahara.

She sat back and picked up her Badoit, tapping the chilled glass of the bottle against her mouth. It would be interesting to know what Cate Wishart was up to these days, though. Marg had been thinking about her ever since she got the letter about the school. She'd gone to art college after Abbeyhill and then what? Marg wracked her brain. It was either PR or advertising, although, according to the rash of names crowding her Christmas cards, she had a brood of kids now so God knows what she was doing. Maybe getting all harried and obsessive like the mums at Marg's work, women who seemed to spin through the day in a blur of diligence and activity, getting it all done, fitting it all in, keeping it all going, just keeping it all going.

She tried to imagine Cate with kids. She'd actually be a great mum, if she was still the same. Daft and loving and down to earth. Everything a mum should be, really. Marg gave a little snort. Like she would know. She tilted the bottle and let the cool water fill her mouth. She'd been a good friend, Cate. The best.

She put the bottle back down and looked at the red-ringed story in front of her. Kind of a shame she wouldn't be seeing her again.

4

'I don't know.' The head of news sat back in his seat and scratched the back of his head. 'Seems a bit speculative. These kinds of warnings are ten a penny nowadays. Charities crying wolf just in case, you know.'

Marg said nothing. She knew it was a good sign that he hadn't dismissed her proposal out of hand. It had been three days since she'd spotted the small piece in the *FT* and she'd done a lot more research since then, identifying and speaking to aid agencies, tracking the relentless pattern of famine and conflict across the region.

She leant forward. 'I think it's going to be another example of the G8 and the UN getting caught with their thumb up their arse. It's the kind of avoidable tragedy they promised to tackle. Perfect example. There have been warnings for months, but they don't even have food stockpiled in the region. Honestly, before you can say "Live Aid" Bob Geldof will be all over this.'

The head of news looked at her. He was a good few years younger, one of the network whizz-kids, but approachable and considered for all that.

'We could get the stringer to take a look,' he said.

Marg shook her head. The stringer for East Africa was a drunken old soak who favoured a panama hat and considered embellishment an essential tool of the trade. 'It's worth more than that.'

'Okay, give me a costing and a game plan. And have you thought of a reporter?'

'Not yet,' said Marg. 'Who's going to be around in the next few weeks?'

'Rick Rutner gets back from Iran at the weekend. He be okay?'

'Fine.' Marg would actually have been happier if it had been someone else. She and Rick only worked well together, business or pleasure, for brief periods. Never more than a long weekend.

'I thought you'd say that.' The head of news flashed her a flat smile, but she didn't respond. Everyone knew she and Rick dated, but she dared anyone to say they let it interfere with work.

Back at her desk, she dug out her diary and looked at possible dates for a trip to Chad. The pages were a riot of red ink. She used red for work appointments, green for Roy, and blue for anything personal. It was going to be tricky to fit it in with all her other commitments, but she didn't want to pass it on to anyone else. A trip would be good for her. She'd been feeling a little unsettled of late. Like she had too much time on her hands. Like she was waiting for something to happen.

Maybe she was getting itchy feet again. She rarely lasted three years in a post before moving on, but she'd only been here eighteen months. Maybe it was the letter about the school that had rattled her. It had made her reflective and Marg didn't like being reflective. She'd never seen the point in revisiting the past. The trick, Marg had always thought, was to keep facing forwards.

'You gotta minute?' Susann Lingenfelder appeared at her elbow. It was less than an hour after the show had finished and her face was still a mask of studio make-up.

Marg snapped the diary shut. 'Sure.'

Susann pulled a seat over and positioned herself so close that their knees touched. She had very bony knees. 'I want to talk something over. Some changes.'

Marg nodded. The Broadcast Awards were due to be announced in a few weeks. She'd been expecting this.

'I'm thinking we should revamp the intro a little. I think it's sounding . . .' She pursed her lips. 'Stale.'

'Which bit?'

Susann slipped into her anchor's voice. 'Hi, I'm Susann Lingenfelder and this is Morning Report. Rise and shine.' She pulled a face. 'It's "rise and shine". It's not sounding right.'

Hallelujah, thought Marg. 'Okaay,' she said.

'It's too perky, you know, I need something with a bit more . . .'

'Gravitas?' said Marg.

Susann nodded. 'That's it. I'm just not sure what.'

'How about "up and at 'em"?'

Susann put her head on one side. 'Really? You think?'

Marg burst out laughing. 'I was kidding, Susann. How about just ending it after "this is Morning Report"?'

Susann paused, nodding slowly. 'I like it. That could work. Hi, I'm Susann Lingenfelder and this is Morning Report. Period.'

'Without actually saying "period",' said Marg.

It was Susann's turn to laugh. 'That's our Marg, blunt as a jackhammer.' She stood up. 'Okay, funny lady, we're going over to Popinjays for brunch. You coming?'

Marg nodded. Of course. No blue ink in the diary to say she couldn't.

'Darling, you have to go.' Cate's mum placed the school letter back on the kitchen counter and picked up her cup of tea. 'Ed, tell her she has to go. It'll be fun.' She leant across and tucked a strand of Cate's hair behind one ear. 'You should have more fun, darling. You really should.'

Ed looked up at Cate from his position on the sitting-room floor where he was ably shoeing a Bratz for Stevie.

'You go if you want to, honey. Don't let your mum bully you into it.' He beamed at both of them. 'And what could be more fun than this little lady here?' He grabbed a squealing Stevie and tucked her under one arm.

The floor was littered with wrapping from the presents they had brought back with them from their holiday. The twins had rushed upstairs to try on their strappy tops and beaded bracelets, and Stevie's giant inflatable dolphin with 'A Gift From the Ligurian Sea' printed on the side was beached on the sofa. Cate fingered the large ceramic necklace they had chosen for her. It felt like a toilet seat round her neck, but she had been appropriately effusive in her thanks. She couldn't wait till Dan saw his gift, a carved wooden figurine of a minstrel with one leg shorter than the other and now wearing a fetching Blu Tack boot to keep him steady. It had become a joke between them, wondering what treasures Joyce and Ed would bring back from their latest jaunt. And their life was one long holiday since Ed had retired from the bank. Two cruises a year and several weeks in Tenerife and the Algarve. Cate couldn't remember what colour her mum's skin tone had been; nowadays she and Ed were permanently copper-hued, if not downright orange.

'You keep out of it, old man.' Joyce gave Ed a warning look but her eyes shone with affection. 'And don't put your back out while you're down there. Lord save us, I don't know who's the bigger kid.'

Cate smiled at them as Stevie clambered on her grampa, convulsed in giggles.

When her dad had died it had seemed as though her mum would never have reason to be light-hearted again. Such a dark time, altered and frightening. And now . . . Cate didn't want to say it was better than it ever possibly could have been because that felt like such a betrayal of the man she sometimes struggled to remember; but she knew that it was. She had been intrigued but slightly nervous about meeting Ed when her mum had finally sat her and her brother down to tell them something was going on. She'd been talking for a while about Mr Watson from the bowling club, and then it became Edward Watson and then just Ed. Cate had already noticed her taking more care than usual to get ready for her Saturday morning match. A little blusher, a shampoo and set when she didn't really need one, the faintest whiff of Coty L'Aimant . . .

Cate knew Ed was a bank manager and had imagined someone prosperously rotund with a good conceit of himself. The man who came through the door that September evening was big and bluff, but he had a warm stretch of a smile and he looked as though he was going to burst with nerves and delight. 'Hello, Cate,' he had said, pumping her arm up and down in greeting. And the way he had looked at her mum. Cate had felt then that someone who could love that much would only bring joy to their lives.

His first wife had died of bowel cancer a decade before and they had never had children. Cate still felt it wrong that his only offspring came by default. He deserved his very own flesh and blood. And when he had held each of her girls hours after their birth, his face had betrayed that he had not stayed fatherless by choice and Cate's heart had broken for him.

'I am thinking about going.' Cate picked up the letter and studied it again. 'I just wish I knew who else would be there, you know, people I liked, like Margie Holland.'

Joyce made a clucking sound and turned to Ed. 'She had this one friend. Right the way through school. Inseparable, they were. She was an odd-looking girl.'.

'Mum, she wasn't odd looking!'

'Well her hair was always a mess,' said Joyce. 'All over the place.'

'It was curly, Mum. And she hated it. Anyway, I thought you liked Margie.'

'I did, darling. She was a good friend to you. Especially when your dad passed on.'

If it hadn't been for Margie . . . He'd gone so suddenly, on the floor of his office as he stood up from the desk to go and get a coffee. A tasteless coffee in a plastic cup from the office vending-machine. A dreadfully ordinary death. Cate had been called out of double English. She could still see Margie's face, questioning and concerned, as she left the classroom.

She'd come round after school when everyone had told her to stay away. Because that's what you did, you tutted and said, 'So sad,' and sent a card, but you didn't confront the grief at its most raw and terrible. Margie had. She sat on the end of Cate's bed and didn't mind the tears and snotters on her skirt, the one she'd hemmed herself to be two inches shorter than everyone else's. Or the great, heaving sobs of Cate's older brother, Tom, whom Margie idolised and had never seen cry, or the blank-faced silence of Cate's mum, numb at the kitchen table with the cup of tea that had long grown cold. And even though she was only sixteen she had said all the right things. She said it was 'fucking not fair'. Which it wasn't. And she said that one day it probably wouldn't hurt so much. Which one day it didn't. And she said you should let it hurt right now, though, because it didn't get much worse than this.

'I hope you do go.' Joyce set her tea on the counter. 'We'll babysit if Dan can't manage. Oh, and look, here he is.' She glanced casually at her watch. 'Better late than never.'

He was late, but Cate forgave him when he gave her a

kiss and whispered 'sorry' against her mouth. Joyce bent her cheek towards him dutifully. 'Dan.'

Cate knew her mum loved him, but it had taken time. She'd been suspicious of his good looks when Cate had first brought him home, uttering only her favourite 'handsome is as handsome does' homily once he had left. Joyce had been quite annoyed when it had cropped up in *Forrest Gump*. She had a saying for every situation. Cate's favourite was 'There's never a pot so crooked that there isn't a lid to fit it.' She'd heard that a lot over the years, after every tearful breakup with a boyfriend. Dan, she thought, made a very good lid.

The twins came tumbling downstairs at the sound of the front door. Emma wore her new top proudly. Jo hated to show any skin and had put hers on over a T-shirt.

'I think Gran and Grampa have been spoiling us again,' said Dan, pinching Jo's cheek. 'I've just been admiring Mummy's lovely pendant.'

'Isn't it beautiful?' Cate gave him her sweetest smile. 'And just wait till you see what they got for you.'

By 6.30 p.m. Stevie had fallen asleep on the sofa, one arm tucked around the Ligurian dolphin, and Ed and Joyce had tiptoed out, blowing kisses as they went.

Dan closed the door to the dishwasher and switched it on. He looked tired too, dark smudgy shadows under his eyes. He wasn't enjoying his work these days, not since the local health trust had decided to merge two of the city hospitals into one. It was a chaotic, ongoing process and one that Dan resented greatly. He hadn't shared much of the detail with her and she'd only started to wonder recently if he was anxious about his own position. Not that he would lose his job, he was too senior for that, but his chance of a further promotion might be scuppered with them bringing in so many new people. Cate knew it probably wasn't the best time to ask him anything, let alone a favour. She went for it anyway.

'Dan, you know this school reunion thing I told you about?'

'Mmm.' He reached into the cupboard and pulled out two wine glasses.

'I'm thinking about going. Would you come with me?'

He turned quickly, looking horrified. 'Would you really want me to?'

'Well, it would be nice if you could. I'd feel a bit odd going on my own. I'm sure most of them will have partners there. And the invite said you could bring your significant other.'

He sighed. 'Honey, I wouldn't know any of them. I'd just be sitting there like a lemon while you talk about old Stinky the maths teacher.'

'We didn't have a maths teacher called Stinky,' Cate snapped. She knew she was sounding petulant but she couldn't help it. One measly reunion dinner in return for countless orifice outings.

'Please, Dan.'

'I'd really rather not. And I'm kind of surprised you want to go, anyway. You haven't mentioned the place in years and it's not like you're still friends with anyone, is it?' He didn't wait for an answer, just handed her a glass of wine and picked up his own, turning to head for the sitting room. 'Are you coming through?'

She shook her head, annoyed and upset, and went, instead, to fetch her sleeping Stevie. She woke as Cate was trying to balance her on a raised knee to brush her teeth, and demanded a story. They snuggled together under the Sugar and Spice bedcover – the irony of which was not lost on Cate. Stevie was a handful; wilful, if you were being kind, downright unruly if you were being honest.

She laid her face on top of her daughter's head as Stevie traced a small, still chubby finger along the words. She was already reading fluently. Her last one grown.

'Baby girl,' Cate murmured into the soft dark of her hair.

Stevie reached the end of the 'Three Billy Goats Gruff', turned the page to the next fairy tale and looked up at her. 'What's a peed pipper?'

'It's Pied Piper, toots.' Cate smiled. 'He was a man who took all the children away from a town.'

'Why?'

How to explain a rather creepy fable about child abduction and broken promises to a five-year-old? 'It's a long story,' said Cate.

Stevie looked back at the book. 'No it's not. It's quite a little one.'

'Well, it's too long for tonight. Maybe tomorrow.' She took the book and laid it on Stevie's bedside table, then leant over her in her quilted cocoon. 'And you do know it's wrong to go away with anyone, don't you?'

Stevie nodded gravely. 'My teacher says you can shout and you can kick them in the chins.'

'I think she meant shins.' Cate patted her leg. 'This bit.'

Stevie nodded again. 'But Emma and Jo say you should kick them in the primates because it hurts the sorest. I would kick them in the primates.'

Cate bit her lip and switched off the light to hide her smile. 'That's fine, baby. If anyone tries to do that you can kick them wherever you want.'

Stevie flipped onto her side and snuggled down until only her nose and forehead were showing. She watched Cate scoop up an armful of small discarded clothes off the floor, sniff them and fold them briskly in the half dark.

'Mummy?'

'Yes.'

'Where are your primates?'

'Night night, sweetheart,' said Cate, gently. 'Time to sleep.'

When she got back downstairs, the twins were lying stretched out on the floor watching *Black Hole High* and Dan was snoring gently on the sofa. She lifted the TV guide off his chest and left him to his slumbers.

She didn't make up her mind until she got home from the school run the following day. She'd settled herself in the office with a cup of coffee, ready to start the research on her latest essay. On the computer screen, the Google searchbox was empty. She leant forward to type in 'Wemyss Ware' and immerse herself in the bold, colourful designs of the distinctive pottery. She typed in Margie Holland instead.

There were more than 200 references and Cate scanned through them quickly: a pet shop owner in Tuscaloosa, a sex therapist in County Durham, someone in Wales who crafted small woodland creatures out of straw, and a nursing manager from Inverness. Nothing that looked like her Margie. She sat back. She could always dig out the address book and try directory enquiries, but she was pretty sure the number wouldn't be listed. She cleared the search field and typed in 'Holland' and 'news' and 'TV', and there it was. Marg Holland. Senior Producer/Editor. Global News Corporation. European Bureau. London. On the flashy website with the little image of the world spinning crazily around the screen. There was no photo, but it had to be her. So she must have changed her name. Or maybe they made her. Marg. God, it sounded awful, and she wasn't even sure how to pronounce it. Was it Marg as in 'margarine', or Marg as in 'Aaargh'? She scribbled the number on a scrap of paper.

It sat beside her notebooks for half an hour until she plucked up the courage to dial. Why not? They'd been so close and she should have probably done this years ago. Margie might not even be there. It might not even be her.

The man on the switchboard was posh and brisk, oblivious to her mounting nerves. 'Putting you through now.'

Cate waited, twirling her pen frantically through her fingers. The background music stopped and a voice spoke abruptly before she'd expected it. 'Studio.'

'Oh, hi, ehm, can I speak to Margie, sorry, Marg Holland, please?' She opted for Marg as in 'Aaargh!'

There was a pause. The voice changed. It sounded surprised and a little wary.

'This is her.'

5

'It's Cate. Catriona Wishart. From school.'

'Cate?'

'Wishart. From school,' Cate repeated. 'Well, Beane now, actually. Cate Beane.'

There was another pause. 'You have got to be kidding. Bean?'

'With two "e"s,' said Cate, hastily.

'As in has-been?'

'As in Sean Bean,' said Cate, 'with another "e" on the end.'

'God, I hope he's worth it,' said Marg. 'Mrs Beane. Mr and Mrs Beane. I'm not getting a good picture here.'

It was so Margie that Cate started to laugh, all the anxiety about making the call slipping away. 'He is worth it,' she said. 'Anyway, what's the deal with Marg? It makes you sound like an extra from *Lord of the Rings*. The Marg awoke from the depths of Kazag Dhum!'

Marg burst out laughing. 'It's a damn sight better than Margie.'

'I liked Margie.'

'Margie doesn't live here any more,' said Marg theatrically. Her voice softened suddenly. 'But it's really good to hear from you. God. Cate. Catriona Wisha . . . Beane. How the hell are you?'

'I'm fine.' Cate grinned broadly. Almost twenty years and they might have last talked yesterday. 'I'm just fine.'

'You've got kids, right? Two boys, isn't it? Or, no, four.'

'Three girls. The twins are eleven, and I've got a five-year-old, Stevie.'

'Stevie?'

'Short for Stephanie.'

'Three girls. Jeez.'

Cate hesitated. 'What about you?' There had never been any hint of a partner in any of the Christmas cards, but then Margie had always said she was never going to get married. Unless Don Johnson asked, and then she'd think about it.

'Nope,' said Marg. 'No husband and no offspring.'

'I got your number off the website,' said Cate. 'High-powered media lady.'

'Something like that,' said Marg. 'I love it. What about you?'

'Not working.' Cate was suddenly annoyed at herself for feeling ashamed. 'I'm doing a course. Interior design. But mostly I'm a mum.'

'And a wife,' added Marg.

'And a wife.'

'What's his first name again? Stan? Something like that?'

'Dan.'

'What does he do?'

'Doctor. Ear, Nose and Throat.'

'Very commendable,' said Marg. 'Holes, but very commendable.'

'Are you seeing anyone?'

'I am,' said Marg. 'His name's Rick.'

'Rick. Rick what?'

There was a pause. 'Rutner.'

'Rick Rutner. God, of course.' Cate nodded. 'The war guy.'

'Technically chief foreign correspondent,' said Marg. 'But yeah, the war guy.'

There was a pause. Cate tried unsuccessfully to stifle a snigger. 'Do you know, I always thought that would make a great porn star name. Rick Rutner. He doesn't do films as well, does he? In his spare time.'

Marg was laughing, too. 'You're not the first person to say that and no, he's not a porn star on the side. He's a reporter, common or garden.'

'Marg Rutner. Has a certain ring to it,' said Cate teasingly. She felt fifteen again, giggling on the phone, Margie at the other end.

'That's not going to happen,' said Marg. 'Anyway, changing the subject, I know why you're calling after years of silence, and the answer's no.'

'So you got the invitation, too?'

'Mmhm. But I'm not going.'

'Why not?'

'God, could you imagine anything worse? We spent five years trying to get out of that place. Well, I did. Why would we want to go back? I'm quite glad they're knocking it down.'

'I thought it might be quite fun,' said Cate, weakly. 'Just to see what everyone is up to. And it's not like they're holding it in the school. It's in a hotel.'

'No way,' said Marg. 'Not if it was in the Albert Hall. Not if you paid me.'

'Oh, go on, please go. It'll be a laugh.' Cate paused. 'It would be great to see you again.'

'It won't be a laugh. It will be an ordeal. But it would be great to meet up. You should come down here. Girls' weekend in London. How about that?'

'I'd love that.' Cate smiled. 'I can't believe it's been so long since we saw each other.'

'When was the last time?' asked Marg.

Cate wracked her brain. 'You came up one summer. I

think you were with the BBC then, in Bristol? We went to St Andrews, remember, because you knew that student.'

'Oh yeah. God, we were babies.'

'Are you sure you won't go?'

'Positive,' said Marg. 'Cross my heart and swear to snog Gary Hamilton.'

'I think you did that already.' Cate laughed. 'Third year. School trip to Stirling Castle.'

'Ew!' said Marg. 'That's one memory I'd erased.'

There was a shuffling noise as Marg put her hand over the phone and talked to someone. 'Cate, I'm going to have to go, but look, give me your number. It's been so great to hear from you.'

Cate rattled off the phone number. 'And you're sure?'

'Absolutely. But we'll meet. Okay?'

'Okay,' said Cate. 'Bye, Margie. Sorry, Marg.'

'Keep in touch,' said Marg.

'I will. And you take care.'

'I mean it,' Marg repeated. 'Keep in touch.'

6

Marg put the phone down. God, Cate Wishart. Cate Beane. What a bloody awful name. What a really lovely surprise.

'Who was that?' The runner was still at her elbow with the package she had brought from the mailroom.

'Long lost friend,' said Marg. 'Not spoken to her for ages. Years.'

'Tracked you down, huh?' The girl snapped her gum. 'You look a bit shocked. She know all your little secrets?'

Marg looked at her coldly, took the pad and scribbled her signature. 'Thanks.' She handed it back brusquely. 'Bye.'

She sat back in her seat. Cate. Did she look the same? She'd always been skinny with long fair hair that she hated to get cut. She suddenly realised that she'd had an image in her head as she had talked to her. A faint impression of a girl grown older. The same face, but rounder. The same hair, but shorter.

She wondered if she was still a klutz, if she still wore Anaïs Anaïs. Marg smiled. The old Cate wore so much of her signature scent that it could take the skin off the back of your throat if you got near her, and she couldn't get through the day without falling over or scraping something, or ripping her tights or hem. If there was a protrusion or stray object in the vicinity, Cate's limbs would find it. You could play join the dots with the bruises she collected on her shins. Just like you could always find her in a crowd by following the trail of her perfume.

She know all your little secrets? Well, yes she did. She knew that Marg had put folded-up tissues in her bra for the first year Christmas dance, she'd even warned her when one of them worked loose and started poking out the neck of her batwing top. She knew she'd had a crush on a rather unsightly fourth-year, who was in the chess club for God's sake, but had a filthy laugh and an attitude to match.

But she also knew all about Marg's mum and offered her own family as a substitute. And she knew what happened at the end of fifth year. She was with her on the floor of her room when all the terror of the future she might not have overwhelmed her. And she had helped her do the pregnancy test, fussing like a little mother, and had rejoiced with her when it wasn't blue and promised that she wouldn't tell. Not anyone. Not ever.

Marg leapt at the heavy press of two hands on her shoulders. 'Jesus Christ!'

'Not quite.' Rick bent low beside her ear and kissed her cheek. 'The next best thing.'

Marg swivelled in her chair. 'What are you doing back? I thought it was another couple of days.'

He stood grinning at her in his blue Ozwald Boateng topped by a sand-coloured jacket. His laptop case was still slung over his shoulder, the one with the singe mark from the Molotov cocktail in Uzbekistan. It was a vanity for him to keep using it. It had only been a very small Molotov cocktail and he wasn't actually carrying the case when it got burnt. But it made a great story for female flight attendants. Marg grinned back, glad to be distracted from her memories. Rick always looked good when he'd just got back from assignment, rough at the edges, a little unkempt. In a couple of days he would have got to the Just For Men and been for a manicure.

'So.' He slung his bag onto a seat and folded his arms, leaning back against the desk. 'I hear we're taking a little trip. Can't bear to be away from me, huh?'

'Yeah, that's it, Rick. I fancy a romantic weekend in one of the world's more impoverished regions.'

'Why Chad?'

'It was one of the eighteen countries given debt relief,' said Marg. 'But it's had bugger all effect. They're still struggling. And in the east they're still getting refugees from Darfur. Good example of international failings ahead of the next G8.'

Rick nodded. 'Okay. When are we off?'

'I'm still organising,' said Marg. 'There's a World Aid project I'm trying to hook up with north of Abeche. Couple of weeks yet, probably.'

'Time for a little R and R, then.' He raised what Marg called his Roger Moore eyebrow.

She grimaced. 'If that means you'd like to go out this weekend, then, yes, that would be possible. So where are you thinking of taking me?'

He leant forward, eyebrow still arched. 'If I said to the heights of . . .'

Marg burst out laughing. 'Jesus, Rick! For a man who makes his living from the spoken word, you're like a walking bloody cliché. Or a seaside postcard.'

He stood up and gathered his belongings. 'And you love me for it.'

'No,' said Marg. 'I like you in spite of it.'

'Just like?' Rick was grinning again. 'Not love?'

Marg grinned back. 'Let's not push it, shall we?'

'Mum, Stevie's not got any clothes on again.' Emma appeared at Cate's elbow as she slid a fistful of spaghetti into the pot of steaming water.

'Well, that's okay. Just leave her.'

'But she's on the chair at the hall window. The neighbours will see her bum.'

Cate shouted without turning round. 'STEVIE. OFF THE CHAIR. AND PUT YOUR PANTS ON!'

'Why does she do that?' Emma picked up a handful of grated cheese from the plate beside the cooker. 'It's gross.'

'It's not gross,' Cate slapped her hand away, 'it's what five-year-olds do. Well, some of them. Actually, not many. And you've had your tea. No pinching mine and Dad's.'

'I bet I didn't do that when I was five.'

'No. But you used to like licking the soles of your shoes.'

'Muum!'

'Well you did. Especially after you'd been outside. Everyone's got something they did when they were little.'

'What did you do?'

Cate put the lid on the pot and turned to lean on the counter. 'Loads. I was a complete clot, always tripping over something. And I used to wrap combs up in my hair. Your gran had to cut one out once.'

Emma grinned and sneaked another hand towards the cheese. 'What about Jo?'

'She put beads up her nose. Don't you remember going to the hospital with her? You were both the same age as Stevie is now. It was a big bead that time. Pink, I think. From a necklace you'd got in a party bag. I think we've still got it somewhere.'

Emma giggled. 'Now that is gross. Oh, Mum, I was going to ask you, could Debs come for a sleepover? This weekend.'

'Not this weekend, honey, but maybe next.'

'Why not this one?'

'Well I'm going to the Ideal Homes Exhibition with Orla tomorrow and I've got a paper to finish, so I'm hoping Dad is going to entertain you lot. But next weekend. Next Saturday? I'll call her mum.'

Jo appeared behind them. 'Dad's home,' she said. 'He's just driving in.'

'Where have you been, mystery girl?' asked Cate. She hadn't seen her since they'd got home from school.

'Reading.'

'Emma's having Debbie for a sleepover next weekend. You want to invite anyone?'

Jo shook her head. 'Nope.'

'Sure?'

'Yeah, Mum. I'm sure.'

Cate watched her disappear into the hall to wait for her dad. Her solitary girl. Emma had been close to Debbie since primary one, but Jo had still to find a kindred spirit. Cate worried sometimes that she didn't have a special friend. She couldn't imagine having gone through school without Margie. Although Jo didn't seem bothered and perhaps it was healthy that she liked her own company.

Dan dropped his bag inside the door, gave the twins a hug, and looked quizzically at Stevie who had arrived at the bottom of the stairs, still sans underwear.

'Hey, pumpkin,' he said. 'Are you not a bit cold?'

Stevie shook her head as her dad enveloped her in a hug. 'I don't like pants,' she said.

'No one actually likes pants,' said Emma, contemptuously. 'But you have to wear them. Mum told you, and anyway, it's the law.'

Stevie looked at her and Emma nodded emphatically. 'The police can check, you know.' A horrified Stevie ran off to get dressed and avoid imminent arrest. Dan gave Emma a reproachful look and came into the kitchen.

'So,' he said. 'We've got one miniature streaker, one know-it-all, and . . .'

'One Jo,' said Cate, smiling and turning back to the pots.

He came up and slipped his arms round her. She pressed

back against him, and for once, he didn't pull away. He seemed to be leaning on her. She felt his breath through her hair.

'Tough day?'

'Mmm.' He buried his face in the back of her neck and she caught hold of his hands which were linked round her waist. He had wonderful hands. Strong and supple. A medic's hands.

'Knackered,' he said. 'I was lucky to get away early.'

'It's not early, Dan. It's after seven.'

'Mmm.' He detached himself and moved to the fridge. 'Drink?'

She nodded and gestured to the bottle of Pinot Noir she had left uncorked on the table. He poured two full glasses and brought her one.

'Cheers.' He took a deep slug and then gave her a quick, unexpected kiss.

'What's that for?' Cate smiled at him.

He shrugged and took another mouthful. 'Tell me what you were up to today. As long as it doesn't involve the National Health Service or a deviated septum or cost benefit analysis.'

Cate put down her wine and stirred a spoonful of crème fraîche into the Bolognese sauce.

'I called Margie today. My old schoolfriend. This morning.'

Dan's face was blank.

'About the reunion,' prompted Cate.

He nodded.

'It was weird, actually. I was really nervous about talking to her but it was absolutely fine. She hasn't changed. Well, apart from her name. She's Marg now.'

'Marg?' said Dan.

'I know.' Cate shook her head.

'As in Marg Helgenberger?'

Cate turned to look at him. 'Who's Marg Helgenberger?'

'The hot one from *CSI*. The redhead.'

Cate stared at him, grinning. 'Since when do you watch *CSI*?'

'Since you've been spending the evenings with your curtains and pelmets,' said Dan. 'Anyway, is she going to go? Marg?'

Cate shook her head and pulled open the oven to retrieve the garlic bread. 'She said she can't imagine anything worse.'

'She sounds very sensible,' said Dan.

Cate handed him a plate. 'Well, I'm going. I think it'll be fun and I'm going to go. On my own.'

'What weekend is it?'

'First in April. I know . . .' she held up her hand, as he started to remonstrate. 'Mum and Ed said they'd babysit if you can't.'

'It's just, there's a conference in Birmingham that I . . .'

'That's fine, Dan. Mum and Ed will cover.' She joined him at the table.

'This looks lovely.' He reached for her face. 'You've got a spot of sauce . . . here.' He wiped her chin and then wiped his hand on her napkin.

'Thanks.'

'So,' he said. 'What have you and the girls got planned for tomorrow?'

She looked at him, confused. 'The exhibition. Ideal Homes. With Orla?'

He sat back suddenly. 'Is that tomorrow? Christ. I'm meant to be going to Aberfoyle with Guy and the others. On the bikes.'

Cate couldn't believe it. 'Dan, you can't be meant to be going. You've known about this for two weeks. You're looking after the kids.'

'Does it have to be tomorrow?' He looked at her pleadingly. 'Couldn't you go on Sunday?'

Cate shook her head. 'It's all organised. Orla's all set and I was going to do my pottery paper on Sunday.'

Dan's mouth tightened. 'Well I'm kind of committed, and frankly . . .' He stopped and sat back in his chair.

Cate took another mouthful of wine. It wasn't as smooth as she'd expected and she felt the bitter tang in her throat as it slipped down. Or maybe she was just finding it hard to swallow.

'Frankly what, Dan?'

'Nothing. It's just . . .'

'It's not often. I don't ask for this kind of thing often.'

He looked up at her. 'Not often? You've been doing this bloody course for . . .'

Cate dropped her fork onto her plate with a clatter. 'Bloody course?'

Dan sighed deeply. 'You know what I mean. Look, honey, I'm sorry. It's not a bloody course. It's a worthwhile venture. And I don't want a fight. Let's not fight.' He slumped in his seat. 'I'll call Guy and cancel.'

Cate shook her head slowly. He'd been working all week. He was stressed. He needed this. 'It's okay,' she said. 'I'll see if Mum and Ed can take the kids for the morning.'

'Are you sure?'

She nodded and he smiled. It was the response he had obviously been expecting. He stood up to fetch another bottle of wine, running his hand through her hair as he passed.

'Joyce and Ed,' he said absently, squatting to peruse the contents of the wine rack. 'What would we do without them?'

Cate watched him. 'I don't know,' she said quietly. 'I really don't know.'

7

'God, Cate, you have to try this!' Orla wriggled on the vibrating stool and let out a long theatrical sigh. 'I tell you, if you had one of these in every home, we'd have no need of husbands.'

'Orla!' Cate giggled as the stand attendant arched an over-plucked eyebrow and looked on disapprovingly.

'We actually sell a lot of these to male clients,' said the attendant drily. 'It releases tension in the lower back.'

'Of course it does,' said Orla. 'Tension. In the lower back.'

Cate grabbed her arm and pulled her away. 'I'm sorry about my friend.' She smiled sweetly at the girl. 'She doesn't get out much.' When they were at a safe distance, she added: 'God, Orla, you're incorrigible.'

'And she was up her own arse, or as much as you can be when you sell giant dildo stools for a living.' Orla snorted. 'Vibrating chairs, fine. But stools? Come on!'

'Look, can we get to the tasteful part of the hall now?' laughed Cate. 'I'm going to have to get back a bit earlier for Mum and Ed, and I'd like to actually see something that doesn't resemble a sex toy before I go.'

Dan had left the house early, long before her mum and Ed had arrived to get the kids. Cate had lain in bed watching him pull on his Lycra. There weren't many men over the age of thirty-five who could carry it off, but Dan could. 'Hey, sexy,' she had said sleepily. 'You going to wear that leotard for me later?'

He laughed. 'It's not a leotard, my sweet, it's high performance sportswear. And only if you're lucky.'

'How do I get lucky?' asked Cate. He hadn't answered, just winked and blew her a kiss as he slipped through the door.

And now it was 11.30 a.m., and he was somewhere on the back roads of Perthshire and she was in the great hall of Glasgow's Scottish Exhibition and Conference Centre, trying to get Orla away from the innovations section where she had found the stool.

Cate looked at her floor plan to find the booth for Chiswick and Hawes who made the fabrics she had been lusting after since she saw them in last month's *Country Homes and Interiors*.

'What is it with you and cloth?' said Orla when Cate pointed out where she was heading.

'It's not cloth. It's fabric. There's a world of difference.'

'Well you go and fondle your linens and I'll go and have a scout about, and find a coffee. Give me a buzz when you're done.'

The Chiswick and Hawes booth was busy and Cate was relieved that she didn't have to chat inconsequentially with the assistants, but could study the fabrics, trailing her hand through books of silk and wool and jacquard, material so heavy, so liquid, it felt like it was pouring through her fingers.

She had always been aware of touch, ever since she could remember. The soft circle on the ear of her toy dog that she stroked to get to sleep. The tweedy roughness of the checked blanket her mum threw down on picnics and days at the beach. The warm weight of a baby fallen asleep in her arms. The sensation of Dan's cheek on hers as he kissed her for the first time.

It had been a surprisingly chaste kiss, given the way he

had been looking at her all evening at that chaotic dinner party in a cold New Town flat. He was still studying and she was an ad exec, with attitude and cash to spare. He had come with a friend of a friend. An afterthought. She knew almost everybody there, but it was him she was most aware of, watching her with his dark eyes across the table as she talked and laughed. And when she left he had come to the door, as if it was his to open, and kissed her on the cheek and smiled, and said her name as she walked down the steps: 'Cate.'

'Can I help you?' A woman in a sleek grey silk shirt bobbed in front of her.

Cate shook her head. 'No, thanks. I'm just indulging.'

'It's gorgeous, isn't it?' said the woman, looking at the book opened before Cate. 'It's our new season's range. Very *Gosford Park*, I think. Sumptuous. See this one,' she pointed at a rich silk brocade, the colour of burnt wood. 'They're using this in the refurbishment of Hopetoun House. In the drawing room.'

'Now, you see, for a space that big I would have gone for this one,' said Cate, lifting another swatch and imagining a fall of heavy green silk at the vast bay windows of the old stately home on the banks of the River Forth.

'Do you have a business?' asked the woman.

'No.' Cate smiled. 'Just a passion. I studied fabrics at art college. I'd love to have used it, but I ended up in advertising instead.'

'Well, I think you've either got it or you don't,' said the woman. 'You know. The eye for it.' She smiled and excused herself to speak to two men who were waiting by the entrance to the booth.

Cate closed the books and picked up one of the glossy brochures, tucking it into her bag. She'd often wondered where she would be if she'd pursued an art-related career instead of settling for the comfort of a corporate wage, and then giving it all up when she fell pregnant with the twins. Maybe she'd have a booth here now. Maybe it would be her fabrics that someone was lusting after.

'You look like you're in a sweetie shop.' Orla appeared at her elbow. 'You done? Because you really need to come and see this.'

'If it looks anything like what I think it might . . .'

Orla laughed. 'No. They've got a home gym section. Tif would have kittens. But you've got to see this thing. It's like a giant hamster ball. You spin around in it in your living room. It's called the Rolover or Rolovater or something like that.'

Cate linked her arm in Orla's. 'Now that's worth seeing.'

'You could get one for Dan,' said Orla. 'Then he wouldn't need to abandon you on weekends to go out on his bike. He could be the boy in a ball.'

Cate laughed. 'I'm thinking more hubby in a bubble.'

Marg turned sideways and stared at herself in the long mirror. The trousers fitted like a dream, high-waisted and long, with the faintest of houndstooth checks and hems that skimmed almost to the bottom of her boot heels. She knotted her shirt at her waist. 'Now that works,' said the assistant. 'Very Katharine Hepburn. But not quite so androgynous,' she added quickly.

Marg smiled patiently. It did work. Standing up. But the minute she sat down the little roll of poochy fat around her stomach that even Roy couldn't shift would poke through the gap, and leave her looking a little muffin-waisted. She reached out for the black silk shirt the girl had brought and whipped off the one she was wearing, ignoring the girl's startled look. Marg didn't do self-conscious. She tucked the silk into the trousers. The shirt had a deep V to a point just below her breastbone, but was so beautifully cut that nothing was going to fall out. She had good boobs, anyway. No need for tissues in her Rigby and Peller balcony bra now.

'I'll need something at the neck.'

The girl nodded enthusiastically. 'Big,' she said. 'I can have something brought up from jewellery.'

'Not too ethnic,' said Marg. 'For this, I'm thinking sleek or maybe baroque.' She sank into the deep leather sofa and took a sip of her champagne while she waited. This was a little different from the stale communal changing rooms of her youth, although the numbers on the receipt presented to her shortly would reflect that.

It was still such a thrill, though, to punch in her PIN or scribble her name. She'd never got over that. Not since the first proper paycheck; peanuts from a small news agency, but enough to go mad in Dorothy Perkins. An orgy of spending. Tops; more than one. A pair of trousers with three buttons at the waist. A skirt with sequins and then, at the till, a belt that gleamed with fake studded gems. The weight of it all in the bags she carried home; no one to say, you can't, it's too much, put it back. No one to place defiantly in your wardrobe the hand-me-downs from a neighbour's older daughter, who had hips as wide as the Clyde and a taste for bri-nylon.

Marg gave a little shudder. She'd never got the idea of vintage. She could still remember the faint stale smell of someone else's skin in the clothes she wore. She wanted new; uncreased and unworn, wrapped in tissue, folded in smooth plastic bags. New like she'd rarely had.

The girl returned, a little breathless and carrying a tray of baubles. She picked up a heavy cross inset with semi-precious stones and hung on a slim velvet ribbon.

'Too Spanish Inquisition,' said Marg, lifting a long string of irregular black pearls on thin silver. 'Now, this I like.' She twisted it around her neck, like beaded barbed wire. 'I'll take it. Trousers and shirt, too.' She checked her watch. 'Actually, I'll just keep them on.' There was just time to drop her bags at home before heading to Popinjays to meet Rick for pre-dinner drinks.

He was in the corner booth, surrounded by a coterie of hangers-on. Rick always had hangers-on, like bees round a honeypot, or, when Marg was feeling less charitable, flies around shite. She sighed. She knew it was unlikely he would be on his own, but just for once it would be nice to not be part of a group. He whistled, low and long, when he saw her, and stood to give her a kiss and make a space for her to sit next to him.

'You look edible,' he said against her ear.

'Just my knickers,' Marg whispered back, and he roared with laughter.

She sat down as he poured her a fluteful of champagne and smiled at the assembled group. Rick's acolytes could be roughly split into three groups. The women, young, smart, invariably blonde with trust funds and good ankles. The men were more of a mixed bunch. There were some journalists from the broadsheets who favoured black polo-necks and drank absinthe, and crossed their legs. And there were always a couple of cameramen, surgically attached to their jeans and pocketed jackets. Marg smiled across at Susann, who had dropped in with her husband, Keller, on their way to *The Lion King*. There was no sign of their two children, offspring so glassily perfect that Marg felt sure they came in a box and were put back each night.

'So,' Rick leant into her. 'Did you miss me?'

'We'll need to see, won't we?' said Marg.

He put his hand on her knee and turned back to the man

on his right to continue talking. Marg took another slug of fizz and interrupted. 'Where are we eating?'

He turned back. 'Elmo's.' He looked at his watch. 'Actually, we'll need to head over soonish. The only table for eight they had was at seven-thirty.'

'Table for eight?'

He looked a little sheepish. 'You don't mind, babe, do you?'

She gave a tight little smile.

'We'll get rid of them all later,' he whispered. 'Just you and me, babe.'

'Just you and me, babe,' sang Marg sarcastically under her breath and drained the bottle of Cristal into her glass. She raised it to the assembled group. 'Cheers!' she said loudly.

It was 2.30 a.m. before they were alone. It had been a good night, though. At least Marg thought it had. She wasn't entirely sure, not after the absinthe. It had tasted like molten metal. And her mouth hurt from laughing. So much giggling. She remembered screaming in hysterics at something that could never be that amusing, as thin trails of smoke from the blonde girls' cigarettes coiled into the air. She clutched Rick's arm. He wasn't doing much better, digging through his pockets feverishly looking for keys, even though they were at her flat and he didn't have a set.

'Come on. Come on. Come on.' She could feel his breath on her neck as she opened the door and got them into the lift. He reached for her before they got to her floor, tugging at the buttons on her black silk shirt. She heard her pearls scatter on the floor. He sniggered. 'Ooops.'

'Rick.' She pushed him off and tried to scrabble for her baubles. The floor of the lift was dusty. She found a fag-end.

'Buy you another one,' he said, pulling her into her hallway and taking her key. In the flat he pushed her onto the sofa and came down on top of her. He was a dead weight. She put her hands on his chest. 'Bed,' she said against his mouth.

'Here.' He fumbled with his trousers. She started to giggle.

'Babe.' They fell onto the rug and it was there, face down in the astrakhan, that she got him all to herself.

8

Cate lay and watched Dan across the bed, his shoulders rising and falling with each slow breath. His hair needed a cut. It had grown to a point at the base of his neck and she wanted to reach out and touch it, but didn't dare, scared he might misconstrue the caress. Scared of another rejection.

He had got home from his cycling at 4 p.m., long after her mum and Ed had left, and had then fallen asleep on the sofa after dinner. And later, when the girls had finally gone to bed and gone quiet, and Cate had brought through some wine and curled into him, he had given her a hug and an excuse. 'Honey, I'm exhausted.'

Cate rolled onto her back and stared at the ceiling. They hadn't had sex for, what was it? Seven weeks now? Eight? Was that normal after fourteen years of marriage? Maybe once every two months was as insatiable as you were likely to get from a thirty-eight-year-old consultant with three children and a fetish for vigorous exercise. Maybe he was over-doing the exercise, maybe that was why it hadn't quite gone right the last couple of times. She'd been so surprised, feeling the weakening in him in the half dark, unsure what to do or say, offering just an 'oh'. He'd given a faint attempt at a laugh and had said 'sorry' almost matter-of-factly and had turned away from her so she couldn't see his face. She'd said it was fine, absolutely fine, and had believed it was. She'd seen enough daytime TV to know it wasn't uncommon.

But he hadn't even tried to come near her since then. Was she being unreasonable? Was it her? She didn't know whom to ask. Not Orla, who probably wouldn't believe her. And not her mum, who would doubtless have a proverb to cover sexual dysfunction. Probably something to do with kitchen implements. A pestle and mortar maybe. Or measuring spoons.

Cate sniggered involuntarily, and Dan stirred and rolled over to face her.

'Moooorniiing.'

'Morning.'

'How's Cate?' He reached over and touched her hair.

'Fine.'

'What time is it?'

'The clock's on your side,' said Cate, 'but to save you looking, it's seven-thirty.'

He stretched again and lay still for a minute before swinging his legs out of bed. 'Think I'll go for a run.'

'Oh.'

He turned back to look at her. 'What?'

'It's Sunday morning, Dan. Can we not have a lie-in?'

'You can. I need the exercise.' He patted his tummy. 'You don't want me to get a big old gut, do you?'

Cate turned over. 'I want you to get a hamster ball,' she said under her breath.

'What?'

'Nothing. I just wondered if you'd make me a cup of tea on your way out, that's all.'

'Sure. Tea for my beloved. Coming right up.'

He disappeared into the en suite and Cate lay and listened to him pee, then wash, then gargle noisily. It was strange how you got so used to someone else, their sounds, their noises, their smells. She remembered their first holiday together when she had sent him out of the room so she could use the loo, not the en suite she had been expecting but a toilet positioned in the corner of the bedroom with just a plastic curtain to screen it. Now, he would happily chat to her while he took a dump.

He emerged and dressed quickly in running shorts and a sweatshirt, flashed her a smile and headed downstairs. She heard him whistling as he put on his trainers, then the sound of the front door shutting and the heavy fall of feet running on the drive.

'Thanks for the tea,' said Cate quietly.

'What's that, Mum?' A face had appeared at the door.

'Nothing, honey,' Cate smiled at Jo. 'Come on.' The twins bounded in, followed a few moments later by Stevie, carrying what looked like her entire collection of soft toys. There was an unseemly scramble as all three of them tried to lie next to her.

'Hey,' said Cate, removing a large purple dog from her face. 'I've only got two sides, unless someone wants to go at my feet.'

'Where's Daddy gone? I saw him in the hall.' Stevie arranged her toys on the duvet and tucked herself under the covers.

'He's gone for a run,' said Cate. 'He'll be back soon.'

Three small forms shifted themselves around until they were comfy, then lay still. 'Now this is nice,' said Cate. 'I like my morning cuddles.'

Emma shifted some more, jabbing bony hips into Cate's side. 'Mum, can you shave your legs? You're all prickly.' She yelped as Cate tweaked her on the arm. 'You are! Why don't you get them waxed? Deb's mum gets hers waxed. Deb went with her. She's going to get her legs waxed when she's bigger. When can I wax my legs?'

'When you have hair on them,' laughed Cate. 'And my legs are fine, thank you very much.'

'I have hair already. I do. Look.' Emma lifted one skinny leg out from under the duvet and held a pinch of skin with a smattering of soft golden down.

'That's not hair. Well, it is hair. But not hair that you need to shave. Or wax.'

'Emma's got hairy legs!' shouted Stevie, and Jo giggled.

'I don't know what you find so funny.' Emma turned to face Stevie. 'You'll get hair on your legs too. And under your arms. And probably on your face. Like a wolf girl.'

'I won't,' whined Stevie.

'Emma.' Cate caught her arm.

'Well, she will.'

'Won't!' shouted Stevie.

'Stop it!' said Cate. 'Stevie, you will get hair . . . in some places, but not till you're all grown up and not all over and anyway you can shave it off, too. And you can help your sister with her moustache while you're at it.'

'Muum!' said an indignant Emma.

'Well, leave her alone,' said Cate. 'Don't dish it out if you can't take it.'

'You sound like Gran,' said Jo. 'Gran says things like that.'

'Well, Gran's very wise. Old ladies generally are.'

'Are you wise now you're an old lady?' asked Stevie.

Cate nodded solemnly at her and turned to Emma, picking up and running a strand of her hair through her fingers. 'Anyway, sweetheart. You shouldn't be in a rush to grow up. Waxing is not something to look forward to.'

Emma grinned at her and cuddled back in, playing with the little rosebud at the neck of Cate's camisole. God, please don't let it come too soon. Cate knew that some of the girls in the twins' class were already in bras, little polka dot concoctions more concave than convex, but still bras. One or two had even started their periods, but the chances were her girls would be later. Cate had been later. One of the last, in fact, because she had been so scrawny. She could still remember the burning shame of wearing a vest when all the other girls were in bras, of one of the boys trying to ping a strap and finding only the weak flap of sturdy cotton. She'd even resorted to wearing the top half of her two-piece swimsuit, until Margie had pointed out that the small raised buttons across the front of it made her look like she had five nipples. Better, Margie had counselled, to be flat-chested than a freak.

Cate laughed out loud.

'What?' asked Jo.

'Nothing. I was just thinking of something when I was at school.'

'What were you like?' Jo shifted to face her.

'Pretty much like I am now, just younger, maybe a little bit more gorgeous.'

'Did you have hairy legs at my age?' asked Jo, now studying her own limbs under the covers. 'Did they have shavers then?'

'Razors,' said Cate, laughing. 'And no, we had to use a sharp stone or an animal tooth. Now, out of the bed, you lot, and let Yeti woman go for her shower. You've insulted your mum enough for a Sunday morning.'

Dan must have gone for one of his ten-mile runs, because breakfast was finished and the kids were squabbling over the computer when he got back drenched in sweat and breathing raggedly. He sat on the front step for a while, then took off his trainers and padded up the hall, leaving damp footprints on the washed oak floorboards.

'Feel better after that,' he said. 'Now, who wants a sweaty cuddle?' He moved towards the children, who ran shrieking into the living room.

'How about Mummy?'

'Mummy would have liked a cup of tea,' said Cate primly, keeping her back to him.

He came right up behind her. She could feel the heat off him, and wanted him suddenly to slip a warm, damp hand up the back of her top, the way he used to do.

He spun her round and pulled her into a bear hug. 'I think Mummy needs a sweaty cuddle, doesn't she?'

The children yelped their assent from the safety of the lounge and Cate smiled weakly.

'And a big kiss,' said Dan. He bent and covered her mouth with warm, salty, but faintly passive lips. She could hear a collective 'Ew!' from the kids.

'Mum and Dad are snogging!' shouted Jo.

'What's snogging?' asked Stevie.

'What they're doing.' Jo made a sucking noise with her mouth. 'It's disgusting. Especially when old people do it.'

Dan pulled back. 'Actually, it's probably just as disgusting when sweaty people do it, too.' He grinned at the girls, patted Cate absently on the rear, and turned to head for the stairs, pulling off his socks as he went. Cate swivelled back to the sink and waited until she heard the shower turn on in the en suite. She counted to twenty, then pushed the hot tap on, full and gushing. In a moment there would be a yelp as the ancient plumbing system struggled with two conflicting needs and the water upstairs changed from blissfully warm to uncomfortably chill.

Serve him right too.

'So, when can you actually say it's a famine?' Rick rolled himself across the sheets and took another bite from the bagel he had brought through from the kitchen. 'What's the tipping point again?'

'You are quite foul, you know that?' Marg watched him

from the bottom of the bed, where she was sitting cross-legged in her Reger knickers with the Sunday papers spread around her.

'What?'

'Stuffing your face with carbohydrates while discussing food shortages in the developing world.'

'Just because you like a liquid breakfast, babe,' said Rick, nodding towards the empty Bloody Mary glass on Marg's side of the bed. 'Ready for another?'

Marg nodded and he padded off towards the drinks cabinet, scratching his bottom as he went. Marg studied him. Rick was one of those men who could look great clothed, but didn't actually have that good a body. His shoulders were broad but carpeted with a thick mat of hair, and a lifetime of travel, dubious food and copious amounts of alcohol had left him with a belly that could look pendulous when he wasn't sucking it in – and he wasn't sucking it in just now. He turned back, saw her watching and winked.

The sudden stab of affection and regret took Marg by surprise. She watched him measure out a good slug of vodka and then a splash of tomato juice into her glass. He was stark naked and utterly at home in her flat, but he didn't belong there. And there would never be anything more than this because neither of them wanted anything more. Although last night hadn't been all that good, from what Marg could remember. She had a sudden fuzzy image of herself on the rug, feeling nauseous, listening to his grunting.

She looked quickly back at the paper on her lap. There had been another mention of Chad in a piece on debt relief in the *Sunday Telegraph*, which had prompted their discussion of starvation over bagels and the hair of the dog.

'You were asking about the tipping point for famine?' she said.

'Mm.' He handed her the Bloody Mary and lay back down.

'The cut-off is fifteen per cent malnutrition in kids. In Niger it was twenty-eight per cent. World Aid say the Abeche corridor in Chad is already looking at twenty-nine per cent. Although this piece is suggesting it might actually be more than a third.'

She folded the paper suddenly and looked up at him. 'Look, how about we go to the Tate? We could have lunch, a wander around?' She wanted to do something that didn't involve want or work or sex, something different and diverting.

Rick stretched and yawned deeply. 'Can't, babe. I'm going to see Mel and Bunty.'

Marg had always found it a little weird that Rick was still so attached to his parents, who were in their late seventies and mouldering away somewhere in Hampshire. She also found it weird that he called them Mel and Bunty. She didn't call her mother by her first name. But then she didn't call her mother at all.

'But I do have time . . .' Rick checked his watch and rolled towards her. 'For a little more lovin'.'

'Actually, Rick, no.' She held him off.

He raised a quizzical eyebrow. 'What? You premenstrual?'

'No. I'm just not in the mood.' She slid off the end of the bed and found her robe.

'Maybe it's the menopause.' He looked perplexed. Rick wasn't used to rejection.

'Maybe,' Marg retorted, 'I just don't want to.'

'Okay.' He shrugged and stood to start dressing, quickly and unselfconsciously. 'Don't know what you're missing, babe.'

'That's just the thing.' Marg threw his trousers at him with a flat little smile. 'I do.'

Marg loathed Sundays. Dead days. When the news was filled with cheating celebrities or pontificating politicians, and she didn't have to work anyway, but she did have to fill the time. Rick had given her a big noisy kiss when he left, her snub forgotten or forgiven. She glanced at her watch. He'd be somewhere on the M25 just now, looking forward to lunch with mummy, arranging another bed for tonight. Probably one of his trust-fund girls.

She took a long hot shower and then took herself off to the Serpentine Gallery via Selfridges, where she got artistic with her plastic in the accessories department and came away with a Mulberry tote in deep burgundy, and a low-slung calfskin belt with a buckle so big you could shoe a horse with it.

She wore them round the gallery, stuffing her smaller bag into the tote and slinging the belt around her jeans where the buckle hung like a shiny gilt sporran.

It was still only 3 p.m. when she got back to the flat. It had started to rain, a light smirr that left little slashes of water across the windows and had made her hair curl just in the dash from the cab to the front door. There was no point in straightening it; she'd be in bed in a few hours, ready for her 3 a.m. alarm. She poured herself a vodka and tonic and stretched out on the sofa, watching the clock above the bookcase, willing it to spin towards sleep and Monday morning. Marg knew what to do with herself on a Monday morning. Monday mornings made sense.

She switched on the television and flicked past the *EastEnders* omnibus and the rerun of *The Railway Children* until she reached Global News. It was the Sunday business show, but she watched it anyway, soothed by the familiar backdrop. She had another vodka and learned something she didn't know about the exchange rate mechanism.

When the commercial break came on, she stood to go to the toilet, but something about the woman on screen made her pause. It was the ad for washing powder, a mum with sleek fair hair not minding that her kids had taken her pants from the washing line and made them into a string of kites. 'For mums who know it's better to fly,' intoned a man's deep voice, 'than get in a flap.'

Marg burst out laughing at the ridiculousness of it all. What mother in her right mind wouldn't slap the little buggers silly for ruining her underwear? But the mum. The mum looked like Cate. At least the Cate Marg had imagined from the phone call. The woman smiled from the screen with her kite of blindingly white and chastely cut knickers. 'Come on,' she said, with a broad bleached smile. 'Come fly a kite.'

Marg knew immediately what she was going to do. What the hell. Weekends were torture anyway. Why the bloody hell not?

It was an answering machine that spoke to her when the ringing finally stopped, but she waited patiently for the beep and then she started to talk.

Cate heard the phone go as she was bent double over the twins' laundry basket trying to extract a soiled sock that had got caught on a piece of loose raffia. She could barely hear the ring above the music from Emma's CD player and Stevie's tuneless and deeply inappropriate singing. 'I wanna know you like a luvva,' she howled, blissfully unaware of the lyrics she was copying. 'I wanna find your secret plaaaaaaaces . . .'

'DAN? DAN! PHONE.' Cate heard the answering machine click on and returned to rooting in the laundry basket. Dan rarely answered the house phone, figuring the call would be for her. The sock came away with a small hole in the toe. She carried the washing downstairs and loaded the machine. When she got through to the family room, he had already pressed play.

'Cate. Hi. Mrs Beane. It's me. Just called for a chat. But

also to say, look, if you promise not to laugh, I'm thinking I might go to that thing. The do. Except I've gone and thrown the bloody invite away. So I'll try you later, or give me a buzz with the details. Except I'll probably have sobered up by then and the answer will be no again. So, we'll see. Hope you're well. And the kids. And Stan. Speak soon. But not after eight p.m. I'll be heading for bed. Early start tomorrow.'

Dan turned to look at her. 'Who the hell was that?'

Cate grinned and reached past him for the phone. 'That,' she said, 'was Margie.'

9

'What made her change her mind?' Orla bent into a squat thrust and bounced up and down gently to the beat of the Mambo Kings. 'Christ on a bike, I'll have thighs like Schwarzenegger after this!'

'Don't know,' said Cate, following suit. 'I'm just really glad she did. You have to meet her when she's up. She's coming to stay for the weekend. It works out quite well. Dan's got a conference in Birmingham so we'll have plenty of space to catch up.'

'Are you not worried it might be a bit awkward?' asked Orla. 'You've not seen her for twenty years. What if she's a complete cow?'

'She always was a complete cow.' Cate bent at the waist and tried to press her head against her knees like the instructor had just done. 'Well, complete cow is a little strong. She was always opinionated, a little prickly. That's what I liked about her.'

'Well, I think she sounds quite terrifying,' said Orla. 'Is she bringing Rick Rutner with her? That would be quite a coup, walking in to your do with Mr Hairy Chest off the news.'

'How do you know he's got a hairy chest?' Cate paused mid-stretch. 'Does he have a hairy chest?'

'God, yeah,' said Orla. 'He's always got his shirt unbuttoned.' She waggled her fingers at her throat. 'I'm quite partial to a man with shagpile, myself.'

Cate giggled. 'Well if he does come I'll introduce you, but I think it's unlikely. I asked her if she'd invited him and she just laughed. I don't actually think it's that serious.'

'She not got kids?'

'Nope.' For a second Cate saw the Margie she had known, clutching her hand on the floor of her room. 'Never wanted them.'

'Could you imagine?' Orla stared into space for an instant. She had four boys, largely because she had kept trying for a girl after the first two. Her house vibrated to the constant hum of the washing machine and various sound systems, her hallway was virtually impassable for piles of shoes and sports kit. She loved everything about it. 'Anyway, you coming for coffee after?'

'Can't.' Cate flopped onto her mat for the stomach exercises. 'I've got to get as much of my next module as possible done before she comes up and the girls have got a netball match after school so I won't get it done then. And I want to head into town first and get myself something to wear that doesn't have shoulder-pads or a sauce stain, or that hasn't been pillaged for a nativity costume.'

'So you're dumping me for your fancy new friend?' Orla turned her head on the mat and grinned at her.

'She's not new.' Cate grinned back. 'She's very old.'

The thing about shopping as a mother, thought Cate, is you always see something for someone else. But all of Stevie's tights were starting to look a little dropped-gusset after her latest growth spurt, and she couldn't resist the soft shaggy fleece gilets she found for the twins, one in blue, one in purple. And Dan needed socks and a new deodorant stick and a water bottle for his bike to replace the one he'd lost in Aberfoyle. Jo always joked that Cate shopped like the contestants on *Supermarket Sweep*, whizzing around stores making precision purchases. But how else did you get it done?

Finally, she started looking for herself and in a small boutique at the far end of George Street found an ankle-length silk cocktail dress in a rich brown, with a subtle paisley pattern. She slipped it over her head in the changing room, enjoying the soft chill of the silk on her bare skin. It fitted well and she twisted from side to side in front of the larger mirror outside, trying to make up her mind. She had wanted to look dazzling but dazzling cost more than she was prepared to pay and this made her look nice. And she was nice and she probably shouldn't be pretending to be anything else.

The attendant came and stood behind her, nodding her head with approval. Cate glanced at her watch. No time to look anywhere else. It was either this or something from the wardrobe. 'I'll take it,' she said.

'It really suits you,' said the girl, swishing open the changing-room curtain for Cate to go in and take it off. She gave an encouraging smile. 'My mum got the exact same one for the golf club dance last week.'

She made it to school in time to collect Stevie and meet the twins on their way to the gym hall for their netball match. They were both in the squad, but Emma made the team more often than Jo. Cate sat Stevie and her *Pony Girl* magazine on a bench next to a pile of odd socks in the changing rooms, and helped hand out the bibs. Jo was on the bench. Again. Cate gave her a big, warm smile when the gym teacher's back was turned, and she smiled back, seemingly unconcerned.

By the time she had laid out the water and oranges for half-time, and retrieved and hung up discarded shirts and skirts from the floor, the match had started. She slipped onto one of the front benches, half carrying Stevie, who had tired of horse tales and wanted to lie across Cate's lap fiddling with the buttons on her cardigan. It wasn't really fair on her, dragging her around after her sisters. Cate didn't know what she would do once Stevie started extracurricular activities too.

She bent to look at her youngest girl. She was so like Dan. Cate ran her fingers through the soft hair just above the curve of Stevie's ear. 'How did you get so lovely?' she whispered.

Stevie looked up at her grumpily. 'I'm not lovely,' she said. 'I'm a beast.'

Cate smiled. 'Well you're a very lovely beast.'

She looked back at the netball court. Emma was playing well, dodging, weaving, spinning on her feet. Her cheeks were pink and her high ponytail whirled above her head. Jo sat on the bench with the other substitutes. But while they were chatting animatedly, Jo seemed to be staring into space. Cate followed her gaze to the back of the gym hall, to the seats where some of the twins' classmates had come to watch. Where Paul was sitting. Emma's friend.

Cate watched the expression on Jo's face. Paul wasn't looking back at her, his attention firmly fixed on the match and on Emma. But Cate knew the look in her daughter's eyes. As a besotted mother, as an infatuated wife, she knew love when she saw it.

The head of World Aid operations in East Africa sighed deeply. 'We had Paris Soir out some months ago,' she said. 'It took a lot of facilitating. We don't have the time for facilitating.'

'We don't need facilitating,' said Marg. 'We look after ourselves. All we need is access. We won't disrupt.'

'It's a small operation where you want to go,' said the woman. 'It should be huge but it's just some nuns.'

'Nuns?'

'Mm. Three nuns. From Ireland. Helping maybe five thousand people.'

Marg felt her heart quicken. She could see the images already in her head. She stopped herself from saying 'That sounds perfect,' but it did. Three nuns doing the work of the G8 nations.

'When could we come?' asked Marg. 'How about next week?'

'Too soon. I'll need to get back to you.'

'Of course. We'll fit in with you.'

There was a pause. 'You haven't promised me that this will change things,' said the woman.

Marg was taken aback. 'I can't say that it will.'

'That's good. Everyone always tells us this will change things if we let the cameras in. But I think, maybe, it changes more the career prospects.'

'I'm not looking for promotion,' said Marg.

'What are you looking for?'

'A good story.' Marg didn't do bullshit. 'Something that makes people think. Maybe act.'

'And would you still be interested five months from now, when the G8 is over?'

'No,' said Marg. 'Not unless George Clooney pops over. Or maybe Sean Penn.'

The woman laughed. Marg saw the runner beckoning to her from the doorway. 'Look, I have to go. We've got a live segment coming up.'

'Okay,' said the woman. 'Can't keep the big political interview waiting, huh? You got the Prime Minister or someone?'

'Someone like that,' said Marg. 'Anyway, I look forward to hearing from you.'

She put the phone down and looked at the runner.

'The squirrel's here,' said the girl.

Marg silently cursed Susann Lingenfelder. This was all her idea, another effort to win anchor of the year. The saddest thing was that in less than a week, the funny end-piece had become the must-see segment of the programme. First, the woman from Delaware who could eat her own weight in hot dogs, then the farmer from Bangladesh who powered a car on nothing more than pig manure, and now the tap-dancing squirrel, just about to open its first show in Blackpool.

'The squirrel's here,' the girl repeated.

'And?' said Marg. 'Do you want me to go and greet it?'

The girl giggled. 'It's got shoes on.'

'Of course it's got shoes on. It's a tap-dancing squirrel.' Marg shook her head. 'I can't believe I just said that. Look, get them set up in the green room and put some newspapers down. I want to make sure it's emptied its bowels before it gets anywhere near Susann. I'm pretty sure you can't get squirrel crap out of Dries Van Noten.'

'Will it need make-up?' asked the girl.

'What do you think?' Marg bent over her console and switched on Susann's earpiece.

'Your rodent's here,' she said.

Susann smiled. 'I should have asked.' She looked up at the booth. 'Is he going to dance on the desk or the floor?'

'Up to you,' said Marg. 'He can dance on your lap if you want.'

'A lap-dancing squirrel,' said Susann. 'I don't think the Broadcasting Standards Authority would go for that.'

'Whatever,' said Marg. 'He'll be on after the Estonian ambassador.'

'Have you seen him?' cooed Susann. 'Is he all cute and furry?'

Marg paused until the title music indicated the commercial

break was ending. 'The squirrel?' she said sweetly. 'Or the ambassador?'

The studio light went to green. 'Hi,' said Susann in a choked voice. 'And welcome back to Morning Report.'

White or black? Black. Marg threw the trousers onto the bed. It always rained in Edinburgh, so white crêpe de Chine probably wasn't a good idea. A top. She raked through the racks in her dressing room until she found the tailored halter neck in a rich burgundy silk. All she needed now were the Jimmy Choos with steel heels and an ankle strap that she had seen in the window of Harvey Nicks. She could stop off tomorrow on her way to the airport.

She couldn't quite believe she was actually doing this. It was ten days since the washing-powder ad and her call to Cate, and she'd only regretted her decision to go three times since then. She still expected the reunion itself to be a dismal affair, filled with women grown plump and dissatisfied, and men who had lost their hair, if not the will to live. But she was intrigued about seeing Cate again. Seeing if she was the washing-powder woman, preternaturally happy and not quite of this world. Or just Cate, living a life she knew nothing about. Maybe she could persuade her not to go to the bloody event after all and they could just have a night out in Edinburgh instead, drinking legally for once and catching up. Catching up. Now that would be odd. Marg Holland. A life distilled. One name change. Six jobs. One affair with a Labour prospective parliamentary candidate; unsuccessful, both him and the relationship. Two awards. One small scar (right buttock) that she liked to say was shrapnel but was actually from falling onto a small wrought-iron fence in Chipping Sodbury while drunk. And on that note, one raging dependence on alcohol. One emerging addiction to teleshopping. And a mild to middling case of Obsessive Compulsive Disorder.

But then Cate knew about the last one even if she hadn't known the proper term. Fidgeting, she'd called it. You and your fidgeting. Standing by the door with a patient smile while Marg checked and looked and checked again. Light switches and bolts and drawers and window catches. The buckle of a school bag, a row of pens. She'd once asked if Marg's mum made her do it. She'd meant told her to do it, forced her, and Marg had said 'yes' and had meant something else that she couldn't quite put into words.

She exhaled slowly. She'd been trying not to think of her mum, telling herself the weekend would be too crammed to pay her a visit, remembering the last time she had tried and was rebuffed before she had even booked a ticket. At Christmas, two years ago. Someone was ailing, probably Aunty Betty. And it wasn't convenient. And the feeling of relief so much stronger than the anger.

She looked in the mirror. She'd scheduled two extra sessions with Roy, and had had her hair cut and coloured, a little blonder than she'd gone before. Although in the Edinburgh smirr it would doubtless crimp into the pubic mop that had dogged her all through school, in the world before straighteners. She shut the case and looked around. There was something else. Something she needed to remember. The hip flask was in, filled with the bison grass vodka Rick had brought back for her from Poland. Nothing worse than an overnighter when all you might be offered was a small glass of bad wine. The file on Chad was in, something to distract her on the plane. The straighteners were there. Please God, let the straighteners be there. She checked. They were.

What was it? She looked around. Of course. The small

box was lying on her dresser, stacked beside her Jo Malone collection. Why hadn't she spotted it against the sleek cream and black packaging?

She'd been amazed when she'd gone into Boots and there it was, still with the same smell. She reached for the bottle of Anaïs Anaïs and tucked it under her neatly folded clothes.

10

Cate prised the lolly stick from the inside handle of the car door and dabbed at the sticky residue with a wet wipe. Damn party bags and their cache of fluorescent, viscous sweets. She'd meant to gut the car before she'd left for the airport, but Jo had lost one of her trainers and it was gym day, and they only found it when Stevie remembered she'd used it as a hovercraft for her plastic hippo in the utility room sink. So it had to be tumble-dried, and they were late for school, and all thoughts of a freshly valeted vehicle in which to pick up an old friend had to be shelved. And now she had just a few minutes in the airport car park to clear away as much child debris as possible. So many bits of paper. Wrappers, torn corners from comics, drawings from long journeys, plastic supermarket bags holding odd socks from sleepovers, or blackening banana skins, scrunched-up tissues sticky with food debris, and worse.

Dan called her Honda the travelling skip and kept his own car as neat and spruced as if it had been autoclaved. Cate swept the last of the debris into a carrier bag, tied the top in a quick, neat knot and stuffed it at the back of the boot. She wondered what Dan would make of Margie, or Marg. She'd need to get used to calling her that. She wondered what she'd make of her. 'What if she's a complete cow?' Orla had said. God, what if she was? What if they had nothing to say to each other after the first few platitudes?

She'd sounded fine on the phone but face to face was different. So great to see you. You look fantastic. How've you been? Me too. Super. Right. Okay. What now? Oh, God.

Cate bent into the driver's seat and peered at herself in the rear-view mirror. She'd managed a little more make-up this morning and some of those blue eye-drops that Orla swore by and made your eyes look sparkly and white, even if you'd been up all night partying, or more realistically, placating a dry-heaving child. She'd picked the cashmere sweater Dan had bought her last Christmas and teamed it with her jeans and good black boots and her smart checked coat. Get going, Cate, she chided herself. You wanted this and you're going to see it through.

She locked the car and walked quickly towards the arrivals hall. Maybe the plane would be late and she'd have a little more time to ready herself. On the concourse she stood before the information screens amid the swirl of busy people who seemed to know exactly where they were going, and what to expect when they got there. She found the flight number. British Airways. Heathrow to Edinburgh. Landed. Five minutes ago. Oh, crap.

She half ran to the arrivals lounge and positioned herself next to a pillar, scanning the stream of people emerging from the sliding doors. Her heart was hammering. Would Margie recognise her? Maybe she should have worn a badge. I'm Cate. Just a bit bigger. So many people. Businessmen and women in suits and coats muttering into mobiles. Grannies, students. Couples. An aircrew, in polished pumps and shiny panstick. And just when she was thinking she might have missed her, Margie came round the corner. The curls had gone, to be replaced by a straight, sharply elegant layered bob, honey blonde and tucked behind her ears.

She was taller than Cate remembered, although that was possibly the spike-heeled boots on endless legs, or maybe the fabulous soft-looking black coat fanning out behind her like a cloak. But the walk was the same. Purposeful and confident and a little ungainly. She looked amazing. Cate stepped forward, the smile stretching across her face. And it was then, when the brown eyes lit with recognition and the perfectly made-up mouth curved into a warm, familiar grin that Cate realised that it was probably going to be okay and that she was probably going to cry.

Marg dropped her bag at her feet. 'Bloody hell, hon. Look at you.' She'd known Cate instantly when she came through the doors. The woman by the pillar in the jeans and soft sweater under the bright check coat. Same smile. Same heart-shaped face. She looked lovely. Not like the washing-powder woman, but real and smiley. Marg hadn't felt nervous about seeing Cate again, but as the plane had bumped down through the cloud cover over Edinburgh, and she caught her first glimpse of the grey city, she had started to feel apprehensive, prepared to find a stranger waiting for her, stilted and unfamiliar.

It was Cate who opened her arms first and Marg stepped in to hug her, a loose, awkward embrace. She gave Cate a kiss and found her ear. 'It's great to see you, hon,' she said.

'You too,' whispered Cate. Some tears spilled from her eyes and she laughed as she dashed them from her cheeks.

'Do I look that bad?' Marg grinned.

'You look fantastic.' Cate dabbed at her eyes with the tissue she had pulled from her coat pocket. 'I'm just a bit overwhelmed, that's all. I thought this would be really strange. But it's you.'

Marg smiled at her. 'It's me. And look at you. Your hair.'

Cate touched her hand to her head. 'I know. Chopped.'

'Never thought I'd see the day.'

'Your curls,' said Cate.

'Frizz,' Marg laughed. 'Tamed. By Mr John Frieda and the technological wonders of GHD. Hell, if Nicole Kidman can do it . . .'

Cate bent to grab her bag but Marg pre-empted her. 'I'll get that.' They turned to walk towards the exit, stealing little sideways glances at each other.

'So,' said Marg, needing to fill the sudden silence. 'What's the plan?'

'Well, I thought we'd stop by the house to drop off your stuff, and then go and grab some lunch before we have to get the kids,' said Cate. 'Then we'll all have dinner at home. Dan's away early on Saturday to this conference, and my mum and Ed are going to babysit while we're at the do.'

'Ed?'

'My stepdad,' said Cate. 'Mum met him about three years after dad died. He's lovely. Really lovely. You'll like him.'

'That's great,' said Marg. 'How is your mum?'

Cate grinned at her. 'Same as ever. She's excited about seeing you. But I'd better warn you now you'll probably get a lecture for being single. And successful.'

'Does she still have all her little sayings?'

'Oh, yeah. A homily for every occasion.'

'I loved them,' said Marg. 'There was never a situation so dire that your mum couldn't make it worse with one of her sayings. What was that one she was always telling us? When life gives you melons . . .'

Cate burst out laughing.

'What?'

'Lemons.' Cate shook her head. 'When life gives you lemons, make lemonade. Not melons.'

'Christ, of course.' Marg started to giggle too. 'Lemons. Not melons.' She paused. 'But talking of melons, hon, I need to ask. Have you had a boob job?'

Cate stopped in the middle of the sky-walk and glanced down at her chest. 'What? No!'

'Well, you were never that size at school. They've come from somewhere.' Marg ignored the curious glances of passers-by, intrigued by two grown giggling women.

Cate could barely speak for laughing. 'It's kids,' she said finally. 'It was after the kids. They grew and they stayed that way.'

'I thought kids made them go all limp and droopy, you know, like spaniels' ears.'

Cate shook her head. 'You've not changed a bit, have you?'

They stood for a moment and looked at each other, and then Marg grinned and linked her arm in Cate's as they continued walking. 'Do you know, I was really quite dreading this, but I think we're going to have a great weekend. Do we have to spoil it by going to this bloody Wanker's Ball tomorrow?'

'Wrecker's Ball,' said Cate. 'And yes, we do.' She moved towards a dark-blue Honda CR-V. 'Here I am.'

'Hold on. You've got something stuck to your bum.' Marg bent over and from the back of Cate's nice coat picked off a thin white tube, hung about with sticky pink tendrils. She held it up. 'What the hell's that?'

'It's a lolly stick,' said Cate ruefully, opening the door and gesturing to the interior of the crumb-strewn car. 'Comes with the territory.'

The house was a smallish sandstone semi-detached in Inverleith with a forlorn pink trike parked in the front garden and a throng of variously sized wellies by the step. Cate opened the door into a long, double-height hallway, floored in beautiful washed wood and hung with a series of antique mirrors that reflected light from a single cupola on the ceiling.

She bent to scoop up a child's red sock lying like a small discarded Christmas stocking on the floor.

'Cate, this is lovely.'

'It's taken us a while.' Cate stashed Marg's bag at the foot of the stairs. 'We've been here four years now and I'm just finishing up the last room. You should have seen it when we moved in. It had been let to students for years, pretty much like a squat. I've tried to keep the original features, just update it a bit.'

'I love this.' Marg trailed her hand along the wrought-iron railings of the curved staircase. 'Very *Gone With the Wind*.'

'It's actually been a bit of a nightmare with Stevie,' said Cate. 'She's got her head stuck through it twice. We had to get the fire brigade round the last time.'

'Have you done it all yourself?'

'It's kind of my hobby. I told you I'm doing that interior design course?'

Marg nodded and wandered up the hallway into a wide, warm kitchen, stopping at the far end in front of a wall of photographs in antique frames, most of them black and white prints of children. 'Your kids?'

Cate moved forward. 'That's the twins. Josie and Emma. And that's Stevie.' Marg nodded. They were beautiful children. She could see Cate in both the older girls, even though they were quite different, but not the small girl, dark-haired and dark-eyed.

'And where's hubby?'

Cate gestured to a wedding portrait. She looked just as she had done at school, with her hair long and loose and wavy. The man beside her was tall, dark and very handsome, but a little serious-looking, Marg thought, with a rather proprietorial grip on Cate's arm.

'He's a looker,' she said.

Cate nodded, her eyes shining.

'Bloody awful dress, though, hon.' Marg eyed the white frothy concoction that Cate had on.

Cate laughed. 'It is pretty much the full meringue, but that's what they were wearing way back then.'

'When was it?'

'Ninety-three. July third.'

'Why wasn't I there?' Marg scanned the crowd of guests behind the wedding party. 'Wasn't I always going to be your bridesmaid or something?'

Cate gave an embarrassed laugh. 'Ehm, yeah, we did talk about that, didn't we? You got an invite, though, but you couldn't come. I think you were in Armenia or somewhere.'

'Armenia? Oh, Azerbaijan. Yeah. Did I send you anything?'

Cate nodded. 'An Alessi kettle. I still have it.'

'How many kettles did you get?'

'Four.'

'But you use mine, right?'

Cate grinned. 'All the time.' She moved across to a large double-doored fridge and peered inside. 'Look, I was planning for us to go out and eat, but I can make something up here if you fancy. Caesar salad?'

'Great,' said Marg. She walked over to a small squashy leather sofa across from a broad oak breakfast bar and sank into it, bending down to unzip her boots. She kicked them off and curled her feet up under her. 'This is weird, isn't it? You have a house. And a husband. You're all grown up'

'It is and it isn't.' Cate lifted a lettuce from the bottom drawer of the fridge and shut the door with her hip. 'We should have done this ages ago. I feel like I saw you yesterday. Really.'

'Why did we leave it so long?' Marg studied her across the room.

'Well,' Cate pulled the lettuce from its plastic wrapping and started running it under the tap in a deep Belfast sink. 'I've been mired in domesticity and you've been a media whizz. Different worlds.'

'You don't look mired.' Marg looked around her. Cate fitted here. A natural habitat.

'I'm not really mired,' said Cate. 'I love it . . . I love them all dearly.'

'Blissfully happy,' said Marg.

Cate looked across at her. 'Happy,' she said. 'I think blissful ends when he's seen you clean your ears with a cotton bud and you're used to him peeing in front of you. Oh, and the kids would run a mile rather than have you kiss them in front of their friends.' For a second, she looked a little forlorn. 'Anyway, what about you and Rick?'

Marg shook her head. 'I've seen him pee, but that was on a roadside in Bukavu. But we'll never get to the ear-cleaning stage. We date. That's it.' She looked around her again and started to laugh.

'What?' asked Cate.

'This is exactly what you wanted, wasn't it?'

Cate's brow furrowed for an instant, then she laughed too. 'Pretty much. God, yeah. I suppose it was.'

'And I'm supposed to be in New York and famous.'

'Doesn't London count?' asked Cate.

'I'm not famous.'

Cate spread the salad leaves into a flat dish and started chopping thin slivers of yellow pepper. 'I've been dying to ask,' she said. 'Why did you change your name?'

'Why did you change yours?' countered Marg.

'It's a little different. I'm still Cate.'

Marg shrugged. 'I did it when I moved from the regions to network. Margie just sounded too damn . . . bouncy. Bad rhyming options, as well. Argie, bargie.'

Cate shot her a quick glance. 'What did your mum think?' She looked suddenly embarrassed at having asked. 'Are you . . . going to see her while you're up? I could drop you off, if you want . . .' She tailed off as Marg started to shake her head.

'I don't think there's time,' said Marg. She had known this would come up but hadn't planned what she would say.

'I'm not trying to pry,' said Cate hesitantly. 'Is she . . . ?'

'Dead? Demented? As much of a bitch as she used to be?'

'God, Margie . . . Marg. That's not what I meant.' Cate dropped her knife on the countertop and stared at her.

Marg stood up. 'I'm sorry, hon. You know how she gets me going.'

'Still?'

'Still.'

'I didn't mean to upset you. Really.' Cate looked distressed.

Marg walked over to the breakfast bar. 'You didn't, Cate. You know what she was like. Well, it's just the same. Except now I don't have to live with it. She's fine, though. Fine.'

'Do you have any contact?'

'Not really,' said Marg. 'I check, you know. I send money up. We talk . . . sometimes.'

Cate dried her hands quickly on a tea towel and moved back to the fridge. 'Do you know, I haven't even offered you anything to drink.' She gave a nervous smile. 'I've got some champagne for tonight, but do you fancy a glass of wine?' She pulled out a bottle of Sauvignon blanc.

Marg eased herself onto one of the high oak stools at the counter, put her elbows on the top, and felt her smile return. 'I thought you'd never ask,' she said.

'Is it short for Marjorie?' Jo leant forward in her seat, as Marg clamped her hands over her ears in mock horror.

'Don't say that word!' said Cate. 'She hates it.'

Jo giggled. 'I wouldn't like to be called Marjorie either. One of the music teachers is called Marjorie and she's got a hair that grows out of her chin. It's kind of thick.'

'See!' Marg twisted round to look at the kids in the back of the car. 'That's what I'm talking about. You think Marjorie, you think lady with a beard. And stout shoes. Probably fat ankles, too. And a great big bosom like a shelf.' She looked at Cate. 'Is it okay to say "bosom"?'

The twins laughed out loud. Stevie studied Marg's chin. Cate watched them in the rear-view mirror, a grin creasing her face. It had been fun to see their reaction when they had tumbled out of school to find their mum standing next to a tall, glamorous stranger in the kind of pointy, high-heeled boots that Emma had been begging Cate to get for months. Marg had shook hands with them all, a little stiffly, but by the time they were halfway home and Marg had started to regale them with inappropriate tales of their mum as a schoolgirl, including the five-nipple swimming top incident, the twins were entranced and Stevie was joining in just for the hell of it.

It was even more fun to see Dan's reaction when he finally got home. Tired of waiting, they'd opened the champagne after Cate had fed the children and Cate felt deliciously dizzy. He dropped his bags at the door and hurried down the hall, turning his dazzling Dan grin on Marg after he'd kissed Cate.

'Sorry, sorry, sorry. Dan.' He held out his hand. Marg shook it warmly, but she didn't do the daft simpering thing that so many women did when they met him for the first time. He seemed to enjoy her company, though, because they talked spiritedly over dinner about the health service and what was happening with the Labour Party and the property markets in London and Edinburgh. And every so often he would reach across and touch Cate, a hand on her arm, a stroke of her hair, in a way that he hadn't done for years. They outlasted him, though. And he took himself off to bed, pleading the need for an early night before tomorrow's conference.

He was still awake, however, when Cate came up two hours later. Her mouth was sore from laughing. Marg was outrageous, and had grown more so with every bottle of wine they had consumed. It was years since Cate had drunk so much. She stumbled into the en suite, where she splashed cold water on her face and struggled out of her jeans and into her pyjamas, hopping across the tiled floor to try and stay upright.

'What in God's name were you doing in there?' said Dan when she emerged.

Cate giggled and curled in beside him, laying a cool hand on his bare chest. He caught hold of it. 'Do we have any wine left?'

'It's a special occasion,' she said. 'Don't be so parsimonious.'

'I think you mean sanctimonious.'

'Don't be that either,' she giggled again.

'You're going to suffer tomorrow morning.'

'I don't care.' Cate stared at the dark shape of his profile. He was looking at the ceiling. She couldn't tell if he was smiling or not. 'She's fab, isn't she? Don't you think?'

'Mm.'

'Do you know, she once dated that guy who does the weather on Channel 6, the one with the really big hands, and you know what they say about big hands.' She hiccuped. 'But Marg said it was inversely proportional. Oh, and she was in Rwanda just after the genocide, and Sierra Leone, all over, really. She's been shot at, you know. Oh, and remember that thing about that guy from the US State

Department and the sheep down in Devon? Well, she says it was all true and the Pentagon had it hushed up. Can you believe that?'

'No,' said Dan. 'Does she know if Elvis is alive?'

'Don't you like her?' She raised herself on one elbow.

He turned to face her. 'I do like her. It's just strange. Seeing you so, I don't know, comfortable – intimate – with someone I've not met.'

Cate bent and kissed him haphazardly on the mouth. 'Are you jealous, Doctor Dan? That I had a life before you?'

'No.' He kissed her back and turned onto his side. 'I'm tired and my drunk wife is keeping me awake.'

Cate lay back on her pillow. He was a little jealous and that was no bad thing. She smiled tipsily to herself in the dark as his breathing steadied slowly into sleep.

'Whose is the rat?' Marg stood in the middle of the twins' bedroom eyeing Hamish, who had retreated to his newspaper nest, leaving only his small pink nose and twitching whiskers visible.

'It's not a rat.' Jo moved across to the cage and flipped down the door. 'It's a hamster. He's called Hamish. Do you want to hold him?'

Marg sat down on the bed in her pyjamas and put her mug of coffee on the bedside table.

'Go on, then.' She held out her hands as Hamish was lowered in.

'Weird,' she said. 'Scratchy little feet.' She peered down at him. 'God, Hamish, have you never heard of Pearl Drops?'

Jo giggled. 'His teeth are meant to be like that. It's from chewing. He chews anything we put in. He likes toilet rolls best.'

Marg looked up at Cate, who was leaning against the door, nursing her own cup of coffee. 'Doesn't he remind you a bit of Mr McCulloch?'

'Who's Mr McCulloch?' asked Jo.

'Chemistry teacher,' said Marg. 'He had long yellow teeth like that. Probably had scratchy little feet as well.' She gave a mock shudder, and Jo giggled and sat down, close, beside her on the bed.

Cate watched them. Both the girls were taken with Marg, but it was Jo, her serious, private Jo who had really connected with her. Marg handed Hamish back and looked on as Jo deftly slipped him back in the cage.

'You like your animals, don't you?' Marg gestured at the posters, and Jo nodded. 'Want to be a vet when you grow up? Your mum wanted to be a vet at one point.'

'Did she?'

'Did I?' asked Cate.

'You did, remember, in primary school, but you got put off when we saw that dog who'd been run over. The Alsatian? Spread all over the road. We almost stood in it.' She turned to Jo. 'At least, we thought it was an Alsatian. The only complete bit left of it was the tail.'

Jo grimaced in horror and Cate shook her head, trying not to laugh.

'What?' Marg looked at her. 'Not okay?'

'Not okay,' said Cate. Outside on the landing Stevie streaked past in a blur of Barbie vest and bare buttocks, and further down the hall a voice rose insistently from the master bedroom.

'Cate. Cate! CAATE!'

Dan was rooting in his sock drawer when she got through. 'I can't find my cummerbund. Have you seen it? The red one.' He seemed frazzled. She stepped past him and unhooked the cummerbund from the rack on the back of the wardrobe door.

'Thanks.' He dropped it haphazardly into his open case.

'Dan, it'll get crushed.' Cate moved over and lifted the silk band, folding it neatly and laying it back on top of his clothes. She ran her hand down the smooth lapel of his dinner jacket which was draped over the end of the bed, then moved over and circled her arms around him. 'I kind of wish I was going to your do.' She raised herself onto her toes and kissed him. 'I'll miss you.'

He kissed her back distractedly. 'Me too. Did you say you'd got me a new deodorant?'

Cate broke away and went into the en suite. The deodorant was on the shelf above the mirror and she peered at her reflection as she reached for it. She hadn't had her shower yet and she looked a little rough after last night's excesses. She pressed her hand to her hair where it felt like it had been backcombed. She'd need Orla's eye-drops as well if she wasn't going to go to the reunion looking like Marilyn Manson.

Dan was already in the hall when she came out. Cate handed him the deodorant and he stuffed it in a side pocket in his case.

'Bye, Marg.' He poked his head round the girls' bedroom door. 'Lovely to meet you. I'm sure I'll see you again.'

Marg raised her hand. 'Yeah, bye, Dan. Have a good conference. I'll keep an eye on your wife.'

The twins and Stevie circled him for a cuddle. He kissed the tops of their heads. 'Be good for your mum and I'll see you tomorrow night.'

Cate followed him downstairs. The taxi had arrived a good five minutes ago, and Cate opened the front door to signal to the driver.

'You got everything?'

Dan nodded and slipped his computer case over his shoulder. He reached out and pressed his hand on Cate's mussed-up hair. 'You need a brush.'

'I need a make-over,' she laughed, 'if I'm going to look eighteen by seven p.m. tonight.'

'Have a good time at your do.' He bent and kissed her quickly on the mouth. 'Behave.'

'Always.' She held the door open for him. 'You too.' He smiled and turned towards the street.

By the time Cate got out of the shower, Marg and the kids were downstairs and in the kitchen.

'What do they eat?' Marg put her hand on Stevie's head. 'This one says she's hungry.'

'Well, not biscuits,' said Cate removing a packet of Penguins from Stevie's fist. 'Not at this time in the morning. I'll put some toast in.' She stepped over the small pile of spilled Shreddies to reach the bread bin. 'And can whoever poured their cereal on the floor instead of into a bowl clear it up? Now.'

'Stevie!' chorused the twins.

Marg perched on one of the stools and pushed a pile of cereal plates further down the counter.

'This is what your house looks like normally, isn't it?' She waved her hand around.

Cate laughed. 'You should be honoured it was so tidy yesterday.'

'If you think this is messy, you should see Mum's office,' said Emma, slipping onto the stool next to Marg. 'Dad says it looks like an atomical bomb went off in there.'

'Atomic bomb,' said Cate.

'What's an atomic bomb?' asked Stevie, standing up and letting small shards of Shreddie crumble through her hands and back onto the floor.

'Well,' Marg cocked her head to one side, 'it's an explosive device which releases a huge amount of energy through nuclear fission. Either plutonium or uranium. It's the kind they dropped on Hiroshima and Nagasa . . .' She spotted Cate's raised eyebrow.

'It's a really big one,' said Cate. 'That makes a big mess of places. And people. Especially people.'

'Thanks for the translation,' laughed Marg. 'Anyway, what's this about an office? Where is it?'

'Upstairs.' Cate had left it off the house tour she'd given Marg yesterday, but wasn't entirely sure why she had.

'Well, let's have a look.'

'What, now?' Cate picked the hot toast gingerly out of the toaster and laid it on the plates.

'Yeah, now,' said Marg. 'You kids can spread this your-selves, can't you?'

The twins nodded and Cate wiped her hands on a tea towel and turned to lead Marg up the stairs.

'It's just for my course, you know. Just somewhere to keep all the stuff. And it's not so much an office as a boxroom.' She reached the door, opened it and flicked on the light. 'Da Daa!'

Marg squeezed past her and stood before the wall of pictures and cuttings and samples.

She whistled. 'Wow. You're really taking this seriously.'

'I'm enjoying it.' Cate stooped to pick up some maga-zines from the floor. 'Although God knows when I'll actu-ally finish. It's just getting the time.'

Marg walked over to the desk and leafed through one of the textbooks, the margins laddered with Cate's neat, painstaking notes.

'You've obviously got a knack for it,' she said. 'The house is lovely. Have you never thought of doing it profession-ally?'

'In mad moments,' said Cate.

'Why mad?' Marg turned to face her and perched on the desk.

Cate waved a hand in the air. 'There's so much going on with the kids, Dan, house.'

'They're all at school now, though, aren't they?'

Cate nodded. 'Stevie started in the autumn.'

'So that's a good, what, six or seven hours to yourself each day?'

Cate gave a hollow laugh. 'To myself? I'm lucky if I get an hour up here. Once I've done the school run, the errands, gone to the gym, cooked dinner, cleaned out the hamster . . .'

'You're letting a hamster get in the way of a career?' Marg

tipped her head to one side and Cate felt herself tense. Fine for her to say, sitting here in her dry-clean-only pyjamas and her hand-tooled leather slippers with no juice stains or unpicked stitching.

'No. I'm letting life get in the way of a career.' She spoke more sharply than she'd meant to and Marg said, 'Ouch!'

Cate smiled. 'I didn't mean it like that. But I like what I'm doing. The mum thing. The house thing. And this thing. It's fine. Everything's balanced out.'

There was a sudden howl from the kitchen and then Emma shouted from the foot of the stairs, 'Muuum. You know the knife for spreading . . . ?'

Cate was out of the room before she could finish the sentence.

'So, Margie.' Cate's mum eased herself back into the sofa and crossed her legs neatly at the ankle. 'How come you've not settled yourself down with a nice London lawyer or someone like that?'

Cate glanced surreptitiously at her watch. It had taken almost an hour for her mum to get to the point. She smiled to herself and concentrated on pouring the tea.

'I guess I've just not met the right man, Joyce,' said Marg good-naturedly.

'Well, he's out there somewhere, dear,' said Joyce, sitting forward to take her cup from Cate. 'As I always say, there's never . . .'

'A POT SO CROOKED THAT THERE ISN'T A LID TO FIT IT!' chorused Marg and Cate.

'What? You're making fun of me.' Cate's mum took an indignant sip of her tea. 'I was just meaning . . .'

'Mum, we've heard them all before,' said Cate. 'Marg isn't a crooked pot. And it's Marg now, not Margie.'

'Well, I must say I prefer Margie,' said Joyce. 'I don't know why you've changed it.'

'That's fine, Joyce.' Marg grinned at her. 'You can call me Margie. And we didn't mean to make fun of you. I'm sure I'll find my lid.'

'And you can call her an interfering old busybody, if you want, my dear,' said Ed, easing himself off the floor where he was attempting a jigsaw with Stevie. 'Now, young lady, come and let your grampa have a breather, and show me this injury you got this morning. What was it again? A Samurai sword?' He sat down heavily in an easy chair and Stevie clambered onto his lap, holding aloft her finger with its Buzz Lightyear band-aid.

'Anyway,' said Cate's mum, giving him a reproachful look. 'Shouldn't you girls be off getting ready? You've only got about an hour before you'll have to leave.'

'Marg, you go on,' said Cate. 'I'll stick the tea stuff in the dishwasher and be right up.'

'No.' Cate's mum stood up and put down her cup. 'I'm on tea dishes. You go and change. Remember this is what you used to do before those school discos.'

She turned to Ed. 'I could never get them out of the room for all the singing and giggling that was going on. Thought they were Madonna, the pair of them, didn't you? You should have heard the racket.'

Cate gave her a grateful hug. 'Thanks, Mum.'

They followed each other up the stairs to the faint, syncopated beat emanating from the twins' bedroom. Cate felt suddenly awkward when they reached the top. She twisted her hand round the banister.

'I think I'll jump in the shower,' she said. 'Freshen up.'

'Mm.' Marg seemed a little discomfited too. She glanced towards the spare room. 'I should probably . . .' Her hands lifted to her hair and mimicked straighteners.

Cate nodded. 'Well, see you in a mo.' She went into the bedroom and pushed the door closed. It was awfully quiet. Her dress was hanging on the outside of the wardrobe and she fingered the cold silk. She had the sudden urge to pick it up and run up the hall, and bounce onto the spare room bed. And they wouldn't stop talking and her mum would have to come upstairs and tell them to keep it down and remind them they had somewhere to be, as she'd done so many times before. And no matter where it was that they were off to – sleepover, disco, concert – it never proved to be quite as much fun as the time getting ready, when it was just the two of them.

God, what did they talk about? Everything and nothing. Boys, classmates, whom they liked and whom they didn't. The size of Gillian Marshall's bust. The injustice of weekend homework, the physics teacher who pressed too close when you needed help modelling atoms. The chances of meeting or marrying a-ha's Morten Harket. How he got his hair to stay that way. What to do with Margie's hair. Sex. When it might happen, what it might feel like. What was happening to their bodies.

She thought of the night her periods had started. She had gone to the loo and seen the faint brownish stain of first blood on her pants and had run back to the bedroom, weak with relief and triumph to tell Margie, who had hugged her and said 'about bloody time' and told her to go and tell her mum. Such a generous thing to do, because when Margie's had started a good eighteen months before, her own mum had simply handed her a pack of looped towels, the old-fashioned kind you had to hang in special knickers, 'like stupid little hammocks,' Margie had said.

And then the later night when Margie said her period hadn't come. Not for four days. And she knew, just knew she was pregnant. He hadn't put the condom on right, not right the way down, and it was loose when he pulled out, the boy with the motorbike whom she didn't even really like anyway. The utter terror in her eyes. Cate, what am I going to do?

And Cate had no idea but fought the rise of panic and promised not to tell a soul, even though she wanted to run and get an adult. The awkwardness of buying a test. The pain of a hand clenched in hers. The agony of time passing until it had worked. Thirty minutes, it had taken, in those days. And then the shock of seeing Margie cry, overwhelmed at her escape.

Cate lifted the dress and stood, biting her lip. They had shared so much. But would it be weird? Marg might look at her like she'd gone mad. Down the hall she heard the click of the bathroom door and then Jo's voice from the bottom of the stairs. 'Mum? Are you up there? Muuuuuuuum?' She hung the dress back on the wardrobe. Too late now. Years too late.

They met again on the upstairs landing and Cate instantly felt a frump. Marg was wearing a beautiful halter top, tailored in rich silk. Her trousers were high-waisted and draped over steel-heeled sandals. 'God, you look amazing,' said Cate. She looked down at her dress. 'I look like I'm off to a barn dance.'

'Crap,' said Marg. 'You look fab; classy. Oh, and here. I meant to give you this earlier.'

She handed over a small box and Cate burst out laughing. 'Anaïs Anaïs. I haven't seen this for ages. I loved this.'

'Go on,' said Marg. 'Splash it all over.'

'I just might.' Cate pulled open the packaging and took a deep sniff. 'God, that takes me back.'

'Give us a smell.' Marg bent forward and breathed in. They smiled at each other.

'Well come on,' said Marg. 'If you insist we have to go, let's get it over with.'

'You know,' said Cate, spraying the perfume down the neck of her dress as they descended the stairs. 'Mum might actually be right. You might just find your lid tonight.'

'Possibly.' Marg started to laugh. 'But I think, being realistic, it's more likely it'll be a load of crooked pots.'

12

It looked, thought Marg, as though a party of middle-aged aunts and uncles had stumbled into the Edinburgh suite of the Sheraton Hotel by mistake. She watched the men and women milling around the tables. So old! Bald, greying, thickening at waist and neck, squeezed into best dresses, kilts and Sunday suits. She heard a guffaw. A man with a big, round face was reddening with laughter. Who the hell was that? Two women gripped each other's wrists in frantic recognition, eyes sweeping the other's shape, hair, outfit.

You look so! So do you! I can't believe! You never are! Have you seen? I know!

Something Burt Bacharach and tinkly issued from the speakers.

'Jesus wept!' said Marg under her breath. 'It's the Village Of The Damned.'

'Behave. We're not even in the door yet.' Cate bent over the table laid out with name cards and seating plans. 'Here's mine. And . . .' She started to laugh.

'What?'

'And here's yours.' She handed across the small plastic tag. Marg peered at it. Marjorie Jean Holland: 1987.

'I am not wearing that. It's not my name and it looks like an RIP.'

Cate giggled. 'Put it on. Mine says Catriona Ann Wishart. You've got to play the part.'

'I'm not wearing it.'

'Yes, you are.' Cate took the tag and reached up to pin it to Marg's top. She smelled of the Anaïs Anaïs. Marg looked down. Cate's fingers were long and slim, but Marg hadn't noticed how lined they had become, a little rough and worn.

'This was such a bad idea.' She peered down at her name tag. 'You know that?'

Cate caught her hand and pulled her towards the room. 'Yeah,' she laughed. 'Isn't it great?'

'Cate? Cate Wishart?' A large woman in a green Ghost dress grabbed Cate by the shoulders.

'Eilish.' Cate stared at the name tag as she bent in for a hug. 'It's lovely to see you.' She turned to Marg. 'Marg, you remember Eilish?'

Marg did remember Eilish, but as a rather slight and mousy girl, not the plus-size lady standing in front of her. The hair was blonde and very done, the jewellery as big as a child might draw.

Eilish scanned her name tag. 'Margie Holland? No!'

'Yes,' said Marg.

'God, you've changed,' said Eilish.

'So have you,' enthused Marg.

Eilish touched her hair and giggled. 'I know. I'm a blondie.'

And the size of a three-seater sofa, thought Marg. She saw Cate's nervous glance and smiled sweetly. And so it continued through the room. Walk a little. Get stopped. Hug. Reminisce. Lie through your teeth. Shriek. Laugh. Marg needed a drink. She looked at the tables. Two bottles of wine on each. Not nearly enough. She tapped Cate, mid-greeting, on the shoulder. 'I'm going to get us a drink. What do you fancy?'

She made her way to the bar, deeply conscious of the stares as she passed each small group, feeling uncharacteristically gauche.

She ordered Cate's gin and tonic and two vodkas and

managed to swallow one surreptitiously before she headed back into the fray. The barman grinned at her as she put the glass back on the counter and raised his eyebrows in sympathy. 'Having fun?' He spoke with a warm Australian drawl. He was very attractive and very young.

'What do you think?'

'I think you're too young to be at a school reunion.' He gave the bar an unnecessary swipe with his cloth.

Marg laughed. 'Thank you for that,' she said. She picked up her drinks. 'You might have just made my night.'

Cate was already seated at their table and deep in conversation with a dark-haired woman by her side. Marg suddenly remembered how at ease Cate was with everyone. Warm and responsive. She felt a sudden and horribly familiar pang of envy. Likeable Cate and Cynical Margie. Beauty and the Bitch.

'Marg. You remember Lucy from the year above?' Cate gestured to the woman at her side. 'And Fay from our class? And this is her husband. I'm sorry, I've forgotten your name already.'

'Gordon,' said the man. He gave Marg a leering smile, his eyes not moving as far up as her face.

'And this is Adam Milner,' said Cate. 'He was two years below us.'

A man with sandy-coloured hair half stood and held out his hand. Marg shook it.

It was a better shake than many she'd had that evening. Firm and confident but not so alpha male that it cut off the blood supply.

'He was the debater,' Cate continued. 'Remember, he won the inter-schools cup?'

Marg didn't remember. Geek, she thought.

'Weren't you the youngest champion they'd ever had?' asked Fay.

Adam laughed ruefully. 'I think you mean geek,' he said, and for a second Marg wondered if she had spoken out loud.

'Don't be daft,' smiled Cate. 'It's a real skill. I'm trying to persuade my two oldest to do speech and debating. It stands you in really good stead for whatever you decide to do.'

'Tallulah's just turned five and we've got her in stage school already,' said Fay. Her husband took a deep slug from his whisky tumbler and continued his leisurely study of Marg's cleavage. Fay's eyes bore into him. She had been a prefect at school, the lead in the choir, and vice-captain of the netball team. There had been nothing that Fay couldn't do. Except, apparently, pick a decent partner.

Fay's voice rose a fraction. 'She's got a real musical skill, so they say. Isn't that right, Gordon? Isn't that what they say? Perfect pitch.'

'Mm,' said Gordon.

'Perfect pitch,' repeated Fay, her voice now growing a little frantic. 'You really should hear her on the piano. And the banjo.'

'Banjo?' said Marg.

Fay nodded vigorously. 'It's fantastic for small motor skills.'

'Motor skills? Isn't she a little young to drive?'

Marg heard Adam Milner laugh as Fay waggled her fingers. 'Dexterity.' She gave a tight and suspicious little smile. 'It's well seeing you don't have kids. You don't, do you?'

Marg shook her head.

'You can tell,' mumbled Gordon.

'Margie Holland,' trilled Fay. 'Abbeyhill's own Bridget Jones.'

'Not really.' Marg finished the last of her second vodka

and set the glass back down on the table slowly. 'She was desperate and I'm not desperate. Can't actually think of anything worse than ending up with the wrong person.' She let her eyes flicker across Gordon before they reached Fay. Stupid bitch and her lecherous prick of a spouse.

'So!' Cate leant forward on the table. 'Isn't this strange?'

'Very,' said Marg as their eyes met.

Fay wasn't finished. 'Well, if you don't have children, what do you do?'

'I'm in news,' said Marg, patiently. 'Television. Producer.'

'How very exciting,' said Fay. 'I never had you down for a high-flier. Did you, Cate? Did you think Margie would be on TV?' She didn't wait for an answer. 'Who are you with? I can't recall seeing you anywhere.'

'Global News Corporation. And I'm not on TV. I produce a TV news show.' Marg spoke slowly, and a little louder, as if she were talking to an aged aunt.

'I prefer CNN myself.' Adam Milner leant onto the table, blocking Fay's line of sight.

'And why is that?' asked Marg tartly, turning to look directly at him.

'More analysis,' he said. 'I sometimes find Global a bit . . .' He paused. 'A bit flighty. For example, last week, you had this decent two-way going on with your man in Afghanistan about the opium trade, and then it's cut off because some footballer's just been arrested for GBH after a barney outside a swanky London club.'

'That's breaking news,' said Marg.

She forgot about Fay, whom Cate was trying to distract with questions about the all-singing, all-dancing Tallulah. She was intrigued by Adam's observations. The tone of Global was something that was constantly being monitored. The board wanted the content and presentation to be glitzier, more like the Newsflash Network, where the women were all buffed and botoxed and the men all gruff and greying. And distracting graphics and thumping theme tunes covered the fact that the content was as trite and simplistic as the copy on a candy wrapper.

'It's not breaking news. It's inconsequential fluff,' said Adam. 'To my life, anyway.' He smiled at her. 'But in general, it's a good network.'

'Well, thanks for that,' said Marg. 'You seem very opinionated for a . . .'

'An architect.'

'Ah, so that's why you're here,' said Marg. 'Can't bear to see an old building pulled down.'

'It would be a travesty.' He leant his elbows on the table. 'There are too few distinctive structures left in Scotland. To ransack this one under the guise of educational progress is criminal.'

Marg watched him closely as he talked. If you'd been asked to describe him, she concluded, you would probably say 'ish'. Tallish, slimmish, boyish. He punctuated his sentences by running his hands through his hair, leaving it sticking up in odd, sandy tufts.

'I sense some letters to the editor,' said Marg, when he had finished.

'Just a few,' he smiled ruefully. 'But I really can't bear it. The quality of our environment is just as important to a sense of well-being as the quality of our . . .'

He was interrupted by a sharp rap from the top table. Abbeyhill's current head-teacher, a rather terrifying-looking lady with an astoundingly large nose, thanked everyone for coming and reminded them to make their bids in the silent auction after they had eaten. A team of waiters swooped in from the edges of the room and placed little towers of avocado and goat's cheese in front of everyone. Marg hadn't realised just how hungry she was, and attacked hers with gusto. Fay laid her hand on Adam's arm and asked him a pointed and inane question about planning regulations.

By the dessert course, her husband had stumbled off in the direction of the bar and had not returned and Adam was still being monopolised. Cate slipped out of her seat and came to sit down beside Marg.

'Having fun?'

'In a manner of speaking,' said Marg.

'Strange to see old faces, isn't it?'

Marg nodded, watching little groups of people rise from the tables and mill around near the dance floor. The band had started to play and Cate tapped her foot to the beat of a Bee Gees number, humming tunelessly under her breath.

Marg felt a sudden rush of affection. They would never have been here, been back together, if it hadn't been for Cate. She reached across and laid her hand on Cate's arm.

'You look like you're having a good time.'

Cate grinned. 'I am.'

'You've got great people skills, you know,' said Marg. 'I've been watching you.'

'Thank you. That's a lovely thing to say.'

'It's also invaluable when you're running your own business,' said Marg.

'Thank you,' Cate repeated. 'But that's not quite so helpful.'

'I'm just saying . . .'

Cate poked her. 'You're just interfering,' she said. 'So, quit it.' She lowered her voice to a whisper. 'Or I'll tell Gorgeous Gordon here that you're gagging for it.' She stood up to let Gordon back into his seat and raised her eyebrows at Marg.

'So, Marg.' Adam Milner bent towards her again, as Gordon tried to attract her attention. 'If you work for Global, you must live in London.'

Marg nodded, gratefully turning her back on the drunk to her right.

'Whereabouts?'

'Battersea.'

'I'm in Maida Vale,' said Adam.

'Oh,' said Marg. 'I just assumed you were based up here.'

Adam shook his head. 'We moved down about five years ago. My wife got a transfer.'

'Did she not fancy coming up with you to help save your old school?'

Adam shook his head. 'She'd have hated it,' he said. 'Probably more so since the divorce.'

'Mm,' said Marg, flatly. She reached for the wine bottle and poured herself another full glass. She held it out to him and he shook his head, a smile playing around his lips. 'You know, most people say, "I'm sorry," when I say that.'

'Why should I be sorry?' Marg put the bottle back down and took a sip from her glass. 'I don't know you from . . .'

'Adam?' He laughed and so did she.

'Are you sorry?' She wasn't sure why she had asked.

'Only for my boys. I've got two boys. Rory and Quinn. Four and seven.' He fished in his jacket pocket and pulled out a wallet from which he eased a photograph. 'This is them.'

Marg studied the print. The two boys were balanced on a fence and smiling broadly at whoever was behind the camera. The smallest one had Adam's sandy hair and clutched a stick. The elder boy, fairer and less like his dad, had his arm around his brother, in a way that suggested he had been told to do it. Both wore thick woollen sweaters that looked as though they had come from a granny's well-used needles.

'Nice,' said Marg. 'They look like they could be in a catalogue.'

'I'll take that as a compliment,' he said. 'They're my handsome twosome.'

'I was thinking knitting catalogue,' added Marg.

He burst out laughing. 'You're just full of the social graces, aren't you, Marjorie Jean Holland?'

'Don't call me that. It's Marg.'

'Well, don't call my boys catalogue kids.'

'Sorry.'

'Well I'm sorry too. Marg.'

They looked at each other. The band struck up a Temptations number. 'Do you want to dance?' he asked suddenly.

'No.'

'Do you want to come and stand opposite me and look vaguely appalled while I dance?'

Marg burst out laughing. Funny guy. But funny wouldn't get her on the floor, not for all the vodka in Finland. 'No, but you go ahead,' she said. 'I can look suitably appalled from here.'

He shrugged and turned to Lucy, who accepted his invitation with alacrity and much better grace. Marg watched them disappear into the throng of people on the dance floor. He seemed to move okay, from the small glimpses she caught through the sway of bodies. Not too jerky, not too energetic, not too uncle-at-a-family-wedding. She made her way to the bar. The Australian waiter must have finished his shift and she was served by a young woman who put too much tonic in her vodka, and worse still, a slice of lemon. She was halfway through it when she was cornered by Eilish, who turned out to have a sense of humour as big as her new shape. They had a good laugh at the absurdity of school reunions, at late thirties' disillusion fuelled by teenage memories and too much table wine.

She was on her way back to look for Cate, and wondering

whether it might be time to call it a night when Adam found her. He held out his hand.

'I said no,' she said.

'Humour me.'

She looked at him. He must have just run his hand through his hair again because it was sticking up at the front, like Tintin's. The vodkas had taken effect, she felt warm with familiar numbness, and a little bit giggly. What was the harm? If nothing else, it would give her and Cate something to laugh about on the way home.

'Just one.' She took his hand. 'But if you do anything disco, I'm leaving.'

Cate sat back in her chair and watched Marg disappear onto the dance floor with Adam. He seemed nice. She smiled to herself, hoping Marg was gentle with him. The small clock by the exit said 11.45 p.m. She'd better phone her mum and let her know they would be later than their midnight estimate.

The corridor outside the function suite was blissfully cool and quiet. Cate found a chair next to the ladies' toilets and fished her mobile from her bag. The phone rang only twice.

'Hello,' whispered her mum.

'It's Cate.'

'Darling. Are you having a lovely time?'

'I am,' said Cate. 'Why are you whispering?'

'Ed's fallen asleep on the sofa,' said her mum. 'I think Stevie tired him out.'

'Oh, Mum, we'll head back,' said Cate. 'I was just ringing to say we might be a little after midnight, but I can find Marg and we'll come home now.'

'Don't be daft,' whispered Joyce. 'You stay on. I'll be waking him in a minute for a cup of tea.'

'How are the kids?'

'Fine. Although Stevie was eating the toothpaste again

and the twins weren't speaking to each other when they went to bed. Emma was making fun of Jo about something. Some boy, I think. I told them they're way too young to be thinking about boys.'

Cate's heart sank. She'd not heard Jo mention Paul since the netball match, and she hadn't been sure how to handle it. Ask her if she wanted to talk? Or let her have her secret crush, no matter that it was on a boy who favoured her sister? She'd decided to leave well alone for the time being. Jo would have been mortified if she thought anyone suspected.

Her mum must have sensed her anxiety 'They're fine, sweetheart. It's just a girl thing. Oh, look, here's sleepyhead all woken up. Morning, old man.'

Cate heard Ed grunt. 'I'll let you go, Mum,' she said. 'We won't be too late.'

'You take your time,' said her mum. 'Enjoy your night.'

Cate switched off the phone and laid it in her lap. The door to the function suite swung open as two people emerged and Cate heard the strains of 'Beyond the Sea'. She suddenly wanted to be with Dan, to be dancing with Dan, not sitting near the loo like a wallflower in her brown and un-dazzling dress.

She picked up the phone and dialled his mobile. He would probably be grumpy if she wakened him, but she wanted to tell him how it had gone, that she was having fun, but not as much as if he were here. It went to voicemail immediately. She searched in her bag for the contact details he had left. The Fortune Hotel in Birmingham. The receptionist was young and friendly. 'I'm afraid that Dr Beane's extension is ringing out,' she said after several minutes of dead air. 'Do you want to leave a message?'

'No, it's okay,' said Cate. 'Actually . . .' She paused. 'Can you tell me if it's possible to switch the phone bell off in the rooms. If you were wanting to sleep?'

'I'm pretty sure it would ring,' said the girl. There was a pause. 'I can try the bar, if you want. I know a few of the delegates are still in there. One or two.'

'No, that's fine.' Cate felt suddenly foolish.

'He's probably just dead to the world,' said the girl kindly.

'Probably,' said Cate. She sat for a moment after she had dropped the phone back in her bag. What was wrong with her? He would be in the bar with Guy laughing at some awful anecdote about adenoids. What was she thinking?

'Hey, hon.' Marg stopped in front of her. 'I thought you'd run out on me.' She held out a business card and laughed. 'Look, I pulled.'

'Who? Adam?'

'I'm just kidding,' said Marg. 'We exchanged cards.' She dropped it into her clutch purse. 'He lives in London and said to give him a call. But I don't think I'm going to need shoring up or re-cladding or whatever he does anytime soon.'

'He seemed really nice,' said Cate. 'Is he single?'

'Newly,' said Marg. 'But don't even go there. He was two years below us for God's sake. He's a baby.'

'He's not a baby,' said Cate. 'He's a grown man. And quite an attractive one.'

'If you like ginger-haired divorcees with two kids,' said Marg. 'Anyway, what are you doing out here?'

'I was just calling my mum.'

'Are you ready to go home?'

'Do you mind?' asked Cate. 'It's just I don't want to keep mum and Ed up too late and the kids will be awake early tomorrow.'

'Of course,' said Marg. She turned to head for the cloakroom, then swivelled back and bent to look into Cate's face. 'You okay?'

Cate looked up at her, then blurted out: 'I can't get hold of Dan.'

'Is that a problem?' Marg took her hand and pulled her to her feet.

'No. I'm just being stupid.' Cate shook her head, embarrassed.

Marg looked at her watch. 'He'll be sound asleep by now, won't he?'

'Well, I tried his room but it just rang out, and the girl on reception said he wouldn't have been able to switch the ringer off. And he didn't answer his mobile.'

Marg stared at her. 'You're worried about this. Has he . . . you know, before . . . ?'

'No. No. God, no. Forget it. Really.' Cate smiled weakly and Marg smiled back.

'Hon, what's come over you? He's not up to anything. Your husband adores you. And as well he might, Mrs Catriona Beane.' She slipped her arm around Cate's waist and guided her towards the cloakroom. 'I told you these things were a bad idea. Play tricks with your mind. Make you feel like a feckless teen when you're a fab thirty-something.'

'In a dull dress,' said Cate. 'With a husband who didn't want to come.'

Marg laughed. 'Well, I'm with Dan on this one, hon. Come on. Let's get out of here and go see what you've got in your drinks' cabinet. I feel a cocktail hour coming on.'

Cate gave her a grateful squeeze. 'Thanks.'

'That,' said Marg, 'is precisely what old best friends that you haven't seen for absolute aeons are for.'

13

'Your hair is weird.' The voice came from the bottom of the bed.

Marg blinked. 'Hello,' she said groggily.

'Your hair is weird.' Stevie stood up as Marg put her hand to her head and felt a thick mat of tangles sticking out above her ear. She yawned. 'You're right. It is weird.'

Stevie grinned and threw a piece of paper onto the duvet before rushing out of the room. She didn't appear to be wearing any pyjamas.

'Thank you!' shouted Marg after her. She lay back down and peered at her watch. 7.30 a.m. Jesus. What ungodly hour was this for a Sunday?

Cate poked her face round the door and held out a cup of coffee. 'I'm sorry. Did she wake you? She was really excited about giving you her picture.'

Marg sat back up and switched on the bedside light. She picked up the piece of paper. 'It's been a long time since someone with no pants on gave me a gift in bed,' she said. She studied the drawing of a large humanoid with a square head and a rather manic grin.

'It's you,' said Cate. 'Apparently.'

'I look like Brigitte Nielsen.'

Cate smiled. 'Mum says she spent ages on it last night. You must have made an impression.' She sat down on the end of the bed. She looked tired. There was an inadequately wiped jam stain on her pyjama top.

Marg took a sip of coffee. 'How long have you been up?'

'Stevie's usually awake at six. The twins have just got going.'

'Jesus,' said Marg.

'You should be used to it,' laughed Cate. 'With your early starts.'

'It's different when it's not work,' said Marg.

'This is work,' said Cate.

'Oops,' said Marg. 'Faux pas number . . .'

'Four,' said Cate. 'I'm counting.' She smiled slyly. 'Anyway, you'll find out how hard it is when you and Adam Milner have a brood of your own.'

'God, can you imagine?' said Marg. 'Lots of little Tintins running around.'

'Tintins?'

'He had hair like Tintin. Sticking up at the front.'

'He did not,' laughed Cate. 'And you're one to talk. Tuftyhead.'

'Tuftyhead? Is that the best you can come up with? Christ, hon, you've lost your touch. Even your five-year-old did better.'

Cate giggled and smoothed her hand across the duvet cover. She didn't seem to want to move.

'Have you talked to Dan?' Marg spoke as lightly as she could, not wanting to pry, not wanting to show how unsettled she'd been by Cate's small panic the night before.

Cate shook her head. 'There's a conference session this morning and he'll be home tonight. I'm just going to leave it.'

'You sure? It might put your mind at rest.'

'I'm sure. I was just being stupid last night.' She continued to stare at the duvet cover, smoothing her hand over the same spot.

'What?' Marg put down her coffee and sat further upright.

'It's nothing, really. It's just—' Cate looked up and sighed.
'It's just what?'

'It's just, I feel I'm so . . . disconnected from him sometimes. I know that sounds stupid, but a few years back it
would never have occurred to me to worry if I couldn't get
hold of him. It's nothing he's done,' she added quickly. 'And
I'm sure he wouldn't. Ever.'

'Of course he wouldn't,' said Marg, wondering if he might,
wondering if he already had. She'd been unable to get the
measure of Dan in just one evening. He seemed affable
enough, but he lacked Cate's instinctive warmth. If Marg
had been asked to describe him she might have said 'closed'.

'We just . . .' Cate ran her hands through her hair. 'I just
feel I've lost touch somehow. We just seem to be kind of
existing at the moment, you know? In parallel almost. Not
together.'

'Hon, if you're this concerned about it why don't you
just talk to him?'

'I've tried,' said Cate. 'But he says I'm being daft. That
it's just that he's busy with work and I'm busy with the kids
and stuff, but . . .' She glanced quickly at the door and
lowered her voice to a whisper. 'We've not had sex for ages.
More than two months.'

'Isn't that actually pretty rampant for a married couple?'
asked Marg.

'I don't know,' said Cate. 'But it's not normal for us.'
She pressed her hand distractedly back on the duvet cover.
'He . . .' She paused and looked up. 'He's found it . . .
difficult.'

'Difficult?' Marg frowned and reached for her coffee.
'Difficult to get it up, you mean?'

'No, no, I don't know. No. Yes. It's probably me,
though. God, I can't believe I'm telling you this.' Cate shifted
uncomfortably and clasped her hands tight between her

knees. A bright spot of colour had centred on each cheek the way they used to when she was asked a question in biology. Miss Wishart, please describe for the class the sex life of the drosophila.

'I don't mind,' said Marg. 'It's nothing to be embarrassed about. Happens to loads of people and there's buckets you can do. Viagra for a start, as an immediate fix. Injections, counselling, penis pump . . .'

Cate gave a little snorting giggle. 'You just made that up.'

'No, really,' said Marg. 'We did a feature on it in my last job. It's like a little Hoover, a vacuum.' She put her coffee down and started motioning with her hands. 'You stick it in, switch it on and ping: hello mama!'

'Ping?' Cate raised her eyebrows.

'Something like that,' said Marg. 'Ping, whoosh, ziiip, whatever noise it makes. It doesn't make a noise, does it? Anyway, the point is it worked. Of course we couldn't show that on screen but the guy's smile was enough. And I think they're actually developing a cream now, you know, that you rub on . . .'

'Oh, God, it's not funny,' said Cate, trying to stop giggling. 'What if it's me? Maybe he just doesn't fancy me any more?'

'It's not you,' said Marg. 'You're a Grade A yummy mummy. These things are mostly down to stress anyway, or something like that. Drink. Age. Circulation. Has he been stressed out?'

Cate nodded. 'Very.'

'Well, then.' Marg shrugged. 'What he needs, what you both need, is a little R and R. A dirty weekend.'

'Just a slightly grubby one would do.' Cate smiled wanly.

'No, seriously. You should get your mum and Ed – who, by the way, is an absolute sweetie – to babysit. And the pair of you head off somewhere fab. A swanky resort. Have dinner, have a spa session, get pissed out of your skulls, get your pump out, pop a pill if you need to, and get yourself shagged good and proper . . .'

'Hi!' said Jo brightly.

Cate leapt off the end of the bed. 'Sweetheart, we didn't see you there.'

Jo came into the room, a little hesitantly, twisting her hands in front of her. 'Hi, Marg.'

'Hi, Jo,' said Marg. 'Your mum and I were just talking about some of the . . . things people were saying last night.' She knew it was feeble but it was the best she could come up with.

Cate stood by the door, her cheeks a little flushed, but if Jo had understood what they were talking about she gave no sign of it. She moved over to the bed and climbed onto the end, curling her legs up underneath her. She was so skinny there was hardly any weight of her to press down on Marg's feet. She sat in an easy 'W' shape, the kind that Marg could never attempt even after a session with Roy. 'Did you have a nice time last night?'

'We did.' Marg nodded. 'Great time.'

Jo glanced round at Cate. 'Did Mum dance?'

'Did Mum dance?' said Marg. 'I couldn't get her to sit down. It was so embarrassing.'

'Was it bad?'

'Have you ever seen *The Office*?' asked Marg.

Jo shook her head.

'Well, let's just say it was . . . energetic. And jerky. Pretty jerky.'

Jo covered her mouth with her hand to stifle a laugh. 'Mum, you never!'

'No, I never,' said Cate, laughing. 'Although when I did dance, I had to dance on my own because Marg was chatting up all the men. And actually, she met a really nice one. Didn't you, Marg?'

'Did you?' Jo giggled again, delighted to be part of such grown-up, gossipy chat.

Marg shook her head. 'Unfortunately not. I met a very nice Australian bartender who could have been my son, and a man who was quite funny – ha, ha, not peculiar – but that's as good as it got. Not boyfriend material.'

'What's boyfriend material?' asked Jo.

'Someone who would make a good boyfriend.' Marg studied Jo. 'Do you have a boyfriend?'

Jo flushed furiously. 'No!'

Cate stepped forward. 'Too young for boyfriends,' she said lightly. She shook her head at Marg.

'Too young? When did we start having boyfriends?' Marg couldn't remember.

'Oh, well into teenage years. Sixteen, maybe.'

'Sixteen! Get real.' Marg saw Cate's warning glance. 'Well, maybe it was sixteen. So long ago I can't remember.'

'Emma has a boyfriend,' said Jo, still flushed. 'His name's Paul.'

'I do not!' Emma wandered into the room and stared indignantly at her sister. 'I do not. You're the one who likes him.'

'No, I don't!' Jo swivelled angrily on the bed, her cheeks burning with embarrassment.

'He's a total . . . gargoyle!'

'Jo! Emma!' said Cate, warningly.

'Have I started something?' asked Marg. She was interrupted by Stevie who burst past Cate and bounced onto the bed. 'Do you like my picture?'

'Very much,' said Marg. 'It's a good likeness.'

'What's a lichens?'

'A very good picture,' said Cate.

Stevie smiled, still looking at Marg. 'Do you want to play horses and cats?'

Marg smiled back. 'Horses and cats. Interesting combination. But do you not need to be dressed for that?'

Jo, clearly relieved that the subject had been changed, tried to push a squawking Stevie off the bed. 'Stevie's bad,' she said. 'She eats toothpaste and she won't wear pants and she sometimes bites the other kids in her class. She's been at the headmistress. Gran says she's the "Very Devil". Ow. Muuum! She pinched me!'

'Okay, okay, enough you lot,' said Cate. 'Out and give Marg some peace.'

'But I just got here,' whined Emma.

'Out!' Cate ushered them towards the door. 'Don't feel you have to get up,' she said over her shoulder.

'I won't,' said Marg.

Cate turned. 'By that I mean you'll get another ten minutes on your own and then they'll all be back. They're like hyenas.'

Marg yawned. 'Down in ten, then,' she said. 'Just give me time to finish my coffee.'

Cate grinned at her. She mouthed 'thank you' above the three small heads.

Marg nodded and mouthed back, 'Shagged. Good and proper.'

Cate gave her the thumbs up just as the door closed and she dissolved into a fresh bout of giggles.

'Jo, can you go down and get her?' Cate stood at the top of the upwards escalator watching Stevie disappear on the downwards one with a cheery wave.

'She'll just come up the other side when I get there,' whined Jo. 'She always does.'

Cate saw Marg check her watch. Damn the misplaced car keys and the roadworks and the lost opportunity for a meaningful, unhurried farewell. 'I know, sweetheart, but Marg's going to miss her plane if we don't hurry up. Go

on. Quick. STEVIE!' She glared at her youngest with such
ferocity that Stevie blanched and hesitated and missed the
jump-off and landed, sorely, on her face. Cate leapt for the
down escalator and followed Jo down to the small howling
form, pushing past travellers with a string of frantic platitudes. 'Sorry, sorry, sorry, excuse me, sorry, so sorry.'

She grabbed Stevie's arm and yanked her to her feet.
We don't smack, she reminded herself. We don't smack.
Especially not in public places, when you're a little
emotional and lot premenstrual. She checked Stevie was
okay then gave her a little shake. 'Not funny,' she said
through gritted teeth. 'Marg's going to miss her plane.'
Stevie's face was streaked with fat tears, the kind that roll
only halfway down and stop, a glistening reminder of
parental shortcomings. She looked up and her eyes flashed
suddenly with rage.

'Poor lamb,' clucked a large lady squeezing past with a fat
flight bag. Cate smiled at her weakly and stepped onto the
escalator. Poor lamb, my arse. You won't be saying that in a
second when we have a full-on, lino-chewing, ear-splitting
tantrum. And here we go.

She rose back towards the second level as heads swivelled towards the rising wail from the small girl tucked under
her arm. By the time she had reached the top again Marg
had hoisted her bag over her shoulder and was looking pointedly at her wrist. 'Look, I'd better dash.'

Cate nodded, mutely, and set a still squalling Stevie down.
'You'd better,' she said. 'Her head starts spinning in a minute.'

Marg pulled her in for a hug. 'Hon, it's been really lovely.'

Cate held on to her. 'It has.'

'Come down,' said Marg. 'For a weekend. Bring everyone.'
She pulled back and grinned. 'Or come on your own.'

'I'll come on my own.' Cate felt the smile stretch across
her face. 'I think I need a girls' weekend.'

'Phone,' said Marg, lifting her hand to her ear as she started to walk backwards. 'We'll get it set up.'

'I will.' Cate pulled the children in around her.

'Bye, kids! Great to meet you. You look after your mum.'

'Byeeee!' They waved enthusiastically as Marg turned and swept up the concourse. Even Stevie joined in, modifying the pitch of her crying and pausing mid-wail to wipe her nose theatrically on the hem of Cate's long cardigan. Marg stopped when she got to the ticket checker and turned for a final wave. Cate raised her hand and shouted, 'Bye!' Marg raised her hand too. Then the soft black coat swirled around her as she slipped through the sliding doors and was gone.

'I fell.' Stevie was the first to reach the front door when they heard Dan's keys in the lock.

'Did you?' Dan dropped his bag and bent to Stevie level. 'Where did you fall?'

'Down the metal stairs. Mummy shouted at me. I fell.'

'What a mean mummy.' Dan grinned at Cate over Stevie's head. 'I'll need to give her a telling off, won't I?'

Stevie nodded. 'A big one. I hurt my nose.' Her dad bent in and kissed it better. 'There, fixed,' he said. 'Now, where are my other girls?'

Jo and Emma descended the stairs and onto him, filled with chatter from the weekend. Cate watched them all from the kitchen. The first time Dan had returned from a trip away, just before they were married, she had run at him and thrown herself up into his arms, legs curling around him. Her lips were chafed from kissing when he had finally let her go. Now, she knew to wait her turn, to wait for the dutiful, husbandly embrace. He disentangled himself from three small bodies and came into the kitchen and folded his arms round her. 'And how's Mean Mum?'

Cate smiled. 'Not to be messed with,' she said, lifting her face for a kiss. 'Especially when you're surfing the escalators at the airport and we're late for Marg's plane.'

'Did she get off okay?' Dan broke away and wandered over to the counter where the mail was stacked. He picked up the envelopes and began flicking through them.

'Fine,' said Cate.

'Good night?' He raked a thumbnail through the bank statement that Cate hadn't got round to opening and studied the contents without looking up.

'Great. Really great. How was the conference?'

'Mm.' His eyes were fixed on the pages in his hands.

'I tried to call you.' Cate kept her voice light. 'You were incommunicado.'

Dan looked up at her. 'Did you get something for ninety-five pounds?'

'My dress,' said Cate, flatly. 'For the reunion.'

'Mum's been spoiling herself.' Dan grinned at Stevie, who had come in to the kitchen, and charged at her dad. Dan dropped the statement back on the counter and pulled Stevie onto his feet, waltzing with her through to the family room. 'But Mummy's worth it, isn't she?'

The children piled on top of him until they all collapsed in a laughing heap in the middle of the room. 'NOOO,' they chorused, 'NOOOO, SHE'S NOT!'

She didn't try again until they were getting ready for bed. Dan was in his pyjama bottoms and hanging up his dinner suit in the wardrobe. She watched him in the dresser mirror as she rubbed face-cream into her cheeks, telling herself that she shouldn't bring it up, knowing that she would.

'I tried to call,' she said again. 'On Saturday evening. Quite late.'

He turned. 'Did you?'

'I couldn't get you on the mobile. Or in your room.'

'Was something wrong?' He seemed genuinely puzzled, rather than guilty, and she felt relieved and a little ridiculous.

'No. I was just hoping you were around. Just for a chat.'

He closed the wardrobe door and came over to her, smiling. 'Chat to me now,' he said. His arms went round her and she turned into him.

'I missed you.'

'It was just a weekend, Cate.' He laughed gently. 'And you were out too. What's up with you?'

'Nothing.' She tilted her head up. 'It's just we never get the weekend away. Together. It's been ages since we've been on our own.'

'That could be nice.' He nodded slowly.

'I could speak to Mum and Ed about babysitting. Maybe we could go to a five-star hotel. Spoil ourselves?'

Dan whistled. 'Pricey.'

'Just for a night.'

'Maybe. Yes, maybe.'

'Is that a yes or a no?' She felt herself tense. It shouldn't be this hard.

'Pushy,' he said with a smile.

'We need a weekend away, Dan.'

'Well, look into it,' he said. 'Although, it can't be next weekend because I've got that thing with Guy in Stirling on Sunday. And the one after that is the Macmillan Nurses auction . . .'

Cate reached up quickly and put her fingers on his lips to quieten him. Then she kissed him, a full, questioning kiss. He opened his mouth on hers, she felt it widen into a half-stifled yawn. 'God, sorry, honey.' He pulled away. 'I'm absolutely done in. Do you mind?'

She swallowed the sob of exasperation that rose suddenly

into her throat and shook her head. He turned and slipped under the covers, rolling himself over to his side. She'd put fresh sheets on; the linen ones, washed so soft they felt like flannel. He stretched himself out indulgently. 'It's nice to be back in your own bed,' he said. 'Night, honey.' He turned towards the wall.

'Night.' Cate turned off the light, glad he couldn't see her face. He fell asleep quite quickly and she lay, quiet and listening until the only sounds she could hear were her own ragged, wakeful breaths and the hamster turning desperately in the dark on his shiny spinning wheel.

14

Marg gently disentangled herself from Susann's bony hug and gripped her hand for a firm shake.

'That's great,' she said. 'You deserve it. Really.'

'No, we do,' gushed Susann, turning to the small group that had gathered round as the broadcast award nominations had been read out. 'Could be a double header,' said Susann. 'If I get the anchor nod and we get the network, too.' She raised her hands in the air and crossed her fingers, a difficult task given the size of the rock that she wore on the middle finger of her right hand. 'Popinjays!' she shouted. 'My treat!' There was an unseemly scramble for the door and the chance to get rat-arsed on Susann's not inconsiderable salary.

'You coming?' Susann paused at Marg's desk, shrugging on her smart check coat. Marg shook her head. As much fun as her weekend had been – and it had been – it had left her way behind on work. She hadn't watched a single bulletin between Friday morning and Sunday night. And now it was midweek and she still had a ton of research to do on Chad and three new end segments to pick before 6 a.m. tomorrow.

'I'm still a bit behind.' Marg smiled apologetically. 'I'm going to have to pass.'

'Wild weekend, huh?' asked Susann, perching on the edge of the desk.

'Pretty sedate, actually. But good. Very good.'

'Meet anyone nice?' Susann inclined her head and flashed Marg her shiniest smile.

'I did,' said Marg, 'but not what you think. An old friend. Girlfriend.'

'And lord, don't we need them?' said Susann. She glanced through the glass wall at the news room. For all that she fronted the show, for all that Marg produced it, the people who had hired them, the people who made the big decisions, the people who controlled were all men. 'You sure?' Susann laid her hand on Marg's arm. 'Quick voddy?'

Marg shook her head again. 'You're on your own, hon.' She watched as Susann crossed the news room and joined the small group trooping down the stairs for the exit. Then she made her way to one of the editing suites. It was dark and quiet and she shuffled quickly through the various packages she wanted to review. There was a copy of Michael Buerk's seminal report from Ethiopia in 1984, the standard by which everything else was judged. And there were the segments she and Rick had filmed in Darfur and Niger. She wanted to remind herself how they had done it previously, anxious not to get formulaic once they arrived in Chad.

The Darfur film started with a wide shot of what had been a village and was now a forlorn circle of small charred ruins. Rick came into view, picking his way between the burnt-out structures. 'This,' he said, 'was Ntobe, home to a community of thirty people. But Ntobe is no more. Its people have gone. On the verge of starvation they have been forced to flee because in this land of want, a war is raging.' He swept his hand across the backdrop then looked straight at the camera. 'To all who see this, it is an unfathomable tragedy.'

'Unfathomable tragedy' was a hard phrase to say, but Rick had wanted to say it because he believed it to be true. Marg smiled at him on screen. He could have turned to drink or snorted himself a supersize nostril, but he'd kept himself intact after years in the job and retained a sense of humour. She could forgive him cheesy when he was this good.

She'd got home to two messages from him, even though he knew she was in Edinburgh. And now he was in Brussels for the week, filling in for the Europe correspondent who had caught bronchitis after a stint on a Norwegian fishing boat for a feature on the cod wars. It had seemed odd to see Rick in a suit and looking so bored. She knew he was bored because he mispronounced the names of half the commissioners; a deliberate ploy, she suspected, to stop him being sent on the EU beat again.

She scribbled some guidance notes and slipped in the tape from Niger. She hadn't forgotten how terrible it had been, but some of the images had faded from her mind. Bodies. Bodies left lying at the side of roads. Mothers, children, fathers. Left to the dust in desperate times. The camera swept over and then settled on the body of a girl. She wore a blue jumper and lay as if she were asleep. Marg stared at the screen. One of the girl's arms was bent at an angle to cradle her head, a final effort to find some comfort when she had finally given up and lain down. She must have been about five or six. She must have been about Stevie's age.

Marg switched off the screen, telling herself she had a headache and she could do this another time. She'd always despised people who said they couldn't bear to watch such things. People are living it, she always said, the least you can do is look at it. But tonight she didn't want to see. Not a small girl dead and alone by the side of a road.

She wandered back to the news room and checked through the provisional running list of features for the following day.

By the time she reached the flat it was almost 7 p.m. She switched on the lounge lights and looked around. Ever since she'd got back from Cate's she'd been finding fault with her apartment. Not the style of it. She liked her furniture, especially her white Heal's sofa. But there was something else, something indefinable. Maybe it was the lighting. Maybe she needed some table lamps, or a new paint scheme, or some throws. Maybe she should get Cate down to advise her.

There was nothing she wanted to watch on television so she settled herself on the chair by the window with a tea mug of her favourite vodka and the batch of new catalogues that she'd stacked on the kitchen counter. She flicked through them absently, occasionally glancing up from the pages of gifts to look at the wet lights of the city outside.

It was the picture that first caught her eye, halfway through a gadgets and gizmos section: a g-string fashioned from small boiled sweets. Marg winced. She'd worn some uncomfortable underwear in her time but that looked positively obstructive. But she had to get one for Cate. She'd die laughing. She might even wear them for Dan and they might even do the trick. Marg slid her purse from her bag. Now these were come-hither knickers. Just what Mrs Catriona Beane needed for a stressed out husband with a bad case of performance anxiety.

It was when she stuffed her credit card back in her wallet that she found the other card. She picked it out and laid it on the arm of the chair. Adam Milner. Architect.

It was an unremarkable card, plain and straightforward, a little like its owner. Marg liked straightforward but she had never wanted ordinary. She picked it back up and dropped it into the large bowl on the coffee table and pushed it down among the matchbooks and loose change and all the other bits and pieces that she wasn't quite sure what to do with.

'Bye, Tintin.' She gave a small regretful smile. Cate would not be pleased.

'That would be a hundred and forty pounds,' said the girl with the soft Scottish voice. 'Per person.'

'Per person?' Cate swallowed.

'That does include a shiatsu massage, dinner for two and a round of golf. Or a falconry lesson.'

'We could do without the buzzards.' Cate gave a small laugh.

'The price would be the same,' said the girl. 'Shall I check availability for you?'

Almost three hundred pounds for a night away. Dan would have kittens. She should find somewhere cheaper. Cate bit her lip. Actually, no, damn it, she shouldn't. It must be two years since they had spent a weekend on their own and he made a decent wage and she was worth it. Every damn penny.

'Could you check availability please,' she said quickly. 'The weekend of the eighteenth, if you have anything then. If you do, I'll take it.'

There was a brief pause. 'Yes, that should be fine. You'll be in one of our Dunsinane rooms. They have a view of the woods. Would you like to sign up for the golf or the falconry now?'

Cate paused. Dan loved his golf, second only to his biking. 'Oh, that's easy,' she said. 'We'll go with the buzzards.'

She could hear the smile in the girl's voice. 'So that's one night in a Dunsinane, a shiatsu massage for two, dinner in the restaurant, and a . . . falconry lesson. That comes to two hundred and eighty pounds, plus VAT. How would you like to pay?'

The light was lasting later into the day, and the girls were still out in the garden. Cate watched them as she tucked her credit card back in her purse. Emma was deep in one of the flower-beds adding to an already fat bunch of daffodils. Stevie was battering a large bit of wood off the old sycamore for reasons that only she knew. Jo was down by the gate, her arms hung over the metal railings, one foot tapping on the ground rhythmically, lost in her own world.

Cate knew what Dan's reaction would be when she told him about the hotel, but she didn't care. Not after Sunday night. She felt a fresh rush of frustration. She'd barely spoken to him for the last three days, although it took two for him to notice. When he'd asked, plaintively, what was wrong, she'd said if he didn't know there was no point in her explaining. He'd shrugged and doubtless assumed she was premenstrual. She was, but she'd also had enough. Enough hoping, enough worrying, enough wheedling. If he wouldn't act, then she would. And Mum had been only too happy to offer to babysit. Again.

She looked at her watch. Time to supervise homework, to run the baths, to finish the essay, to clean out the hamster. But first. She picked up a pen from the large tin on her desk and drew a big red circle round 18 April on the diary on the wall. She stood back, then redrew it so it more resembled a heart, if a rather misshapen one. She smiled to herself. Marg would be proud.

15

A week later, the heart had grown a smiley face, two legs, a belly button, and an arrow through its middle with a drop of blood at its tip, courtesy of the girls who were prone to doodle with Cate's collection of coloured pens whenever they came in.

Cate glanced back at the book in front of her and studied the pictures of the great Jacobean houses, tracing her hand over the images of strapwork parapets, barley twist chimneys and basket finials that enlivened the solid stone dwellings. And the lights. Everywhere lights. Great fireplaces, burning torches, candles in windows and on thresholds.

She'd been pleasantly surprised when she'd called to find out how much she had left to do before she could get her diploma. God, she was on a roll. Last week she'd booked the night away with Dan. This week she'd sorted out what needed to be done to finish the course. The last few essays and tutorials she could handle. The dissertation would take much more effort. She had picked Jacobean banqueting houses as her topic when she'd first started. She loved their style, extravagantly ornamental but solidly liveable. And she adored the idea of a banqueting house, a whole structure devoted solely to dining, not a reclaimed oak table adorned with Ribena rings and fading felt-tip curlicues and rocked by a wobbly leg. Ten thousand words and she would be done. Cate Beane Dip.ID. Her eyes flickered over to the manila folder on the bookshelf that held her precious cuttings. She knew they didn't have enough money to even think of buying anything just now. But maybe they could just go and look, just in case, just to see.

The cuckoo clock that her mum and Ed had brought back from Lausanne gave the loud click that signalled it was about to peal. The bird was long gone, ripped from its perch some years back by a rather vicious little girl from Stevie's toddler group. A forlorn piece of coiled wire sprang out and gave a series of disembodied calls. Nine o'clock. It was getting late. She'd need to get them into bed before Dan got back from the gym. She smiled. He'd been amazingly unfazed by the cost of their night away, beyond a low whistle when she had mentioned the price. She knew he was getting a little irritated that she'd felt it necessary to repeat the date to him on so many occasions, but she'd have happily tattooed it on his forehead if it helped him remember.

The door opened slowly and Jo's face appeared.

'Hey, sweetheart.' Cate closed the book on the Jacobites and pushed back her chair. 'What you up to?'

'Nothing much.' Jo wandered in and stood by the desk. 'What are you doing?'

'I'm thinking about my dissertation,' said Cate. 'It's the last big essay I need to do for my course.'

Jo pursed her lips and nodded distractedly.

Cate pulled her onto her knee, even though she was far too big. She didn't resist like she sometimes did.

'What are the girls up to?' asked Cate. There was no school tomorrow because it was an in-service day, and Debs had come round for a sleepover.

'They've been doing each other's hair and they're talking about boys now.' Jo pulled a face.

'And you don't want to talk about boys?'

Jo shook her head and leant back against Cate.

'You know if you ever want to talk to me about anything, you can?' Cate laid her face on the top of Jo's head.

'Mmhm,' said Jo.

'Really. Anything.'

'I know.'

'So, is there anything you want to talk about?' She caught Jo's ponytail and started braiding it gently. 'Anything you want to ask?'

Jo turned slightly. 'Can I have my ears pierced?'

'No.' Cate laughed. 'And the answer will be no until you're at least, oh, fourteen.'

'But Muum, loads of people have their ears pierced already.'

'You're not loads of people,' said Cate, tightening her arms round Jo. 'You're my girl. My amazing girl.'

'Why am I amazing?' Jo played with Cate's fingers, twisting her wedding and engagement rings in concentric circles.

'You're bright, you're funny, you're beautiful.'

'I'm not beautiful,' said Jo. 'I have a long face.'

'Who says you have a long face?'

'In art we had to do self-portraits and the teacher said I'd made mine too round, that it should be long because I have a long face.'

'What shape is the teacher's face?' asked Cate.

'Kind of square.'

'Like SpongeBob SquarePants?' said Cate.

Jo giggled. 'Yeah. Kind of.'

They sat in silence for a while, until Jo said, 'Is Marg going to come up again?'

'I hope so,' said Cate. 'I need to phone her. Did you like her?'

Jo nodded vigorously. 'She was fun.' She giggled again. 'Remember what she said about Hamish's teeth and that dog you saw squashed on the road?'

Cate glanced at the clock again. It was too late to call tonight, but tomorrow afternoon, when Marg had finished work. She'd call then.

The door swung open again and Stevie strode in.

'Hey, baby,' said Cate. 'You ready for bed?'

Stevie shook her head and put her hands on her hips, her favoured pose to deliver important news. 'Debs wanted Hamish out and he's gone for a walk.'

Cate slipped Jo off her knee and sat upright. 'Gone for a walk. Where?'

'I don't know. He went under the door. He made himself flat like this.' Stevie pressed her hands together. She smiled broadly. 'You know, Mummy, he goes down the stairs very well.'

Marg squinted at the clock. Jesus, what time was it? 9.20 p.m. Who the hell was calling at this hour? Her mobile juddered on the bedside table, shrieking at her shrilly. She snatched it up. Something must be happening somewhere. Something big.

'Marg Holland,' she barked.

'Hi.' The voice was warm and a little uncertain. 'It's Adam. Adam Milner.'

Marg shook her head, trying to focus. Her instinct was to say, 'What the fuck?' But she opted for a short, sharp, 'Hi.'

'Is this a bad time?'

'It is, actually,' said Marg. She sat up and rubbed a hand across her eyes. 'I was asleep.'

There was a pause. He must have been looking at his watch. 'It's not even nine-thirty.'

'I get up at three in the morning.'

'Oh, Christ, of course you do. Morning show. God, I'm sorry. This wasn't a good start.'

'To what?'

'To asking you out.'

It was Marg's turn to pause. 'You want to ask me out? On a date?'

'A date sounds very teenage, very Abbeyhill,' said Adam, 'but yes.'

'Why?'

He burst out laughing. 'I knew this wouldn't be easy. Let's just say I enjoyed your company. I'd like to see you.'

'Well, that's very nice of you,' said Marg. 'But . . .' She stifled a yawn. 'Ehm, no.'

'No?'

'No.'

'Dinner? A nice dinner?'

'I said no.'

'Why no?'

Marg sighed. 'Well, since you asked, you're two years younger than me. You have an ex-wife and two children. Oh, and I'm seeing someone. And I don't feel like it. And you woke me up. I don't like being woken up.'

'Well, I'm sorry for that. Again.' Marg heard the laugh in his voice. 'But as for the other stuff, it's just dinner. Not a lifetime commitment.'

Marg laughed in spite of herself. 'Well, thanks for making that clear, but no.'

'And that's a definite no?'

'Is there another kind?'

'No.'

'I'm going to try and get back to sleep now,' said Marg. 'It was nice to hear from you.'

'Liar.' She could tell he was smiling.

'Okay, it was deeply inconvenient but not totally unpleasant to hear from you.'

'I can live with that,' he laughed.

'You're going to have to.' Marg stifled another yawn. 'Bye, Adam.'

She put the phone back on the nightstand and flopped backwards into the bed. God. Adam Milner. She had a sudden ridiculous image of herself sitting in Popinjays across from a boy with tufted hair. She smiled and reached for the phone again.

'Hellosteviespeakingcanisaywhoiscalling?' The sentence came out in a rush of burbling enthusiasm.

Marg sighed. Why did parents let their kids answer the phone? They didn't let them operate heavy machinery or do taxes, but they were happy to give them free rein when it came to telecommunications. She'd once had to call a cabinet minister three times on deadline before his four-year-old consented to take the phone to his father. Marg guessed it was her threat to reach down the phone and throttle his Tigger that finally did it. 'Hi, Stevie,' she said slowly. 'It's Marg here. I thought you would be in bed by now.'

'We don't have school tomorrow. Mummy lets us stay up late when we don't have school tomorrow and Daddy's not here.'

'Is Mummy there?'

'Yes.'

'Can I speak to her?'

'Debs let Hamish out,' said Stevie, importantly. 'He went for a walk and he's gone inside one of the seats. Mummy's looking for him.'

There was a pause, a shriek and a muffled curse.

'I think she found him,' said Marg.

Stevie sniggered. 'Mummy said "shit".'

'I'll bet she did.' Marg smiled. 'Look, it's obviously not a good time. Tell Mummy I'll phone back tomorrow. Say it was Marg.'

'It's okay,' said Stevie brightly, 'she's not bleeding. Mummy? Are you bleeding? It's the lady who came.'

'What lady?' Marg heard Cate say.

'The big one. With the yellow hair.'

'Hi.' Cate came on the line sounding breathless and a little confused.

'Hello,' said Marg.

Cate giggled. 'Oh, hi. I was expecting Big Bird. I think she meant to say tall and blonde. We'll need to work on her descriptive skills. Anyway. Hi! How are you?'

'I'm fine,' said Marg. 'More importantly, how's Hamish?'

'Bloody hamster.' Cate lowered her voice. 'He got up inside the sofa leg. That's the second time he's bitten me.'

'Did he break the skin?'

'Yes,' said Cate. 'But I'll survive.'

'Don't you need a tetanus shot or something?'

'He's a hamster, not a badger,' laughed Cate. 'Anyway, I'm glad you phoned. I was going to call you. But I thought it would be too late.'

'It would have been. But I was wakened up.'

'Wakened up? By what?'

'By whom?' said Marg.

'Okay, by whom?' said Cate.

'Tintin.' Marg grinned at the phone in the dark of her bedroom.

'Adam!' Cate sounded thrilled. 'Just now? What did he want? Did he ask you out?'

'He did. Woke me up to ask me out.'

'Are you going?' There was a shuffling noise as Cate settled herself into a chair.

'Nooo,' said Marg.

'Why not?'

'He's a baby, Cate. And I don't fancy him. And if I thought

I was going to meet someone at a dismal dinner dance to try and save a building I would knock down myself with a wrecker's ball then I'd end it all now.'

'You're mad,' Cate giggled. 'He's a nice man.'

'Nice is not good,' said Marg.

'Nice *is* good,' replied Cate. 'Hold on.' She broke away for an instant. 'Stevie, no. No Jammie Dodgers. Upstairs. Toilet and teeth. Daddy'll be home any minute and I don't want him to catch you still up. Now. Nooo. Now. Jo! Can you take her, please? No, don't hold her like that. She'll fall on her head . . . Sorry.' She turned her attention back to the phone.

'Dan out?' Marg spoke casually.

'Oh, he goes to this training thing at the university on a Thursday,' Cate sounded relaxed. 'For his cycling.'

'Mmm,' said Marg.

'Anyway,' said Cate. 'I really think you should give this guy a go. Just one date. See how you get on. You don't have to commit to anything.'

'I'm seeing Rick,' said Marg.

'Technically,' said Cate. 'But you said it wasn't exclusive, didn't you? He sees other people, too.'

'That's not the point,' said Marg. 'I'm not looking for anyone else.'

'You're mad.' Cate laughed. 'But it's lovely to hear from you. Jo and I were just talking about you.'

'So,' Marg was wide awake now and made herself comfy in a nest of white duvet, 'apart from hamster rescue, what else have you been up to?'

'Well, I took your advice and I've booked a night away for Dan and me. I was going to phone and tell you.'

'Clever girl. I hope it's somewhere gratuitously expensive.'

'Almost three hundred quid a night.'

'Perfect.' Marg grinned. 'Is he pleased?'

'I don't think pleased is the right word,' Cate laughed. 'But he was surprisingly okay about it. He doesn't know about the buzzards yet, though.'

'Buzzards?'

'Long story,' said Cate. 'But you'll be doubly pleased because I've also looked into getting my course finished and the diploma up on the wall. It should take me about another three months, less if I really get down to it.'

'That's great,' said Marg. 'Then you can look at getting yourself set up.'

'And you can look at butting out,' laughed Cate. 'One step at a time, okay? Course finished. Diploma. Then we'll see.'

'But you don't actually need your diploma to set yourself up, do you? It's not like physiotherapy. You could be doing it now.'

'Not listening!' sang Cate. She paused. 'Christ, it sounds like Stevie's flushed herself down the loo up there. I'll need to go, and you'll need to get back to bed.'

'Stevie said they're off school tomorrow.' Marg was reluctant to ring off.

'Mm. In-service day. It's a real pain. So I'm taking the twins shopping tomorrow morning and spending the afternoon in the soft play area.'

'Soft play,' said Marg. 'Is that these rooms for kids like padded cells?'

Cate laughed. 'It's more Hieronymous Bosch for the under-tens. It would be your worst nightmare.'

'You still coming down for a weekend?'

'Of course. You'll need to let me know when suits.'

'I will.'

'I'm going to have to go,' said Cate. 'I'll call you next

week to sort out the weekend thing. Night, Marjorie Jean.'
A smile came into her voice, 'Hope Hergé brings you sweet
dreams.'

'What the hell's Hergé?'

'Go look it up,' said Cate with a laugh, 'and ponder the
error of your ways.'

16

Aid agencies could rarely afford the kind of rent that secured a lift, so Marg made her way slowly up the uneven stone stairs of the old furniture store in King's Cross, following the trail of misery on the posters that adorned every landing. Chechnya. Sudan. Sierra Leone. East Timor. The door at the top had a security entry system, so she pressed the buzzer and announced herself when the intercom crackled into life with a short and unintelligible greeting. 'Marg Holland. Global News.'

Nobody answered but the lock clicked back and she pushed the door open and stepped into the world of good deeds. The receptionist was pleasant enough, settling her on a low, stained couch with a cup of Fair Trade tea and a well-thumbed copy of the *Guardian*. But she got precious few smiles from anyone else as she waited for the agency director to come off the phone.

Marg always thought aid workers and journalists were like an old married couple grown tired and contemptuous of each other, but knowing they should stick together for the sake of family. Most of the people around her now were under thirty and not unattractive, but with earnest, scrubbed faces unsullied by the phoney gloss of brand-name cosmetics. Even with the most translucent layer of Laura Mercier and a slick of volumising mascara Marg felt a little too much like a department-store perfume girl.

She watched them at their desks. She had toyed with the

idea of aid work after college, but when she had explored it further she'd discovered that while the work was attractively risky, the pay was unattractively crap.

Her experiences with the NGO community since had proved to her that they weren't a breed of bohemian superheroes, but were as prone to dysfunction as any other demographic, maybe even more so. The war-zone parties thrown by NGOs were some of the most debauched she'd ever been to, and on her first overseas assignment in Rwanda, with conflict and crisis all around them, the in-country head of a French aid agency had propositioned her mid-interview. 'If you get lonely – and I think you look like a lonely girl,' he had said, 'that is my tent.' She had looked, not at the tent, but at his moustache still carrying traces of the rice he had eaten for supper, and his wedding ring, and the thickish squeeze of hairy flesh poking through the shirt buttons over his belly, and had given him a smile that could freeze mercury. She'd had cause to use it often since. A tall woman with a thatch of red frizz and the kind of frown lines that only stress of global proportions can bring emerged from an office and interrupted her reverie. She strode over and shook Marg's hand with a grip like a welder. 'Marg? Nice to meet you. Sorry I kept you waiting. We've had a bit of a . . . situation in Angola.'

'I saw that,' said Marg. It was just last night that the wires had reported that two World Aid workers had been kidnapped, along with a local guide, by separatist rebels. 'Are they okay?'

The woman gave her a quick, wary glance as she led her into the office.

'I'm just asking to be polite,' said Marg. 'Not for a story.'

'I don't know.' The director dropped into the seat behind a desk heaving with brochures and bits of paper. 'We have someone trying to make contact with the group.' She rubbed her hands together distractedly. 'It's getting to be a habit now, wherever we are. It's money. Always money. They think we're rich.' She gave a harsh, hollow laugh.

Marg nodded and slipped into the low chair opposite, peering through the stiff fronds of a long-dead spider plant.

'So,' the woman let out a deep sigh and balanced her elbows on the desk, 'Chad. We need to talk.'

'We do,' said Marg. It was World Aid who had asked for the meeting and Marg had agreed out of courtesy. She didn't need their permission to turn up at their project, but if their passage could be eased by a half-hour conversation, then Marg was happy to oblige. No point in alienating anybody before they had even arrived in the country.

'Firstly, safety.' The woman looked up at her. 'It's your responsibility. We can't guarantee you anything. No backup. No help if things get . . . complicated. You are there on your own. Free agents.'

Marg nodded. 'We're pretty self-contained.'

'If the situation worsens from the way it is now,' the woman continued, 'we reserve the right to cancel everything; any interviews, any filming. It's all off.'

'I know,' said Marg.

'Just so you do.' The director sat back in her chair. 'I have to tell you there was some concern about you coming.' She held up a hand. 'By "you", I mean Global. The coverage has been getting a little . . . how shall I say . . .'

If she says 'flighty', thought Marg, I'm going to reach across and slap her.

'A little . . . insubstantial,' said the woman.

'How so?'

'It's too much celebrity. Do I need to know that Wayne Rooney is the new muse for Gucci?'

'It was Andy Murray actually, but I take your point,' said Marg.

The woman laughed. 'Good answer.'

'So,' said Marg, keen to change the subject, 'tell me about the nuns.'

The director leant forward and smiled. 'Leonora is this big.' She held her hand out at a level little higher than the desk. 'You could crush her like an eggshell, yet she takes on the world. She's been there two years now, the same as Grainne. Ann is newer.'

'How old are they?'

The woman shook her head. 'They could all be grand-mothers. They're with the Sisters of Mercy, but they work under our auspices.' She sighed deeply. 'We are so stretched. We rely on them more than we should. Last month they had almost eight thousand people through the feeding station. They do first aid, too. Leonora is a nurse. It's amazing.'

'They sound incredible,' said Marg. 'I'm looking forward to meeting them.'

'What kind of coverage are you planning? Is it a one-off or a series of reports?'

'Depends what the situation is when we get out there,' said Marg. 'At the moment it's a package, one longer feature tied in with the G8. But I won't know until we get there.'

'You won't stay long?'

Marg shook her head. 'We won't be any kind of burden. Really. If Leonora and the others want us out of there, we're out of there. That okay?'

The director nodded. 'Who's the reporter?'

'Richard Rutner.'

The woman's eyebrows lifted fractionally. Everyone knew Rick. Probably half the women out in the general office had come across him, or been cross with him, or come under him.

'Rick's very experienced,' said Marg, keeping a straight face.

'I'm sure he is.' The eyebrows stayed aloft.

Marg smiled slowly. 'I'm sure the nuns will . . . take to him.'

The director let out a roar of laughter and slapped the desk, sending up a fine spray of dust from a pile of old newspapers. 'Leonora and Richard Rutner. A match made in heaven.' She rocked back in her chair and kept giggling.

Marg grinned. If anyone could charm the Sisters of Mercy it would be Rick. She'd seen him melt the toughest of toothless old crones on many an assignment. Once he'd even got access to a notorious Macedonian mobster through the man's aged mother, a woman so stooped and wrinkled she might have been a prune, but who flushed like a teenager under Rick's fatuous flattery.

'Well,' the director sat back again, 'I think that's all. Thank you for coming in, Marg. I appreciate the courtesy. I've let our in-country head know when you plan to be out, and I emailed you the project details a while back. You got them?'

Marg nodded as the woman stood to show her to the door. 'And what is Mr Rick Rutner working on just now?' She reached out to shake hands again.

'Not quite such an important assignment,' said Marg, gripping the outstretched hand warmly. 'He's buying me lunch.'

'If I have to talk about another fucking haddock quota . . .' Rick raised himself from his seat in the window of Popinjays and gave Marg a noisy, wet kiss. 'Hey, babe. Thank Christ you're not Belgian or smell of cod.'

'Thank you.' Marg laughed and slipped into the chair beside him. 'I think.'

'I swear, if they send me back to Brussels, I'm resigning. I'll go and work for E! or GMTV.'

'It's not that bad,' said Marg soothingly. 'And you do it

so well.' She slipped into her best Rick impersonation. 'This is Rick Rutner for Global, bringing you breaking news on scallop stocks.'

'Fuck you.' He gave a broad smile and leant towards her. 'And I do hope that's on the table.'

'God, Rick.' She shook her head and reached across to take a deep slug from his vodka and tonic. She'd only seen him briefly since he'd got back from the EU the previous day and she wasn't quite ready for a full Rick onslaught.

'Talking of which,' he gave another grin, 'I need to stay at your place for a couple of days on the weekend of the eighteenth. I'm getting my apartment spruced up. That okay, babe?'

'Spruced up?' Marg was perplexed and a little panicked. 'How long for?'

'Two nights. Three, tops.'

'Why?'

He sighed. 'It's this fucking thing the publicity department want me to do. You know the *Saturday Post* do this lifestyle crap in the magazine about people who travel all the time and what their homes are like? Well, apparently, they want to do my flat. The foreign correspondent on home soil. That kind of thing. The only good part of it is they give you up to a thousand quid to get it smart enough for the photos. I can get it done myself, or they'll send an interior designer round to help. You know, lick of paint, new rug.'

Marg forgot her flat-sharing reservations and gripped his arm. 'An interior designer? You get an interior designer in?'

'Yeah. Not to do the whole thing, just to style it up a bit. But, hell, if I can get it repainted by the broadsheets then I'm gonna.'

'This is too perfect!'

Rick looked confused. 'That I'm moving in?'

'No! No, listen. You don't have to use their designer, do you?'

He shook his head.

'You know my friend Cate? Well, you don't, but she's this friend from school. Haven't seen her for ages, but I stayed with her for that Wrecker's Ball thing. Well, she has this great style and I've been trying to persuade her to get herself set up as an interior designer.'

Rick looked sceptical.

'No, listen,' said Marg. 'We get her down, give her the money. She gets a credit in a national broadsheet, a bit of experience. She's in the middle of a diploma for design anyway. She's an art college grad, she has great taste and she needs this. Trust me. You could be launching the career of the next Martha Stewart.'

'Bad choice,' said Rick.

'Okay, the next Anouska Hempel.'

He shrugged. 'Babe, if it makes you happy. But no animal skins. Or shagpile. Or stags' heads. Or those blinds that look like big knickers.'

Marg laughed and leant across to kiss him. 'No Austrian blinds, I promise. And thanks. You won't regret it.'

He raised his glass to her. 'So, what's my reward?'

Marg scrabbled in her bag for her mobile. 'A weekend with your favourite girl,' she said. 'Fish free.'

'Cheers, babe.' Rick drained his drink. 'You've got a deal.'

Cate smoothed the newspaper out on the floor of the girls' bedroom and folded it neatly to fit into the base of Hamish's cage. She knew she should get the girls to clean him out, but it often wasn't worth the fuss of nagging and reminding and nagging and reminding until the smell of hamster pee soaked into newsprint got so bad that she couldn't stand it any longer. She always caved in long before they did.

Over near the door – firmly closed – Hamish moved around tentatively in the new exercise ball she had bought him, a miniature version of the one Orla had found at the Ideal Homes Exhibition. She waggled her finger at him warningly. It still sported a bandage, although since they'd run out of the flesh-coloured ones she'd had to resort to one of Stevie's bright green Buzz Lightyear affairs that had drawn admiring comments from a small boy in the Tesco checkout queue. 'Mummy, look! That lady's got a Buzz bangie.' Cate had held her finger aloft and said, 'To infinity and beyond!' but he had looked at her like she was addled and had moved behind his mother's legs.

She placed the fresh dish of water into the cage and crushed the old lining and bedding into a soiled, soggy ball. Hamish, growing more confident in his new contraption, trundled past her and under Jo's wardrobe. She made a grab for him but missed. Bloody hamster! She lay flat on her front and peered underneath.

Hamish had reached the wall and was rolling along it at a brisk pace. He stopped suddenly against a slim book that had been pushed into the furthest corner near one of the rear legs. Cate stretched out and pulled the book towards her, hoping Hamish would follow. It was a notebook she had given Jo the previous year, hardbacked and decorated with two fat cupids taken from an Italian cathedral fresco. A sticker had been pasted in the top right-hand corner of the cover. 'Diary. Josephine Gail Beane.'

Cate felt the weight of the book in her hands. The thin silk of the page marker lay almost a third of the way through. God, it would be so easy, so handy. A shortcut to her daughter's soul. She had no idea Jo had been keeping a diary. Emma had started on her birthday but had given up after a week, bored with the mundanities of an eleven-year-old's existence. But Jo. Jo had always been scornful of journals. Cate flicked through the pages in a quick blur and saw a riot of spluttering ink and exclamation marks and what looked like a heart shape or a pair of lips, she wasn't sure which. She snapped it shut feeling suddenly ashamed. Hamish re-emerged and bumped into her knee before rolling across towards the washing basket.

'You're right,' she said quickly. 'Bad mother. Bad, bad mother.' She bent down again and pushed the book back under the wardrobe, positioning the page marker almost exactly as it had been. Knowing Jo, there would probably be a James Bond trap for curious parents, a cunningly placed hair, a strategic piece of carpet fluff, possible even a hamster dropping.

The phone started to ring and Cate jumped to her feet, glad of the distraction. She shut the door on Hamish and the hidden diary and sprinted downstairs, catching the call just as it switched to the answering machine.

It wasn't a good line but she could make out that it was Marg and that she was excited. She held the phone close to her ear and listened intently, eyes widening in surprise. She spoke only when Marg had stopped.

'What! I can't. No. It's not possible. It's really sweet of you. No. Really. No. There's absolutely no way. I couldn't. Could I?'

17

'Of course you bloody could.' Marg sounded frustrated. 'This is the perfect opportunity. You get your work show-cased in a national newspaper. A national paper. Jesus, Cate, chances like this don't come around that often.'

'I don't do . . . work,' said Cate. She dropped onto the easy chair. 'It's a hobby. Marg, how can I? And anyway, it's the weekend I'm meant to be going away with Dan.'

'So, postpone it. It's not like he's never cancelled anything before, is it? Reschedule it for the following weekend or another time.'

'But the kids.'

'Your mum and Ed will help out, or hey – how about their dad? Maybe he could lend a hand.'

'Marg,' said Cate warningly. Her heart was hammering with a mix of panic and elation. God, what an opportunity. £1,000 to dress an apartment, a photo spread in the *Saturday Post.*

'Look, you were going to come down for the weekend anyway,' said Marg. 'We just bring it forward and add an extra day. Or two.'

'I don't know.'

'Well I do. I'm not letting you back out of this.'

'I'll think about it. I'll need to check with Dan and Mum.'

'You've got till the end of today. Rick'll have to tell them he's got his own designer.'

Cate swallowed. 'Okay, I will. I'll phone you early evening.

I promise. And you're sure he's okay about this, that they'll be okay about it?'

'They'll be fine and he's delighted. Although you'll have your work cut out for you – he's got all the style sense of a haddock.'

Cate heard a muffled and laughing profanity. 'I'll call you,' she said. 'Tonight.'

'Make it work, Cate.'

'I'm going to try. Really.'

'Trying's not good enough,' said Marg. 'You're coming down. Even if I have to come up and get you.'

Cate put the phone back on the console and stood up. She looked in the mirror. Her cheeks were flushed and her eyes bright and panicked. God. Oh my God. There was a faint dunt from above her head. Christ! Poor Hamish was still trundling around the bedroom in his ball. She ran up the stairs making mental lists as she went. There was a netball match on that Saturday morning. She'd have to call the school and get someone else to help out and someone to ferry the girls there and back because Dan would have no idea where they were supposed to be. And Stevie had a party at roughly the same time. Present still to be bought, wrapped, labelled. And the twins had the dentist on Friday after school. Oh God, how could she do this?

She pulled Hamish from his ball and shoved him back in his cage where he tottered off to his bed. Her mind was spinning. Do you ever think of doing it professionally? His own designer. Are you going to let a hamster get in the way of a career?

In the office she slipped into her seat and looked around her, instinct and excitement overriding the low buzz of panic.

Rick Rutner. Reporter. Not porn star. Well travelled.

Serious. A trunk, an old travelling trunk. She could see it now in the corner of a sitting room, placed as though it had always been there. If he didn't have one, she could get one at a secondhand sale. She saw herself and Marg browsing a market on a bright Portobello morning. Chiswick and Hawes. Some of their soft, mossy cushions and a Harris Tweed throw for a couch or the back of a chair, although that could be half the budget gone right there. An old reading lamp, too, like the ones in a library. And stacks of books and magazines. Reading matter. Everywhere. Especially in the loo.

She scribbled some notes and looked at the calendar. Realistically, she'd need to wait and see what his flat looked like – God, it'd probably be an Austin Powers pad if what Marg said about him was true. If she was being sensible she'd need a day to assess, a day or even two to source, another to buy, and two more to dress. Five, maybe six days. A very long weekend. She inhaled sharply and picked up the phone before guilt and terror got the better of her.

It was Ed who answered. 'Hey, sweetheart. How are you? I'd get your mum but she's out at her Ladies' League. She's not due back till after four.'

'That's fine, Ed. I'll call back.' She paused. 'Actually, I need to ask you this now. It's a huge favour. Really huge.'

'Of course,' he said. 'What is it?'

'You know you're looking after the kids the weekend that Dan and I are away? Well, I've been given the chance to go to London instead and do some interior design. For a newspaper article. It's Marg's boyfriend's apartment. But it would mean me being away Friday and maybe even Monday, too.'

She paused. It sounded too much as she said it. She couldn't. 'Oh, God, Ed, it won't work. No, look, forget it. Honestly.'

Ed jumped in. 'What won't work? That sounds just great, sweetheart. For a newspaper. Fancy that. How did that come up?'

'Marg heard about it,' said Cate. 'Oh, God. Ed, I don't know what to do. I'd love to do it, really love to, but I've booked the hotel, and Dan will probably have a fit and I wouldn't get back until Monday night, and the kids . . .' She tailed off.

'Now, what's that thing your mum says again?' said Ed. 'You can please all of the people some of the time and some of the people all of the time but you can't please all of the people all of the time. Wasn't it Abe Lincoln who came up with that?'

'I always thought it was Yoda from *Star Wars*,' said Cate weakly.

Ed laughed. 'Well, whoever it was, you please yourself, sweetheart. And I think that means you should go to London. You know, when opportunity knocks and all that . . . you grab it.'

Cate smiled. 'You've been living with mum too long,' she said.

He laughed again. 'And you know we love spending time with the girls, and we were going to anyway with you and Dan off on the night out. So don't worry about that side of it. We'll work it out.'

'You're wonderful.' Cate felt suddenly like she wanted to burst into tears. 'You're the best dad.'

She knew that he was smiling. 'It's no trouble,' he added. 'You go off and get yourself prepared. I've no doubt your mum will call later with . . . advice. You can tell her when you need us round. We'll be there.'

She told the kids on the way back from school. There was a prolonged, perplexed silence and then Stevie and Emma spoke simultaneously.

'Can I have a present?'

'Can I come too?'

'It's not definite yet,' said Cate. 'I still need to sort it out with Daddy. But if I do go, yes, I'll get you all presents, but you can't come with me.'

'Why not?' whined Emma. 'Debs' mum took her and she said you have to go into Topshop because they've got this toilet that's like a fountain.'

'A toilet like a fountain,' said Cate. 'That doesn't sound very pleasant.'

'Can I have a Barbie Pegasus?' interrupted Stevie.

'Not the loo,' Emma giggled. 'The sink thing. It's like a big fountain and you wash your hands in it. And they've got a whole bit just for belts. A whole bit. Please, Mum. Pleeease? We never get to go anywhere. Pleeeeease?'

Cate shook her head. 'Honey, you can't. I'm going to be working all the time.'

'But it's not work,' said Emma. 'It's just sorting out someone's house.'

'It is work,' said Cate. 'It's called a commission.'

'Who's going to look after us?' asked Jo, ever practical.

'Dad,' said Cate. 'And Gran and Grampa are going to help out lots, too.'

'Can I have a Disco Bratz?' asked Stevie.

'Maybe,' said Cate. 'I'll get something nice.'

'When will you come home?' asked Jo.

'Probably Tuesday,' said Cate. 'Maybe Wednesday.'

'Can I have a Barty Bear?' said Stevie. 'That's what I really want. A Barty Bear.'

'Too big,' said Cate. 'It would need its own seat on the plane.'

'Does Dad not want to go too?' asked Jo.

'Dad doesn't know yet,' said Cate. She angled the rear-view mirror and gave them all a big, beaming smile that belied her nerves. What she should have said was, Dad doesn't know yet and I have no idea how I'm going to tell him.

In the end, and because he was late, she went for the blunt approach. She let him put his bag on the bottom step and sling his coat over the banister, then she met him in the hall and pulled him into the kitchen. She needed to get him before the kids came down and blurted it all out for her.

'What?' he laughed at her as she turned to face him.

'Dan. I've been asked to go to London to do some interior design stuff. Well, it's Marg's boyfriend, Rick. His flat. It needs to be done up for a photo spread and she's suggested I do it.'

Dan leant against the counter. He looked confused. 'Marg asked you to go to London to do up her boyfriend's flat?'

'No. Well, kind of. Rick's been asked to do this thing about his flat for the style section of the *Saturday Post*, because he's a foreign correspondent. And he gets to have a designer help him get it ready.'

'You?'

She wished he hadn't sounded so surprised. 'Me,' she said. She lifted the lid of the pasta pot and gave the steaming contents a quick but unnecessary stir.

'Wow!' He smiled at her.

'The thing is,' she ploughed on. 'It's the weekend of the eighteenth. Well, it would be a bit longer than the weekend. Friday to probably Tuesday. But I've spoken to Mum and Ed and they're more than happy to help out and the kids are fine about it, and I was planning to go down and see Marg sometime anyway, and . . .'

'That weekend? I thought we were away that weekend.'

'We are. We were.' She bit her lip. 'But we can rebook it for another time.' She grabbed his hands again. 'Dan, it's just an amazing opportunity and I'd really love to do it. And Mum and Ed will be here.'

He shrugged. 'I suppose. If you want.'

She noticed, even in her relief, that he had relinquished their weekend away more easily than she had expected.

'So you're getting paid for this?' He moved across to the fridge and peered in.

'Not exactly.' She turned and gave the pasta another stir. 'There's a thousand-pound budget, but it's not a fee. As such. Marg and Rick are going to pay up-front for anything I need to buy and they'll get the money back. I'll need to buy a plane ticket down. That's all. No hotel or anything.'

'So you're paying to go to London to do up someone's flat for no fee? Sounds like a good deal.' He gave a flat laugh.

'It's an opportunity, Dan.'

'Okay, okay.' He held up his hands. 'When will you be leaving?'

'On the Friday. I'll be back either late on Sunday or maybe Monday.'

The children tumbled into the kitchen.

'Mum's getting me a Barty Bear,' said Stevie. 'In London.'

'Is she now?' Dan looked up at her and Cate shook her head.

He gathered them into him. 'Well, looks like it's just you lot and me,' he said. 'Mummy's abandoning us.'

Cate lifted the pot from the hob and drained the pasta over the sink, breathing in the hot damp steam, relieved the asking was over. He came up behind her and put his hands on her hips.

'I'm sorry about the weekend,' she said.

'It's fine.'

She turned to face him. 'Are you okay with this?'

'I'll have to be.' He gave a quick smile. 'If it's what you want.'

'It is.' She reached up to kiss him back and handed him the ladle. 'And I've got another favour to ask. Can you serve this up for me? I need to make a quick call.'

18

Cate leant back in the seat and savoured the rising surge in her stomach as the plane lifted into the sky. It was cloudy, and the aircraft jolted a little as it climbed through the cumulus towards the flat blue and the certain sun that lay above.

Below, in the disappearing grey jumble of buildings was a house papered in Post-its, like some strange yellow blight. Pasta Carbonara: must be eaten by Sunday. Debs' mum to pick up and drop off after netball. Check sports kit: bib, shorts, polo shirt, trainers. Hair must be tied back on both sides. Make sure Stevie wears clothes at all times. Dentist: Friday 3.45 p.m. Hamish: clean out. Do Not Let Out Of Ball! Piano practice: 10 minutes a night or no TV. DO. NOT. EAT. THE. TOOTHPASTE.

Preparing to invade a small nation would have been easier, but if there was anything she had forgotten it was too late. She closed her eyes. Five days in London.

She gave a little unbidden laugh and the man beside her snapped his newspaper closer to his face. He hadn't said a word as he squeezed in beside her in his dull blue suit that had gone shiny on the bum. She glanced at him, wanting to push the paper down and say, 'I'm a designer, you know. I'm flying to London for a spread in a Saturday broadsheet.' She picked up the inflight magazine instead and flicked through the sticky, curling pages. Dan had been a little panicked-looking when he had left for work. But she had got a proper kiss and an admonition to phone often and not to let Marg lead her astray. Her mum and Ed had run her to the airport and would be in charge today and then pop in over the weekend before they took over again on Monday.

The girls had been clingy when she dropped them at school and had given her a real cuddle, apparently not minding who saw. She had promised Emma she would go to Topshop and see the toilet fountain on her behalf and buy her a belt. Jo said she didn't know what she wanted. Stevie wanted so much that she had laboured over a list, now tucked in Cate's bag.

The plane levelled out and the seat-belt sign pinged off. Cate plucked at a loose thread on her long cardigan and lost herself in imagined textures and vivid colour schemes.

The trolley was approaching, laden with cans and bottles and packets of crisps. 'Can I get you a drink?' The attendant flashed a flat, practised smile.

The surly man with the shiny bum shook his head without looking up.

Cate nodded. 'Yes please,' she said. 'I'll have a mineral water.' She paused and gave a smile. 'And a large gin and tonic.'

Rick dropped his bag in the hall and shut the door with a hefty back-kick.

'It's like being married.' He grinned at Marg. 'How's it feel, Mrs Rutner? Should I carry you over the threshold?'

'Try it and you'll lose an arm.' Marg pushed his bag under the hall table with her foot. 'This is not a marital experiment. It's a necessary evil.'

'Darling,' said Rick affectedly, as Marg handed him his own key. 'You say the sweetest things.'

She gave him a grim smile. She knew she was being tetchy but it had been a bitch of a morning. Not only had the live link to Amman failed mid-segment, but Susann had choked during an interview with the new Secretary of State for Culture.

The minister had almost completely lost her voice after an all-night debate, and what Susann had meant to say to her was 'Last night has left you a little hoarse.' But somewhere before the end of the word came one of those unexpected throat seizures that every anchor dreads, and what she said was 'Last night has left you a little hoar.' She had recovered well, but had become hysterical once the show was over, worried that she might have ruined her chances for the best anchor nod, or, worse still, would be a dead cert for the next TV's funniest bloopers show.

'Right,' said Marg, leading the way into the lounge. 'Some ground rules. I get that back once the weekend is over. And no food – or trust-fund girls – in the bed. Oh, and no shaving clippings in the sink.'

Rick clipped the key onto his keyring and jangled it in her face. 'Does that go for you too?'

'God, Rick.' Marg shook her head and checked her watch. 'I'll need to get a move on. Cate's plane will be here soon. I'm going to take her past your apartment and then we'll meet you in Popinjays, right? You will be nice?'

'Of course.'

'I mean it, Rick. Don't be a drunken arse, okay?'

He grinned at her, threw her his own keys, and headed for the bathroom. 'Does that go for you too?' he said again and shut the door before she could respond.

Marg slumped onto her sofa. It had seemed such a good idea at the time but she really wasn't sure how it would work.

Cate had asked if she could stay at Rick's to give her as much time in the flat as possible. So she wouldn't be here, but Rick would.

It's just a weekend, Marg told herself as she heard the

loo flush. Although you'll be spending next weekend and a good few days after with him as well in Chad.

Rick emerged, still zipping up, and she stood to go in after him. He waved his hand in front of his face. 'I'd leave it a couple of minutes if I were you, babe. Health and safety reasons.'

Marg sighed. 'God, Rick,' she said. For the second time in less than five minutes.

'Well?' Marg took a step forward and peered into Cate's face. She'd hardly said anything since she stepped through the door, just moved through the rooms of Rick's apartment, quietly taking everything in. The cleaning lady had done a sterling job but it was still a bit of a jumble of odd pieces of furniture and overstuffed bookcases and bare floorboards. It wasn't often that Marg stayed there. So many people had a key to Rick's that there was every chance of being wakened by a cameraman buddy using it as a crash pad at the end of a boozy night, or a trust-fund girl expecting to find a space in the bed. Rick was often double-booked.

'It's not what I imagined,' said Cate slowly. She turned and flashed a broad smile. 'But it's fab. It's ideal. Really. I love the books. I was hoping there'd be loads of books. And these.' She moved over to the window and pushed back the curtains to reveal the broad wooden shutters that Marg had never noticed. 'These are beautiful. It's so rare to find them on British buildings these days. They're so much more functional. Keep the noise out well, too.'

'Or in,' said Marg. 'There's been the odd party in here.'

'I'll bet.' Cate pulled the shutters closed with a hefty yank. 'Is it going to be a lot of work?'

Cate shook her head. 'Not too bad. He's okay with me doing a bit of painting?'

'The only thing he doesn't want is Austrian blinds. Or a stag's head.'

Cate laughed. 'I'm looking forward to meeting him.' She moved across to the large cupboard. 'Can I look in here? Or is an It Girl going to fall out?'

Marg smiled. 'Did I tell you he told the paper he was flying down an up-and-coming designer from Edinburgh? I think they're expecting wall-to-wall tartan.' She checked her watch. 'Actually, we'd better get a move on. He's been in Popinjays for a couple of hours. If we don't get there soon, he won't be able to form a sensible sentence. Stick your stuff in the spare room. The bed's made up in there.'

'And you're okay to help out tomorrow?' Cate lugged her bag over to the small room off the lounge. 'It'll be an early start. I want to go to Camden Market, and a couple of the design shops near Bond Street. And a paint store. And maybe a haberdasher's.'

'A haberdasher's?'

'For a tailor's dummy,' said Cate. 'To hang his flak-jacket on. He has a flak-jacket?'

Marg nodded, then smiled broadly. 'This is more like it,' she said. 'Look at you. This is your mad moment, hon. You enjoy it.'

'I will. I am,' said Cate. 'And thanks so much for thinking of me for it. Really. I know I was a bit of wimp when you called, but I still can't believe I'm doing this.'

'You'll be great,' said Marg.

'I know I will,' said Cate.

'We'll still be able to go out, too, won't we?' said Marg. 'It won't all be rag-rolling and stencilling.'

Cate nodded. 'I've got some shopping to do for the girls. Apparently there's a toilet like a fountain in the Oxford Street Topshop. Emma wants me to see it.'

'I was thinking more Harvey Nicks and cocktails,' said Marg.

'Do they have a fountain in their toilet?' Cate laughed.

'Do you know,' said Marg, 'I don't think they do.' She glanced at her watch again. 'Anyway we need to get a move on and meet your first client. Doesn't that sound weird? Your first client.'

'My first client,' said Cate. 'Richard Rutner. International Man of Mystery.'

Or drunken arse. Marg looked across the broad floor of Popinjays to the group in the corner and the man at its middle, red-faced and guffawing. He looked up and caught sight of her through unsteady eyes. 'Babe!' She should have known.

Marg led Cate across to the corner booth with a heavy heart. 'Cate, this is Rick. Rick, this is Cate.'

If Cate was surprised that her first client was completely sozzled she didn't give it away, but flashed Rick a warm, broad smile and shook hands, then plonked herself down among them all as if she were a regular.

Rick leant across and patted Cate's knee. 'This is my very own House Doctor,' he said. 'She's going to transform my humble abode into a palace, aren't you?'

'That's the plan,' said Cate brightly.

Rick stopped the waiter for more glasses and poured Cate a large measure of wine. She accepted it graciously and held it up to him. 'Cheers,' she said. 'It's lovely to meet you.'

'You too.' He emptied what was left of the bottle into a glass for Marg. 'I hope Marg here told you I don't want any frilly curtains or animal heads or tartan. Nothing too Glenbogle.'

Cate didn't flinch. 'Of course,' she said, taking a sip of her drink. 'But you're still keen on the disco ball, right?'

Rick looked at her quizzically for an instant then gave a loud guffaw. 'I like her, babe,' he said to Marg over Cate's head. 'She's a find.' For some ridiculous reason Marg felt herself relax. Cate had passed the Rutner test. He waved the empty bottle in her direction.

'Get us another, babe, eh? While I talk to my designer here.'

Marg raised her eyebrows at Cate and headed for the bar. She looked back as she waited for the wine. Cate was leaning in towards Rick, nodding vigorously at something he was saying, her face all smiles. Marg felt a little rush of pleasure. Cate. Here in London, and having fun.

'Have you got my Barty Bear?' Stevie was breathless with anticipation.

'No, baby. I said I'd get you something nice, but it might not be a Barty Bear. Are you being a good girl for Daddy?'

'I'm being very good,' said Stevie. 'I only ate a little bit of toothpaste.'

'Only a little bit,' said Cate. 'None would be better, but you're trying and that's good. Well, I miss you, toots, but I'll see you soon, okay?'

'Byeee!' shouted Stevie and the phone was discarded. Cate pushed open the shutter on one of the windows and peered into the street, still alive with people at 9 p.m.

The room around her was covered in dust-sheets, the walls damp with undercoat and primer. A work in progress.

'Hey.' Dan sounded weary. 'Stevie's gone to get the twins. They'll be down in a sec.'

'How are you doing?' Cate gave a gentle laugh.

'Knackered.'

'When did Mum and Ed leave?'

'You just missed them,' said Dan.

'So how come you're knackered?' she wanted to say.

'Oh, Orla phoned,' said Dan. 'She thought it was tomorrow you went down. She wanted to wish you luck.'

'I'll call her,' said Cate.

There was an unfilled pause. 'I'm having a good time,' she said.

'Mm.'

'We're going to really get down to it tomorrow. A couple of markets and fabric stores.'

'What's he like? Marg's man.'

'He's really different from how he comes across on TV,' said Cate. 'Completely unreconstructed and drinks like a navvy, but he's actually quite a sweetheart underneath. He's got a good heart.'

'Sounds like it,' said Dan dubiously.

'No, really, he has.'

'So you might be back down for the wedding?'

'God, no.' Cate laughed. 'They're really similar and they're great together but they just don't seem to . . . fit. You know?'

'Here are the girls.' Dan disappeared from the line and Jo and Emma came on, one after the other, filled with urgent updates from planet pre-teen. Debs, it transpired, had now had one ear pierced twice, which, according to Jo, wasn't fair because neither Jo nor Emma had Any Holes Anywhere, and the dentist said Emma might need a brace for the tooth that still hadn't settled into place.

'They're like these big metal contraptions,' said Emma theatrically, when it was her turn to talk. 'I'm not wearing it, Mum. I'm not.'

'It's "contraption", sweetheart, and don't get in a panic. It's not for sure that you need one.'

She suddenly wanted to be home. With her girls who mispronounced and wanted piercings, and ate toothpaste, and needed her there.

'We'll talk about it when I get home.'

'Have you been able to get the belt yet?'

'Not yet,' said Cate, 'but I will. And I'll take a picture of the fountain on my phone.'

'Thanks, Mum.'

Dan came back on the line. 'Better go,' he said. 'Time for the bedtime battle.'

'I miss you all,' said Cate.

Dan must have held the phone out because his voice faded slightly as he shouted to the girls. 'Do we miss Mum?'

There was an assortment of 'yes's and giggles and 'no's but amongst it all Cate couldn't hear Dan's answer. She couldn't hear if he'd said anything at all.

19

'For a cushion?' Marg raised her eyebrows sharply. 'Ninety-five quid for a cushion?'

'Sssh.' Cate frowned at her and glanced quickly at the assistants bent over the old scrolled cash desk in the corner of the Chiswick and Hawes showroom. They didn't seem to have heard. 'I'm not buying that one and you don't exactly shop at Ikea, do you?' she retorted.

'No. But I've never paid ninety-five pounds for a cushion, especially one this small.' Marg dropped the tiny green velvet square back onto the display sofa. 'I never saw the point of cushions, anyway. What is the point of cushions?'

'Comfort,' said Cate. 'For cuddling into.'

'Isn't that what men are for?'

'You can't pummel a man into the right shape,' said Cate.

'No?' Marg cocked her head and they both laughed.

Marg looked at her watch. She was obviously getting bored. 'Are we done after this? Because if I don't get a cocktail down my gullet soon I'm going to throw a wobbly just like Stevie did at the airport.'

Cate grinned. Marg had been a trooper. Three trips back to the flat already with a dressmaker's dummy from a haberdasher's in Pimlico, enough paint to rag-roll Tower Bridge, and a beautifully battered old suitcase they found at a market, plastered with labels from long-gone airlines. TWA, Pan Am and Caledonian. She deserved a break, even though Cate didn't want to stop.

Her internal Stevie alarm had wakened her at 6 a.m. and she'd spent an hour and a half on the walls and shifting furniture around.

It was a beautiful morning, cool and bright, and she'd walked until she found a small café two streets away from Rick's, where she had a pain au chocolat and a cup of strong dark coffee for breakfast. There was a small florist's opposite and Cate had sat and watched the owner arrange deep tubs of exotic blooms: china pinks, heliotrope and leopard lilies. She'd brought her small sketchbook with the layouts she'd planned and she sat and doodled, and smiled, occasionally, at no one but herself, because she had all the time in the world to work at what she loved on a glorious London day.

She handed Marg an armful of cushions. 'Okay. We'll stop for a late lunch. But then I'll need to get right back into it. I'll just get these four.'

'Why not four the same?' asked Marg. She eyed the mismatched red squares. 'These ones look a little . . . boudoir.'

'Because these go better.' Cate lifted a small silk cushion and laid it against an almost burgundy brocade affair. 'See the sheen on this when you turn it? It's almost exactly the same shade as this one. And it's Rick's favourite colour.'

'Red is his favourite colour? I never knew that. How do you know that?'

Cate smiled. 'I asked him.'

'Makes sense.' Marg shrugged and turned to follow her towards the till. 'It matches his eyes.'

Now, this was dazzling. Cate lifted the sleeve of an Alice Temperley dress and let it slide over her wrist in a slither of colourful silk jersey.

'I love her stuff,' said Marg, glancing casually at the price tag. 'Sexy as hell and comfortable too. You don't often get that.'

'Do you have any?' Cate looked round at her. She'd already noticed that the pewter wrap-over blouse Marg was wearing with her jeans probably cost more than Cate's own entire ensemble, which, from the feet up, went Barratts, Wallis, Tesco, Tesco. Oh, and Marks and Spencer for the knickers. A machine-washable girl.

'One or two,' said Marg. She looked a little uncomfortable and Cate smiled to herself. Marg had often been uncomfortable about her clothes but only because she had so few. There wasn't much money in the Holland household, although Marg's mum had a job as an administrator at the teacher training college. Cate had often felt aggrieved on Marg's behalf that she found the spare cash for bingo every Friday night, but never to spoil her daughter with something gorgeous and unexpected. A strappy little top for the school disco; the jeans with flowers up the side that everyone was wearing. Cate had lent things when she could, and had rejoiced with Marg when she had got a Saturday job and splurged her first day's wages on a long pink stripy top, which might have made her look like a stick of candy rock, but must have made her feel a million dollars.

'You can try it on.' Marg caught hold of the back of Cate's coat and pulled her away from the rack of slinky dresses towards the escalators. 'But only after lunch. Drinkies first.'

'Do you remember going down town on a Saturday?' said Cate, allowing herself to be hauled away from Harvey Nicks' designer glories. 'They never had anything like this in Tammy Girl, did they?'

Marg gave a little shudder. 'I think most of my wardrobe was a hundred per cent nylon then. Remember those trousers that got all static when my thighs rubbed together?'

Cate snorted with laughter. 'God, I'd forgotten about them. Your sparky pants.'

'Could you say that a bit louder?' said Marg. 'I don't think the woman buying blusher on the ground floor heard you.'

Cate giggled. 'You put on a better light show than the school disco.'

'All right,' said Marg. 'Do you want me to bring up your swimsuit bra again?'

'No,' said Cate. 'That wouldn't be nice.' She waited until they had stepped onto the moving stairway and then leant forwards. 'Sparky pants,' she whispered.

'Five-nipple freak,' whispered back Marg. The woman behind them looked studiously at her feet.

They waited only a few minutes before a waitress led them to a table for two in the mid-section of the restaurant. Marg ordered two Kir Royals and when they were brought on a small silver tray, she handed one to Cate and raised the other.

'Cheers, my dear. Are you having fun?'

'Loads,' said Cate. 'This is such a hoot. Thank you.'

'You're welcome.' Marg picked up the menu. 'I'm glad you came down. I don't do stuff like this very often. You know. Lunch on the weekend with a girlfriend.'

'I'm glad I came, too.' Cate sat back and looked round at the other diners and the beautifully laid table and the sleek, polished glasses. 'It's not often I get a lunch when I can finish a sentence without being interrupted by someone who needs to be sponged down or told off.'

Marg smiled. 'I had noticed. It's like a kind of affliction that mums get.' She put her drink down and adopted a different accent.

'So, anyway, I was saying to him that we need to try and

organise – HOW MANY TIMES DO I HAVE TO TELL
YOU NOT TO PICK YOUR NOSE? DIRTY, DIRTY
BOY! So, anyway, he thinks . . . I SAID NOT ON YOUR
SLEEVE! NOT. ON. YOUR. SLEEVE!'

Cate giggled hysterically as half the restaurant swivelled
to watch Marg's performance.

'I'm not that bad,' she said.

'No.' Marg picked up her drink. 'You're not as bad as
some I've come across, but you're still afflicted.'

Cate took a long slow sip of her Kir and studied Marg.
'Do you think you and Rick will ever have kids?'

'God, no. Where did that come from?'

'I don't know,' said Cate. 'He's lovely, actually. I like
him.'

'So do I. But not for his DNA.'

'Well, if not him, anyone? Do you think you ever will?'

Marg shook her head.

'Adam Milner?' Cate smiled slyly.

Marg raised her eyebrows and looked at her.

'Do you know, we should give him a call while I'm down
and he could advise us on the architectural merit of Rick's
flat.'

Marg kept looking at her.

'No?'

'Why are you trying to pair me off?' Marg sat back and
eyed Cate accusingly. 'Why is it that those of you who've
got married and had kids try to get the rest of us to do the
same? To confirm that you've done the right thing? To
convince yourself that you have?'

'Maybe,' said Cate, smiling. 'I don't know. It's just you
deserve someone nice.'

'I do, but I don't need someone nice. Especially not to
father children. It's not going to happen.'

'Really not?'

'Really not,' said Marg. She paused and leant forward. 'Remember . . . at school?'

Cate nodded, knowing instantly what she meant.

'I still have that feeling. A kind of panic that it might happen. I just really don't want it. Them. Kids. And I'm not going to suddenly change my mind. I'm not going to go all Angelina Jolie and head off to Cambodia for a small orphan or two. I don't have a biological clock. I don't want kids. I don't want to be a mum.' She took a sip of her drink. 'Strange, isn't it, considering I had such a good role model?'

Cate smiled gently. 'But you're good with them. Jo thinks you're fab. Stevie, too.'

'Well, you're good with hamsters but that doesn't mean you should breed them,' said Marg.

Cate laughed. 'I suppose you're getting on a bit, anyway. Those ovaries must be shrivelling up in there. Like pitted prunes.'

'Bitch.' Marg grinned. 'At least my boobs are still above my waist. Without underwiring.'

'I'm not going to dignify that with a response.' Cate scrabbled in her bag at the sound of her mobile.

She looked quickly at the screen. 'I'm going to tell Dan you're being disrespectful to his beloved wife.'

She pressed the phone to her ear. 'Hey!'

'Hey.' There was a pause.

'How are we all?' asked Cate. 'I was going to call tonight at bedtime.'

'We're fine,' said Dan, slowly. 'Well, actually . . .'

'What?'

'I'm calling to see if you know what might remove a henna tattoo?'

'A henna tattoo?' said Cate, puzzled. 'From what?'

'From Stevie.'

184

'What!'

'It was at the party,' said Dan, weakly. 'She wanted a tattoo done.'

'Where?'

'At the party,' Dan repeated.

'No, where? On her arm? On her forehead? Where?'

'Cheek,' said Dan. 'Right cheek.'

'And you let her?'

'She wanted it,' said Dan. 'I didn't see the harm.'

'Didn't see the harm! Dan, these things are dreadful. Debs got one on her arm last year and it took months to come off. Months!'

'Well, I didn't know, did I? I'm not a tattoo artist.'

'Jesus,' said Cate.

'You won't want to know what shape it is, then?'

'Oh, God,' said Cate. 'It's not a death's head or a pentangle or something like that, is it?'

'It's meant to be a hummingbird but it looks more like a . . .' He lowered his voice. 'Bat.'

'How big?'

'Not very.'

'How big?'

'Two inches?'

'Jesus, Dan!'

'Okay, okay.' He sounded annoyed. 'Mea culpa. Bad Dad. Oh, and you might as well know, we forgot to take the present as well. But the mum was very pleasant and I said you'd hand it in at school next week. And Stevie's here, she wants to tell you herself.'

She heard the phone change hands and then a small and slightly wobbly voice.

'Mummy, I've got a smudge on my face. I don't like it.'

'Oh, baby, I know. Daddy told me. But don't worry, it'll come off. Promise.'

'I don't like it.' Stevie started to cry and Cate pressed the phone so tight to her ear that it hurt.

'I know you don't, baby girl. But don't cry. We'll get it all sorted. Don't you . . .'

'Come here, pumpkin.' Dan lifted Stevie away and passed the phone to Jo. Cate could hear the softness of his voice in the background. 'It's fine. Grampa Ed's gone to get some special soap and soon there'll be no smudges on your face. Not anywhere, okay?'

'Mmhm,' sniffed Stevie.

'It's huge, Mum,' whispered Jo. 'It's kind of like those big bats. You know the ones we saw in that programme that hang upside down and eat apples?'

'A fruit bat,' said Cate. 'Oh, God.'

'Do you want to speak to Dad again?'

'Please.'

Dan sounded terse. 'Yes.'

'I thought Mum and Ed were going to take her to the party,' said Cate.

'They were, but Ed's been a bit wheezy and your mum wanted to take him to the out-of-hours GP. They're here now, though. Your mum's suggesting white spirit.' He paused. 'She says it would take the stain out of a sinner's soul.'

'White spirit! No, Dan, don't let her put white spirit on Stevie's face.'

'Calm down, I won't. Ed's got some of that special gel soap, the abrasive stuff that takes car oil off. That should do the trick. Unless you can think of anything else.'

'How about make-up remover pads? There should be some in the bathroom cupboard.'

'Tried that. No joy.'

'My poor girl,' said Cate.

'Well, we're getting it sorted,' said Dan. 'She'll be fine.'

'Phone me and let me know if it works, and give her a big hug from me. Okay?'

He sighed. 'Okay. Bye.'

Cate laid the phone on the table.

'Family drama?' said Marg, taking a sip from her glass.

'Dan took Stevie to a birthday party and let her get a henna tattoo on her cheek. It won't come off. Apparently it's the size and appearance of a fruit bat.'

Marg smiled. 'Very rock 'n' roll.'

'It's not funny,' said Cate tersely, taking a deep slug from her own glass. 'He should have known. These things are the devil to remove.'

'It's just ink, Cate,' said Marg. 'It'll shift.'

Cate looked up sharply. 'How would you know?' She knew she was sounding harsh, that she was taking out her frustration on Marg when it should be directed at Dan for being such a dope, and at herself for not being there to stop it happening in the first place.

'It'll shift,' Marg repeated. 'Don't get so wound up about it.'

'I'm not getting wound up.' Cate took another mouthful of Kir.

'Yes, you are. You're doing that martyred mum thing.'

'What martyred mum thing?'

'Where you expect everything to fall to pieces when you're not around and you're probably secretly pleased when it does. I see it all the time at work.' Marg waved her hands affectedly in the air. 'Flap. Flap. My husband's an arse. The kids have called the fire brigade.'

'I didn't do that!' Cate sat forward. What the hell did Marg know?

'You did,' said Marg. 'It was unnecessary.'

'Why was it unnecessary?'

'Well, he's doing the looking-after this weekend, which you

should be pleased about. They're half his after all. So you should just leave him to it. And Stevie got to go to a party . . .'

'Without the present,' said Cate. 'And she came away looking like a Maori warrior.'

'Okay, without the present. But Dan got her to the party. Presumably she had fun and she got a mark on her face that he's trying to get off. Small crisis. Not many dead.'

'So suddenly you're the great mothering and relationship expert?' said Cate stiffly.

Marg sat back and smiled. 'You're getting pissed at me, aren't you?'

'Yes I am. God, Margie. Marg.' Cate grimaced. 'You pick your moments. We were having fun.'

Marg was still smiling. 'We used to fight like this a lot,' she said. 'Remember?'

'Only because you're so bloody opinionated.'

'I tell it like I see it.'

'You always did.'

'And you always used to go into a huff,' said Marg. 'Just like now. Just like Stevie, actually.'

Cate stifled a giggle. 'You know nothing,' she said.

Marg took another drink and studied Cate across the table. 'Didn't that feel good?'

'No,' said Cate. 'What?'

'Having a fight. It's good we did. Don't you think we've been unnaturally nice to each other since you got back in touch?'

'You did this deliberately?' Cate's eyes widened.

'No,' said Marg. 'You were being unreasonable. Most times you're probably right to be annoyed at him if he's not pulling his weight, but not this one. He was a bit of an arse but he's dealing with it. Let it go.'

'He called to ask what to do,' said Cate.

'Or maybe he called to let you know.' Marg paused and stretched, a smile still playing around her lips. 'So, anyway, now I'm going to go to the loo while you call back and see if they've got the condor off Stevie's face yet.'

'Bat,' said Cate. 'Fruit bat.'

Marg stood to head for the Ladies'. 'I'll see if it's got a fountain,' she said.

'You do that.' Cate picked up the phone. 'And if it does, jump in it.'

20

Wherever Rick was last night it must have been smoky, or he had spent most of it singing. Marg watched him in the green glow of the bedside clock. He was still asleep, flat on his back, with his mouth ever so slightly agape. He was breathing heavily and each exhalation crackled slightly in his throat. She wasn't sure what time he'd got in, she'd just been dimly aware of the heavy press of a body next to her and the faintly sour smell of stale alcohol and late-night tapas. She'd turned from her favourite side to face the wall.

The clock said 3.12 a.m. Cate was probably up and at it already even though Marg had left her at 9 p.m., by then onto painting the ceiling in Rick's living room and wittering on about cornices and decals. She smiled. It felt good to know that Cate was just a few miles away, and in her element.

If Marg was being honest she had been a little nervous once Cate had confirmed that she could come down, wondering if she would be out of her depth. But she seemed to really know what she was doing and the flat was looking better already, fresher and smarter. And the red cushions did look fab, piled casually on Rick's ancient leather sofa with an old and faded Navajo-style throw that Cate had found wrapped around Rick's collection of LPs at the back of the It Girl cupboard and had sent out with Marg to have speed-cleaned and pressed. The weekend had been fun, too, even with Cate's flap over the henna tattoo, which had apparently come off, almost completely, with some of Ed's wonder soap.

Stevie and her tattoo. Rick and his flat. It seemed so strange that she and Cate could slip into each other's lives after an absence of twenty years. Marg felt a sudden pang of regret. If she'd just thought to call . . . It shouldn't have taken a crumbling comprehensive to get them back together. But she knew that if Cate hadn't called she would never have thought to; that Cate would have been consigned to her past until so much time had gone by that she might even struggle to remember her name. That friend I had at school.

Rick snorted suddenly and Marg turned back to look at him. His eyes opened momentarily, squinting and unfocused, and then shut again. He rolled a little closer and Marg shifted away. This was getting tedious. They'd slept in the same bed for more than two nights in a row before but she had always known he would be buggering off back to his own place when he woke.

Do you think you and Rick will ever have kids? Marg studied Rick's face, his masculine mouth sagged slightly open. She tried to summon a picture of her and Rick sitting at a mealtime table, spooning mush into a mewling toddler. Rick pushing a buggy, her breastfeeding. She pressed her hands to her stomach and imagined something growing inside, the way she'd done when she was a teenager. It didn't feel right. It wasn't going to happen. Not with him. Not ever.

She swung her legs out of the bed and sat on the edge, stretching.

'Babe,' he murmured sleepily, and an arm flapped over the empty space she had just left.

She stood and wandered down the hall towards the

bathroom. She'd begged off decorating duties after work today to finish up her preparations for Chad. She'd had an email from World Aid to say the nuns were prepared for their arrival and were looking forward to meeting Rick. The director had finished it with one of those irritating winking emoticons – ;-) and Marg had replied with her own version, which she'd hoped resembled Rick looking suitably horrified – §8-o. Or pissed.

Rick was paying another visit to his parents but had promised to meet her at his flat tonight to see what Cate had done. Cate had seemed confident of having it all finished by day's end, keen to get home in time to see the girls after school the following afternoon.

The bathroom light was still on and the extractor fan whirring noisily. He'd left the tap dripping as well, and Marg turned it off sharply. The loo seat was up. He hadn't flushed, but he had splashed. 'God, Rick,' she said.

'I've really just concentrated on two rooms.' Cate held the door to the living room tight shut and gestured for them to head down the hall. 'I looked back through the old *Saturday Posts* and they seem to do just two and the bathroom's always one of them. So . . .' She opened the door and Marg and Rick stepped inside.

Rick made a 'Whoo!' noise. Marg couldn't believe it was the same space. The walls had been newly painted in a light wash of smoky blue, and the old shower curtain had gone to be replaced by a bevelled glass screen drawn across the bath. A small antique table sat at its side, piled high with books and magazines. The bright blue blind with the yellow fish that Rick had never replaced had disappeared; a drop of sheer white gauze in its place, decorated with the faintest gothic script.

'I went with the idea of a print room. Words,' said Cate.

She looked at Rick. 'I know you said you like to read in here; in the bath, or on the loo.'

Marg touched the glass bath screen. 'You did this? You fitted this?'

Cate nodded. 'It's quite easy. It looks so much better and you don't get that wet-nylon-sticking-to-the-bum thing going on.' She laughed, watching their faces closely.

'And this?' Marg gestured to the floor where smart black and white check tiles had replaced the old cork covering that Rick had had down forever.

'It's a bit of a cheat,' said Cate. 'It comes on a roll, but it's great quality. Easy to keep clean, too.' She glanced at Marg, who didn't imagine it had been very pleasant being anywhere too close to the floor of the Rutner lavatory.

'And this . . .' Cate pointed to an antique free-standing toilet roll holder. 'I hope you don't mind that I took the old one off the wall. I noticed when you sit on the loo, your knees kind of knocked into it, so this one you can move around.'

Rick wasn't paying any attention. He was studying the walls, where a series of old maps had been hung above a new towel rail.

'Look at this,' he said to Marg. 'Persia. Iran.' He turned to Cate. 'Where did you get this?'

'Well, Marg said you'd been in Tehran just a couple of weeks back, so I chose that one. And I know you did that series in the Antarctic last year. This one shows the route of the Amundsen expedition. That's the Ross Ice Shelf.'

'Where they had their main camp,' said Rick. 'We flew over that.'

'There's this fabulous map store in Hammersmith,' continued Cate, 'like something out of Dickens. Musty and completely overstocked. I read about them in a magazine article a few years back and I phoned them and ordered these two. I picked them up yesterday – oh, and they'll be sending you the bill shortly.'

Rick nodded. 'And look at this.' He pointed to a wooden newspaper rack, like the ones that libraries have, fixed to the wall and hung with a selection of Sunday broadsheets.

'Well, I thought you could do research or plan your next trip while you're . . . sitting here.' She gestured to the loo. The seat and lid had been replaced with wooden ones, warm-hued and solid.

'She changed the loo seat,' said Marg. Marg would have no idea how to change a loo seat.

Rick grinned. 'This is going to be my bunker,' he said. 'I love it. Can't wait to see the lounge. Lead on.'

'There's not such a big difference in here,' said Cate when they reached the end of the hall. 'I've tried to use your pieces, with just a fresh mix of colours and a couple of extras. And I've tweaked the lighting.'

She wasn't entirely right. The room had been transformed. The end walls, where the bookcases were, were now a deep red, almost the colour of a Bloody Mary. She'd moved the chairs and sofas around, too, to create two distinct areas, a lounge and a study, where she'd placed the battered suit-case next to Rick's desk table. The curtains had come down to show off the shutters, and there were two new rugs in place of the large green rectangle of carpet, now rolled and stacked in the hall ready for a skip.

'My lord, she's a big girl.' Marg turned. Rick had pulled open his flak-jacket draped around the dressmaker's dummy and found that the dummy was female.

'You'll need to give her a name,' said Marg. 'She needs a name.'

'Bertha,' he said. 'I'm going to call her Bertha. Better watch out, babe. She's a hottie.'

'She won't laugh at your jokes,' said Marg.

'You don't laugh at my jokes,' Rick replied.

'I would if they were funny.' Marg turned to grin at Cate, and suddenly noticed how exhausted she looked and the tiny flecks of paint still in her hair.

'Did you get any sleep last night, hon?'

'Not much.'

Rick came over and kissed Cate enthusiastically on the cheek. 'Thanks, Cate. You've really done a sterling job. I like it. I love it.' He smiled at them both. 'Hey, I might even keep it this way.'

'When does the photographer come?' asked Cate

'First thing Thursday morning,' said Rick. 'Don't worry. I won't touch a thing.'

'I've listed everything I bought and used, and the price of it,' said Cate, pointing to a piece of A4 on the desk.

'Well, you keep what's left,' said Rick. 'You deserve it.'

'Thanks,' said Cate meekly.

'How much was left?' asked Marg.

'Fifteen pounds and thirty-six pence,' said Cate. 'Oh, until I got this. I forgot, Rick, there's one last thing.'

She swung open the cupboard door and fiddled with something that was hanging on the back of it. The strains of 'Rudolph the Red-Nosed Reindeer' filled the room and Rick exploded with laughter at the sight of the plush deer head, mounted on a fake backboard.

'Your stag's head,' giggled Cate.' I saw it in a charity shop on the way back this morning and I couldn't resist. You squeeze the nose to set it off. It was only six quid, so feel free to bin it if you want.'

She turned to Marg. 'Oh, and this is for you. As a thanks for bringing me down. And I didn't want you to feel left out.' She picked up a flat, square package from the sofa and handed it across.

Marg sat down and lifted away the tissue. It was a drawing,

a simple charcoal portrait encased in a sleek ashwood frame. She sat and stared at it quietly.

Rick peered over her shoulder. 'Nice,' he said.

'It's me.' Marg felt suddenly choked. She looked at the girl with the big smile and the crazy hair, then up at Cate. 'You did this at school for fifth-year art. You got an "A".'

Cate smiled gently. 'Well, you got me the Anaïs Anaïs, so I wanted to give you something. I thought it would go well in your apartment, maybe near the Peter Howson. Then I can say I've been hung with the greats.' She tried to laugh.

'Thank you,' said Marg.

'You're welcome.'

They looked at each other.

'Shit. Blub alert,' said Rick. 'Right, while you pair have a howl, I'm going to get the bubbly.' He headed for the kitchen, pinching Rudolph's nose as he passed. The two women sat together on the couch.

'You are really good at this,' said Marg. 'You know that?'

'Thank you.'

Marg placed the drawing beside her. 'He'll need to give the paper a name. For when they do the strap-line on the photos. You know, room styled by Cate Beane, or Catriona Beane, or Beane Designs. Designing Beane. Beane and Done It.'

Cate laughed. 'God, ehm, I don't know. Probably Cate Beane.'

'You sure?'

'Why not?' Cate frowned.

'Just don't think it's got the right ring to it,' said Marg. 'No offence to Dan.'

They sat for a moment.

'How about Catriona Wishart,' said Cate, finally.

'Better,' said Marg. 'Catriona Wishart it is. Room styled by Catriona Wishart.'

On the back of the cupboard door, Rudolph the cheap plush reindeer warbled his way to a shuddering and dramatic close.

Cate sat on the sofa and curled up her legs, pulling the Navajo throw around her for warmth. She was too excited to sleep, even though she was exhausted. Rick had really loved it, and she could tell Marg was impressed. Cate knew she'd been a little worried about getting her roped in. She looked around her. But it did look good and it had been a joy to do: to have a budget, to have the time, to have the space and the chance.

She turned her wrist and glanced at her watch. It was only 9.20 p.m., but both Marg and Rick had work first thing and had headed off just after 8.30 p.m.

She'd already said goodnight to the girls, but Mum and Ed would have gone home by now and Dan would be on his own. She could tell him everything in more detail. She could play him Rudolph. She could hear his voice.

It was her mum who answered. 'Oh, darling, he popped out about an hour ago.'

'Popped out?' said Cate. 'Where?'

'Just to the pub,' said her mum. 'One of his cycling friends phoned.'

'Guy.' Cate sighed.

'No,' said Mum, pleasantly. 'It was a Gillian.'

Cate felt a strange clutch of anxiety in her chest. She knew there were women in the cycling group, at least one consultant and a radiographer. It shouldn't matter that one of them had called for him. Although why would they phone the house when Cate wasn't there, when they'd never phoned before? Well, not that she knew about anyway.

'Darling, are you still there?'

'Mm,' said Cate.

'They'd been for a run and Dan couldn't go, but they were in a pub near the dry-ski slope. I just told him to head off. There wasn't much to be done. He took the bike. To get a bit of exercise. You know he's been so wound up these last few months, working so hard with all these changes at the hospital. Ed and I were just talking about it the other day.'

'That was nice of you to let him go,' said Cate blankly. 'Which pub?' She wasn't sure why she was asking.

'I think it was called Hunters. I can't really remember.' There was a pause. 'She was with the cycling group, Cate. A friend.'

'I know,' said Cate. 'I was just a little taken aback there, you know, a strange woman phoning the house for Dan when I'm not around.' She gave a flat, forced laugh.

'You're being silly, darling. And she didn't phone the house. It was his mobile. And she was very nice.'

'On his mobile? You talked to her?'

'Oh, don't make a fuss. I heard it go while he was up with the girls and I just assumed it would be you, so I answered it.'

'Oh,' said Cate. This felt worse. Much worse.

'Anyway,' said her mum, pointedly, 'the girls are missing you. They'll be glad to see you home. Oh, and Stevie's convinced you've got her a Barty Bear. Isn't that one of these things that's almost full size?'

'It is and I did,' said Cate. 'Guilty working mum and all that.'

'Well it's not really work, is it, dear?' said her mum.

She shouldn't have called home. 'Actually, Mum, it really is. Work.'

'Well, all right, dear. But don't get yourself in a state about Dan. A quick drink with friends. And here's you gallivanting around London.' She gave a gentle tut.

'Night, Mum,' said Cate. 'Thanks for all your help. I'll see you tomorrow.'

'Night, darling.'

She sat and looked at the phone for a second then picked it up and went to text, typing quickly, like the twins had shown her. 'How's th pub and lady frnd? Mine's a gin.' She pressed the send button and instantly regretted it. He'd either be irritated or confused. Either way, she'd have to explain herself. She laid the phone back beside her and waited for it to ring.

At 11.45 p.m., long past closing time, she switched it off so she didn't have to listen to its stubborn silence, and lay in the warm glow of the rooms she had transformed, trying to will away the cold thoughts that were crowding in on her.

21

'Going live in ten.' Marg watched as Susann seamlessly brought her interview to a close and read the next intro right to the second that the feed from Karachi started to run.

Marg sat back and exhaled loudly. She'd hardly had time to think since she'd arrived at work, let alone wake Cate with a 7.30 a.m. alarm call, as she'd promised to try and do. They'd only been on air for about half an hour when the political editor had called in a flap, saying something significant was happening in Whitehall, possibly concerning the foreign secretary. The minister had been under fire for some months now, after some ill-judged remarks at a Buckingham Palace banquet to honour the South Korean president. He'd had a little too much Chateau Lafitte and had suggested, within earshot of the press pack, that stuffed corgi might make an interesting hors d'oeuvre for the international guests.

An hour ago the political editor had called back to say there was a rumour that it would be a resignation speech. 'Confirm it,' Marg had barked. 'Two sources if you can.'

She glanced at the clock. Ten minutes to go until the programme ended and still nothing. Shit. She checked the other channels. It hadn't broken anywhere else yet but it was bound to have reached them in some form or other, and she wanted it first. She tried the political editor's mobile to get an update. It was engaged. A good sign.

The clock ticked onwards. Susann started a two-way with the Paris correspondent. The end-piece was all lined up, but Marg didn't want to finish the show with a story about a naked hiker traversing the Alps. She wanted something meaningful. She wanted a good old-fashioned scoop.

She called the political producer in the Westminster studio.

'It's going to be tight,' the producer said. 'He's out in the corridor. Hold on . . . Earpiece in, earpiece in . . .' She sounded panicked.

The phone changed hands. 'Got it,' said the political editor. 'He's going.'

'Are you sure?' Marg felt her heart leap.

'Completely,' he said. 'Get me on air. The BBC have got wind of it.'

'Live to you in thirty seconds.'

'Live to Westminster. Thirty seconds,' she shouted to the studio. 'Susann. Breaking news, in ten.'

The Westminster producer had rattled out an intro into the system and Susann took a breath and started to talk even before the producer had finished typing.

'And now, some breaking news. Global understands that the British foreign secretary is to issue a statement later today announcing that he is to step down. That is, the British foreign secretary is to resign today.' Susann cocked her head as if she were listening to an urgent message in her ear. She wasn't, but Marg knew she thought such gestures made it seem slicker, more immediate. The breaking news strap-line appeared and the screen behind Susann flooded with red. Jesus God, thought Marg, let it be right.

'Our political editor is with us now. I understand this is something you have been able to confirm in the last few minutes?' said Susann.

His tie was askew, and his big, florid face was pink with panic and exertion, but Marg could have kissed him.

'That's right, Susann. We have been able to confirm that the British foreign secretary will announce his resignation later today.' He took a breath. 'As you know, the minister has been under pressure . . .'

Marg imagined the panic in other news rooms, the horrible sinking feeling in the pit of the stomach, the scrabble to confirm, to catch up, the shouted profanities from editors' offices. WHY THE FUCK DON'T WE HAVE THIS?!

Marg had experienced several why-the-fuck moments in her career. It felt perversely good to know someone else was going through it right now. She looked up at the clock. Three minutes to go. I love this job, she thought.

'Again, great work.' The head of news lifted his file of papers from the table and beamed at everyone sitting around it. The daily de-brief could sometimes be an ordeal, but not today. 'Two full minutes ahead of the Beeb,' he repeated. 'Great work, everyone. Great work.'

At the far end of the table, Rick slouched in his chair, rolling slightly from side to side on its castors. Domestic politics bored him. Attaboys that weren't directed his way bored him.

'Shame about the naked climber,' he said to no one in particular. 'I was wondering what our policy was on full-frontal? Were we going to pixellate his Matterhorn?'

There was a half-hearted giggle from some in the room, and a far too enthusiastic laugh from the arts correspondent. She was young and averagely pretty. And pretty average at her job.

Rick swivelled to face her and winked. Marg watched them from the far end of the table. The weekend sleepover had been a little too much, and although she was looking forward to the Chad trip, she didn't relish another whole weekend in Rick's company. He was annoying her.

He caught her looking at him as they all stood to leave and grinned. Marg didn't like the way the arts correspondent looked at her too.

It was just a quick glance, but her expression was unusual. Marg couldn't quite place it. Antagonism, maybe. Envy, possibly. She hoped to God it wasn't pity.

'Marg, call on line two.' One of the administrators interrupted her thoughts.

'Can you take a message and I'll call right back?' It was probably Cate phoning to say she'd got up herself thank you very much and had arrived home safely, but Marg had had too much coffee that morning, and she badly needed a pee.

The secretary spoke into the phone. 'He says he can wait. I'll put him on hold.'

'Who is it?'

The secretary looked at the note she had scribbled. 'Abbeyhill High Benevolent Fund. Does that means anything to you?'

Marg walked back to her desk. 'I'll take it.' Christ, he was persistent. She would give him that. She pressed the blinking red light and said, 'Marg Holland,' in a rather formal way.

'Marg, hi. It's Adam Milner.' There was a pause. 'Is this a better time?'

'Time, yes, place, no. I'm at work.'

'So am I,' he said. 'I assumed you'd have finished your show.'

'Just,' said Marg.

'Can you talk, or do you want me to call back?'

'I can talk.'

'I was wondering if you were free this weekend. For dinner.' He said it slowly, as if he knew what the answer would be.

'I'm in Chad this weekend,' she said. 'Sorry.'

'That's not the kind of brush-off I was expecting.' There was a smile in his voice.

'It's not a brush-off,' said Marg. 'It's a fact.'

'Okay.' He sounded encouraged. 'Well, how about today?'

'Today?'

'Lunch,' he said. 'It's too early for your bedtime. You must be about finished your shift. Lunch. Today. Spur of the moment. By your hesitation I assume you don't have anything else planned and can't think of an excuse quick enough.'

She found herself smiling. 'All right then.'

'Okay?' He sounded surprised. 'Great.'

'When and where?' asked Marg.

'How about noon. Covent Garden. Do you know the new brasserie with the metal sculpture over the door? Café Fortis, I think.'

'I know the one. Okay, I'll see you then.'

She put the phone down, wondering why she had so readily agreed to meet him. At the far end of the news room the arts correspondent was spinning in her chair, glancing around. She caught Marg's eye and flashed her a tight little smile. Oh, what harm could it do? thought Marg. At the very least, she could do with some diverting company and a decent lunch.

He was taller than she remembered, but then she was wearing flats, and for reasons she had tried not to think about, a fresh slick of lipstick.

He leant forward and gave her a kiss on the cheek. He smelled of soap. 'It's great to see you,' he said, and looked like he meant it.

She sat down opposite him and hung her bag neatly and diagonally over the back of the chair. His hair was more closely-cropped than it had been at the Wrecker's Ball and he suited it better. Not so boyish. Not so Tintin.

'Is it too early for wine?' He handed her a menu.

'It's never too early for wine,' she said. 'And I deserve a drink.'

'Good day?'

'Weren't you watching? Not too flighty today, eh?'

He shook his head.

'We scooped everyone else on the foreign secretary's resignation.'

'You did? Great! No, I had the boys an extra two days.' He sat back to let the waiter fill his glass with water. 'On handover days I'm lucky if I get out the door wearing all my clothes.'

'How often do you have them?'

'Every second weekend through until the Monday morning. And every Thursday night.' He looked up. 'My ex does kick-boxing on a Thursday night.'

'Because of you?'

He laughed. 'Maybe. No, it's amicable. Well, as amicable as these things get. She's a great girl. Really.'

'So how come you're not with her?'

He laughed again at her bluntness. 'She met someone else. Well, that's not strictly true. We started falling apart, and she met someone else.'

'Am I supposed to say sorry right about now?' said Marg.

'It would be a little out of character, don't you think?'

She looked at him. 'Sorry,' she said.

'Thank you.' He was still grinning. 'So, anyway,' he said. 'Chad. What's happening in Chad?'

'War and want,' said Marg. 'And just over two months till the G8 decide what not to do about it again.'

'Whereabouts are you going?'

'Near Abeche. It's . . .'

'In the east, I know.'

205

'You've been?'

He shook his head. 'I did my VSO in Sudan. I know the region.'

'You? You did Voluntary Service Overseas? In Sudan?' She hadn't expected this.

He grinned. 'Why the surprise?'

'I don't know. I never had you figured for an aid worker.'

'I wasn't. Not really. Water engineer. It was a project near Habila.'

'When?'

He sat back and furrowed his brow. 'Oh, years ago now. After uni.'

'How does an architect become a water engineer?' Marg laid her elbows on the table.

'I trained in structural engineering. Architecture was post-grad. It helps to know what underpins a building, how to actually put it together. It was a great grounding but I didn't want to go straight into corporate life. And I couldn't afford a gap year in the traditional sense.'

'Very worthy of you,' said Marg. 'Are you religious?'

He laughed out loud. 'You're a real treat, you know that. No. I'm not religious.'

'I just wondered,' said Marg. She sat back and shifted her knife and fork. They had been lying out of kilter when she arrived and she was finding it hard to get them just right, dead straight, parallel to the place-mat.

'Do you know?' He leant forward. 'If you were one of my boys I'd tell you to stop playing with your cutlery. That's about the fourth time you've fiddled with them. I think they're just about perfect.'

She forced a laugh. 'Habit,' she said. 'I like order.'

'You're in a strange line of work for someone who likes order,' he said. 'You deal almost exclusively in chaos.'

'Maybe that's why,' she said. 'But thanks, anyway, for

pointing out my faults.' She looked at him and he looked back, his eyes warm with humour, but direct and unsettling for all that. She was relieved that the waiter picked that moment to come and take their order.

It was the waiter who brought the lunch to a close, hovering just within eyesight, with the bill in his hand.

'I think they want us out of here.' Adam motioned for him to come over.

Marg checked her watch. Jesus, 2.15 p.m. She can't have been in here for two hours. 'God, I've got to go. I didn't realise it was so late.'

'I enjoyed that.' He handed her her coat as they walked out into the air.

'So did I,' said Marg. He'd been a lot better company, a lot more interesting than she had expected.

They stopped on the pavement. Marg waited for him to ask if he could call her again. She had decided, somewhere between the antipasti and the *torta di mandorle*, that she would say 'maybe'. When she was back, maybe.

He bent forward and kissed her on the cheek. 'Have a safe trip,' he said against her skin.

She air-kissed him back, careful to not let her lips make contact.

'Thanks. I will. And thanks again. For lunch.' She paused, waiting.

'Bye.' He stood and looked at her for a moment then grinned broadly and started to walk backwards. He turned after a few seconds with the briefest of waves and she watched him stride towards the underground. Beneath his black overcoat, folded back by the wind, even though she was a little put out, she noticed that he had rather good legs.

★

'Muuummy!' Stevie hurled herself through the school door and charged at Cate.

'Hey, baby.' Cate grabbed her for a tight, protracted hug. 'I missed you.' She pressed her hand on Stevie's cheek where the faint imprint of the bat-shaped hummingbird still lingered.

'Did you get it? Did you?!'

Cate set her back down and shushed her. 'You'll need to wait and see. I said I'd get you something nice and I did, but you'll have to wait till we're home.'

Stevie hopped excitedly on one foot, holding tight to Cate's hand while they waited on the twins. 'Daddy let us have Corn Pops for breakfast and he spilled the orange juice. On his shoe. Daddy said it was a godawfulmess. What's a godawfulmess? And my teacher said it's okay I forgot my snack and my gym shoes. I just used my bare feet.'

'Well, that's good then.' Cate smiled down at her.

It was lovely to be back, deciphering five-year-olds' semantics, clutching tight a small, soft hand.

The twins rewarded her with warm smiles, but kept their hugs until they were back at the house. Dan had obviously made a decent stab at keeping the downstairs presentable, and Cate could see her mum's hand in the neat piles of toys and books stacked on the edge of the stairs to be taken up, and in the fresh milk and bread in the fridge.

But the kids' bedrooms were apocalyptic, the washing baskets were full to bursting and Hamish was smelling decidedly rank.

'Did no one think to change him?' Cate knelt on the floor of the twins' room, sorting washing into piles.

'Sorry, Mum.' Emma twirled before the mirror in one of the three new belts Cate had bought.

'I meant to,' said Jo, 'but I just forgot.' She fingered the fringed leather bag on her lap. Cate had struggled over what to get her and the bag was a last-minute purchase at the Topshop till.

'Do you like it, honey?'

Jo nodded and placed it beside her on the bed. 'Thanks, Mum.'

Cate stood up, balancing the wash-basket on one hip. 'Well, I tell you what, if I go down again, you'll just have to come down with me and pick something for yourself.'

'Are you going down again?' Emma stopped mid-twirl.

'Probably not,' said Cate. 'This was just a one-off. But you never know.' She looked round the room. 'Although, I don't think I can afford to go away again, because it looks like you lot just had one wild party without me.'

Stevie appeared at the door, still carrying Barty Bear, even though her arms must have been getting tired. She hauled him across to where Cate was standing. 'Did he really sit beside you all the way home? In his own seat?'

'Really,' said Cate. She didn't have the heart to tell her he had been stuffed, plush arse over elbow, into an overhead bin by an impatient steward.

'Barty's hungry,' said Stevie. 'Listen.' She pressed his stomach and he let out a long whistling 'Wheeee!'

Jo giggled. 'He sounds like he's farting.'

'He's not,' said Stevie indignantly. 'He's hungry.'

'I think he's meant to be growling,' said Cate.

'I'm going to call him farty bear,' taunted Jo.

'Muuum,' wailed Stevie.

'Girls!' said Cate. She beamed at them suddenly. Bickering siblings, an armful of washing and a malodorous hamster. She was well and truly home.

For once, he wasn't late. He came straight into the kitchen and caught her round the waist and pulled her in to him.

It was a good kiss and she put her hand up to his cheek as he pulled away.

'Hey,' she said.

'Hey.' He looked her up and down and then stretched out a hand towards her stomach. He started to laugh and she looked down.

'Press here,' he read from Barty's sticker that one of the girls must have stuck to her somewhere between homework and starting tea. 'What happens if I press here?'

'That's for you to find out.' Cate giggled.

'That sounds like an invitation.' He pulled the sticker off slowly and stuck it to the side of a cabinet. 'Don't lose that. I think I might need to use it later.'

She felt the catch in her throat. 'I should go away more often,' she said.

'No.' He bent in and kissed her again. 'No, you shouldn't.'

She watched him walk into the sitting room to greet the girls. Shouldn't she be dancing round the kitchen? Wasn't this what she had been looking for for months now – Dan as he used to be? But she couldn't shake the thought, however daft, that it just might have something to do with guilt.

She waited until he came back into the kitchen and was washing his hands at the sink.

'Did you get a text?' she said. 'Last night.'

He turned his head briefly. 'Oh, yeah. A weird one. What was that about?'

'Mum said you were out with a girlfriend. I was checking up on you.' She kept her voice light.

'Oh, Gill.'

Gill. Not Gillian. Gill.

'Gill's in the group,' he said. 'They'd been down to Heriot and back. Joyce said I should head off and meet them.' He was still at the sink and she couldn't properly see his face in the reflection from the window. He seemed to be looking down.

'Why didn't you text me back?'

He turned. She could tell nothing from his expression, which was still playful, but a little puzzled. 'I don't text, Cate, and you were just kidding, right?' He dried his hands, still watching her.

'Yeah.' She summoned her best smile. Her confident smile. Her Cate smile. 'Yeah,' she said. 'I was just kidding.'

22

'Did you see the way Tif looked in that unitard?' Orla lifted a second mini doughnut off the plate and settled herself back in her chair.

Cate nodded. Tif had taken that morning's Fab Abs class wearing the kind of fuchsia one-piece that would make most women resemble a sweet potato.

'She's incredible.' Orla grinned. 'Christ, if I could flex my pelvis like that I'd have my old man's undivided attention.'

Cate pressed a finger into the sugar that had fallen from her doughnut. She ought to have had Dan's undivided attention on Tuesday. He had given all the signals. But when she had raised herself over him in the bedroom she had felt him tense almost imperceptibly and he had caught her hand as it drifted downwards. 'Tired,' he had said, trying to laugh. 'Must be all this childminding.'

She had scanned his face in the half dark, not sure what she was looking for, not sure what she might see.

When he rolled heavily to his side, she had lain for a moment studying the familiar curved lines of the ceiling cornicing, listening to his wakeful breaths.

'Dan.'

'Mmm.' He hadn't sounded drowsy.

'Is it . . . is there something wrong, something we should be doing?'

He had paused long enough for his 'About what?' to sound fake.

Cate had inhaled slowly. 'Sex. Us. Why it's . . . not happening.'

She had sensed him stiffen, heard him sigh. His hand had reached out and landed on her face. He patted her nose.

'Stop obsessing,' he had said. 'It's fine. I'm just tired. That's all. Sleep.'

And he hadn't really touched her since, beyond the dutiful hug and hometime kiss, and he didn't seem to have noticed that the 'press here' sticker was still on the cabinet where he had left it. A statement of intent. She'd left it where it was, hoping he might catch sight of it and remember how he had felt when she came home.

She put the sugar to her lips.

'Hoi, dozy,' said Orla. 'Come back wherever you are. Lost in London?'

Cate sat up straight. 'Sorry.' She flashed a warm smile. She knew Orla had been feeling a little neglected in the past few weeks. Cate had missed so many gym sessions, her arms and legs felt like they were about to seize up after just one class. 'I'm just a bit preoccupied, you know, waiting for this article to come out.'

'Tomorrow!' smiled Orla. 'Can't wait to see it.'

Cate nodded.

'Do you think it will change anything?'

'No. I doubt it. But if I ever do take it further, it will be great to have that, and Marg said the paper's photographer seemed happy with it when they came out yesterday to take the pictures.'

'Did her lover boy like it?'

'He did, although he's not really her lover boy. Well, he is. I don't know. It's an odd relationship they've got going on.'

'Shag buddy,' said Orla.

'Pardon?'

'Shag buddy. A friend you shag.'

'What do you know about shag buddies?'

Orla tapped the side of her nose. 'I know these things. I read the gossip mags in the hairdresser.'

'No you don't,' laughed Cate. 'You buy them.'

'Okay, I buy them.'

'Although, Rick's got competition.' Cate bent forward for another doughnut. 'She had lunch on Tuesday with a guy we were at school with. Two years below us. He's an architect now, really nice guy. But not her type.'

Cate had been taken aback when Marg had admitted she'd met up with Adam Milner. Marg had played it down, of course. Just a lunch. Keep him off my back. Rude not to. And she had got a little riled when Cate had dared to sound pleased. But it might be good if something came of it. Marg's relationship with Rick was a curious one. On paper they seemed perfect, but in practice it didn't quite work, it seemed just a little too functional, a little too convenient. Although Marg as a surrogate mother to two small boys? Dealing with an ex-wife? Maybe not.

'Strange how at school two years is a complete generation gap,' said Orla. 'But now you couldn't even call him a toy boy. They didn't go out at school, did they?'

'God, no. She can't even remember him.'

''Cos sometimes those first crushes never leave you.'

For an instant Cate saw Jo's face staring at Paul, high in the gods of the sports hall. She leant forward. 'I've been meaning to ask you. How did you handle it when your boys started getting into girls?'

'Do you want to rephrase that?' said Orla.

Cate laughed. 'You know what I mean.'

'You're not there yet, are you?'

'Almost,' said Cate. 'Jo's been . . . well, I know she's got a thing for this boy who's actually a friend of Emma's.'

'You've done all the puberty stuff, haven't you, the sex talk?'

Cate nodded. They'd done the sex talk, although when she'd found herself drawing two stick figures to try and explain the missionary position – the hangman version of *The Joy of Sex* – she'd gone out and bought a book. The twins had read it avidly. But the only question they'd had was 'What's a fantasy?' And when Cate had explained, asked if she'd ever had one.

Only involving your dad, she'd said. Which wasn't strictly true. She'd always had a bit of a thing for Willem Dafoe, and there was that bearded man who did the Sunday night gardening programme and something about the way he handled seedlings. Although that was one she wouldn't be sharing with anyone.

'Yeah, we've done the sex talk. It's the emotional side I'm not sure how to advise on.'

'Tricky,' said Orla. 'There's not much you can tell them. Although, if you think about it, there's really only one rule.'

'And what's that?' asked Cate, swirling the dregs of her coffee in the bottom of the cup.

'Never want someone more than they want you.' Orla took a final bite of doughnut. 'That,' she said through a mouthful of sugar, 'ish a one-way ticket to torment.'

Marg sealed the bottle of insect repellent in a zip-lock pouch and added it to the growing row of small plastic bags laid out on the bed.

It was the strongest you could get, and the last time she'd used it, in Mogadishu, it had taken the paint off a metal chair in the lodging they'd slept in. God knows what it did to your skin. But the doctor had said she should only avoid it if she was thinking of getting pregnant. Which she wasn't.

That should be almost everything. The malaria medi-cine was in, two packs of Immodium, mosquito net, sleeping-bag, the breakfast bars, boxes of pens and note-books for handing out to children; likewise, three large bags of fruit sweets. She'd get the cigarettes in duty free. A couple of packets of Silk Cut could get you through many a tricky situation. Fags for Peace, Rick called them. A sarong for squatting by the roadside. Toilet paper, two rolls, and enough wet wipes to clean the Glastonbury hordes.

Her clothes were piled neatly on a chair, and were prob-ably best described as utilitarian. Three pairs of chinos with a little bit of stretch. Three long-sleeved shirts. A fleece, a waterproof, and two pairs of boots. Stout, brown, and utterly devoid of style. Her TAG Heuer watch was in the cupboard safe, replaced by a cheap digital affair, likewise her Chanel sunglasses, replaced with some plastic ones she'd got free with £50 of petrol. She left her straighteners, regretfully, on the top of the dresser. There was no point in packing them. It wasn't as if she was on camera, and Rick and the rest of the crew had seen her frizz before. Harpo Hair, as Rick liked to call it. Lip balm and tinted moisturiser was as much make-up as she would need when she might not be washing for a couple of days. Anyway, she liked the feeling of being stripped down to the bare essentials. Less to itemise, less to check, less to worry about. She pulled the zip shut on her old holdall, stowed it beside the bed and carried what was left of her vodka through to the lounge to finish off her paperwork.

The office had asked her to update her next-of-kin details before she left, something they did every few years. It was just common sense in a business with mortality and divorce rates almost twice the national average, but Marg still resented it. Her details never changed. Next of kin: Mrs

Carol B. Holland. The B was for Buchanan. Or Bloody Awful Mother.

She'd often wondered what her mother's reaction would be if someone ever did come to the door to say the jeep had overturned or the plane had gone down, or the bad men had come. Vague disinterest? A query about the value of her estate? A flat, regretful smile followed by a night at the bingo? She knew Rick was horrified whenever she talked of her mum this way. He adored his parents and he just didn't understand. She didn't hit me. She wasn't a drunk, or particularly abusive. She just didn't get me and I didn't get her. She tried to remember when she had first realised theirs was not the biscuit-tin version of maternal love. She'd noticed, of course, the way other mums were around their daughters, mums like Cate's. The affection that went with the impatient tug of a shirt collar, a button fastened with a gentle tut, the birthday cards that said 'all our love', not 'from Mum'. Her mum would come to school events but there was defiance in the way she sat in the audience, bag clasped tight on her knee, shoulders drawn in, a posture that screamed 'I should not be here'.

And, in truth, she shouldn't have been. It was her Aunty Betty who had let the cat out of the bag, fuelled by a little too much sweet stout one sour Christmas when Marg was about eleven.

'It's not as though she chose to be in this position,' she had said sharply after Marg and her mum had had another row and her mum had slammed out to the garden to get some air, with her cigarettes and her ever-present cloud of bitterness. Marg had asked what that meant and had been told. She had learned more then about her dad than her mum had ever let on. How he hadn't wanted the responsibility of a child, or at least said he didn't, but the feckless bastard was now quite well set up in Falkirk with a wife and a family of two, thank you very much. 'Your half brother and sister,' Aunty Betty had slurred accusingly, as if Marg herself had conjured them up, these people who sounded like they didn't quite exist.

Marg had always known her dad was still alive, but she had invented a better story for school: that he had fallen from the Forth Road Bridge while inspecting it for rust. So much more poetic than a deadbeat who didn't want to know. And sometimes she had almost come to believe it herself, seeing in her dreams a splayed silhouette plunging silently from the elegant span of concrete into the wide, stirring grey of the river below. She confessed the lie to Cate in primary seven and had felt swamped by guilt when Cate's dad did die when they were in fifth year.

She stuck her pen in the corner of her mouth. This year, the details form had a separate box for emergency contact. It seemed a bit sad to put the office number, and there was no point in listing Rick. After a moment's thought, she scribbled Cate's name and address. Might as well have someone who knew her and might make something of an effort to help her out.

Friday night laughter carried up from the street. It was 10.30 p.m. and she ought to be thinking of bed.

The flight was leaving tomorrow at 10 a.m., so she would have a bit of a lie-in and then just enough time to grab the *Post* and phone Cate to congratulate her. She could actually have done with a chat just now, but it was probably too late to phone the Beanes, and Rick was out with his broadsheet buddies, a pre-trip ritual he couldn't miss.

She looked at the bowl on her coffee table and for a strange instant she thought about calling Adam Milner. He shouldn't have his boys this weekend. Maybe he was home and looking for some conversation. They'd had a really good chat at lunch on Tuesday, although she was a little disconcerted at the way he had left it. She saw him walking backwards with his broad, knowing grin.

Get a grip, Marg. She stood instead and switched off the lights until only the orange glow from the street lit up the flat. Then, in the half dark, she started her checks, round the rooms and up the hall, past the print of the smiling girl, until she reached the bedroom and the sanctuary of sleep.

23

It was the tiniest of small print. The size of text they use for disclaimers or to hide the inevitable catch. Batteries not included. May contain nuts. Can cause blindness if inserted into eye socket.

For Cate, though, it could have been neon and fifteen feet high. There, underneath the photograph of Rick reclining on his sofa, seemingly engrossed in a copy of *Paris Match*: 'Rooms styled by Catriona Wishart. Catriona Wishart Interiors. Edinburgh.' Catriona Wishart Interiors! That must have been Marg. Oh my God.

'Well, let's see.' Dan peered over her shoulder, leaning against her as he scanned the page. He'd taken the bike down to get the papers and she could feel the warmth of him through the thin Lycra of his cycling top. Upstairs the intermittent thump of two small feet signalled that Stevie was awake and jumping off her chest of drawers.

'He's older than I thought.'

Cate nudged him in the ribs. 'The rooms, Dan.'

He laughed. 'They look great. Nice loo. Why don't we have newspapers in our loo?'

'Because we have three kids so they'd end up being used as loo roll, or made into paper boats for the bath. I pull enough out of that plughole without having to worry about wet newsprint.' She turned to face him. 'Really, you like them?'

He kissed her quickly on her hair. 'I do. You should be

chuffed. It's a national paper. Some folk would kill for that kind of advertising.' He moved to the sink to fill his water bottle. 'I see you used Wishart,' he said after a moment.

She turned to look at him. 'It was a spur of the moment thing, really. We just thought it . . . sounded better. You don't mind?'

He laughed. 'You can call yourself what you want.'

Cate took the paper over to the table and spread it out. 'I still can't believe it.' The photograph of the bathroom hadn't quite caught the extent of everything she'd done, but they'd used the caption 'Print Room', and Rick had made great play in the accompanying interview of Bertha the buxom haberdasher's dummy, who had a prominent position in the pictures of the lounge.

"'She's the only woman in my life at the moment," says Rutner, still determinedly single at the age of 45. "Not many women understand the kind of life I need to lead."'

Only woman in my life? Determinedly single? Cate scanned through the rest of the piece but there was no mention of Marg, or anyone who might be Marg. She felt slighted on her behalf. He could at least have alluded to her in some form, or acknowledged their relationship, even in an oblique way.

However, Marg hadn't mentioned anything Rick had said in the piece when she'd wakened them all at 7 a.m. to say she'd just picked up a copy at the airport and it looked fab. 'You're on your way, hon,' she had said.

'No, you are,' Cate had laughed. 'To Chad.'

Her coffee had grown cold, but she sipped at it anyway and stared at her handiwork in full colour in the national press.

Dan appeared at the door carrying Stevie on his back. 'One base jumper ready for breakfast,' he said, setting her down in the kitchen.

'Are the twins awake?' Cate stood up and folded the paper away.

He shook his head. 'One of them is snoring, so I just left them to it. The hamster's up, though.'

Stevie grabbed Dan's arm and tried to swing herself back on to him. 'I want to go with Daddy. I can go on my bike.' Cate had a sudden image of a five-year-old careering along beside the cycle group on her pink and purple Daisy Racer with the shiny tassels on the handle-bars.

She smiled. 'You can't, baby. We're meeting Gran and Grampa for lunch because they're going off on holiday tomorrow. Remember? It's at the café with the play area. The one you like. Although . . .' She paused and looked up at Dan. 'Maybe we could meet Daddy later, for a coffee or something, when he's on his way back.'

Dan shook his head. 'A bunch of sweaty guys?'

'And girls,' said Cate. She didn't phrase it as a question, and he just smiled and shrugged on his waterproof jacket.

'I've not seen Guy for ages,' continued Cate and Dan raised his eyebrows. She didn't like Guy and he knew that. He was an arrogant man, cold to his wife but warmly genial to anyone who gave him the time of day. Especially women under forty.

'I'll be back about three-thirty,' said Dan. 'I'll see you all then.'

She went to the door with him, watching as he squatted low to unlock the bike chain and clip on his water bottle. He looked so fit and she was suddenly aware of her dressing gown, soft and warm but a little saggy with age. She pulled the belt tightly and ran her hands through her hair.

'Maybe we could get a bottle of champagne in tonight,' she said. 'To celebrate.'

For an instant he looked confused. 'Celebrate?'

'The paper, Dan.'

'Oh, yeah, of course. Good idea. Yeah. Well, bye. I'll see you later.' He leant forward, not to kiss her, but to pull the door shut behind him.

'Have fun,' said Cate weakly as it closed with a click. She stood quietly in the hall for a moment before a loud squelching drew her back to the kitchen.

'I poured the juice myself.' Stevie looked up proudly from the seat by the counter as a large pool of Florida orange, with bits, spread across the granite top. Cate sighed and touched her hand to Stevie's cheek, still ever so faintly hennaed. 'Yes, you did, baby girl. Although it might have been helpful if you'd got most of it in the glass.'

'Six copies!' said Joyce. 'I think the newsagent thought he'd taken leave of his senses. And he's been down the bowling club already and handed most of them out.'

Cate beamed at Ed, who was looking a little sheepish across the table. 'Well, I'm proud of our girl here,' he said. 'No shame in that.' He winked at Cate. 'You must be pleased as punch.'

'I am,' said Cate. 'I've stuck my copy up in the study.'

'I still think you should have used your married name,' said her mum, keeping one eye on Stevie who appeared to be taking exception to a small boy in the play area at the far end of the restaurant. 'It's what you are now. A Beane. If I was Dan I would have been a bit put out by that.'

'Well, he wasn't,' said Cate. 'He was fine about it.' She raised her eyebrows to Ed, who raised his back. 'And anyway,' continued Cate, 'if I do set up on my own, I want to have something that's completely separate from family life.'

'What do you mean, set up on your own?' said her mum.

'If I ever set up a design business,' said Cate.

'But you're not going to, are you? Oh, Stevie, no. Not his ears, love . . .' She stood up quickly to go and intervene and Ed reached across and laid a hand over Cate's.

'Don't you listen,' he said. 'That's a great thing you've got there in the paper. If you get the chance to do more like that then I think you should. Really. Why shouldn't you use your skills?' He sat back and laughed. 'But that's just between you and me, okay?'

Cate mouthed 'okay' and 'thank you' and laughed with him.

Joyce returned with Stevie and sat her back down between Jo and Emma, who were trying not to look bored. The restaurant had been her mum's idea but the twins were too big for it now. Too big for soft play and too old for Happy Meals. They picked idly at what was left of their ice-creams.

'Shall we order coffee?' asked her mum, and Jo looked up, quickly and beseechingly at Cate. She took the cue.

'Actually, Mum, I think we'll head off. We'll need to stop at the supermarket, and Dan should be back soon.' She reached for her purse, but Ed pre-empted her. 'No. My treat. We're not going to see you for two weeks.'

Outside at the cars, the girls clustered around Joyce and Ed for a cuddle.

'I hope you have a great time,' said Cate. 'When does your flight leave?'

'Some ungodly hour,' said Joyce. 'But by lunchtime I'll be on the sands of Albufeira. She pulled up her coat sleeve and inspected her wrist. 'Can't come soon enough. I'm as pale as a ghost.'

'Can I go too?' asked Stevie from under Ed's cap, which he'd placed on her head.

'I wish you could, lovely,' said Joyce. 'Maybe another time. But I'll bring you something nice. All of you.'

'I'm sure you will,' said Cate, giving her mum a kiss on the cheek. She thought she saw the faintest smile curve the corners of Ed's mouth. She moved to hug him.

'Bye, sweetheart,' he said. 'And well done, again. I'm proud of you.'

They drove off with a loud toot as Cate was fastening Stevie's seat belt. She waved a hand in the air without looking up. Stevie lifted something from the back seat and waved it in Cate's face. 'Grampa forgot his hat.'

'Well, you keep it safe.' Cate dropped it back on Stevie's head. 'He won't need it in Portugal. We'll give it to him when he gets home.'

Stevie sniffed loudly. 'It smells like Grampa,' she said.

'And what does Grampa smell like?' asked Cate, as she slid into the driver's seat.

'Toasty,' said Stevie, after a moment's thought.

'That's a good word,' said Cate.

'Why?'

'Because it means warm.'

The jeep bounced over a pothole and Marg caught hold of the bar above her head and held on. In the front seat beside the driver Rick dozed, his head dunting on and off the window. The flight had got late into Ndjamena and by the time their internal flight to Abeche had set them down, the light was starting to go. Marg checked her watch. It would be a good few hours before they reached Madayouna, where they would spend the night before pressing on tomorrow towards the camp and the nuns.

She looked through the windscreen. The road was edged with a thin line of people. Women with children wrapped to their backs and loads balanced on their heads. Men grouped in small, intermittent shacks. She cracked open the window next to her and took a breath of warm, woodsmoked air. Soon there would be no one walking by the roadside, soon the fires and the yellow lights would go out and all movement would cease. Because, when the dark comes in Africa, it often seemed to Marg, everything stops and holds its breath.

24

'I know, sweetheart. I know.' Leonora MacMahon spoke softly and reassuringly as her fingers deftly removed the bloody dressing on the woman's side. The bullet must have pierced her bowel and Marg tried not to gag as the small ragged hole was exposed and the stench rose around them. The woman moaned a little and the man at her side laid a gentle but ineffectual hand on her shoulder. She wasn't so much a woman as a girl, thought Marg, maybe mid- to late teens, with soft, frightened eyes.

'There,' said Leonora, after she had cleaned the wound and stuck on a fresh patch of gauze. She lifted the girl's dress back over her shoulder and helped her to her feet. No time to sit and gather strength. No time for niceties when you live in one of the more pitiless corners of the world.

The nun turned to Marg and gave a quick smile. She was barely five feet tall, as the director of World Aid had said, and she looked like the kind of little old lady you might see standing on Dublin's Grafton Street with a stout handbag hung on her arm and nothing more significant to do than take tea at Bewleys and then the bus home. Leonora pulled the bloodied gloves from her hands, dropped them in a plastic bucket and tucked a stray wisp of grey hair back from her eyes. 'Now,' she said and turned her attention to the pregnant woman who had slipped wordlessly into the room and sat herself down carefully on the small metal chair vacated by the woman with the bullet wound.

'Do you still need me?' asked Marg. She'd been in the makeshift clinic for an hour, helping out as Leonora had asked her to do. Despite World Aid's rules, the nuns had given them a warm welcome when they had arrived the previous night, and had offered a room for them to sleep in instead of them using the jeeps.

It was just four walls and a bare floor and a small high window hung with cardboard and an old blanket, but very welcome for all that. They were able to stash their gear and put down mats and sleeping bags. Not that Marg had slept much. She never did when she was on assignment; too much running through her mind to blank out. No drink to help her on her way. She'd lain awake and watched the others sleep and then the rat, pressed against the shadows by the wall, which had started for the safety of a pile of sandbags, running neatly along the edge of Rick's makeshift bed. Marg didn't mind rats. There was something oddly comforting about them, something expected in a world where little else made much sense.

'Not just now,' said Leonora. 'Maybe later. Thank you.'

Marg walked to the door and watched the long, patient queue snaking around the compound of three flat buildings. Over the small rise beyond the gates were some five thousand people, stateless, homeless, camped under plastic and sacking. Hungry, sickening, looking to three Irish nuns for strength, maybe even survival. A story at every step, but only a few minutes of air-time in which to tell them. Marg sighed. It was such an ordinary kind of tragedy, far too common, expected, even. No great waves, no violent shaking of the earth by which to measure the magnitude.

It was getting hot and the lucky ones had been able to find some respite under the protruding corrugated iron roofs of the buildings. In the centre of the compound, under a canopy, a baby hung listlessly in the weighing machine. Most of them had cried at the rough indignity of the procedure. The greatest fear was always for those that didn't. Marg watched the mother lift the child from the straps and fold his wasted body into her as Grainne clipped a small plastic bracelet to his spindly wrist. His defeated silence had bought him a meal.

Rick appeared round the corner, carrying a low table. He set it up near the weighing station then came and joined Marg on the decking. They stood in silence for a moment, watching. Beyond the compound wall they could see the cameraman getting his tracking shots of the camp. He had found the desiccated carcass of a cow and had bent low in the dust to film through the horns.

'Think we can persuade the G8 to stage their next meeting here instead of a five-star resort?' asked Rick finally.

'Probably not,' said Marg. 'I don't think the room service is up to scratch.'

Rick looked at her. 'What are you thinking? Grainne says there's a woman here who lost one child to malnutrition last week and whose other one is pretty bad. Unlikely to die while we're here, though.'

The baby won't die on deadline. The curse of the profession: the bigger the tragedy, the more visual the horror, the better the story.

'Maybe,' said Marg. 'But I don't like death-watching.' The truth was it had been done so often that Marg thought it had become devalued. She wanted something different; something that could encompass not just the scale of suffering but the dreadful inevitability of the situation, despite all the West's fancy promises. Probably best just to hand the microphone to Leonora and let her give the politicians what for.

Rick laid his hand on her shoulder. 'I told Grainne I'd help her get the feeding tables up. I'll speak to you later.'

Marg watched him cross the compound and turn his smile on Grainne, who beamed back at him. He had told her within minutes of their arrival that he was useless at pronouncing names, so he would call her Granny. She must have been sixty-five if she was a day, but she had giggled like a girl. Marg laughed to herself. Good old Rick. She became aware of someone behind her, and turned. It was a boy who had been hanging around the clinic entrance for most of the morning. He was small enough that he might have been under ten, but his eyes looked older. He grinned at her, a warm stretch of a smile. She grinned back. 'Hello.'

He said nothing, but kept smiling.

'What's your name?'

He kept his eyes on her, still smiling, but said nothing.

'I'm Marg.'

'Mark,' said the boy.

'No, Marg. G,g,g. Margg.'

'Mark.' His smile stretched further. 'G,g,g.'

Leonora appeared at the doorway and laid her hands on his shoulders. 'Amodu, can you get Ann for me, please? I need her help with one of our ladies here.'

He nodded and slipped off the decking, still beaming.

'He speaks English?' said Marg.

'A little.' The women watched him run across the compound on long, skinny legs. He wore flip-flops that were too big for him and a T-shirt that was too small. It was faded green and the logo on the front said 'Miami Beach Life' over a picture of a smiling sun in a cap and sunglasses. 'He's my special helper,' said Leonora. 'He lifts when we can't. He's better than some of the men. He likes to watch at the clinic. Wants to be a doctor when he grows up.'

'How old is he?'

'Oh, I don't know, my dear,' said Leonora, laying her hand briefly on Marg's arm. 'They're not big on birthdays in this part of the world.'

'Roughly,' said Marg.

'Maybe eleven?' said Leonora. 'He doesn't know. But these two, here' – she pointed to a small boy and girl sitting quietly by the corner of one of the buildings, a little apart from the queue – 'they're his.'

'His?'

'His brother and sister. He looks after them.'

'What about his family? Parents?'

Leonora shrugged her shoulders. 'He lived with his grandmother but he doesn't know where she is now. Displaced. Dead. They had to leave and somewhere along the way they got separated.'

'Amodu?' said Marg.

Leonora nodded. 'He's a good boy.'

Amodu came back with Ann and the nuns disappeared back into the clinic to see to the pregnant woman. Marg stayed out on the decking, mulling over her filming options. She thought the boy had gone in with them but she became aware of him again, standing just behind her, leaning against the wall as she was leaning against one of the pillars.

He had crossed his leg at the ankle, just as she had.

'Copycat,' she said with a smile.

'Mark,' he said, and smiled back.

'If there were three men on a boat and it filled with water and they each had a bucket and it takes two minutes to fill the bucket how long would it take them to get all the water out?' Emma sat back and bit the end of her pencil.

Cate looked up from her textbook. 'Three men?'

Emma nodded.

'And how big is the boat?'

Emma looked at the sheet. 'Thirty-six cubic metres.'

'Why is the boat filled with water?' asked Stevie.

'Doesn't matter,' said Emma impatiently. 'It's homework.'

'But why?'

Cate laid her hand on Stevie's arm. 'You get on with your drawing, toots.'

At the opposite end of the table, Jo sat smiling smugly. She was already on to her English.

Emma looked expectantly at Cate.

'I'm not doing it for you, honey,' said Cate. 'It's division and multiplication. You need to work out how many bucketfuls it would take to empty the boat. What size are the buckets?'

'Six litres,' said Emma petulantly. 'But I don't get it.'

'Well you need to have a good long think,' said Cate. She went back to her reading and Emma bent over her jotter. Beneath the table, Hamish trundled around in his exercise ball.

'I drew a fairy.' Stevie held up her piece of paper. Cate looked up, smiling patiently. It had seemed like a good idea to bring her books down at homework time so they could all study together, only it hadn't been the quiet hive of activity she had imagined.

'So you did. It's lovely. But honey, please don't suck the end of the felt-tip pens. You're getting green lips.'

'It looks more like Shrek than a fairy,' said Emma contemptuously.

'Emma.' Cate tapped her pen on the side of Emma's jotter. 'Men in the boat.'

Stevie stuck her tongue out at her sister and slipped off the chair to go and check her face in the mirror. The room went quiet.

'Whereabouts is Marg again?' Jo peered at the front cover of her atlas and Cate indicated for her to hand it over. She found the page for Africa, located Chad and handed it back with her thumb pressed on the spot. 'There. She's in the east of the country.'

'I wish I lived there,' said Jo, studying the page.

'You probably don't,' said Cate. 'Maybe for a visit, but where she's going, the people have hardly any food.'

'Why?' Stevie climbed back onto her chair.

How to explain internecine conflict, harvest fluctuations and the culpability of Western governments? 'They just don't,' said Cate.

'Can't they go to the shops like we do?' asked Stevie.

Cate smiled at her. 'No, sweetie, they can't just go to the shops like we do.' She looked back at her book.

'Which one is the isosceles triangle again?'

Cate glanced up. 'What's happened to the men in the boat?'

Emma shook her head. 'I'm going to come back to it. Which one is the isosceles?'

Cate sighed. 'I honestly can't remember, honey. Is it the one where all the sides are the same?'

'Dad would know,' said Emma.

'Yes, he would, but he's not here.'

'Can I phone him?'

'No. Dad's got meetings tonight. Get your maths book. It'll be in there.'

'I don't know where it is,' whined Emma.

Cate looked imploringly at Jo. 'Isosceles?'

'It's the one with two sides the same,' said Jo. 'Equilateral is the one with all the sides the same.'

'Thank you,' said Cate.

Jo grinned and swung backwards in her chair. Emma bent back over her book. The hamster ball crossed the kitchen floor and disappeared into the family room.

'Do you know,' said Jo, after a moment, 'Hamish is the only boy in the house.'

'He is,' said Cate absently, without looking up.

Jo looked round the table. 'It would be weird if it was just girls in the house, wouldn't it? If Hamish and Dad didn't live here.'

Cate looked up quickly. 'That's not going to happen,' she said.

'I know,' said Jo. 'But it would be weird, wouldn't it?'

'Yes,' said Cate. She managed a smile. 'It would be weird.'

25

'I could stop at any one of these shacks and find a story so terrible it would be hard to comprehend.' Rick walked slowly towards the camera position clasping and unclasping his hands. 'Rape, starvation, murder, intimidation. These people have experienced it all.' He came to a halt and stretched his arm out to indicate the camp around him. 'They thought they might find some comfort here after crossing the border from Darfur to Chad. But nature had other ideas. Three years of drought and the continued intransigence of Western governments mean they have walked from purgatory . . .' He paused for effect. '. . . into hell.'

He glanced questioningly at Marg. 'Still too strong?'

Marg sighed and clicked off her stopwatch. 'Still too strong, and a touch too quick. Why don't you start from a little further back? And tone it down, Rick. Less of the four horsemen. Okay?'

'Horsemen?' He looked puzzled.

'Of the apocalypse,' said Marg. She waved her hand in front of her face to ward off the flies, large and black and insistent. 'War, famine, plague, pestilence. I think you had them all in there.'

Rick gave a quick, flat smile and wandered back to his starting point, talking as he went, trying to re-form his piece to camera. It was growing hotter and if he didn't nail it soon he'd start to sweat. Rick had a horror of damp underarms. People who couldn't be roused by conflict or tragedy wrote letters about correspondents' sweaty armpits. So the shirt would need to be changed and everything would get delayed a little more and they had to get it all done today because they were heading off tomorrow.

The curious crowd that had gathered around them stood, quietly intrigued at the strange goings-on in their midst. On its fringes, smiling his big warm grin, was Amodu. He had been waiting outside the room when they had got up that morning, his brother and sister already installed by the edge of the clinic building, sitting patiently in the dust. Marg had beckoned him over and slipped him two small notebooks and a pack of pencils to give them. The girl had tucked hers quickly into the folds of her faded dress, and the boy had sat on his. They were too precious to use.

Amodu had returned to the decking and settled himself down as Rick and the cameraman had a fag and Marg sorted through her notes. He must have sat near to her for a good half-hour, saying nothing but smiling every time she looked up, before Leonora had called for him and he had sped off.

Marg reset the stopwatch and raised her hand to Rick, who nodded that he was good to go.

'And running in four, three, two, one . . .' She counted him in.

'I could stop at any one of these shacks and find a story so terrible it would be hard to comprehend,' repeated Rick. 'Rape, murder, starvation, terror. These people have experienced it all.' He stopped walking again. 'They thought they might find some comfort here after crossing the border from Darfur to Chad. But nature had other ideas. Drought, locusts, too little aid. These people have found no relief. People whom the G8 nations promised to help. People who should not be suffering this way in the twenty-first century, in this modern world.'

Marg smiled at him. 'Spot on. Good job. I'm happy if you are.'

He nodded.

'Just the nuns, then,' said Marg. They'd already done their interviews with some of the camp's inhabitants, including the woman whose child had died the previous week. She gave her own halting explanation of the loss through the voice of the interpreter, her other child lying listlessly on her lap taking sharp, shallow breaths. Rick, who had persuaded Marg that they should include the woman's story, had only alluded to her surviving child's prognosis on camera once they were away and out of earshot. Now they just needed Leonora, Grainne and Ann to have their say.

Marg beckoned to Amodu and he pushed his way through to her.

'Amodu, can you please go and ask Leonora if she can come up now. We're ready for her.'

He beamed, nodded and sprinted off towards the compound.

'I think you've got a fan.' Rick slipped his pack of cigarettes from his pocket and tapped one into his mouth. He held it out to her and she shook her head. It was the second time he had offered her one that day. He should have remembered she'd quit last year.

'He wants to be a doctor,' she said.

Rick flicked up the lid of his lighter as they watched the boy disappear into the compound, running as fast as he could on long, bony limbs. He lit the cigarette and took a long, slow drag. 'Poor little sod,' he said.

Cate watched the rain bounce off the paving stones by the edge of the lawn.

She ought to be staring at the computer screen but she was finding the dissertation heavier going than she had thought it would be. Ten thousand words. And where was she now? She pressed the word count. 1,351. Crap. Think Jacobean. Think Jacobean. Her eyes drifted across to the wall and the double-page spread from the *Saturday Post* tacked up on the corkboard.

'Richard Rutner on The Home Front' screamed the headline. She wondered how he and Marg were getting on in Chad.

She had sensed Marg's frustration at having to share her apartment with him when she was down in London, but maybe it was different when they were on the road together. Although, Marg had always needed her own space and Cate had always known when to make herself scarce. When the faint furrow had first appeared between the eyebrows on a day gone on too long. Not so much a frown line as an early warning system.

Cate smiled and stared back at the screen. Jacobean. Think Jacobean. She sat for a moment then quickly closed her essay and pulled up Google. She laid her elbows on the desk, poised. God, what to type? Can't get it up. Loss of libido. My husband doesn't fancy me any more.

She went for 'lack of interest' + 'sex' + 'men', and there, among the welter of post-pregnancy, get-that-thing-away-from-me websites was what she needed. Impotence: the physics and psychology.

She read for a good ten minutes, feeling a rush of relief. This was it, it had to be. It was all there: high achiever, stressed out, avoiding intimacy, prone to moodiness and in denial. And it wasn't so very unusual. She scrolled down the screen until she found the treatment section and gave a little laugh.

Marg was right, there was a vaccum device, and Viagra, and both could have the desired effect. But relationship issues might also need to be resolved and there was no pill

for them. 'Communication is the key,' read the last paragraph. 'The first and most important thing you need to do
is talk.' Cate pressed print. One night, when the time was
right, they would talk. They absolutely had to. It said so
here.

A thunderous rattle from downstairs signalled that the
washing machine was on its final spin. In the utility room,
she waited until it had come to a squeaking stop, then transferred a tumble of the girls' wet clothes into the dryer and
lifted a fresh armful from the laundry bin.

Dan's chinos came out last. She didn't really like him in
them. He had good legs but they got obscured in the swathes
of shapeless beige cotton. They were the staple of his work
wardrobe, though. Chinos and a smart shirt and the white
coat that shouldn't still have the effect on her that it did.

It was as she was stuffing the trousers into the washer in
a jumble of boxers and blue socks and pyjamas that she
spotted a small corner of paper poking from the pocket.
She never normally checked his pockets because he never
left anything in them: small change was always transferred
to the ceramic bowl on the kitchen counter and anything
else went in the bin. She pulled at the paper, feeling a sudden
stab of anxiety. This was a TV-movie moment. The surren-
dered wife sorting through the laundry. A husband's moment
of carelessness. A forgotten receipt. Scanties not meant for
her. A necklace she would never wear. Maybe it wasn't erec-
tile dysfunction, maybe it was just the opposite.

She unfolded the small rectangular piece of paper. It was
a receipt.

She studied the print and sat back slowly on her heels.
'Gel Botz. The comfortable alternative. Men's Lge. £10.99.'

Cycling pants. Padded cycling pants. She burst out
laughing at her own stupidity, and stuffed the chinos into
the machine, staying close to the floor for a moment after

she had switched it on to watch the clothes curl and spin together as the water poured in and the bubbles formed that would wash away all the dirt. Through in the hall, the phone started to ring.

The voice, when she answered it, was Home Counties and very brisk. 'Could I speak to Catriona Wishart, please?'

'Speaking,' said Cate tentatively.

'Oh, hello. I'm phoning from the features department of the *Saturday Post*. We've had a call from a lady who saw your work in last week's paper. The Rick Rutner feature? She was keen to get in touch with you but she couldn't find Catriona Wishart Interiors listed in directory enquiries. I said I'd pass on her details, rather than handing out your number. Do you have a pen?'

Cate's heart leapt. 'Ehm. Yes. Yes I do.' She reached for the nearest writing implement, a fat green crayon that Stevie had left on the corner of the sofa. 'Great. Fire away.' She scribbled the name and number on the phone pad. She didn't recognise the code, probably somewhere in England. Her heart was thumping.

'I'd like to ask,' said the voice. 'If we get other calls, do you mind if I pass on this number? It would just make things easier, from our end. This is your business number, isn't it?'

'Not technically,' said Cate. 'But I don't mind at all if you give it to people who saw the article. Not at all.'

'Lovely. Well, best of luck.'

'Thanks,' said Cate. 'Thanks very much.'

She put the phone down and tore the piece of paper from the pad, running her eyes over the number. It might be nothing, just someone wondering where she'd got Bertha, the haberdasher's dummy, or even Rudolph the singing reindeer, which Rick had insisted appear in the background of one of the shots. Or, maybe . . . ?

She looked up at herself in the hall mirror. She was flushed, two red circles on her cheeks like inexpertly applied rouge. She always blushed like that when she was anxious, or embarrassed, or excited. Mostly, when she was excited. Cate Beane, she said silently to the beaming woman in the mirror, repeat after me. In the grand scheme of things, notwithstanding the odd marital hiccup, you have a Perfect. Bloody. Life.

26

'Hey, Harpo, wakey wakey.' Rick kicked the bottom of Marg's sleeping-bag. 'We'll need to get a move on if we're going to meet the plane. Shift it.'

Marg yawned and rubbed a hand across her eyes, trying not to feel anywhere near the mass of curls that had sprouted on her head. 'What time is it?' she said croakily. She'd wakened at 3 a.m. from the most bizarre dream. She was dancing with Adam Milner at some crowded, indefinable ball, and Cate had been there but she was waltzing with Rick. Marg could hear them giggling and she kept trying to steer Adam across the floor to find out what was so funny. Only he kept moving her in a different direction and had laughed at her and called her Marjorie Jean as she grew angrier at him with every dip and twirl.

'It's the back of five,' said Rick. 'Leonora's up already. Bags are in the jeep. It's just you we need.'

Marg pulled her knees up out of her sleeping-bag, shivering, even though she was fully dressed. In less than a day she would have access to a hot shower and a generous vodka. Thank the lord for plumbing and the Poles.

There was movement in the camp already, even though it was still early. Thin spirals of smoke from the fires curled up into the lightening sky and Marg could hear the steady murmur of voices and coughing, and the occasional wail of a child roused from fitful sleep.

She found Leonora in the clinic, getting ready for the long, steady queue that would soon come over the rise.

'Is that you all set, my dear?' The nun laid the small metal dish she was holding back on the table and accompanied Marg out onto the decking.

'Thanks for everything,' said Marg. 'Really.' Across in the middle of the compound, Rick had found Grainne and had grabbed her in a bear hug. She shrieked with feigned outrage.

Leonora watched them. 'The baby died, you know,' she said suddenly. 'Last night.'

'I'm sorry,' said Marg.

Leonora shrugged. 'She only had the two.'

They stood for a moment in silence. 'Do you need to use the sat-phone again before we go?' asked Marg. They'd let the nuns call home on it the day they had arrived. Leonora shook her head. 'Not unless you've got a direct line to Downing Street or the White House, now, do you?'

Marg gave a weak smile. 'Is Amodu here? I was hoping to see him before we headed off. To say thanks.'

'I haven't seen him yet,' said Leonora. 'His sister was a bit poorly yesterday.'

'Poorly?'

Leonora patted her chest. 'Bad cough. Very bad.'

'It's just . . .' Marg held out her rolled-up sleeping-bag and waterproof jacket. 'I wanted to give him this. It's not much, but it's . . .' She put them down on the decking, feeling a bit inadequate. 'Can you make sure he gets them?'

Leonora nodded and gave her a gentle smile. 'He's a good boy, isn't he?'

'He helped us out a lot with our filming yesterday,' said Marg. 'Found us some families to talk to. He doesn't ever stop smiling, does he?'

Rick was signalling to her from the compound gates.

'Got to go.' She shook Leonora's hand warmly. 'Thanks again. And all the very best.'

Leonora nodded. 'Stay safe, my dear,' she said.

'You too,' said Marg.

It was as the jeep had started its bumpy way along the track by the edge of the camp that Marg spotted him. He was walking towards the compound and he broke into a run when he saw the vehicles.

Marg tapped the driver on the shoulder. 'Just a minute.' She waited until the jeep came to a dusty stop then nipped out of the back door and walked towards the boy with her hand outstretched.

'Bye, Amodu. Thanks for all your help.'

'Bye, bye.' He smiled and nodded and grasped her hand tightly, and Marg squeezed back. Then she turned and got back in the jeep. He walked alongside it as it negotiated the potholes, beaming in the window at them all. The car gathered speed and he started to run, waving.

Marg wound down the window. 'Special helper,' she shouted and gave him a thumbs up. He stopped in the track as the jeep sped off and raised his hand high in the air.

'Mark!' he shouted. 'G,g,g.' The smile never left his face.

'I don't want to go in after-school club,' wailed Stevie. 'It smells in after-school club.'

Cate removed the mangled tube of fromage frais from Stevie's hand and gave her yoghurty face a swift wipe with a piece of kitchen roll. 'It does not smell in after-school club,' she said.

'It does,' said Stevie petulantly. 'It smells of toes.'

'Toes?'

Emma slid out of her seat, nodding gravely. 'Actually, Mum, it's the same room where they keep the lost property.'

Cate looked at her, perplexed.

'It's mostly gym socks,' said Emma. 'That aren't clean.'

'Oh,' said Cate.

'Toes,' announced Stevie grumpily. 'Smelly toes.'

'Well, it's just for one afternoon,' said Cate. 'And it's really unusual for you to have to go, but I can't be sure I'll be back in time from the Borders. With the traffic and everything.' She thought she saw Dan flatten his lips behind his raised mug of tea. He'd been pretty underwhelmed about the possibility of her getting more work, even though she wasn't entirely sure yet what the job might entail or that she would be offered it. It had taken her a day to pluck up the courage to phone the number scribbled on the pad in green crayon. It turned out to be a woman from Bath relocating north who had bought an old house near Peebles and was looking for a designer to help her rid it of decades worth of chintz and swirly carpets.

'I'm just a hopeless case when it comes to decorating,' the woman had said. 'I'd put up woodchip and lantern shades if I could get away with it.'

She had seemed unbothered when Cate had explained she was just starting out, probably figuring that she would be grateful and cheap. And before she knew it, she had agreed to go down the following week to take a look.

'So you might actually get paid for this one?' Dan had said when she had told him that night.

'If I get it. I know they're speaking to a couple of other designers.' Other designers. Hark at me, she thought.

'How much?'

'It's normal to charge around fifteen per cent of the design costs.'

'So, on something of around ten thousand pounds that would be . . .'

'Quite a lot,' Cate had said. 'Although there would have to be some initial outlay.'

'Outlay?' Dan tilted his head.

'Well, she would get the big stuff – the sofas and so on, but I'd probably have to source and choose the soft furnishings, curtains, rugs, flooring, paint . . .' She tailed off.

'How much?' Dan's mouth settled into a flat, disapproving line.

'I don't know at this stage. It might be quite a lot initially, but we'd get it back, with extra. I thought we could use the savings account. If I get the job.'

Dan ran his hand over his face. 'God, Cate. How do you know she's kosher? Have you just got her word she'll pay you?'

Cate stiffened. 'I don't know, Dan. I might not even get the job. But I want to try. It's not like I'm raiding the kids' pocket money or anything. It's a short-term outlay for a long-term benefit.'

He had stood up and stared moodily into his coffee cup. 'It's a big commitment. Are you ready for it?'

'Are you?'

He hadn't answered.

She scrubbed at the yoghurt traces on the table. The twins had disappeared upstairs, ostensibly to finish off their home-work, but she could hear Robbie Williams crooning sugges-tively to them through the ceiling. Stevie was dancing silently in the sitting room with a small blue gonk and Dan was standing at the sink, looking at his reflection in the dark-ening glass of the window.

She moved up behind him, reached round to drop the paper in the bin, then linked her arms across his chest and pressed into his back. She didn't want to fight tonight. Not with the print-out from the impotence website, ready and folded in her bedside drawer. 'So, grumpy,' she said. 'If I haven't bankrupted us by taking on dodgy clients, and once

246

Mum and Ed are back, will I try and rebook this weekend away?'

'Mmm,' he murmured.

'Mmm that would be nice, or mmm I'd rather chew my own hand off?'

He gave a little laugh and she pulled back and nipped him quickly on the bum. 'And when we do go, will you wear your Gel Botz for me?'

He turned, looking confused, and she grinned at him, wanting to see his eyes light with mischief or amusement, with anything. 'I thought you were looking a little broad in the beam,' she said.

A smile creased his tired face and he reached round to slap her on the bum. 'Right back at you,' he said. 'Only your padding's real.'

She opened her mouth to remonstrate but the phone started to ring. It was Stevie who reached it first, twirling across the room to grab the receiver.

'Hellosteviespeakingcanisaywh . . . ?'

Cate saw Stevie's face crease into a smile, then a flash of puzzlement. She turned and held out the receiver.

'It's Granny.' She wrinkled her nose. 'She sounds funny.'

Cate glanced at Dan. They never called when they were away. Not once in fifteen years of travelling. Not even when Mum's case had fallen from the gangway of the *Paradise Princess* and half of Anguilla had watched her foundation garment float off across the Caribbean Sea.

The line was faint and Cate had to press the phone tight against her ear to hear her mum's voice. Her throat felt suddenly dry.

'Cate.' Her mum sounded choked, bewildered.

'Mum. What is it?'

'He's gone. Cate, he's gone.'

'Mum.' She felt the blood drain from her face. 'Mum,

what is it? What's happened?' Even in her panic she realised it was a stupid thing to ask, because she had known in that first awful instant what was about to come. From the corner of her eye she saw Dan move quickly towards her.

'Cate. He's gone. Ed. Your dad. He's dead.'

27

'Are you really sure I can't go through?' Cate looked pleadingly at the man in the grey overalls behind the desk.

He shook his head reluctantly. 'I'm sorry, love. Restricted
access. You'll need to wait till . . .' He paused. 'Till the hearse
arrives.'

The sliding doors swooshed apart as one of his colleagues
emerged and Cate caught a glimpse of the interior of the
airport's freight hangar. It was open to the tarmac and filled
with crates and boxes and low-bedded trolleys and animal
cages carrying family pets. And somewhere among them,
Ed's coffin. Returned to them like damaged goods. 'When
the hearse gets here, love, you'll get through then,' the man
repeated. 'Have you got someone coming. To meet you?'

'My mother and my brother,' said Cate blankly. She sat
back down on the hard orange plastic seat in the waiting
area. She had offered immediately to go out to Portugal but
Tom, her brother, had insisted that he should bring their
mum and Ed back. And now they were somewhere on the
air side of the terminal completing paperwork, and she was
waiting here, within yards of a man she had adored and
couldn't reach.

'Do you want a cup of tea or something?' The man bent
before her. 'It's just the office machine. Not great, but you're
welcome to it.'

She smiled at his kindness. 'No, it's okay. I'm fine. Thank
you.'

And the truth was that she *was* fine. Fine in that numb, driven way when you can't stop for an instant because if you do you know the grief will engulf you.

Telling the girls had been the worst. Dan had gone to get the twins from their room and had held Cate's hand tight as she had spoken to them.

'It was a heart attack. His heart stopped beating. It happened when he was having a nap. He just slipped away and then Granny couldn't wake him.' So, a good death, but far too soon. For him. For all of them.

'I don't want him to be dead,' Stevie had said instantly and her lip had gone wobbly and she had been lifted up into Dan's arms and cried noisily and angrily into his chest.

The twins had sat still as statues until Emma burst into tears and Jo clutched her sister's hand and said, 'Oh, Mum,' and Cate's tears had come as well.

And Dan had held it together, even though she could see his own shock and hurt. And Marg was coming. She would be here tonight for the funeral. She'd insisted when Cate had phoned to tell her, even though she must be up to her eyes in work, being just back from Africa and all. Cate had needed her to know, though, and had been surprised at how much. Maybe it was because of the last time. Maybe because she needed someone to tell her that it was fucking not fair to lose your dad. Not twice in one lifetime.

The small side door opened and Cate's mum and brother walked in. Cate leapt to her feet. Her mum, still in her bright holiday clothes, seemed smaller, diminished by loss. Her eyes were shadowed with fatigue but they lit with tears and relief when she saw Cate.

'Darling.'

'Mum.' They held each other as Tom pressed his hands into their shoulders. The man in the overalls slipped out of the room.

'Are you okay?' Cate's mum pulled back and put her hand to her cheek, and Cate nodded, mutely.

'Good,' said her mum. 'That's good. And the girls?'

'They're very upset,' said Cate. 'But they've been great. Dan, too. They want to see you.'

Her mum nodded and gave a loud sniff. 'Good. Good. Good.' She looked around. 'Now. Tom. Cate. We need to get him home.'

Tom went off to locate someone who could help, and it was while he was gone that the man in overalls reappeared.

'The hearse is here,' he said. 'If you're ready?'

'Can I go through now?' asked Cate.

The man nodded gently. 'Yes, love. You can go through to him now.'

Marg peered down through the thin drifts of cloud at the brown hills below. They were only ten minutes out of Edinburgh and the nose of the plane was down, so this must be somewhere near Selkirk. She studied the structure of the landscape through the faint opaque distortion of the thickened glass. Thin stretches of road, small grey clusters of villages, the occasional solitary house way up a track, like a misplaced Monopoly piece. Marg wondered what would make you want to live on the edges of life like that. Cate, she knew, dreamed of a remote farmhouse where the nearest neighbour might be miles away across hill and field, but Marg couldn't imagine being so removed.

The last time she had come out of the air it was into London and as the plane curved across the heart of the city, so big you couldn't see its edges, she had felt the familiar rush of pleasure. She liked her own space but she liked it in a city so loud and busy and crowded that you needn't ever have a moment's silence if the thought of one unsettled you.

The office had been fine when she said she needed to take some personal days, even though they were obviously a little surprised. Marg never took personal days.

But when she explained it was for a funeral, a friend's father, they had said, yes, of course. The package on Chad was being held for another week, anyway, to coincide with a pre-G8 conference in Geneva. It was looking good, though, in the two days she had had to work on it. They had stopped in Ndjamena to film an interview with the Chadian Minister for the Interior, and then Rick had been diverted unexpectedly to South Africa where a great white shark had broken through a cage during a tourist dive at Fish Hoek and had taken the leg off a middle-aged matron from Antwerp.

Marg smiled at the memory of Rick on yesterday's show, looking not unlike an elephant seal in black neoprene, plunging into the waves for his piece to camera. The largest thing to come near him was a curious sunfish. The news room christened him Keiko, until Marg had suggested that Free Willy might be more appropriate. The arts correspondent had found that particularly funny.

It had been a relief, actually, to have him out of the way. He could be a complete pest when it came to editing, wanting to make sure he came across with the right mix of gravitas and beefcake. Lots of side profiles – all chest and above – and long, meaningful pauses, which wasted precious seconds of air-time.

The package was pretty powerful, though, especially the interview with Leonora, whose gentle but steely outrage said more about the obscenity of the situation than any Rick Rutner monologue. There were some fantastic shots of her working in the clinic, with the long queue outside. And here and there, throughout the three minutes of time, there were glimpses of Amodu. Marg liked the fact that he was in the film, not displayed for all to see but watching from the sidelines as he had when they were there, with his big broad smile.

'Ladies and gentlemen, we are making our final approach into Edinburgh. Please make sure your seat backs are in the upright position and your tray tables are safely stowed. Cabin crew, seats for landing.'

Marg laid her head against the back of the seat as the plane swung out across the Forth estuary to line up for the runways of Turnhouse. Cate had sounded shattered when she had called. God, it just wasn't fair. First her dad and now Ed. Marg wondered how the girls were doing. Even though she had only seen Ed with them briefly, it was obvious he doted on them and vice versa, especially Stevie. Pant-hating, toothpaste-eating Stevie. The very devil and the apple of her grampa's eye.

She listened to the rattle of the wheels grinding down from the underbelly of the aircraft. The last time, she had walked to Cate's house straight from school, even though it was a good mile and a half. She hadn't been sure what she should say, and still hadn't worked it out by the time she reached the neat bungalow where almost all the lights were out. But she had known that she had to say something.

She couldn't even remember who had opened the door. Had it been Tom? Or a neighbour? She remembered Cate's mum had been in the kitchen, though, her back towards the hall. She was sitting at the table with her head in one hand, so still that Marg thought she might be asleep, while women Marg didn't recognise moved around her, white-faced and tearful.

Cate was up in her room, curled in a tight ball on her bed as if she had wanted it to swallow her. Marg had come in and closed the door quietly. She had seen Cate upset before. When her goldfish had died in primary four, when she'd tripped on the stage and everyone had seen her knickers in the third-year performance of *South Pacific*. When the boys had pulled at her shirt expecting to find a bra strap and had roared with mocking laughter when they found she wore a vest. But never like this. This was something horribly real; huge and awful.

Marg had sat on the end of the bed and had started to speak. And at first Cate hadn't moved, just shaken noiselessly with great gulping sobs, but then she turned and laid her head on Marg's knee.

Marg wasn't sure now what words she'd used, something about the bloody unfairness of it all. And when she had finished talking she had stroked Cate's hair, damp in places from so much crying and had fought back her own tears, thinking of the man she had conjured up twisting helplessly towards the sea, and then the real man whom Cate had loved dying so unexpectedly on this most ordinary of days.

The plane landed with a solid bump and taxied briskly across the rain-slicked tarmac towards the terminal. On most flights, Marg was one of the first to her feet and could extricate her bag from the overhead bin in seconds. Tonight, she sat patiently until almost everyone else had disembarked, gathering her thoughts. Then she stood and made for the stairs.

She came through the doors of the arrivals hall and went straight to Cate, dropping her bag without caring how it fell.

'Hon, I'm so sorry.'

Cate bent into her, and her shoulders started to shake gently with fresh sobs.

'It's not fair,' said Marg into her hair. 'Really. It's not bloody fair.'

Cate pulled back and wiped her hand across her eyes. She looked exhausted and empty. 'I'm glad you're here and I'm okay. Really. I'm okay.'

Marg took her gently by the shoulders and looked straight into her eyes. 'You don't have to be,' she said. 'Cate, that's the one thing you don't have to be.'

28

'My grampa died.' Stevie placed a large square box on Marg's knee and balanced herself on one leg, hopping gently up and down. 'Do you want to play jungles?'

'We could do that.' Marg looked down at the box which was decorated with coloured cartoon animals, then up again at Stevie, whose best dress was decorated with two large chocolate stains as well as some large appliqué flowers.

'I'm sorry about your grampa,' said Marg.

Stevie nodded gravely, still hopping. 'It's a tragic loss.'

'It is.' Marg wondered how often Stevie had heard that phrase since she had got up that morning. Marg had heard it herself several times, from the pursed lips of the elderly women now crowding Cate's kitchen and dining room in a tutting, tearful huddle, and the men standing stiffly in blazers and slacks through in the lounge, doubtless trying not to wonder who might be next.

It had been a good funeral, though, as funerals go. Warm tributes from those who knew Ed best: bad jokes about his throwing arm and permatan from his bowling club buddies; a particularly lovely speech from Cate's mum, who had thanked him for eighteen good, good years; and Cate, a smiling and genial Cate, who had read one of his favourite poems, Hugh MacDiarmid's 'The Little White Rose'. She had got through it without crying, only letting the tears come later when the coffin shuddered through the curtains at the crematorium, and he really was gone.

'Right.' Marg got down on her knees with Stevie. 'Jungles. Talk me through it.'

'Well,' said Stevie, 'there's all these animals and if you land on them, no, if you get to the space, no, if you land on them, when you're on the space you get a thing from this bit and you put it in your other thing.' She looked up. 'Okay?'

'Not really,' said Marg. 'But let's give it a whirl.' She watched Stevie set out a series of small plastic animals on the board. She didn't sit still for an instant, jiggling around, humming under her breath, talking to herself like a miniature crazy you might cross the road to avoid. It was strange the way children rationalised life's shittiest times. Marg found it quite refreshing. My grampa died. Do you want to play jungles?

Cate passed by the door, carrying a tray of sandwiches and smiled gratefully when she saw Marg down on her knees and about to play a board game for the first time in three decades. Cate's friend, Orla, a lovely bouncy Irish girl, followed her with plates and napkins, and Dan brought up the rear, a half-empty bottle of Glenlivet in his hands. Even Marg could tell he was being more attentive. He seemed to be always at Cate's side and there had barely been a moment throughout the funeral when he wasn't holding her hand.

'What animal do you want to be?' Stevie held out a small fistful of creatures. 'You can't be the tiger because I want to be the tiger.'

'Okay,' said Marg. 'I'll be the wolf?' She picked up a grey dog-like creature.

'That's not a wolf,' Stevie giggled. 'It's a hyena.'

'Okay, hyena.'

'They laugh like this,' said Stevie. 'Heh, heh, heh, heh, heh.' She cocked her head to one side. 'Can you do that?'

Marg nodded. 'If I had to. Absolutely.'

Stevie looked at her expectantly.

'Heh, heh, heh, heh, heh,' said Marg.

'That sounds more like a witch,' said Stevie. 'But you can't be a witch because it's about animals. You have to be a hyena.'

'I'll work on the laugh,' said Marg. She looked up. Jo was leaning against the door-frame, watching them.

'Hey,' said Marg. 'Want to join in?'

'Is she cheating yet?' Jo folded herself onto the floor next to them. Both she and Emma had seemed much less resilient than Stevie about their loss, both had cried at the funeral, and Jo's eyes were still red-rimmed.

'I don't cheat!' said Stevie indignantly.

'You do too,' said Jo. She turned to Marg. 'She counts all wrong and gets further along the board when you're not looking.'

'Don't.'

'You do.'

'DON'T!'

Through in the kitchen, Marg could hear another ruckus erupting, the jerky sobs of someone building up to a full-blown indulgent wail. She sat back on her heels and looked through the doorway. Cate had been collared by a largish woman in a black cardigan, who was weeping inappropriately on her shoulder.

Marg jumped to her feet. 'I tell you what, Jo, why don't you play for me and make sure Stevie doesn't cheat? I need to go and talk to your mum.' She breezed into the kitchen. 'Cate, can I pull you away for a sec? We seem to have run out of . . . cheese footballs.'

Cate smiled weakly in gratitude and extricated herself from the woman's grasp.

'I'm sorry,' she said gently. 'I have to go.'

'So terrible,' sniffed the woman, turning towards Marg. 'Such a tragic loss.'

Marg flashed her a mercury-freezing smile for her over-emoting and guided Cate out into the hall.

'Thanks.' Cate leant against the banisters and exhaled noisily when the door was firmly shut and the woman had found another shoulder to dampen. 'I have absolutely no idea who that was.'

Marg glanced at her watch. 'Do you want to go somewhere for a drink? Quick escape?'

Cate shook her head. 'I can't.' She glanced around her then reached out and grabbed Marg's hand. 'But come with me. I want to show you something.'

She pulled Marg up the stairs and led her to the office, closing the door behind them. 'Here,' she pointed to a small piece of paper, scribbled with a phone number and name in what looked like green crayon and pinned to her cork-board beside the article from the *Saturday Post*.

'What am I looking at?' said Marg.

'A possible commission. All because of the *Post* piece.'

'You serious?'

Cate nodded. 'The paper phoned last week because this woman had been trying to get in touch with me. She'd seen the article. Anyway, she's moving up to the Borders. From Bath. It's a big old house and they need help getting it done up. It's not positive I'll get it, but I'm going to go down next week and have a look. I was supposed to do it today actually, but, obviously, I had to postpone.' She touched her fingers to the card. 'I think Dan assumed I would drop the whole thing. You know, with Ed . . .'

'Why?'

Cate shrugged. 'I think he's worried he's going to be left holding Fort Beane if it takes off.'

'When it takes off,' said Marg. 'You've got to pursue it.'

'I know,' said Cate. 'Ed wouldn't approve if I didn't. He was so great about it all. Adamant that I should go for it.' Her eyes welled with tears, and Marg leant across and touched her arm.

'He was a sweetheart,' she said, 'and a really smart guy.'

They stood for a moment, saying nothing.

'How are things with Dan?' asked Marg, tentatively. 'Have you had your weekend away yet?'

Cate shook her head. 'Not yet. And everything's fine. Really. He's been lovely.' She gave a flat laugh. 'You'll like this, though. I had another daft moment about a week ago. I found a receipt in his pocket. For underwear. But it was just gel pants for his cycling. Large size. For men.'

'Maybe he's just seeing a hefty lass,' said Marg. She held her hands wide apart. 'Big fat arse. Or maybe it's a hefty lass with piles.'

Cate reached across and slapped her on the arm. 'They were for him.'

Marg smiled. 'Course they were. Oh, and talking of pants, I've got a present for you. I'll need to send them up.'

'I don't like the sound of that.' Cate pulled a face. 'They're not crotchless, are they?'

'They're very tasteful,' said Marg. 'Literally.' She settled herself onto the floor, leaning her back against the wall. 'This is like being in your old bedroom.'

'It's about the same size.' Cate shimmied down against the other wall until her knees were almost touching Marg's.

Marg looked around. 'You got any menthol fags hidden anywhere?'

Cate shook her head.

'Miniatures of Famous Grouse? Bottle of Advocaat? Kahlua?'

Cate smiled. 'Nope.'

'What have you got?'

Cate pulled open a drawer in the chest next to her and peered in. 'Lots of paper-clips, Sellotape, and Smarties. A tube of Smarties.'

'Go on then.' Marg held out her hand and took the sweets, tipping out a small handful. She picked out a red one and held it up. 'Remember we used to do lipstick with these?' She sucked it and wiped it on her lips. 'How do I look?'

'Like Gloria Swanson,' Cate giggled. 'But not in a good way.'

'Thanks a bunch.' Marg wiped her hand across her mouth.

'Now you look like Stevie,' said Cate. 'It's all over your cheek.'

'I'll say it's blusher.'

Cate upended the tube and found a brown Smartie, licked it and rubbed it on her chin. 'Beauty spot?'

'Large mole,' laughed Marg. 'Or emerging boil.'

Cate gave her chin a wipe and laid her head back against the wall, looking out through the window.

'Is it okay to laugh, do you think?' She turned back to Marg. 'Is it okay to laugh today?'

'Absolutely,' said Marg. 'I don't think Ed would be averse to a bit of Smartie face-painting. If he was here.'

'Oh, God, yes. He'd do the full Coco.' Cate smiled at the thought.

Marg slipped another Smartie from the tube and popped it in her mouth. 'How's your mum bearing up?'

'She really is fine,' said Cate, holding out her hand for another sweet too. 'She's going to stay with us for a couple more days and then she's going to go down to Tom's for a week or so. After that . . .' She paused. 'I think she'll stay in the house. I don't know, though. Haven't really thought that far ahead.'

The door swung open suddenly and Dan poked his head round. 'Here you are. I've been looking for you.' He gestured to Cate. 'Some of them are starting to leave – finally.' He peered at them both. 'What's that on your faces? What have you been doing?'

'Giving each other a make-over,' said Marg. She handed the Smartie tube to Cate and got to her feet. 'Actually, I need to be heading off, too.'

'Are you sure?' Cate let Dan pull her up.

Marg nodded. 'Yeah, I should.'

'I'll give you a run to the airport,' said Cate, but Marg shook her head.

'No. I'll call a taxi.'

'Don't be daft,' said Cate. 'I'll take you. I'd like to.'

Marg shook her head again. 'Honestly, hon. You've got enough going on here. And I want to make a stop-off on the way anyway. I've got a little time before the flight.'

Cate hesitated. She looked surprised. 'Oh, okay. Good. That's good.'

The taxi arrived as Cate was ushering another batch of mourners out of the door. Marg shrugged on her coat and picked up her bag. The twins were in the hall too, with Dan, who had Stevie balanced on his shoulders. They clustered around as Cate took her out onto the step.

'Phone me when your thing is on, and we'll watch.'

Marg nodded. 'It's next week sometime. I'll let you know. And let me know how it goes with the job. And we should arrange another weekend. For sure. Either up here or in London.' She turned and waved at Dan and the girls. 'Bye you lot. See you sometime.'

The taxi driver had the boot open and was standing waiting in the drizzle. Cate pulled her in for a hug, and held on. Marg couldn't see her face, but she knew she was about to cry again.

'You'll be fine, hon,' she said.

'Thank you,' Cate whispered. 'Again.'

★

The Ford Focus pulled to a stop outside the row of narrow terraced houses. It was raining quite heavily now and the wipers whisked rapidly back and forward across the windscreen like frantically waving arms. Marg leant forward.

'Can you wait?' she asked the driver. 'It might be a while. Maybe half an hour or so?' The taxi driver nodded and settled back in his seat, pulling a red-top tabloid from the side pocket. Marg shut the rear door and headed for the house, the one with the uneven path and the faded green door. The smell of the sea was strong. It was just one street away; she used to be able to reach it in a matter of minutes and watch the giant tankers and merchant craft slip past on the industrial end of the great river.

She stood for a moment on the front step, then took a sharp breath and pressed the bell. It sounded through the door, a shrill echo. Drrring.

It was a while before she was aware of any kind of movement. She heard keys turning in more than one lock and then the door was pulled back and she was hit by a waft of warm, stale air that smelled of toast and old nicotine and something that needed cleaning. The woman on the other side kept one hand on the edge of the door and looked at her, her mouth moving slowly into a flat, surprised smile.

'Well, well, well.'

'Hello, Mum,' said Marg. 'Long time no see.'

The thin grey cat coiled itself around her mother's legs and looked haughtily at Marg. Marg couldn't remember its name. Titch, Mitch, something like that. Bitch, maybe. They were in the kitchen, and Marg had sat herself down at the table. Her mum was over near the sink, pouring boiling water into the two mugs she had pulled from the hooks under the cabinets. She shuffled across to the fridge in her sheepskin slippers. She was moving more slowly than she had the last time Marg had seen her. It was probably her bad ankles. Or bad hips. Or bad back. Because there was always something that had been bad about her mum, but never quite so bad that it couldn't be made worse by something Marg had done.

'So.' Her mum set down two mugs of weak tea and eased herself into a chair opposite. 'What brings you up this weather?'

'Cate,' said Marg. 'You remember Cate Wishart from school? Well her stepfather died. I went to the funeral.' She took a quick sip of tea and burnt her tongue.

Her mum nodded blankly and her eyes slipped to Marg's jacket, which she had slung over the back of the kitchen chair. She leant across and rubbed a brown-tipped finger across the fabric. 'Nice,' she said.

Marg ignored her. 'It was Cate's stepdad. Remember, she lost her dad while we were at school?'

'Mm,' said her mum, nodding, although she clearly didn't remember. 'And how is Cate?'

'She's fine. She has three kids now. All girls.'

'Well, well.' Her mum took another sip of tea and let her gaze drift out of the window. 'And how's work?'

'Fine. Great. I was in Africa last week. Chad.'

'Chad.' Her mum nodded again. The clock above the cooker, the one that Marg had always hated because it reminded her of exam rooms, clicked noisily onto the half hour. And now would be the time, thought Marg, that you might say, Chad. Really? What took you there? What was it like? What was the story? Tell me all about it.'

'And how are you keeping?' asked Marg.

Her mum gave a tight little smile and reached for her pack of cigarettes, slipping one out and lighting it with a deep, needy drag. 'Oh, you know. Hip's playing up again. And the sciatica's got worse. Constant pain, it is. Constant.

Shouldn't complain, though, eh?' She tapped the side of her head. 'Still got my faculties.'

'You probably shouldn't be smoking, you know.' Marg gestured at the cigarettes.

'One of the few pleasures,' said her mum. 'Won't deny me that, will you?'

Marg stared into the dull brown of her tea. This was agony. She should never have come.

The grey cat had climbed onto the countertop and sat watching her, its coiled tail flicking nervously.

'There's a lot of new houses around,' said Marg. 'Almost didn't recognise the street.'

'Mm,' said her mum. 'Lot of new houses. Pricey, too. Two bedrooms and they're asking a hundred and fifty thousand quid.' She rested her elbows on the table, her cigarette aloft, pluming a thin spiral of grey smoke. 'More money than sense, a lot of people.'

Marg found herself nodding and followed the thinning waft of smoke up to the ceiling. There was a faint wash of tobacco brown around the light fitting and in the corners, and Marg felt her stomach turn. She stretched her hands out on the table and felt something sharp and crusted under her fingers, something old and edible left to solidify in the thin pine cracks. She lifted her hands quickly and saw her mum glance across; a slow look, and then a measured breath.

'Would have tidied if I'd known you were coming.' There was a pause. 'Would have got the best china out.'

And there it was, the first sharp stab of sarcasm. Marg felt herself shrink. Bare legs and a nightie, toes clenching under the table in slippers a size and a half too big. Bought for thrift and growth. The figure at the sink, back turned but mouth moving. Not good enough for our Marjorie, is it? Well, la de bloody da. The sing-songy tone. The stale, cluttered home with all the detritus of a life let go. The abject distance between the people who lived here. A mother and daughter. She suddenly wanted to leap up and grab some kitchen roll and bleach and scrub at the table with its aged crusted stains and make a clear space all around her; just a small space, empty and clean, free of taint.

She looked across at her mum. 'No you wouldn't have,' she said quickly.

'Pardon?' Her mum paused mid-drag and stared at her.

'Tidied,' said Marg. She hadn't meant to pick a fight. Maybe it was the funeral; a family's real, felt, loss. Maybe it was being with Cate again. Her throat tightened against the rise of rage and hurt. 'You wouldn't have tidied, Mum. If you'd known I was coming.'

Her mum tapped her cigarette sharply in the ashtray. 'What a thing to say!' Smoke surged from her mouth with her words. She lifted the cigarette and jabbed it in Marg's direction. 'You've got a cheek.' Her lips pursed with indignation. 'Turning up here saying things like that. The bloody cheek of it!'

'Turning up here?' Marg gave a hollow laugh. 'What, like a bad penny? Like a bad smell?'

The cat, sensing the rising agitation, dropped silently from the countertop and stalked out of the room. Marg watched it go, its tail high with disapproval or disdain. She turned back to her mum, her heart hammering now. 'Would you rather I'd called, or would you have found some excuse to stop me coming? Like you did last time, Mum. Remember? Two Christmases ago. It's not convenient. Aunty Betty's not keeping well. Maybe next year.'

'So, what, I've to jump every time you want, no, deign, to come calling?' Her mum's face contracted with contempt.

Marg sat back in her chair. 'Every time?' She repeated the words, then shook her head. 'I've not been up for four years, Mum. Four fucking years!'

'Don't speak to me like that,' spat her mum. 'Don't you speak to me like that!'

'Or what?' Marg sat back in her chair. 'Or what? You'll send me to my room? You'll treat me like dirt? Send me to Coventry? Been there, Mum. Done that.'

Her mum stood up quickly and moved across to the sink, clattering her mug onto the drainer. 'I don't know what your game is,' she said. She tapped her cigarette into the sink and held it back to her mouth.

Marg watched her inhale. A sudden weariness came over her. This was so horribly, horribly familiar. The rhythm of her youth. The sharpness of unkind words, the gnawing tension in the pit of her stomach. She leant on the table and laid her face on her raised hands. The clock slipped to the quarter hour. Somewhere on the river a klaxon sounded. Marg remembered the sound of the klaxons, clarion calls from the big ships. The ones she sometimes wished could spirit her away, if she just got down to the shore in time.

'Where are you going?' they would ask. Anywhere but here.

She tilted her head. Her mum had folded her arms and was looking out through the window, past the neighbour's whirligig, with its limp pennant of damp washing, to the grey sheets of rain beyond. One of her hands was shaking gently.

'Why did you keep me?'

It wasn't the first time Marg had ever asked, but it was the first time she had wanted to hear the truth.

There was no response.

Marg sat back and twisted her hands together. 'Christ, Mum. Look at us. You don't give a fuck where I've been, what I've been doing. And I had to force myself to come and see you and I'm sitting here wanting to run for the bloody door and you'd be holding it wide open if you could, wouldn't you? So, why? You had options. Why did you keep me?'

Her mum laid her cigarette on the edge of the sink. She didn't turn but eventually she gave a little shrug. 'You did all right,' she said.

'What? When?' said Marg. 'Now? Yeah, I do all right now.'

'You did all right,' her mum repeated.

Marg shook her head vehemently, even though she knew her mum wasn't looking. 'No, I didn't, actually. I did not do all right.'

She pushed her chair back, crowded suddenly by images and feelings. A girl in her room in an empty house. The heat of angry tears. The awkward pity of friends.

She looked up. 'Do you know?' she said. 'I first had sex at fifteen.'

Her mum swivelled to the side, not the full way round, but enough to show the pursing of her mouth in shock.

Marg gave a bitter laugh. 'Not a clue what I was doing because you'd told me fuck all. And then just before I left school, I had to take a pregnancy test. Upstairs. Cate was with me. And you had no fucking idea because you were at the bingo. And God, I was really scared. So fucking scared. Do you know why? Because I didn't want a child. And I still don't. Not then and not now. Why do you think that is, Mum?'

There was no movement from the figure at the sink, but she could hear her mum's breathing, raised and ragged.

'Maybe,' said Marg, 'because a child is just a huge fucking problem, a huge fucking inconvenience, the worst thing that could happen. Something that sours your whole fucking life. Isn't that right, Mum?'

Her mum turned, her face white with anger. 'You have no right to say this to me,' she said. She flicked her cigarette into the sink and pressed her hands together in agitation.

'I've got every right,' said Marg. 'And I'd really like to know. Why did you keep me? Really. Why?'

Her mum gave what sounded like a snort and shook her head. 'You're a piece of work,' she said again.

'Yeah, I am,' said Marg. 'And you made me. So, what was it? You couldn't bear to be parted from me? You thought I might come in handy one day? You thought Daddy dearest might have a crisis of conscience and come back for us?' There must have been something in the last words she had spoken because she saw her mum's face change. The mouth, set in a tight, angry line, opened suddenly in a wordless shout.

'That's it, isn't it?' said Marg. 'You thought my dad might come back?'

Her mum drew a breath. It was a while before she spoke, as if she couldn't quite find the words. 'We would have been just right,' she said finally. 'If you hadn't come.'

'If I hadn't come,' repeated Marg, slowly. She laughed suddenly at the awful absurdity of it all. 'Fuck's sake, Mum, it wasn't an immaculate bloody conception. You both had something to do with it.'

Her mum shook her head. 'We never planned . . .'

'Yeah, I know that, you told me that bit, remember? You and Aunty Betty.' Marg cut her off. 'And then he buggered off and you hung on to me, hoping he'd come back. And at some point you realised it wasn't going to happen but it was too late then to do anything else.'

'We would have been just right,' repeated her mum.

'No, see, Mum, that can't be right,' said Marg bitterly, suddenly wanting to hurt, to wound. 'Because he's got a wife and kids, two kids. In Falkirk. He's probably a grampa, for God's sake. It probably wasn't just me he didn't want. He didn't know me. But he knew you.'

'Don't you say that to me!' spat her mum again. The

voice was shrill, but Marg saw that her shoulders had dropped. She looked suddenly tiny, stooped by the window, hollowed out by a lifetime's discontent. Marg felt a quick wave of shame and the anger went from her voice.

'God, Mum. You could have moved on. You could have found someone else.' She saw Cate's mum with Ed, laughing in a kitchen.

Her mum reached forward and scraped her pack of cigarettes from the table, lighting one unsteadily.

'You should have moved on, Mum,' said Marg again, quietly. 'I have.'

'Well, good for you.' The sarcasm had returned and Marg sat back in her chair. She looked up at her mum, who was drawing fiercely on her cigarette. Her eyes were bright, but not with tears, and Marg realised she had never seen her mum cry, although she must have done – surely she must have done, in bitterness and despair?

'Mum.'

She saw her mum's eyes slip to the clock. The cat had reappeared, crossed the floor carefully and wound itself back round her mum's ankles. Her mum glanced down and her expression changed instinctively to reveal a flash of affection.

Marg watched them for a moment and then stood slowly, knowing she was being dismissed, no words left to say.

She lifted her jacket from the chair and shrugged it on, then fished into her bag for her purse and pulled out a fistful of notes, laying them in a clumsy heap on the table.

'Do you need . . . ?'

'Good of you,' said her mum, flatly, as though nothing had passed between them. She turned and moved in front of Marg down the hallway and snapped back the locks. Marg hesitated on the step, unwilling, suddenly, to leave like this, the way she had left so many times before.

'Mum . . .'

'Kept him waiting, I see.' Her mum was looking past her to the Ford Focus. Her eyes were blank. 'Well, bye then.'

It was the response she should have expected, the one that maybe she deserved. Marg turned and walked down the path. She heard the click of the first lock even before she had reached the end.

'That you, love?' The driver folded his paper and tucked it back into the side pocket of the driver's door. 'That wasn't too long.'

Marg nodded curtly. 'Airport, please.'

The driver shifted the Focus into gear and pulled away from the pavement. The wipers started their frantic farewell. 'Going somewhere nice?' he said brightly, as they rounded the corner and the river came into view. 'Somewhere nice and warm?'

'Mmm,' said Marg. She didn't want to talk. Not right now. 'Can I have a look at your paper?' she said. For a second she thought about heading back to Cate's.

It was an instinctive reaction. When she couldn't bear it at her mum's she went to Cate's. But not this time. Not this Cate. All grown up with a family of her own, grieving for a man who had loved her back.

Marg opened the paper. The Page 3 Girl gave her a dazzling grin, but she hardly noticed. All she needed was a barrier, a wall of newsprint, so she could sit in the badly sprung back seat with her head bent low and no one could see that the wetness on her cheeks hadn't come from the rain.

29

It wasn't exactly what you would call a capsule collection. Cate stood back and studied the rack of clothes in the wardrobe. No signature colour. No definitive look. And when had she started wearing so many cardigans? She lifted the sleeve of a long grey lambswool one with a tissue balled in its pocket like some sort of growth.

At college her wardrobe could not have been described as anything other than quirky. But skinny leggings under the tight, darted fifties dresses she found at church sales had long since given way to washability and elasticated waists.

She found the suit in its clear plastic carrier at the end, next to the tiered skirt she hadn't worn for years, and pair of cream linen shorts her mum had brought her back from Venice, so gathered at the waist that they looked like a nappy when she had put them on. She'd been unable to come downstairs and show them off for laughing. Her mum had been offended. Ed had said, 'I told you so.'

She closed the blinds quickly, not wanting to do a Stevie and flash the neighbours, and slipped off her jeans. The suit trousers slid easily enough past her knees, but she had to do the wriggle and jump to get them up over her thighs and bum and now the zip gaped mockingly at her, an un-traversable divide.

Only your padding's real. Bloody hell.

She waddled across to the mirror, clutching the trousers

closed. Okay, so she had last worn the damn things more than ten years ago, but she wasn't that much heavier, surely? Or maybe the flesh had just moved around on her, like one of those morphing Plasticine figures, everything sliding downwards.

The suit jacket still fitted but only just, and the cut was much too boxy. Cate draped the suit on the bed and dropped the linen shorts on top of it. Charity shop for both, and if she got this job, she'd go on a splurge. A couple of sharp suits and a dazzling dress. Maybe even an Alice Temperley. With a pair of vertiginous heels. Real fuck-me-now shoes. Glossy and strapped and spiky. She smiled weakly at herself in the mirror in her pants and bra and black trouser socks, almost through at the toe. Yawn on me now, Dr Dan.

The woman who emerged from the house to meet her had managed to get into her suit. It was soft, swishy and the colour of pale toffee, a shade or two darker than her short, bobbed hair. Cate made a mental note. No primary colours. No plaid. Neutral tones. Think Hamptons, sea-washed.

'This is lovely.' Cate stepped from the car and stretched out her hand. 'Very Robert Louis Stevenson.' It was a beautiful house, tucked behind a copse of trees off the main Edinburgh to Peebles road. Whitewashed and four-square in that no-nonsense Scottish way, but with little flourishes, like the studded wooden outer door and the spired windows on the upper floor. She couldn't tell exactly how much land was around it, but there were fields to the back and a wide stretch of lawn to each side, a little unkempt but lined by well-stocked herbaceous borders.

The woman shook her hand firmly. 'It is lovely,' she said. 'To be honest we got it for the paddock. My eldest's a horse freak. But I've been wanting an older property for ages. We were in a new house in Bath, bit of a monstrosity, actually.

Fake dado-rails, that kind of thing. I can't stand fake, can you?'

Cate shook her head.

'As I said on the phone, I loved what you did with the bathroom in the newspaper. Inspired. I love reading on the loo. Only place you can get away from the damn kids sometimes.'

'Thanks,' said Cate. The woman was not what she had expected from the phone call, much more glamorous than she had sounded – and much more highly strung.

'Really, we're looking for a complete overhaul inside.' The woman started towards the front door. 'I'd better warn you, it was an elderly couple who had it, so nothing's been done for bloody decades and it smells of piss and antiseptic. I have no idea where to start. I know what I don't like but I'm pretty crap on deciding what I do.'

'Okay,' said Cate. She had already spied the diamonds on the woman's ring finger. 'Does your husband have any firm ideas on what he might want?'

'Husband?' The woman turned and gave a snort. 'He's shacked up in Didcot with his catering manager. That's why I'm up here. But let's see. What would he like? Oh yeah, fake tits, fake tan and a brain the size of a walnut probably.'

Cate fought the urge to giggle hysterically. 'Oh,' she said. 'I'm sorry.' This she had not been expecting.

The woman laid her hand on Cate's arm and gave a tight little laugh. 'Don't be. I'm not. Well, there was a time. But I think you've only got so much weeping and wailing in you. And then you realise what an utter fucking bastard he actually is and you move on, don't you?'

She seemed to be waiting for an answer, so Cate nodded, blankly.

'Anyway, listen to me wittering on. Bitter old hag.' The woman giggled. 'That's his description, by the way, not mine.

Come on in and tell me what you think. As you can see, I'm not one for bullshit.'

Cate glanced at the clock on the dashboard. As long as the traffic was okay she'd be in plenty of time to get the girls from after-school club. She felt a surge of nerves and excitement. Please let me get it. As Emma would say, 'Pleeeeeease!' Behind the dark paint and the swirly carpets, the house was a dream. High ceilings, cornices, wood panelling, a claw-foot bath, and even a room with two walls' worth of William Morris wallpaper. Not to everyone's taste, but lovely if she could tone down all the dark, distracting colours around it.

She hoped she'd done enough to persuade the woman to give her the job; at least she'd asked Cate to do a proposal. And Cate had had a good giggle as she was shown round, the woman castigating her ex at every opportunity. Cate smiled. There were things she knew about this man that maybe only his GP did. Or the receptionist in the Genito-Urinary clinic. God, imagine hating your spouse so much that you could find pleasure in describing his wonky willy to a complete stranger.

She tried to imagine feeling that way about Dan. What if it hadn't been a receipt for Gel Botz, Men's Lge, in his trouser pocket, but one for a g-string in a size so small it could never have been for her? But it wasn't a g-string, and it was a good day, after so many dark ones, and if she played her cards right, she might get a proper commission on her own merits. She switched on the radio and tapped her fingers on the wheel to something blandly bright and boppy.

Stevie was right, the room they used for the after-school kids did smell a little of toes, and Cate promised the girls a TV tea for their ordeal with the unwashed socks. They charged up the hall of the house like a small herd of buffalo, churning up the rug and leaving piles of discarded shoes and bags.

'Messages!' shouted Emma and pressed the button on the answering machine. Cate bent over to get the knot out of Stevie's shoelace and listen to her continuing and convoluted tale about a major primary one infraction involving the fish tank and someone's Fruit Winder. She was dimly aware of the voices. One was Orla and one was Dan.

'Orla wants to know if you're going to bums 'n' tums tomorrow, and Dad's going to be laaate,' sang Emma from the door to the family room. 'Don't make tea for him!' She disappeared into the kitchen and went straight for the cupboards.

'Okay,' said Cate quietly and to no one in particular. 'I won't.'

She bent and scooped up the mail and carried it into the kitchen. Phone bill, wine club promotion, two businessy letters for Dan, and a postcard.

Cate dropped the other letters on the counter. She turned the card over slowly, and put a hand to her mouth. Jo, who had sat down at the counter to eat a bag of crisps, looked over at her.

'Mum?'

Cate tried to smile at her, the tears welling in her eyes.

'It's a postcard, sweetheart. Grampa must have sent it. They're always late.' At the mention of his name, Emma and Stevie came through from the family room.

Cate cleared her throat and sat up beside Jo at the counter. 'It's okay. It's good. Listen.' She started to read.

'A big hello from the Algarve. Can you spot Gran swimming on the front of the card?' Cate held it up and the girls gave a weak laugh at the large cartoon whale superimposed on the waves. 'Nice and hot. Today we took a pedalo out and tomorrow we're taking a bus trip to see the cliffs. A big hug to all our girls. And our designing woman! Much love, Grampa Ed and Gran.'

'I don't want Grampa to be dead.' Stevie's voice wavered.

Cate pulled her onto her knee. 'I know, sweetheart. I don't either.' She sat for a moment with her face buried in Stevie's hair, looking at the words.

'Will you keep it?' asked Jo. She reached across the counter and touched the edge of the card.

'Of course,' said Cate. 'Of course I'll keep it.'

She set Stevie down, gave them all a hug and shooed them back through to the cartoons, then she found a drawing-pin and carried the postcard upstairs. There wasn't much space on the corkboard, so she shunted the newspaper article to one side and stuck the card next to it, with the writing facing out. Cate pressed her fingers to the script and let the tears come afresh as she read it again. 'Thank you,' she whispered.

Marg sat back in her seat and took another slug of rapidly cooling coffee. Sod the French and their high-rise hostage crisis. The breaking story had well and truly chewed up the schedule and Chad had been shunted far down the running order, just two segments away from the Swede with the musical armpits who would end the show in – Marg checked the clock – six minutes.

Down in the studio, Susann brought her two-way with the Paris correspondent to a close. 'Thanks for that update. We'll obviously bring you any further developments as we get them. Now,' she swivelled seamlessly to face the other camera, 'it is less than two months until the leaders of the G8 nations meet for a fresh round of talks on how to tackle world poverty. We've been here before, of course. But poverty still claims thirty thousand children each day in the developing world. Chief foreign correspondent Richard Rutner travelled to Chad to visit one project trying to do what the world's most powerful nations seem unable to.'

The piece started with a long shot of the compound. The camp was just visible in the background, flagged with the ever-present coils of smoke. The camera focused slowly in on figures moving in the foreground: Leonora, Grainne and Ann, busy at the weighing station.

Rick's voiceover kicked in. 'These are the Sisters of Mercy. Three Irish nuns at work in a continent still blighted by immeasurable want.'

Marg watched intently, keeping one eye on the newswires and the screens around her. If there was any more breaking news in the next three minutes she would throw the biggest hissy fit Canary Wharf had ever seen.

Rick appeared on camera, walking through the camp. 'I could stop at any one of these shacks and find a story so terrible . . .'

Marg relaxed a little. It was looking good. She noticed some of her colleagues go quiet when the mother of the sick child came on. Rick had added a new voiceover. 'The day after we filmed this, the infant in Agathe's lap died also. Both her children gone.' Leonora was on after the Chadian Minister for the Interior. They had framed the shot so Rick was visible as he talked to her, her diminutive figure neatly emphasised against his six-foot-two bulk.

'Sister Leonora, if you had anything to say to the leaders of the world's most powerful nations, what would it be?'

Leonora gave a gentle smile. 'If I had anything to say,' she repeated, 'I'd say, come and spend a day here. Meet these people who have found themselves here. Walk with them for just a day. And you could find . . .' She turned away from Rick to look directly into the camera. 'You could find that the decisions on how to stop this might seem that little bit easier, might come that little bit quicker.'

The picture froze on her face and Susann turned back towards Camera 1. 'Sister Leonora MacMahon ending that report from Richard Rutner.'

Marg exhaled. The programme editor laid his hand on Marg's shoulder and when she turned, gave her the thumbs up. Marg grinned. I know. Bloody fantastic. Sister Leonora MacMahon, you're an absolute star.

'Why kick-boxing?' Roy turned and ran backwards in front of Marg.

'I don't know,' puffed Marg. 'Someone mentioned it the other day, and sometimes you just feel like kicking the living shit out of something, or someone. Don't you?' She'd been feeling like that ever since she got back from Edinburgh. Angry at herself for going to see her mum, angry at her mum for being everything Marg had known she would be. Angry for crying when she had promised herself so many years back that she would shed no more tears over a relationship not worth fixing.

Roy laughed. 'How about T'ai Chi?'

'Sod that,' said Marg. 'I need something full contact.'

'How about tae kwon do?' Roy signalled to her to stop.

'Maybe.' Marg put her hands on her hips, breathing heavily. 'Do you get to kick?'

'Yup,' said Roy. 'But not to maim.' He paused and tilted his head at the sound of muffled beeping. 'Either that's your phone or your arse is singing.'

Marg blew him a kiss and dug in her bumbag for her mobile. It was a text. 'Saw Chad. Grt wrk. Bck 1 pce?' It was too abbreviated for Cate and too verbose for Rick, whose texts rarely got more literary than 'Fck?' or 'Drnk?' And it was unlikely to be the director of World Aid. It must be Adam Milner. No one else outside the office knew she had been there. There was no name attached and she didn't immediately recognise the number, but she felt a strange little frisson of gratification that he had got in touch.

'Can it wait?' asked Roy. 'Because you've got two more circuits of the duck pond.'

Marg nodded and tucked the phone back in her bag, swivelling it round to her back. It could wait. After his non-committal farewell at their lunch, he could wait and wonder. She bent into a stretch. For a little while, at least.

30

'Is it the Abbeyhill Benevolent Fund guy again?' Marg walked briskly towards her desk and the blinking red light on her phone. It had been three days since the unanswered text and she was a little surprised he had lasted so long. Silence usually worked wonders, but generally a little quicker than this.

'No.' The admin girl looked down at her pad. 'It's a woman. World Aid.'

Marg slipped quickly into her chair and picked up the receiver. 'Hello?'

'Marg? Hi. Is this a good time?'

'Hi, yeah, it's fine.' It suddenly struck Marg that it was a little strange she hadn't heard from the charity before now. They'd given World Aid a good spin in the piece, the kind of publicity aid agencies crave, the kind that gets the phones ringing with donations. But the director didn't sound in a thankful or congratulatory mood.

'I just wanted to let you know we're having to pull Leonora and the others out. It's got too unstable.'

'What?' Marg felt her blood freeze. 'When?'

'Well, there have been some incursions into the camp in the last two days. Local militia. But last night, there was shooting, apparently. Two dead.'

Marg had a sudden terrible image of a frightened boy in flip-flops and a faded green T-shirt. 'Do you know who was killed?'

'No.' The woman sighed. 'I don't know. I think it was a man and a child, but I don't know.'

'Leonora. The others. They're okay?'

'As much as they can be,' said the woman. 'They'll be pulled out tomorrow. We've got a team going up from Abeche to get them.' She gave a grim laugh. 'As you can imagine, they're not that keen to be withdrawn.'

'So what happens to the camp?' Marg knew it was a stupid question, one she wouldn't normally ask. Nothing would happen. The nuns would leave and be forced to stay away until it was deemed safe enough for them to return. The rest could take their chance with the marauders and with Mother Nature.

'We'll go back in as soon as it's safe,' said the director patiently. 'It's frustrating.'

'There was a boy,' Marg said. 'He was kind of helping them out. He was about eleven.'

She heard the woman sigh down the line. 'I don't know what to tell you. There's maybe five, six thousand people there.'

'But sometimes you can evacuate local staff, too, can't you?'

'It's just the nuns, Marg,' said the woman. Her voice softened. 'But if I hear anything else, I'll let you know.' She paused. 'It was a nice piece you did. Thanks.'

'You're welcome,' said Marg quietly. She put the phone down. Rick was at the far side of the news room, perched on the arts correspondent's desk. Marg raised her hand and caught his eye and he stood, a little reluctantly, she noticed, and wandered over.

'What's up?'

'I've just had World Aid on,' said Marg. 'They're moving the nuns out. The Janjaweed were at the camp. Two people were shot last night. An adult and a child.'

'Shit.' Rick sat down on the edge of the desk. 'Grainne and the others all right?'

Marg nodded. 'The nuns are fine, but not everyone else.' Her eyes suddenly felt hot and stinging.

Rick looked astounded. He bent forward. 'Are you crying?'

'No, I'm not crying.' Marg dashed her hand across her cheeks. Christ, twice in one week. What the hell was wrong with her? Maybe Rick was right and she was menopausal. 'I'm just frustrated,' she said. 'They're just in such a bloody awful situation and, hey, guess what? It gets worse. And now there's no one to help out. Not even a four-foot-eleven Irish nun, for fuck's sake.'

'What's up with you?' Rick put his hand on her arm and lowered his voice. She knew he had good reason to ask. They'd been in worse places, seen worse suffering and she'd never reacted like this.

'Remember the boy?' Marg glanced up at him.

'What boy?' He looked puzzled.

'Never mind.' She shook her head and Rick patted her arm ineffectually and stood up.

'Look, I'm going to go to lunch,' he said.

'I'm not hungry,' said Marg.

He looked a little sheepish. 'No. I'm going to lunch.'

Marg looked up. The arts correspondent was shrugging on her jacket and trying not to look in Marg's direction.

'Fine,' snapped Marg. 'Great. Go.'

'It'll be okay, babe. They'll be back in situ soon.' He shrugged. 'It is bloody awful. But, hey . . .'

She watched him walk across the room. But, hey? Rick needs his lunch, and a post-prandial shag.

She sat for a moment until the lift doors had closed, then she bent down and dug in her bag for her mobile. She needed to speak to someone who might have something more profound to say than 'but, hey'. She found the text message and pressed reply, then moved her fingers quickly over the keys. 'Back 1pce. Tuf trip, tho. Situ now worse.' By the time she got back from the coffee machine with her own lunch – a cereal bar and another cup of bitter coffee – the phone face was illuminated with an incoming text message. Read Now? She pressed the button. 'Talk it thru? Café Fortis 7 p.m.?' This time, he'd signed it: 'Adm.'

She hesitated only very briefly then keyed in the two-letter reply. 'OK.'

Maybe it was the three vodkas she'd had with Susann in Popinjays, or maybe it was noticing the lingering pat Rick gave the arts correspondent when they got back from lunch, but Adam looked rather agreeable when he stood up from the table in his dark suit and open-necked white shirt. She let her lips touch his cheek this time in greeting and felt his grip on her upper arm as he responded in kind.

'Sorry I'm late.' She tried to sound breathless with purpose rather than hoarse from the pub.

He smiled and settled his napkin back on his knee as they sat down. 'So. Tough trip?'

'Mm. This ours?' She reached for the bottle of wine at the table's edge without waiting for him to answer, and poured herself a large glass.

'That bad, huh?' His smiled broadened.

She took a long deep slug. 'Not so much while we were there, but I just got word today that the nuns are being pulled out because there's been some trouble in the camp. Shooting.'

He raised an eyebrow. 'From within the camp?'

'No. Militia. Janjaweed.'

He shook his head. 'Bastards.'

'Exactly,' said Marg. 'Bastards.'

'Was anyone . . . ?'

'Two dead,' said Marg. She took another drink and then bent forward. 'I know it's not huge, in the grand scheme of things. But you know, just after we've been out. And it's such a small operation they're running . . .'

She fiddled with her salad fork, then remembered Adam's comments at their previous meeting and dropped her hands into her lap. 'We met this boy there,' she said. 'He was maybe eleven. Just a good kid, holding it together in a fucking awful situation. He was looking after his sister and brother.'

'Little surrogate dad,' said Adam.

'Yeah. Pretty much. He wanted to be a doctor.'

Adam put down his menu. 'You know, when I was in Habila, there was a girl. Same kind of thing, a bit older, though. She had four siblings who relied on her. Bright girl. Really bright. She wanted to be a teacher, but you just think, no way, love, you'll be lucky to see forty with your health intact. Anyway, I kept in touch with the project and heard, four years ago, she sat her exams. She's probably teaching now.'

Marg smiled. 'That's great. I needed to hear that. This boy, Amodu, he couldn't get the hang of Marg. I tried to spell it for him but he ended up calling me Mark. Ggg.'

There must have been something about her face that made him stretch across and put his hand over hers.

'He'll be doing okay. He's obviously a resourceful lad.'

'Has to be,' said Marg. She took another deep draught of wine and they sat in silence for a few moments. 'I don't know why it's bugging me so much. This one.' She shrugged. 'Anyway, I should ask, how are your boys?'

'Fine.' He ran his hands through his hair, and for a second she thought about reaching across and patting down the tuft he had created. 'Well, Rory's being a real handful at the moment. He might be four but we're still getting the terrible twos from him. He's been potty-trained for a good eighteen

months now, but every couple of weeks we get the equiva-
lent of a dirty protest.'

'Nice.' Marg wondered why she had noticed that he said
'we'.

Adam laughed. 'You probably don't want this kind of
detail, do you?'

'Generally not, but after today, it's kind of nice to hear
something utterly inane.' She held up a hand. 'Not too
many specifics, though. You can leave out consistency and
appearance. Oh, and anything cute they said as well. It
might sound astoundingly witty to you, but for the rest of
us it's not big and it's not clever. Save it for the granny
who knits their sweaters.'

He burst out laughing and bent forward to top up her
glass. She grinned back at him and felt the tension that had
been swamping her start to ease. Okay, he was two years
younger. Okay, his hair was standing on end. Okay, she
should know better. But, hey.

'I'd really prefer if we got a cab.' Marg peered out from
under the restaurant canopy. It wasn't raining but the air
was damp and misty enough to wreak crinkling havoc on
her hair.

'Come on.' He reached for her hand and pulled her out
onto the pavement and she felt the vaguest flash of disap-
pointment when he let it go as they started to walk.

'Is this absolutely necessary?'

'It's nice to get some fresh air, and I want to show you
something. It's not far.'

The streets were Friday night busy and it occurred to
Marg that they looked just like any of the other couples
walking briskly to or from party, dinner, pub. Adam had
headed east and after about half a mile he stopped in
front of a new apartment block, not quite finished, but

with the sale sign prominently displayed. Marg looked up at the structure. It was a bold design, with a series of turret-like structures on the front that mimicked the outline of the older Victorian buildings around it.

'You buying here?' she asked.

He shook his head. 'What do you think?'

'It's okay. A bit . . . tubular bells.' She took a step back. 'Or maybe a desk-tidy. But stylish. Why?'

'Because I designed it.'

'Oh,' said Marg. 'In that case it's a stunning example of cutting-edge architecture.'

'I knew you'd be honest.' He laughed and stretched his hand towards her face. 'And you've got a curl.'

'The technical term is frizz.' She reached up to tuck it behind her ear, uncharacteristically self-conscious.

'It looks good.' His hand traced briefly down her cheek as he took it away. He glanced towards the road. A taxi had stopped at the lights. 'Anyway,' he said, 'we can get your cab now. I just wanted to have a look at this at night. And see what you thought. It's a bit more out there than anything else I've done.'

They didn't talk much on the way home. Marg sat and watched the fragranced tree on the rear-view mirror swinging with each bump and turn, wondering what she would say when the journey came to an end. The taxi stopped outside her block and Adam got out, but not before she heard him ask the driver to wait.

Marg took a breath. Such a strange day. Too much emotion, too much drink. She spoke quickly, before she thought better of it.

'Do you want to come up?'

He took a step towards her. 'Yes. But I can't. I've got to pick the boys up first thing.'

She looked at him. 'You could . . . go from here.'

He bent forward unexpectedly and kissed her. His lips were warm. He tasted of espresso.

'I can't,' he said, pulling just away from her mouth. 'But I'd like to see you. Again.'

'Okay.'

'Okay.' He smiled and walked backwards towards the cab. She turned for the door and took the stairs. In the hallway of the apartment she laid her head against the wall, feeling the cold of the plaster through her frizzing hair.

She hadn't put the lights on and she could just make out her reflection in the mirror above the desk.

Quite a week. You cried over your mum and an eleven-year-old you'd known for three days. Rick's shagging the arts correspondent and you've initiated a date with the school debating champ who's two years younger than you, but not so desperate, it seems, that he wants to spend the night. Way to go, Marg. She gave a tipsy laugh and reached for the phone. She knew it was late, but this Cate had to hear.

'Shit!' Cate's foot connected with the pedal on Dan's bike, propped in the dark against the hall cupboard. Ow, ow, ow, ow, ow. She hobbled into the family room and reached the phone just as the answering machine clicked on. 'Hello?'

It was Marg. 'Hey, it's me. Did I wake you?'

'Not really,' said Cate. 'I'd just gone to bed. Did you get my message?'

'No.' Marg sounded confused. 'I phoned you.'

'Yeah, but I left you a message,' said Cate. 'I thought that's why you were phoning.'

'What was it about?'

'I got the commission.' Cate sat down on the sofa and rubbed her foot. 'I got the job. I just heard this evening.'

'Fantastic. Wow. Cate, that's great.'

Cate grinned. 'I know. It's this woman who's moving up

from Bath. She's an absolute hoot. She's got a big fat divorce settlement . . .'

'A big fat what?'

'Divorce settlement,' repeated Cate. 'Are you pissed?'

'A little.'

Cate laughed. 'So, if you haven't played my message yet, why are you phoning?' She peered at the wall clock. 'At quarter to midnight.'

'I've just been on a date,' said Marg. 'At least I think it was a date.'

'Adam!' Cate lowered her voice suddenly. 'Is he still there?'

'No. He didn't want to come up. Stay the night.' She sounded suddenly deflated.

'That can be good,' said Cate quickly, trying to wonder why it might.

'How can that be good?'

'He's not just after sex.' Cate curled her legs up under her.

'Well, maybe I was.' There was a short giggle. 'I mean, Rick's shagging the arts correspondent.'

'Is he? Do you mind?' She couldn't tell from Marg's voice if she did.

'Not really. It's par for the course. It was the personal finance correspondent last year, and he'll probably move on to the home news editor next.'

'These are all women, right?'

Marg laughed. 'Yeah, they're all women.'

Cate giggled. 'You know, you're my very own soap opera. Are you going to see him again? Adam?'

'I think so.' Marg paused. 'I need to ask you, though, is this really creepy? I quite like him. But is it creepy?'

'Why would it be creepy? He's a lovely guy. He's single. You're single.'

'I don't know. I keep thinking of the school thing.'

'Well, you need to get over that,' said Cate. 'You're not seventeen any more.'

'If I was, he would be fifteen. Maybe even fourteen. Fucking hell.'

'Stop it!' Cate laughed. 'He's a man. All grown up.'

'That's really exciting about the commission,' said Marg.

'Yeah. I've been pinching myself since she phoned.'

'Is Dan pleased?'

'Kind of,' said Cate. 'He's happy I'll be getting paid, but not so happy that we have to fork out for it first.'

'I don't see what his problem is,' said Marg. 'It's not exactly charity work you're doing.'

'I know.' Cate sighed. 'It's just a bit new for him, I suppose.'

'Well tell him to get used to it,' said Marg. 'And to get grateful.'

Cate gave a little snort.

'Anyway,' said Marg. 'How are the rest of you? How's your mum?'

'Mum's okay. She's back up next week and we're going to talk about what she wants to do.'

'And how are you coping?' asked Marg.

'I'm fine,' said Cate. 'Really. I miss him. The girls, too. I keep thinking we'll see him like we usually do at weekends.'

'I bet you do,' said Marg.

They both fell quiet. 'Anyway,' said Cate, after a moment. 'I should go. The twins have got a netball match early tomorrow, and we need to get ready for the duck race on Sunday.'

'Duck race?'

'It's a big fundraising thing the hospital does. You race these rubber ducks down the Water of Leith. The kids love it. Dan hates it. But we all go.' She paused and lowered her voice again. 'And I want to try and get a look at this woman from the bike group who's been calling him.'

'Really? What woman?'

'Well, she phoned him once. While I was in London.'

Marg gave a little snort. 'One phone call does not constitute infidelity – and I thought you said he had problems in that department anyway?'

'Marg!' Cate held the phone closer to her ear, even though she knew there was no way Dan would have heard.

'Well, doesn't he?'

'You are so pissed,' said Cate. 'Otherwise you'd realise how rude you're being.'

'Sorry,' slurred Marg. She sniggered. 'Or maybe this'll be the one he bought the pants for. Big lass. Broad in the beam.'

'You think you're very funny, don't you?'

'Know so,' said Marg. 'But don't fret about it, hon. It'll be some sad spinster matron with well-developed calves who's got a crush on him.'

'Old, broad arse and well-developed calves. I'm sticking to that picture,' said Cate. 'Anyway, I need to go.'

'I'm really pleased about the commission,' said Marg. 'You know the next step is to get a company set up, and business cards, and . . .'

'You know the next step is to go to bed,' said Cate. 'Goodnight.'

'You too. Speak soon?'

'Speak soon.'

Cate made her way back to the bedroom, avoiding the bike and the creaking fifth stair. Dan had oiled the hamster wheel but she could tell from the faint trundling from the twins' bedroom that Hamish was on it. She poked her head round the door. Emma was curled towards the wall with the duvet pulled almost to the top of her head. Jo was on her back, one arm outstretched over the edge of the bed with the hand slightly curled. Cate moved closer and looked down at her in the half-light from the hall lamp. There was nothing more beautiful on earth than your sleeping child. Even a cynical eleven-year-old whose forehead was creased and folded into a vaguely worried frown.

'My lovely girl,' whispered Cate, hoping it might filter through to whatever dreams Jo was having. She pulled the door almost shut behind her and tiptoed back into the master bedroom.

'Who was that?' Dan sounded groggy.

'Marg.' She slipped under the duvet and curled towards him, not quite touching him. His eyes were shut.

'She okay? Why was she phoning at this time of night?'

'She was excited. She wanted to tell me something.'

He opened his eyes sleepily. 'Man?'

Cate nodded.

He gave what sounded like a snort. 'Young love, eh?' He rolled onto his back and shut his eyes. 'Can we sleep now?'

'Mm,' murmured Cate. She stayed where she was, watching his profile. Young love, eh? Remember that.

31

'You look lovely.' Cate stood back and studied the ensemble Stevie had picked out herself for duck race day. 'Only, I might rethink the footwear.'

Stevie looked down at the thick slipper socks she was wearing below her red plaid skirt and pink stripy top. 'But they've got ducks on them,' she said, puzzled. 'That's why I choosed them.'

'Chose them,' said Cate. 'And they're fab, poppet, but they're a bit too thick to fit in your shoes.'

'But I'm going to wear my wellies.'

'Oh you are, are you?' Cate kept her smile in check. 'Well, you'll look very Vivienne Westwood.'

'What's that?' asked Stevie.

'Stylish and non-conformist. And non-conformist means you dress the way you want. Now go and brush teeth, toots, and find your hairbrush. The last time I saw it, it was on the big sofa in the living room. Next to Barty Bear.'

'It's his brush now,' said Stevie. 'I'll need to borrow it.'

'Ask nicely. I'm sure he'll hand it over.'

She went into the hall and shouted up the stairs to the twins who were giving much more time and consideration to their outfits than their sister.

Dan's voice echoed back from the bedroom. 'Caate, have you seen my check shirt?'

'DAMP!' she yelled back.

'Pale blue sweater?'

'DIRTY!'

There was a pause.

'GEL BOTZ ARE CLEAN!' she shouted.

'THANKS!'

'What are jelbots?' Emma came down the stairs, followed by Jo. They both had jeans on, but different tops, and Emma had the spangliest silver eyelids outside of Las Vegas. Cate met her on the bottom step and tilted her head up. 'You look lovely, puss, but way too much make-up here. You'll need to wipe some of that off.'

'Muuum.'

'No, honey, seriously. Less is more. Go wipe. Not all of it, but at least a bit.'

'I told you,' said Jo, as Emma passed her to head for the bathroom. 'You look like a Bratz doll.'

'Yeah and you look like a Cabbage Patch Kid! Bumhead!'

'Bumhead!' said Cate. 'What's with bumhead?'

'Actually,' Dan appeared at the top of the stairs, buttoning a light-green cord shirt and tucking it into his chinos, 'no one looks like a bumhead. You all look rather nice.'

Stevie stopped mid-brush and gave him a twirl.

'Now Mummy,' said Dan, and Cate pirouetted in front of him in her tiered silk skirt and wrap top. The beaded choker she had guided him to for her last birthday jangled at her neck as she turned. He whistled loudly and she grinned up at him.

'Shall we tell Mummy?' he said, walking down slowly, still smiling.

'Tell Mummy what?' Cate looked at him.

Jo sniggered. 'You skirt's waaay up at the back. You've tucked it into your pants.'

By the time they had found a parking space and walked as quickly as Stevie's wellies would allow to the Botanic Garden, the race was about to get under way. There was just time to buy five small, numbered plastic ducks and hand them to the officials who were piling them into the river across Inverleith Terrace. They would be fished out again and the winner proclaimed down at Quilts Wynd, before the water widened as it rushed towards the sea. Some ducks escaped every year, of course, and it was Jo who had decided the previous year that it must be rather nice for the men on the ships that plied the Forth to spot a small yellow bath toy or two bobbing past on an unknown journey. Cate had offered to drive home, so Dan headed off to the drinks end of the marquee to find a beer for himself and something suitably soft for her. Most of the guests were up that end and Cate had always suspected that duck race day was really just an excuse for a giant medics' piss-up. She saw Dan launch into conversation with a snowy-haired man. Her mineral water would obviously be a while, so she took the girls, who were hanging awkwardly around her, through to the children's tent where they descended on the buffet with ill-disguised glee.

'I'll be back in ten minutes,' she said. 'Try to eat some of the fruit, not just rubbish, and keep an eye on Stevie. No wandering out of here. Okay?'

They nodded, piling their plastic plates high with hot-dogs and curly chips. At the far end, beside a rather sad tray of oranges and bruised grapes, was a giant tower of marshmallows and a tray of chocolate finger biscuits. The only drinks available seemed to be fizzy and primary-coloured. Great, thought Cate. Sore tummies all round for the journey home. She walked back through to the main tent. It was busier now and she couldn't immediately spot Dan.

She chatted to one of the receptionists from his depart-ment and a colleague of his whose name she could never remember, and had almost reached the bar when she felt the hand on her shoulder.

'Cate.'

She turned and her heart sank. 'Guy.'

He bent and kissed her on the cheek, slipping one hand round her waist. She could feel herself recoil instinctively at his touch. His hand was always just a fraction too mobile, as if he were trying to feel through the fabric.

'And how is the lovely Cate?'

'I'm okay.' She took a little step back and folded her arms loosely across her chest.

'Dan told me about your uncle.' Guy arranged his features into something approximating sympathy.

'My stepdad, Ed,' said Cate. 'And . . . thank you. It's been a really big shock.'

'Mmm,' said Guy. His eyes swept the room, as if he were looking for better company. He can't have spotted any because he looked back at her. 'And what else is going on with you? Where are your girls?'

'Through in the kids' tent,' said Cate. 'And actually, things are changing a bit for me. I'm doing some design work now. Just starting up really. Dan might have said.'

He clearly hadn't. 'Grrreat,' said Guy. He sounded like the tiger from the cereal ad. His eyes swung round the room again.

'Is your wife here?' asked Cate brightly.

He gave her a lazy smile. 'She finds all this awfully dull.'

Or maybe, thought Cate, she can't stand to watch you make a complete arse of yourself over some flint-eyed bimbo for the thousandth time in your marriage, you feckless prick.

'Shame,' she said. 'Anyway, have you seen Dan?'

He shook his head. 'Not yet.'

'Well, if you do, can you tell him that I've popped into

the glasshouse for a bit. Just for a look around.' She suddenly
needed to get away.

'Mm.' Guy bent in for another embrace, but she gave
him a quick pat on the back instead, swerved neatly round
him and out of the tent, checking the back of her skirt
surreptitiously as she went in case she was flashing again.
The girls were fine, sitting in a circle with the other offspring
watching some kind of juggling show. She waved to them,
motioned to her watch, and held up ten fingers. They smiled
and nodded. Stevie's mouth looked suspiciously red.

In the tropical house she sat down on one of the benches
and took a deep breath of the hot, damp air. She'd always
loved it in here, especially as a child, lying flat on the pond
edge with Tom to watch the golden fish come up and round
their mouths into perfect, astonished 'O's.

The stag-horn ferns on the far side were bent into a wide,
low curve, unmoved by any wind. Something like that would
look great in the new lounge of the Peebles house, something prehistoric, a profusion of vivid green to counter all
the muted tones. Her head was buzzing with ideas. Tonight,
when the kids were down, she'd get some work done. She'd
have to. She was meeting the woman again next week and
she still hadn't got to the fabric shop to pick up the sample
books she'd ordered. It was a good kind of panic she was
feeling, though. Driven by excitement, rather than fear.

'What are you doing hiding away in here?' Dan held the
heavy metal and glass door open and Cate felt a blast of
cool air from outside. He held out a bottle of mineral water.
'I got your drink.' He seemed a little annoyed.

'Daydreaming.' She stood up as he came in. 'Don't you
love the heat in here?' He stared into the pond. She moved
beside him. 'Remember in Queensland? The rainforest?' It
had been their honeymoon, lying warm and damp next to

each other. Watching lizards skitter across the wall. Touching all the time.

'Have you abandoned the girls?' he said.

She should have said, 'No, have you?' But she didn't. 'They're watching the show.'

He turned and held the door open for her and they stepped out of the warmth.

'I saw Guy,' said Cate, as they walked towards the tents. 'He told me you were in here.'

She linked her arm in his. 'Are the rest of the bike group here? It would be nice to meet them.' Even though she knew it was ridiculous, she had found herself scanning the marquee for someone whose face she didn't know, someone who might be looking at her with more than polite and passing interest.

He attempted a shrug. 'Don't know.'

'How about Gill?' She gave him a dig in the ribs. 'The mystery Gill. She here?' She laughed and made it sound carefree.

'I said I don't know.' He spoke sharply without turning to look at her.

'Okay. You don't need to snap. I'm just having a laugh. What's up with you?'

He loosened his arm from hers and cracked his knuckles loudly, something he only did when he was stressed. 'It's all this centralisation stuff. They're talking now about shifting the whole damn microbiology lab to the Western as well.'

'They're talking about it on duck race day?' said Cate.

'Yeah,' he said tersely, 'on duck race day.'

They reached the marquees. 'I'll get the girls,' said Cate. 'And we'll come and find you.'

Dan paused. 'Right now?'

'Is that a problem?' Cate stopped in front of the children's tent and turned to face him. He gave her a pained look. 'It's just . . . There's a couple of people I need to speak to about this. I'm sorry, love, do you mind? Give me half an hour. I just wanted to bring you your drink.'

'You want me to stay in the children's tent?' said Cate.

'No. Yes. No. Whatever.' He cracked his knuckles again.

'Fine,' said Cate coldly. 'We'll leave you be. I'll go get my face painted. Maybe they do bats here as well.'

It was almost an hour before she saw him again. The girls were well ensconced in the kids' corner and she sat and chatted with some of the other watching mums, enjoying the inconsequential banter about nits, and the waiting list for swimming lessons, and finding a party outfit for an eleven-year-old that didn't make them look like Courtney Love. Stevie came and climbed onto Cate's knee. She smelled of something falsely fruity and felt hot.

At 2 p.m., they were told to gather in the main tent for the announcement of the race winner. Cate led the girls over to Dan. He was in a group of men and women, deep in conversation, but he broke off to introduce them. 'My wife, Cate, and these are my girls, Emma, Jo, Stevie.' He took Stevie's hand and beamed. The good dad.

Cate smiled at them all. None of the women looked fit enough to be cycling regularly. She checked their calves just in case.

Up on the stage, the hospital manager had launched into his prizewinning preamble, the same tired anecdotes as last year. Cate stifled a yawn. There was a shriek from the stage microphone as he bent bent closer to name the winning duck.

Cate saw Stevie tug at Dan's hand. 'My tummy's sore,' she said plaintively. Dan gave her a quick pat on the head and turned back to the stage.

'And the winner is . . .'

Stevie looked across at Cate. 'Mummy!'

'Number 234!'

Cate realised what was about to come. In a sea of ducks and doctors, and amid polite applause, she reacted first, jumping forward and holding out her cupped hands instinctively as a five-year-old high on cherryade and pink marshmallows vomited colourfully and copiously into them.

'You've got to see the funny side.' Cate carried her balled-up skirt and top out of the en suite and held out her hand for Dan's shirt.

'Would that be the smell in the car on the way home, or having to apologise to the chief registrar?'

'He only got a little bit on his shoes, and anyway, who wears patent slip-ons to a duck race?' said Cate.

'Is that a rhetorical question?'

Cate sighed. 'Dan, I know you don't particularly enjoy these things, but why are you so grumpy? It's not Stevie's fault she was sick. The only things available for her to eat were utter junk. At a medics' day out. She had three glasses of cherryade, for God's sake.'

He stood up from the end of the bed. 'I know. I know. Maybe next year we should just give it a miss.'

She watched him rummage aimlessly in the wardrobe. The girls were downstairs engrossed in a DVD. It probably wasn't the best time, but when was she going to get the chance? And if he was already a little put out by the day's events, what she was about to say might not be such a shock to the system. She laid the sour-smelling bundle of clothes on the dresser top and took a breath.

'Dan.'

'Mm.'

'Can we talk?'

'About what?' He didn't even try to disguise his sigh, a slow, pained exhalation. He kept his back to her.

'Us.' She sat on the end of the bed and knitted her fingers together, not sure where or how to start. 'You know. The way we've not been able . . .'

He twisted his head to look at her, frowning.

'The way we've not been able to sleep together . . . have sex.'

She saw his face change, but ploughed on, knowing she had to keep going now. 'It's just, we haven't been together for weeks and weeks now, ages. And the last time we did, well, the last three times, well, it didn't really work . . . and I just thought that . . .'

'What?' He hadn't moved but his voice had grown cold. 'You just thought what?'

God, this was harder than she'd expected. 'I just thought you . . .'

He interrupted her sharply. 'You just thought I haven't been . . . servicing you properly?'

'Servicing? Dan!' Cate felt her face redden with exasperation. She pressed her hands on the covers to steady herself. 'That's not what I meant. It's just, it's obviously a problem, I mean an issue. And I had a look on the net, at a couple of sites and there's loads we can do. At the very least we need to talk about it. Shouldn't we?'

'You looked on the web.' He dropped the T-shirt onto the bed behind her and ran his hands through his hair, leaving them there, clenched and pressed to his scalp. His eyes were shut. 'Christ,' he said finally. 'Jesus Christ.'

Cate stood up. 'What? Dan. Talk to me. What? Is it me?' She felt the faint rise of panic in her chest.

He was shaking his head now, but she didn't find it remotely reassuring. 'I can't believe you're doing this. Cate, I'm up to my eyes in it at work with all this crap that's going on. Up to my eyes, and you're harping on about this, you're searching the web for problems we can have.'

She took a sharp breath. 'Dan, it is a problem. We can't just ignore it.'

'I get it,' he said, bluntly, reaching to pick up the T-shirt he had just discarded. 'Your husband's a fucking dud in bed. Fine. Point taken.'

'Dan!'

'Well that's what you're saying, isn't it?' He looked accusingly at her.

'No, Dan. That's not what I'm saying. I'm trying to have a grown-up conversation about this. Trying to find out what's wrong.' She felt her exasperation give way to anger. 'God, Dan. What's going on with you? I feel like I'm dancing on eggshells with you all the time. You're just so . . . so . . . blinking semi-detached.'

He gave a hollow laugh. 'Is that a designing analogy, is it? Blinking semi-detached?'

'No,' she said. 'It's an observation from your wife.'

'And you're good at that, aren't you?'

'At what?'

'Observing.'

'What does that mean?'

He shook his head. 'Questions. Watching. Always watching. Where are you? What are you doing? Where are you going? Why can't we go away? Who was that?' He was spitting the words out. 'I'm really sorry about Ed, Cate, really sorry. But you need to stop with the . . . with the . . . you need to . . .'

'What?' She felt the panic grow within her. This was not how it was meant to have gone. 'Dan?'

He stared at her then reached back into the wardrobe and grabbed his tracksuit bottoms. 'I need to get out,' he said flatly. 'I'm going for a ride.'

. She took a step towards him. 'Dan, you can't. You've had too much to drink.'

'If that's an observation from my wife . . .' He paused and looked at her coldly. '. . . then why do you sound like my bloody mother?'

She wasn't sure how long she stood there next to the pile of vomit-spattered clothes, but she heard the familiar thuds and dunts of the bike being pulled from the understairs cupboard and then the sound of the door. She went into the bathroom and bent over the sink, hardly aware of the chill of ceramic against her hands. She felt sick. And she hadn't touched cherryade or marshmallows all day.

Bzzhhzzzhzh.

Oh bugger off, whoever you are. Marg laid her head back against the sofa and ignored the buzzer. It was probably for the young couple in the next flat over. They had way too many friends, some of whom hadn't mastered basic intercom usage. She turned up the volume on the TV.

'If I tilt it this way, you can see the princess cut of this beautiful ring to its best effect,' said the man with the lazy eye and the mahogany tan.

Bzhhzzhhzhzhzzhhzh.

Marg glanced at her watch. Seven-thirty on a Sunday evening. It wouldn't be a courier, and she was pretty sure it wouldn't be Rick. He'd be crawling into a bed somewhere else in the city. She stood and walked to the door. Whoever it was, she'd send them packing. She needed to be asleep in just over an hour.

'Uh huh.'

'Marg? It's Adam.'

Her stomach gave a sudden and unexpected lurch. 'Oh.'

'Hi.' There was an expectant, crackling silence. 'Can I come up?'

She hesitated. Christ. Fuck.

'Ehm, yeah. Sure. Come on in. Top floor. Second on the right.'

She pressed the button and then sprinted for the bedroom. FUUUUCK! No time to straighten hair. Just enough for a slick of smoothing serum and a swipe of lip gloss. Bare feet rather than bedsocks. She pulled off her cashmere knee-highs. God, he'd be halfway up by now. In the sitting room, she bundled the catalogues under the coffee table, and switched the channel from QVC to CNN just as she heard the first knock. She took a deep breath, walked briskly into the hall, dimmed the hall light and opened the door.

'Hi.' His breathing was quickened, as if he had taken the stairs two at a time. He wasn't smiling.

She stood holding the edge of the door like some kind of support, or barrier. She wasn't sure which.

'Hi,' she said. 'Again.'

He put one arm on the doorjamb. She looked at him expectantly.

'The other night.' He stopped as if he was figuring out what to say. 'The other night. I wanted to stay.' His eyes drifted for an almost imperceptible second and she glanced down. Fuck. Bra. No bra. Fuck.

She folded one arm across her as casually as she could. 'Your kids?'

'I've just dropped them off at their mum's. They've got the dentist. First thing tomorrow.'

'Oh.' She tried to smile but her lips stuck to her teeth. 'Do . . . did you want to go out?'

He shook his head and took a step towards her.

'Do you want a drink?' She glanced unnecessarily at her watch. 'It'll have to be a quick one because I've got my three a.m. start. But we ca . . .'

'No.' He was still moving. 'I don't want a drink.'

'Do you . . . ?' He bent in suddenly and kissed her, pressing her back against the wall. She let go of the door and it swung slowly shut. She took a breath against his mouth, short and sharp. He pulled back and stared at her again. His eyes seemed darker. If it was to stop it would be now. A gentle push, a weak joke, head for the kitchen, mix a drink. Keep talking. Above all, keep talking.

She looked up at him, said nothing and raised her face to his.

32

'Milk?' Adam stood blinking in the middle of the kitchen, still post-coital sleepy.

'Fridge.' Marg waved her hand towards the sink. 'Door next to the dishwasher.'

He looked around blankly 'Dishwasher?'

She laughed. 'One down from the sink.'

He bent and retrieved the carton and poured a quick glug into the mug of coffee steaming on the countertop. 'Sure you don't want one?'

She shook her head. 'I get something in the office.'

'I'd need a drip of it if I had to get up at this hour every day.'

She watched him raise the mug to his lips. His shirt was wrongly buttoned, done in haste and in the dark after the alarm had shrieked reproachfully at them just before 3.15 a.m. He looked younger without his jacket, without the attitude and the darkened eyes of last night.

She still wasn't quite sure what to make of it, what to make of him. When she had briefly imagined sex with him, in the way that she always did when she met somebody new, somebody possible, she had envisaged something much less assured, much less absorbing. But he had a good body. Slimmer than she usually went for, but sinewy and in pretty good shape. And practically hairless compared to Rick.

She realised he was watching her. Maybe he was thinking

the same way about her. Stouter than I go for, but in pretty good nick. Hairier, though, than the ex. She smiled and he grinned back.

'What?' He put his coffee down.

'Nothing.'

The buzzer sounded. 'Driver,' said Marg, and Adam turned to reach for his jacket. He stopped halfway down the hall to look at the pencil drawing hanging beside the Peter Howson.

'Is that . . . ?'

'Me. Yes. Cate did it at school.'

He looked closer at the smiling girl then shook his head. 'Nope, can't say I remember you.'

'How could you not?' Marg gave him a shove to move him on. 'I was a fifth-year goddess.'

'And modest with it,' he said.

She ushered him through the door first, then stopped suddenly.

'Go ahead and I'll catch up. I've just got to grab something.' She ran back to the kitchen and switched on the light. Kettle. Why did he have to use the damn kettle? She pulled the plug from the wall and draped the flex over the edge of the counter, where she could see it when she turned to check again at the door. Off. Absolutely off. Fridge door shut. A quick press to check. Another for luck. She flicked the light switch, and felt its upright position with her fingers as she left the room. A quick check of the loo: toilet seat down, floor clean. She ran back to the front door.

The lift had come and he was holding the doors apart for her. She stepped in beside him and pressed the button for the lobby. The doors pinged shut.

He turned to face her and leant back against the lift wall, smiling as they sank slowly towards the street.

'There's a name for that, you know,' he said finally.

'Name for what?'

'Checking everything. Twice. And rearranging your cutlery so it's straight.'

'I wasn't checking anything.' She dug in her bag, trying to look too busy to care.

He watched her, still smiling. 'You don't talk to your paper-clips, do you? I used to work with a woman who talked to her paper-clips. She couldn't pick one up without wondering how the one next to it might be feeling. Would they mind? Were they related? You see, her theory was that you might use paper-clips one at a time, in fact you could argue they were designed to be used that way, but they were also designed to be linked. She couldn't quite get over that.'

Marg burst out laughing, despite the flash of irritation at his observation. 'I'm not that bad.'

'It's not necessarily bad,' he said. 'She had quite a little soap opera going on in her desk drawer. The secret life of paper-clips. She had a touch of Obsessive Compulsive Disorder too.'

'I don't have OCD,' said Marg. 'I'm just careful. And anyway, did your mother never tell you it's incredibly rude to point out what you imagine are other people's faults?'

'It's not a fault,' he said. 'It's a foible. Everyone has them. I quite like your foibles.'

'That's plural, is it?' She raised her eyebrows.

'Oh yeah.'

The lift bounced gently onto the ground floor and the doors swished apart. The lobby was half dark and Adam stopped her before she reached the exit and the waiting cab. It was a long kiss.

'So,' Marg looked up at him, 'where do we go from here?'

He held open the door for her. 'Canary Wharf . . . then, who knows?'

'I can't have you turning up at the door every night,' she said. 'If that's one of your foibles.'

'You could turn up at mine.'

'I don't know where you live.'

'Well, you'll need to come and see, won't you?'

Marg signalled to the cab driver that she would just be a moment. 'Well, you'll need to invite me.'

'Consider yourself invited.' He raised his hand and started to walk backwards. 'I'll call.'

'Okay.' She moved to step into the car then paused. 'How are you going to get home?'

'I'm going to hike it for a bit.' He smiled and kept his eyes on her. 'It looks,' he said, without glancing at the sky, 'like it's going to be a pretty decent day.'

'Oh my God, that it so Richard Gere in *An Officer and a Gentleman*!'

There wasn't much that could bring Susann out of her cubicle mid-haka, but Marg's casual confession about her Sunday night visitor had done the trick.

'He just turned up? At the door? For sex?' Susann fanned herself with her hand. 'Well, fuck me.'

'No,' said Marg, 'fuck me,' and they burst out laughing.

Susann moved over to the mirror and bared her teeth in a cartoon smile to check for lipstick smears. 'Christ, you wouldn't catch Keller doing something like that. He's got so fucking regimented. Condoms: check; mood lighting: check; bath sheet: check.'

'Bath sheet?' said Marg.

Susann held up a hand. 'Eight hundred thread count Egyptian cotton bed linen. He's obsessed with it.'

'Anal.' Marg pulled a face.

'Only on his birthday,' sniggered Susann, and they were off again.

The runner popped her head round the door, a little surprised to see the programme's two mainstays giggling like six-year-olds.

'Well,' said Susann, giving her hair a last, unnecessary pat. 'He sounds like a keeper, this one. But either way, you enjoy it while it lasts, girl. In a matter of weeks he could be defuzzing his navel with your Ladyshave.'

'Please tell me Keller didn't do that,' said Marg, as they left the loo and strode up the corridor to deconstruct a waking world.

'No.' Susann winked. 'But are you absolutely sure that Rick never has?'

The man from the valet service sucked his teeth sharply and surveyed the interior of the Honda. He shook his head. 'Who'd you have in here, love? The Hibs squad?'

'Children,' said Cate weakly. 'Three girls.'

The man pointed his chewed pen at the brownish mark on the edge of the back seat, stuck about with bits of fluff and a small leaf. 'I don't know what that is, love, but I don't think it'll come off easy.'

'It's toffee-apple,' said Cate. She handed him the keys. 'Do what you can. I just need it to look a bit more like a company car than a play-bus.'

'I'm not a miracle worker,' said the man. 'Might take about an hour.'

'That's okay,' said Cate. 'I've got shopping and stuff to do.'

Stuff. She was instantly annoyed at herself for playing it down. I have business to do; samples to pick up, fabrics and furniture to source. I have work to do. She emerged from the garage and walked towards the backstreet boutiques of the New Town. It had started to rain and she pulled her small black umbrella from her bag and bent her face under it. On any other day the rain wouldn't have mattered because this would be her idea of utter heaven. Time and cash to spend on what she loved. But she still felt sick, and the rain wasn't helping. Even though Dan had apologised when he got back and slipped in beside her, a distant figure across the bed, chilled from the night air. It's work, he had said. A lot going on. Big changes. I shouldn't have snapped. I'm sorry. We'll be fine. She had said a quiet 'okay' and had rolled to her side. But it wasn't okay. It was unsettling and it was getting a little scary.

She ducked into the newsagent's on the corner of Frederick Street and bought a *Scotsman*. It was property day. She could buy a coffee later and daydream over beautiful old stone with impossible price tags. She stood patiently at the counter as the elderly lady in front of her fussed over her small change.

The magazines were stacked beside her in shiny, beckoning rows. It was ages since she'd bought a woman's glossy. She picked one up and studied the cover. THE MIDDAY MAKEOVER. IS RED THE NEW GREY? REAWAKEN YOUR MAN'S INNER ANIMAL. Reawaken your man's inner animal? She gave a flat little laugh. And what might that be? In Dan's case, probably a giant sloth. Or maybe that was just with her. She put the magazine back on the shelf. Get yourself shagged good and proper, Marg had said. A few weeks back she might have thought that was the answer. But, now, after the yawn, after Gill, after yesterday, especially after yesterday, she wasn't so sure.

'Oh, I'm sorry, dear.' The elderly woman turned as the handful of coins she had been counting out slipped from hands bent and clawed like Tif's and rolled across the floor. The girl behind the counter raised her eyebrows at Cate, but Cate smiled and stooped to retrieve the money. She handed it back to the woman, then her own sixty pence to

311

the sales girl. She got to the door first, and held it open for the woman.

'Thank you, dear.' The woman shuffled through and adjusted her Rainmate over a tight, bluish perm. 'Never rains but it pours, eh?'

Cate nodded and raised her umbrella. It was one of her mum's favourite expressions.

'Off somewhere nice, though?' said the woman brightly, gripping the handle of her tartan shopping trolley.

Cate smiled at her again. 'Yes,' she said, with a silent thanks for the reminder. 'Yes, I am.'

Christ, designers must have killer biceps. Cate lugged the sample books from the boot of the car and rested them on her knee while she picked up the two bags of supermarket shopping and clenched the handle of the jumbo pack of toilet roll between her teeth. The grumpy valet man had done a sterling job. Even the toffee-apple stain had been scrubbed away to a vague stickiness. Cate had removed the small forest of fragranced trees that he had seen fit to hang around the interior, though.

The girls had rushed ahead into the house, and she glanced up to watch Jo as she kicked off her school shoes in the hall. Cate had known the minute she emerged from school that something was wrong. Jo looked drawn, and her smile had been forced and she hadn't had a single caustic comment for her sisters all the way home. She was first out of her seat when the Honda had come to a stop.

Cate carried her fabric books and plastic bags into the family room and deposited them on the couch. It wasn't quite 5 p.m. Enough time to call her client and update her before tea. She was on her way up to the study when the yelling started in the twins' bedroom and Emma appeared at the top of the stairs in full flounce.

'Mum, Jo just swore at me. She called me a stupid bitch!'

Cate sighed. 'What is it with you two? Why did she swear at you?'

'I don't know,' said Emma. 'She's just gone totally mental.'

'Well, there must be a reason,' said Cate. 'What is it?'

Emma shrugged unconvincingly.

'Emma?'

Emma glanced backwards towards the closed bedroom door and took a deep breath. 'Well. It's just. It's . . . Look, Paul asked if I'd be his partner at the Spring Fling with him and I said no, because I don't like him in that way? And I'm kind of hoping . . . well, anyway, I said he should ask Jo, because I know she likes him, but I didn't, like, say that to him, and he said, "Yeah, right!" Like that: "Yeah, right!" And Jo kind of . . . she kind of heard. And . . .' She drew another breath and held out her hands, exhausted of all possibilities.

Cate gestured for Emma to go downstairs. 'It's okay, love. Can you go and get a snack for Stevie while I talk to her? No crisps and at least one piece of fruit.'

'Does a Fruit Winder count?'

'No.'

'A Frube?'

'No. From the fruit bowl. Fruit from the fruit bowl.'

She pushed open the twins' bedroom door and slipped in. Jo was on her bed, furiously engrossed in a book she had read before.

'Hey, sweetheart.' Cate sat on the end of the bed and put her hand on Jo's leg. There was nothing to her beneath the thin polyester of her black school trousers. 'You okay?'

'I'm fine.'

'You shouldn't have called your sister a stupid bitch.'

'Well, she's always bugging me,' said Jo angrily. 'I just want a bit of space, you know. I don't even have anywhere

I can go.' She looked up and her voice cracked slightly. 'I
need my own room, Mum. You do other people's rooms.
Why can't I have a room?'

Cate bent forward to hug her. 'You're right, sweetheart.
We'll have to look at that.'

Jo pulled back. 'You promise?'

'I promise,' said Cate. She reached out and touched Jo's
cheek. 'Emma told me, love. What happened with Paul.'

Jo dropped her head. 'I don't want to talk about it.'

'Honey.'

'Mum, I don't want to talk about it.'

Cate sat for a moment. 'Well, that's okay, but it's good if
something's upset you to talk it through. Everyone needs to
do that. It helps.'

'Do you?' Jo looked back up at her. 'Need to talk to
people.'

'Of course.'

'Who do you talk to?'

Cate started to say 'your dad' but found herself hesi-
tating. 'Granny and Orla,' she said. 'And Dad. And Marg.'
She smiled. 'Marg's good for telling things to. She usually
knows how to sort it out.'

Jo gave a little smile back. She flicked the pages of her
book. 'Do you wish you'd known her all the time?' she asked
finally. 'I mean, right through?'

Cate nodded. 'Yes, I do. I'm annoyed I let us lose touch.
Well we both did. But it would have been pretty great to
have her around. She could have been your Aunty Marg.'

'Aunty Marg,' said Jo.

And God, thought Cate, wouldn't she have been great at
this. Jo's head was down again. Cate put her hand back on
Jo's leg. 'Anyway, if you don't want to talk, that's fine, but
if you do, you just say, okay?'

Jo nodded and Cate stood and turned for the door. She

paused as she opened it. 'And maybe tonight after home-work and tea we could talk about getting you two girls into your own rooms. How we might do that. All right?'

Jo didn't look up but she nodded vigorously.

'I'll give you a shout when dinner's ready, puss.' Cate bent to pick up Emma's discarded school sweatshirt and drape it over a chair.

'Mum.'

Cate turned. Jo had closed the book and moved to the edge of the bed.

'It hurt.' Her face collapsed in fresh, remembered pain. 'Mum. It really hurt.'

'I know,' said Cate, going to her. 'My lovely girl, I know.'

33

Marg bent and peered at the photos crowded on the top of the tall blond-wood bureau. God, she was gorgeous. Not what Marg had expected at all.

'Is this your wife?'

'Ex,' said Adam. 'Yeah.' He put the bottle of wine between his knees and pulled sharply at the cork. It emerged with a fat, satisfied pop.

It was a group shot. Adam and her and the boys. She stood at one edge, he at the other, their hands linked behind the children. Even though her eyes were screwed up tight at a hot sun, it was a pretty face with sharply defined cheekbones and a wide, generous smile. Her free hand was raised to push back thick dark hair from her cheek.

'She's very attractive.'

Adam handed Marg a glass of wine. 'What were you expecting? An orc?'

'No.' Marg took the drink. 'But she could pass for Helena Christensen.' She bent her head and looked at the photo again. 'On a dim day.'

He laughed. 'On a dim day. A perfect Marg compliment.'

'You know what I mean.' She took a sip of her wine.

'See this one.' He came and stood next to her and pointed to a small print of the boys at a beach. 'Just after this was taken Rory poked Quinn in the eye with that stick – he loves his sticks – and we sat in A&E in Brighton for four hours.'

'Happy times,' said Marg.

'It's a good shot, though.' Adam looked at the picture fondly.

She had to agree. The boys were running full tilt towards the camera like miniature warriors, mouths open and screaming with delight and feigned aggression.

A short, stout terrier chased behind them.

'That your dog?'

'Yeah. That's Hamish. He died last year. My old boy.'

'Hamish?' said Marg. 'I know a hamster called Hamish.'

Adam grinned. 'You? You know a hamster? That's not a phrase I expected ever to come out of your mouth.'

'My friend Cate who was at the ball, her kids have one. It's a bit of an escape artist. And a biter.'

He leant across and kissed her suddenly on the cheek.

'What's that for?'

Adam laughed. 'For knowing a hamster called Hamish. Anyway, do you want to see the rest of the house? Bring your wine if you want. I don't mind spills. Bit of Beaujolais would make a welcome change from Ribena. Or pee.'

'I'll try and control myself,' said Marg.

She followed him back into the hall and up the thin, sanded staircase. Like the photo of his ex, the house was not what Marg had imagined. She'd expected something sleek and steely and impersonal, a showcase for his work. Not the shambling two-storey terraced affair with the battered blue front door.

She had thought twice about going. By the time he had phoned to invite her, Sunday night had seemed surreal. Cate had wanted to know if she was dating when she'd called midweek, asking to talk about anything other than Dan. Marg had gone for 'not yet'. She hadn't had to deal with Rick either because he was in Lagos. Not that he would mind because this is what they did. No strings. Free agents.

Come and go as they please. His fling with the arts correspondent appeared to have been brutally brief, though,
because the poor girl had taken to dressing like a puritan
and had been glowering at everyone for the past few days.

'This is the boys' room.' Adam led her into a large bright
blue bedroom with bunk-beds and a toy-strewn floor.
'Apologies for the mess, but it's important for them to feel
like it's their space and they can do what they want. So I
tend not to tidy it up too much.'

Marg walked further in, stepping over fallen Action Men
and small discarded clothes and a herd of soft toy animals
that had been strung together with what looked like a skip-
ping rope. Muscled superheroes smiled down cheesily from
the walls. Marg made a space for her wine glass on a small
desk and bent down to pick up a large and curiously shaped
spiky plastic orb. It expanded suddenly in her hands and
she dropped it.

'What the hell's that?'

Adam laughed. 'It's a Hoberman ball. You can get inside
it once it's expanded all the way. Or try this.' He put the
orb over Marg's head and closed it around her face. 'You
look like that guy out of *Hellraiser*.'

'Very Marquis de Sade.' Marg gingerly removed the toy
from her head and threw it back at him. 'And the point of
it would be . . . ?'

'It's fun,' said Adam. He dropped the orb onto the lower
bunk. 'The kids love it.' He picked up her wine, handed it
to her and grinned. 'Come and see my room now.'

Marg smiled back at him. 'Is it fun, too?'

He gestured into a wide whitewashed room dominated
by a large sleigh bed. 'No toys,' he said, 'but the bed's good
for bouncing. Or so the boys tell me.'

The viewing was curtailed by the sound of the phone.
'Excuse me.' Adam headed downstairs and Marg followed

him slowly, pausing to study a series of black and white prints of buildings on the wall.

He was perched on the arm of the sofa when she wandered into the lounge. 'You did? All by yourself? Wow! High-five for the biggest boy.' He gestured for her to come in. 'Of course. No, we'll go for sure. I need to see that. Did you get your badge? Two weeks. Okay. Yup. Of course. All right. Put him on. And well done that boy, I'm really proud of you.'

He slid onto the sofa still clutching the phone. 'Hey, Rory boy. How are you?' It must have been a long answer because he sat quietly, nodding and smiling in turn.

'Well, I told Quinn we'd go swimming when you're over. You like that? Okay. No. Not this weekend. Well, maybe. We'll see.' He sat quietly again then grinned.

'What am I doing? Well, I've got a friend here. We're going to go for lunch. Her name's Marg. No. Maargg. Yes, it's a girl. A grown-up one.' He looked up at Marg and winked, utterly unselfconscious. 'What's she like? Very tall with big metal teeth. No, I'm kidding. She's nice. Funny. She liked your Hoberman.' There was a pause. 'No, Rory, she doesn't want to keep it. Rory. She doesn't want to keep it.' He raised his eyebrows at Marg. 'Okay. I'll tell her. And I'll see you on Friday night, boyo, okay? Bye. I love you too. Bye.'

He leant over the edge of the sofa and replaced the phone. 'Quinn swam fifty metres this morning.'

'Is that good?' Marg sat down on the seat nearest the door.

'When you're eight, yes. It's Olympian.'

For a second Marg thought she saw a flash of sadness in his eyes. 'Should you be going to see him?' She wasn't sure of divorced dad etiquette.

'I'll see him on Friday. We'll go swimming then.' He looked

across at her. 'Oh, and you're not to take Rory's Hoberman away with you. He's very possessive.'

'I'll get my own,' she said. She toyed with the stem of her wine glass. 'Are they used to you . . . having people over?'

'You mean women? A woman?' He smiled. 'There have been one or two. And they're okay with it. Well, Rory's fine. He's young enough that it doesn't seem too odd to him. But it's been hard for Quinn.'

'And you've been divorced how long?' She'd been wanting to ask and it seemed like the right time.

'Divorced for six months. Separated for fifteen.'

'That's a pretty low average,' said Marg. 'One or two dates in almost two years.'

'They weren't dates. They lasted longer. Anyway, what about you? What's your average? I seem to remember you telling me you were seeing someone.' He stretched his arm along the back of the sofa.

'Kind of,' said Marg.

'Kind of? Does that mean off and on?'

'It means occasionally.'

He studied her face. 'And ongoing?'

She wasn't sure what the answer to that should be, so instead she said: 'We're being watched.'

'What?' He looked puzzled.

'We're being watched.' She pointed behind his arm to a small green plastic soldier poking out from the back of the sofa cushion.

'Oh, that's where they are. We almost had a full-scale incident over them a week ago. Rory thought Quinn had taken them.' He reached down behind the cushion and pulled out a handful of troops, setting them down on the coffee table and spacing them out, ready for action.

'This is a pretty sick link,' he said, as he moved the figures around. 'But have you heard anything more from Chad?'

Marg nodded. 'I got through to Leonora just a couple of days ago. She's one of the nuns. They're in Ndjamena now because it's still too volatile, so they've no idea what's happening in the camp now they're away. Don't even know if it's still there. They might all have dispersed.'

It had been a frustratingly faint link, but reassuring to hear Leonora's voice, even though she had no good news to impart. She couldn't say where Amodu was, just that he had not been caught up in the original incident. She had hoped he was among the ones who had left at the same time as the nuns had. She hadn't seen him on the morning they had gone and she had taken that as a good sign.

Marg had found it strangely heartening that Leonora hadn't added, 'I'm sure he'll be okay.' Because she had no way of knowing that he would be. She did say that he had been delighted with Marg's jacket and had worn it solidly for three days despite the heat and the fact that the arms were far too long.

'It's nice of you to call,' she had said finally, and Marg had known that she meant it.

'Too small a crisis.' Adam interrupted her thoughts.

'Far too small.' She watched him position the small plastic army, feeling the sudden urge to reach across and topple them all with one angry swipe. For a boy she hardly knew, left to fend for himself.

'So, are you going to take me for this lunch?'

'Do you not want to finish the tour?' Adam paused, a small green commando clutched in his fist.

'Lunch.' Marg stood up. 'I'm getting toy overload.'

'That's a pity.' Adam stood too and dropped the last few soldiers back onto the sofa.

'Why?'

'Well, it was Quinn's birthday last week. He had his main party with his schoolfriends and his mum, but I've said I'll have a barbecue here for him, too, at the weekend. It's just some kids from round here and a couple of my friends.'

Marg found herself shaking her head even before he had finished speaking. Too soon. Way too soon. 'I don't think that's a good idea.'

'Why?' He laughed gently. 'It's not a big deal. Very casual. Just drop by.'

Just drop by. She hesitated.

'Go on.' He stepped back to let her through the door. 'It'll be good. Casual.'

'Maybe,' she said. 'Maybe. Can I think about it?'

She thought about it most of the way through lunch and all of the way home, in the cab and in the lift and across the living room, up to the point where she lifted the phone.

'What in God's name,' she said, when the ringing stopped, 'do you get an eight-year-old for a gift?'

'Boy or girl?' Cate tucked the phone under her chin and handed the bin-bag to Dan. He mouthed 'Who is it?' with a look of such annoyance that she thought for a second of saying, 'None of your business', or 'Gill'. Just to see what he would do. She cupped her hand over the receiver and whispered 'Marg' then took the phone through into the living room and curled on the sofa. She watched him tie the yellow handles in an irritated knot and get ketchup on his fingers as he did so.

'Something gadgety, probably. Boys love gadgets. Listening devices. Night vision goggles.'

'You get these for kids?' Marg sounded horrified.

'God, yeah. Just go to Woolworths. There's a whole selection of spy stuff. Intruder alarms. Invisible ink pens . . .'

'Mini JetStream for covert rendition flights?' asked Marg.

'Possibly.' Cate laughed. 'I have to ask. Is this research for work or what I think it is?'

'I don't know what you think it is, but Adam's having a barbecue for his oldest. Quinn. He asked if I'd drop by.'

'Oh my lord,' giggled Cate. 'She's meeting the kids.'

'It really isn't a big deal.'

She could imagine the expression on Marg's face. 'Of course not,' said Cate.

'Really.'

'I know. Really.'

'So, you think a gadget?' There was a short pause. 'God, Cate. What the hell am I doing? I don't want to go to Woolworths. I don't want to meet his kids. I don't want to be Daddy's special friend. This is a bad idea. Such a bad idea.'

'No, it's not. Marg, it's fine. And I was just kidding. It's not a big deal. He's got kids. You're seeing him, you're going to meet them sometime or other.'

'I'm not . . . seeing him.'

'Well, what would you call it?'

'I don't know,' said Marg.

Cate sighed. 'Marg, people this age – our age – tend to come with stuff. Kids, exes, nasal hair, mortgages, droopy bits. You're not signing on to be a full-time stepmum just by turning up at a barbecue, for God's sake.'

'Okay.' Marg sounded a little sheepish.

'Okay,' said Cate. 'So go to Woolies, buy something for a prepubescent James Bond, and go and enjoy it. Remember to smile. And don't drink too much. And don't swear. Oh, and don't wear anything that's dry-clean only.'

'Well, aren't you full of common sense today?' said Marg, archly.

'I always was the sensible one,' laughed Cate.

'Then have you set up your own business yet?'

'No,' said Cate. 'But that doesn't mean I'm not sensible.'

'You can do it on the Internet, you know. In about an

hour. Pick a name, send off your seventy quid and Companies House will do the rest. You need to look into it.'

'Maybe I have,' said Cate.

'Or maybe you're going to go and do it right now, after I've hung up.'

'Maybe I will.'

'You take my advice and I'll take yours,' said Marg. 'Deal?'

'Deal,' said Cate. 'Woolworths, some spy stuff and you'll be all set.' She started to laugh.

'What?'

'I'm imagining you on a bouncy castle.' Cate stood up to carry the phone back through to the family room and her ketchup-covered husband. 'Please tell me there's going to be a bouncy castle?'

34

'Are you really sure about the colour, darling?' Cate's mum took a step back and looked at the swipe of crimson paint she had just rolled onto the wall of the spare bedroom. 'It's a little . . .' she lowered her voice to a concerned whisper, 'house of ill repute.'

Cate laughed and nodded towards Jo, brushing rhythmically on the far wall in time to an inaudible tune on her iPod. 'She wanted a red wall, and how do you know what the inside of a house of ill repute looks like, anyway?'

Her mum gave her a disapproving slap on the leg and dipped her roller back into the paint. She held it still for a moment, dripping bloodily over the plastic tray. 'Well, there was that time on our Bangkok stopover. I mean, it looked like a teahouse from the outside, for heaven's sake. How were we to know?' A little giggle escaped and Cate reached across and put her hand on her mum's arm. It was the first hint of a laugh since she had returned from Tom's.

'You should have seen Ed's face when he realised. Fair tickled, he was.'

'Was that one of the services on offer?' said Cate slyly. It was lovely to see her mum like this, eyes lit with memory, able to recall more with fondness than with pain.

'Cate!' Her mum glared at her, but the smile still curved the corners of her mouth. 'Anyway,' she picked up the roller and gestured towards the curtains, 'you know what they say about mixing red and green.'

Kirsty Scott

'You get brown?' said Cate innocently.

'Should never be seen,' said Joyce, 'except upon a fairy queen.'

'Or Santa's elves,' said Stevie suddenly, turning from her empty paint tray and waving her dry roller in the air. Stevie and emulsion didn't mix.

'You're right, poppet,' said Joyce. 'Or Santa's elves. And how's that invisible paint going on?'

Cate watched Jo swing her brush across the wall. She had been so delighted when she'd been told she could not only have the spare room, but could pick a colour scheme for it. Paul had not been mentioned since. Maybe she was more like her mum than Cate had realised, able to distract herself from heartache with fabric and gloss. Although it had been a struggle to fit in buying the paint and finding a free afternoon to start, with the job in the Borders so near to completion. Cate had been up and down the road to Peebles so many times in the last week that she drove now on autopilot, no need to keep the Scottish tourer map clenched between her knees.

The door flew open and Emma came sailing in, breathless with excitement. 'Everyone, look at this. Do you like Daddy's new hairdo?' She turned to usher in Dan. Or someone who looked like Dan but had just enlisted in the US Marines.

'Oh my God.' Cate dropped her roller in the tray and stood up. His soft dark hair had been shorn almost to the wood. 'Dan. That's a bit severe.'

He rubbed his hand across his head. 'I like it. Easier to keep.' He winked at the girls.

Joyce bent her head to one side to study him. 'It takes years off, Dan, I must say.'

'You think?' He looked back at her nonchalantly.

'I think it's cool,' said Emma. 'He looks like Vin Diesel.'

'Vin Diesel's bald,' said Jo, contemptuously.

326

'Yes,' said Cate, 'he is.' She walked over and touched Dan's head. It felt rough. She felt a fresh rush of anxiety. Why in God's name?

'I just wanted a change,' he said, as if he had heard her thoughts. 'I was booked in to get it done a week on Saturday but Guy's organised an overnighter to Galloway, so I nipped into the barber's on the way home.'

'An overnighter?' Cate looked at him.

He gave a quick forgive-me grin. 'There's a time trial event at Lochmaben. We thought we'd take a run down, but it'll finish too late to get back up in daylight. Anyway,' he looked around the room, not waiting for her response, 'it's like a scene from *Little Women* in here. You've all been very industrious.'

'Mummy's going to paint me a Ural in my room when we're finished,' said Stevie.

'Mural,' said Cate. 'And it won't be today.'

Dan folded his arms and leant against the doorjamb. 'Well, Mummy's going to be very busy with all her painting and . . . whatnot.'

It was the 'whatnot' that got her. That and the overnighter and the hair she hadn't been expecting and the fact that she didn't have a clue what was going on in his head any more.

'Actually,' she said, 'Mummy has been quite industrious today. Not only have I been painting, but I set up my own business. You're looking at the CEO of Catriona Wishart Interiors.'

It had been as ludicrously easy as Marg had said. Some online forms to fill in, a debit card payment, a name to choose and it was done. The letter would be on its way from Companies House.

There was a puzzled silence in the half-painted room.

'Who's Catriona Wishart?' asked Stevie.

'You did what?' asked her mum.
'Why?' said Dan.

Of the three balloons tied to the gatepost, one had burst and the other two were so overblown that the image of the footballer printed onto them was now more Maradona than Michael Owen. The smell of charcoaled chicken drifted over the top of the house with the occasional peal of laughter and the odd warlike cry. Marg took a breath and pressed the bell. Just an hour. That's all. It's no big deal.

The door was opened by a skinny boy of indeterminate age wielding a plastic light sabre, who ran back down the long hall without so much as a word. Marg followed him, slipping off her jacket and laying it neatly on the pile of coats at the bottom of the stairs. An older woman in the kitchen wrestling with a jumbo-sized bag of crisps gave her a guarded smile and gestured to the garden when she asked for Adam. Marg felt surprisingly pleased to see him hunched over the barbecue trying to position pieces of chicken breast. His face brightened when he turned at her hand on his arm.

'You made it.' He bent and kissed her quickly and on the mouth, then took her hand. She was aware of the furtive glances from some of the other adults clustered around the lawn. She was relieved that they didn't all look particularly younger than her.

'Quinn, Rory, come here. There's someone I want you to meet.' He gestured to a group of children hanging like lemurs from a small, lopsided climbing-frame. One boy peeled away and came to stand awkwardly by Adam's side.

'Where's Rory?'

'Under the bush,' said Quinn, as if it were the obvious place to be.

'Rory!' Adam bent and peered into a thick leylandii. 'Out.'

328

A small and grubby figure emerged, clutching a thin stick. His top read 'Big Trouble'. 'Boys, this is Marg, my friend I told you about. Marg, this is Quinn and Rory.' He put his hand on top of each of their heads as he said their names.

'Hi.' She stretched out her hand and they shook it in turn with all the wary curiosity of small border guards. Rory's was damply warm and faintly sticky and Marg fought the temptation to wipe it on her Miss Sixty jeans. She handed over the flat wrapped parcel to Quinn. 'That's for you. Belated birthday.'

He glanced quickly at her, then at his dad, then muttered, 'Thanks.'

'You didn't have to,' said Adam. 'Really.'

'You can't turn up at a party without a present, can you?' She looked at the boys with what she hoped was a dazzling grin. They looked back at her as if she were speaking Latvian.

'Well, open it.' Adam gestured to the present and Quinn tore off the paper self-consciously. He looked, puzzled, at the folder inside.

'It's a bit off-the-wall,' said Marg. 'But I wasn't sure what to get. I'm not that great in toy shops.'

'What is it?' Rory stood on tiptoe to stare at the documents.

'It's a sponsorship,' said Marg. 'It means you're sponsoring a boy who lives in Africa. In a country called Chad. His name's Faisal and he's seven, I think. They don't have a lot of money where he lives, so this means he can go to school and his family get help . . .' She tailed off. 'He'll write to you, too. You'll get letters.'

Adam put his hand on her arm, then turned to his son. 'That's a really great gift, Quinn.'

'Uhm, yeah. Thank you. Thanks.' Quinn closed the folder and stood holding it awkwardly.

'Why is it a boy?' Rory raised his head and looked at Marg, deeply confused.

'Well, it's a boy in Africa,' said Adam. 'We're going to sponsor him. Marg's arranged it.'

'What does sponsor mean?'

'It means we kind of look after him a bit,' said Adam. 'Help out with things.'

'Is he going to come and live here?' asked Rory.

'No,' said Adam patiently. 'He lives in Africa. Marg went to the country that he lives in. It's called Chad.'

Quinn shot a glance at his friends in the corner. 'Thanks,' he said, again, staring down at his shoes. 'It's . . . neat.'

Which is probably eight-year-old for utter bloody crap, thought Marg. Should have listened to Cate. Should have gone with the spy stuff.

She smiled weakly at him as he handed the gift to Adam and ran off to the far end of the garden. Rory stood still looking at her, then turned to a small group of grown-ups setting out paper plates at a nearby table.

'That lady,' he said gravely, 'got Quinn a boy.'

'A boy?' said one of the men.

'A boy. She got him a boy for his birthday. He's from Chav. He's going to come and live with us. Because that lady got him.'

Adam ran his hand through his hair and caught Rory by the shoulder. 'Hey, scout. It's Chad, with a "d". And he's not coming to live with us.'

He let Rory go and turned back to Marg. 'You need some wine.' She nodded. You have no bloody idea how much. He led her over to the food table and poured her a paper cup from a box of supermarket Chardonnay.

'Somebody brought it,' he said, handing the cup over. He seemed on edge.

'It'll be fine.' She took a sip. It wasn't. It was tepid and really rather bad.

'It's a great gift.' He poured himself a cup.

'The wine?'

He laughed and raised his cup to hers. 'The sponsorship.'

'But night vision goggles might have gone down better.' She drained the wine and held out her cup for more.

'No. Really . . .'

'Adam.' The older woman from the kitchen appeared at his elbow. 'I'm sorry to interrupt, but someone's been at the cake.'

'At the cake?'

'They've eaten the goalposts.'

'Jesus, not the goalposts.' He sighed and put down his cup. 'Excuse me. Will you be okay?'

She held up her hands. 'I'm fine. I'll mingle. Go.'

She dispensed another cup of wine and glanced round the garden. Quinn was still at the climbing-frame with the other boys, but upended now from a narrow metal bar. Rory had disappeared, possibly back under the bush.

She wandered over to the group of adults by the food table and introduced herself. They were pleasant, but parents, and one by one were called away on toilet trips or bump-and-graze emergencies until she found herself on her own again with her cup of bad white and her heels sinking slowly into the grass.

'Would you like a Smartie hat?' A plump girl with a heavy fringe tapped her on the arm and held out a plate of what looked like chocolate-dipped marshmallows.

'Pardon?'

'A Smartie hat?'

'No, I'm good,' said Marg.

'Wotsit?' The girl proffered another dish half filled with bright orange pellets.

'No, really, I'm fine. Thanks.'

She waited until Adam reappeared after salvaging the cake, but he was then called to tend to Rory who had got some mud in his eye, and to sort out an altercation at the climbing-frame involving an even smaller boy, as round as he was tall. Marg went to find her coat and call a cab. It came quicker than she had expected and she thought, briefly, of leaving without saying anything. Adam was still in the garden, acting as referee at a rather brutal game of touch rugby.

She went to the back door and gestured to him. He came running over.

'Adam, I'm going to head off. Thanks. For asking me.'

'Are you? Well . . .'

'Say bye to Quinn for me. And Rory.'

He followed her into the kitchen and down the hall. 'I was hoping you might hang on,' he said when they reached the door. 'They'll all be leaving. We could have a drink.'

'No, it's fine. Honestly. You've got your hands full.' She opened the door.

'Marg.' He looked suddenly serious. 'I'm glad you came. Thanks. And for the present. Really.' A blue balloon bobbed past him and out into the front garden where it impaled itself with a weary pop on the first sharp point of a holly bush.

'You should get back in,' said Marg.

He nodded. 'I'll call you, then.'

'Sure. Bye.' She walked smartly to the cab and climbed in, shutting the door on the shrieks of laughter still drifting over the roof of the house and the awkward silence that had descended on its front. The cab pulled away from the kerb and swung round in a loop. She didn't look back.

'Where you headed?' The driver glanced at her in the rear-view mirror.

'Canary Wharf.'

'Anywhere in particular?'

'Popinjays?' asked Marg. 'You know Popinjays? The bar?'

The driver nodded. 'Popinjays it is.'

She settled back against the seat and watched the unfamiliar streets blur past. Family homes. Strangers' homes. What in God's name had she been thinking? She dug out her mobile and dialled.

'Hey,' she said when she heard the familiar voice. 'You up for a late lunch?'

Rick laughed. 'I'm always up,' he said, 'for my favourite girl.'

35

'And live to Ankara in three . . . two . . . one.' Marg saw the quick, concerned glance from the programme editor. She'd cut it too close. Susann swivelled frantically to address the correspondent filling the screen behind her like a giant looming shadow. Marg sat back and rubbed her temples. Her head was still thumping. Too much vodka on Saturday and too much soul-searching on a hungover Sunday. God, what a weekend.

She looked at the clock. Only three minutes to go. Rick had slipped into the seat beside Susann during a brief segment of video, ready for a discussion about anarchist groups and the offer they had received from a mainstream environmental agency to join them in the run-up to the G8. It was an unexpected development, breaking news, and he'd had maybe five minutes to prepare. She watched him dust off his lapels and bare his teeth in a smiling snarl to the powder girl in the low-slung trousers.

She hadn't said anything to him about the birthday party, not in Popinjays and not back at his flat where she hadn't been in any fit state to say very much at all. Rick was never at his conversational best during sex, beyond the odd grunted 'woaah', and she'd needed a lot more vodka than usual to get her in the mood, if you could call her state of anaesthetised angst anything like in the mood.

Not that he would have been intrigued or felt in any way threatened if she had talked about Adam and the boys. He was indifferent to children and her other dalliances had not interested him. Dalliances. Was that what it was?

'Marg!' She snapped back and saw that Rick was waiting to be counted in. 'Live to Rick in two . . . one . . .' She rushed the words. Susann's mouth hardened into an irritated line.

'Bad night?' The programme editor didn't turn his head.

'Bad weekend,' said Marg. 'Sorry.' She concentrated on Rick and what he was saying. He always settled himself with a little lift of his shoulders, like a Tommy Cooper shrug. It was his only onscreen tic. Everything else was blandly smooth and assured. She watched him talk, watched the marvellous mouth spout what sounded like good common sense.

'These radical anti-capitalists, they have a choice, Susann. And it's a stark one. They can stick with what they know, the undeniable excitement of living with chaos, or they can grow up and embrace something really quite ordinary, something they may have despised, but which may prove to be much, much more rewarding in the long run. The fascinating thing about this situation is that no one can predict how they will react to this unforeseen development. No one knows what they will decide to do.'

Marg bent over the microphone a little more swiftly than she needed to. 'And that,' she said flatly, 'is a wrap.'

She leant on the console for a moment, rubbing her head with her hands. 'Fuck,' she said softly. The programme editor glanced across at her warily.

'You need some more personal days this week?'

She glared up at him. 'No!'

'Okay.' He held his hands up. 'You'll need to be on better from for Friday, though. You remembering about Friday?'

She looked at him, puzzled. 'What's happening on Friday?'

'Take Your Daughter to Work Day. I'm bringing in my youngest. She's nine. Don't want you being all Sweary Mary on me. There's a few words she hasn't learned yet.'

'Take your daughter to work?' said Marg. 'Why?'

'New company thing. There's notices all over. You not seen them? Susann's bringing her girl as well. It's to show them there's nothing they can't do. You know, all that equal opportunities crap. I know you don't have kids, but you got a niece or something? You could bring her. As long as it's a girl, it's all right.'

Marg ignored his last suggestion. 'So what you're saying is that on Friday the place is going to be overrun with children?'

'Pretty much. Yeah.' He stood and gathered his papers and slapped her on the back with them. 'Don't be such a Roald Dahl witch, Marg. It'll be a laugh.'

'Yeah.' Marg dropped her head back into her hands. 'Won't it just.'

'Bad day?' Roy turned and jogged backwards as Marg laboured up the hill behind him.

'Why does everyone keep asking me if I'm having a bad day?'

'Oh, I don't know.' Roy slowed down, springing from foot to foot like a boxer jumping rope. 'Maybe 'cos you've got a face like fizz and you can't run the length of yourself. Would that be it?'

'Thanks.' Marg imagined a baseball bat connecting with his shins. See how springy you could be after that, Roy, sweetie.

'You need to sweat it out, love. Leave all these global issues in your wake.' Roy jumped higher, knees to chest.

'It's not global,' puffed Marg. 'It's personal.'

'Well sweat him out of your system, then.' Roy winked. 'Whoever he is.'

'That's just it.' Marg stopped and put her hands on her hips, breathing heavily. 'Whoever he is.'

'More than one, eh? Marg, Marg, Marg.'

'Can we talk about something else?'

'Okay.' Roy grinned. 'How much did you have to drink at the weekend?'

'Not enough.' Marg felt the faint vibration of her phone in her hip-pack. She zipped it open and peered at the name, wondering why she felt a rush of guilt and relief when she saw it.

'I need to take this.' She perched on a nearby wall, not minding the damp, and stretched her right leg out in front of her, flexing her toes up and down as Roy was motioning her to do.

'Hi.'

'Hi. It's me.' Me. Not Adam.

'I wanted to call . . .' He stopped. There was a long pause. 'You know, in my head it went differently. Saturday. It went better. You didn't have a God-awful time, the boys were charm personified and I'd just got a crate of Pouilly Fumé delivered. Oh, and the loo was clean.'

'I didn't use the loo.'

'Well, that's a mercy,' he said. 'And you don't want to know why.'

She gave a little laugh. 'It was fine.'

'You're lying. You hated it.'

'Well, it wasn't really my thing.' She switched legs as Roy tapped his watch.

'You sound out of puff,' said Adam. 'Have I caught you at a bad time?'

'I'm exercising,' she said. 'With my trainer.'

'Is that ducks I can hear?'

'Yeah. I run round the pond. Battersea Park.'

'I take the boys there sometimes. They like the children's zoo.'

'Mm,' said Marg.

There was another pause. 'They come with me, Marg,' he said.

'To the park?' She knew it wasn't what he had meant.

'No. They come with me.'

'I know.' But not all the time, she said in her head.

'I'd like to see you again.'

She was a little surprised at how quickly she answered. 'Okay.'

'Is that Global News speak for "anything to get this guy off my back", or "I'd quite like to, but I'm a little wary because of last time"?'

'The latter,' said Marg. She stood up. Roy had started to jog on the spot again.

'Good. I'll see you tonight.'

'Tonight? I didn't say anything about tonight.'

'I can finish at six. An early dinner. I'll have you in bed by nine. Promise.' The connection was weak. She couldn't tell if there was laughter in his voice.

'Okay,' she said.

'I'm not completely convinced about the triffid.' The woman stood back and narrowed her eyes at the large stag-horn fern sitting beside the bay window in a low, barrelled planter. She paused and looked across at Cate, standing expectantly by the lounge door. 'Apart from that . . . Love it. Absolutely love it.'

Cate laughed out loud. 'Thank goodness.'

'I don't think you're meant to sound so relieved,' said the woman with a broad smile. 'Cocky, yeah. Totally unsurprised, absolutely. Of course you love it! Dahling! What's not to love? That kind of thing.'

'I'll work on that for my next client.' Cate beamed. 'But I am relieved – I'm pleased – that you like it.'

'What else have you got lined up?' The woman trailed

her hand through the rough, mossy silk of the curtains as Cate came in and sat on the arm of the sofa.

'Nothing specific,' said Cate. 'I have a mural to paint for a . . . bedroom.' She didn't need to know it was SpongeBob SquarePants and for Stevie.

The woman glanced across at her. 'I would imagine you'll be pretty busy before too long. Good designers are hard to find. The designer we had do the house in Bath was a disaster. He had this idea of what would look good and he really just went with that. It all ended up a bit footballer's wife. You know, ruched everything, gold-plated taps, naked lady statues on the patio – actually, that was probably the ex – anyway, point is, you got a sense of me and what I might like. I appreciate that.'

'Thank you.'

'You should give me some of your business cards and I'll pass them on. Can't beat word of mouth.'

Business cards. Shit. Should have got business cards.

'I don't have any with me,' said Cate, as casually as she could. 'But I'll send some down to you.'

'Well, I'm glad I got you on the way up. Next year, my dear, I won't be able to afford your pick for one lousy lamp-shade. Even if I can squeeze any more cash out of the duplic-itous shagging bastard. Oh, and talking of filthy lucre . . .' She turned to a table by the wall and picked up a cheque. 'I made it out to Catriona Wishart Interiors. Is that right?'

'Perfect.' Cate took it with a smile and glanced quickly at the numbers, trying not to show her excitement. Four numbers, all in a row, with no decimal point to blunt their impact. Bloody hell. She felt like hopping up and down on the spot, like Stevie did when Cate caved at the checkout and dropped something sweet and unexpected into the basket.

By the time she reached the Edinburgh city bypass she

had decided that the Alice Temperley dress and the fuck-me shoes could wait. A house fund. A separate account that she could add to, that would maintain the dream. Every job, a little bit more. And in maybe five years' time? She smiled to herself in the slow lane and pulled out to overtake a dawdling bread van.

It was only when the outline of the hospital came into view that the doubts set in. It was an impressive building, in a sleek, clinical way, but Cate hated the fact that it faced the city so squarely, with its back turned to the gentle, pleasing folds of the Pentland Hills. She imagined Dan, purposeful in hospital white, pausing mid-examination.

Dr Beane, I'm sorry to interrupt but we've just learned your wife's gone and set up a slush fund to squirrel away the money she gets from her, from her . . .

From her whatnot? says Dan.

She wondered what he would think of her plan. They hadn't had anything like a proper conversation since duck race day. That was the beauty and the peril of having children, so easy just to communicate about them and through them. Stevie's got a wobbly tooth. Are you impotent or having an affair?

Her fingers tightened around the wheel. How could she be thinking this way? How could she not know?

The traffic slowed to a steady crawl as the hospital off-ramp approached. Cate glanced at the building and the low sun winking sharply off the myriad panes of smoky glass. He was in there. Dan. She felt a sudden surge of anxiety. God, she would need to try again. They had to sort this out. Otherwise where would they end up? A sexless old couple slumped in sour silence across an expanse of bed or table. Or maybe even apart. She parked a fair distance from the house, in the street with all the small shops, the bank and the printers and the rather racy boutique she'd always avoided on the grounds that she might come out looking like Christina Aguilera. And once she had finished her errands she nipped into the small Greek restaurant and booked a table, a booth, tucked in the corner. Somewhere they could talk.

36

'I've refused to go anywhere I might be served by someone dressed as a soft toy.' Marg tucked the phone under her chin and sifted through the rail of clothes in her wardrobe.

Cate laughed. 'I'm just delighted you're going at all. I think it's great, really. How on earth did he persuade you?'

'I don't know. I'm a mug. I didn't think it was necessary. But we had a really good night out earlier in the week, and they've got a day off school, and he phoned and . . . I don't know.'

'Well, they're a big part of his life,' said Cate. 'It's good you get to know them.'

'I'm not going to adopt them,' said Marg.

'No,' said Cate. 'But if you keep seeing him, you're going to keep seeing them. Occasionally. You are going to keep seeing him, aren't you?'

Marg ignored her. 'And how are the Beanes?'

There was a pause. 'The girls are great,' said Cate, a little too brightly. 'Dan's a bit grumpy, though, because I've put my money from the last commission in a separate account.'

'You need to get him sorted out,' said Marg.

'I know. I'm taking him out to dinner tomorrow with some of it. A proper date. See if we can't get past this . . .' She paused.

'Duff patch?' said Marg.

'I think it's more than that.' Cate's voice changed and Marg felt instantly guilty for being so flippant.

'Hon, it'll be fine. Really.'

'I hope so,' said Cate. 'We just need to thrash it all out.'

Marg couldn't resist. 'Did you mean to say that?'

There was a giggle. 'Chance would be a fine thing,' said Cate.

'God, remember we used to talk about sex all the time?' Marg moved across and sat on the end of her bed. 'How you did it, who you would do it with . . . Remember that film we got in place of sex ed in second year, with the Austrian guy, the one about . . .'

'Elephant seals,' interjected Cate.

'God. Yeah. Ze bull seal inserts ze penis in ze female. He duss not notice he iss almost suffocating her.'

'I was quite terrified by it all,' said Cate.

'I think that was the idea. Scare us out of doing anything.'

The line went quiet for a moment.

'You never thought, though, that they might not be able to do it, did you?' said Cate finally. 'You know, boys. Men.' There was another pause. 'Or that they might not want to. You just assumed they could. And would.'

'It's not that, hon. It's not that he doesn't want to.' Marg lay back against the pillows. 'Come on. Focus on tomorrow. It's a start, and you'll get it sorted out. Where are you going anyway? Somewhere fancy?'

'Not terribly.' Cate's voice lightened a little. 'Got a new blouse which is, though. Actually it's more of a bodice. Stripy – kind of *Moulin Rouge*.'

Marg whistled. 'I never sent you up those pants.'

'Keep them,' laughed Cate. 'Sounds like you're more likely to use them than I am.'

'And how's work?'

'Well, there isn't any . . . but –' she obviously anticipated Marg's squawk of outrage – 'I'm looking at advertising. I've got business cards ordered. Tif's put up a notice at the gym.

I know the next job's not going to drop into my lap. I'm going to have to work at it. It'll come.'

'Attagirl.'

'You should get going,' said Cate. 'It's almost noon.'

'Have a good date,' said Marg. 'Be good.'

'You too.' Cate laughed. 'Be nice.'

The boys must have been told to be on their best behaviour because they were sitting stiffly in their seats when Marg arrived at the restaurant.

'Hello.' She bent in to kiss Adam on the cheek then took her seat with a broad smile.

'How are you two?'

'Fine,' said Quinn, with a shy smile. Rory eased a finger up his nose and studied Marg carefully.

Adam tugged at Rory's arm to dislodge the digit and indicated to him to answer.

'I'm fine,' he said, with a hint of petulance. He wiped his finger on the tablecloth.

'So.' Marg picked up the menu, aware that her voice was half an octave higher than it ought to be. 'What's your favourite thing to eat at this restaurant?'

'Ice-cream!' shouted Rory, raising his arms in the air and sending his glass of orange juice toppling onto the floor.

'Nice one, scout.' Adam shot him a recriminating glance and bent to clean up the mess. Rory's lip wobbled.

'I think that was my fault,' said Marg quickly.

Rory froze mid-pout and looked at her. His hair was a little too long and it fell over eyes fringed with thick, curving lashes. Wasted on a boy, thought Marg.

'It was her fault,' Rory said to his dad.

'Oh, it was, was it?' said Adam, emerging from beneath the table with a pile of sticky orange napkins.

'She said so.' Rory pointed at Marg.

'Her name's Marg,' said Adam.

'Hi,' said Marg.

'Hello,' said Rory. He looked as if he might start to giggle. She winked at him and he winked back, both eyes at once.

By the time the pizzas and the half-bottle of Montepulciano were cleared away it was all going rather well. They weren't so bad. Quinn was obviously a bright boy, quiet and thoughtful, a little unsure of himself, maybe. Rory was a handful and had managed two toilet trips and a tantrum over a stray slice of tomato that someone had dared leave on his pizza Margherita. Marg watched them interact with Adam. She was no expert but he seemed like a good dad, fun and loving.

'Right.' Adam clapped his hands together. 'Who's for ice-cream?'

'Me, me, me, me, me!' Rory wriggled furiously in his chair.

Adam looked at Marg. She shook her head. 'I'll pass. Just an espresso for me.'

'Are you su . . . ?' His phone started to ring and he dug in his pocket and pulled it out. His face changed when he saw the number. 'Excuse me.' She wondered if it was the wife.

'Hi. What? When? Shit!'

The boys looked at each other and sniggered. Adam held up a warning finger.

'I thought he wasn't due in until Monday,' he said into the phone. 'Well, no, frankly, I can't. Where's the site manager?' He ran his free hand through his hair. Up went the fringe. 'Christ. What a f . . . freaking mess. Look, I'll see what I can do. Okay. I'll call you back. Give me five minutes.'

He put the phone on the table and leant forward. 'Look, boys, Dad's going to have to go back into work for a bit. Something's come up. I'm really sorry. We'll have ice-cream tonight. I'll need to phone Mum and see if she's in.' He turned to Marg, picking up the phone again as he did so. 'I'm so sorry about this. A client's come in early from Dubai and he's turned up down on site. I'm going to have to go. This could be an utter bloody disaster.'

She nodded and bent to pick up her bag. 'It's fine.'

'But I want my ice-cream.' Rory's face contracted with rage.

'I know, Rory.' Adam spoke firmly. 'We'll have some tonight. At home.'

'I want ice-cream HERE!'

'Rory!'

She wasn't sure if it was Adam's frustration, or the thought of another incoherent tantrum, or the crestfallen look on Quinn's face, but Marg spoke before she really thought about what she was going to say.

'Actually, if the boys are okay with it, why don't you go and solve your problem and I'll sit here and they can have their ice-cream? How long will you be?'

'Yeah, yeah, yeah, yeah!' shouted Rory.

'I don't know.' Adam looked at her with what could only be described as utter disbelief. 'Are you sure?'

She wasn't, not anywhere near, but she said, 'Absolutely,' with as much conviction as she could muster.

He turned to the boys. 'Would you stay here with Marg while I go and sort out my work thing?'

They nodded.

'Well, okay then.' He stood up, then bent quickly and kissed her on the mouth. 'Thanks. Really. Thanks.' He turned to the boys. 'Be good, okay?' He ruffled their hair. 'I'll be as quick as I can.'

He grabbed his jacket and turned to head for the door.

'Don't be long,' Marg called after him in a rather half-hearted way. The boys were looking at her when she turned back. Expectantly. Interview panels had seemed less daunting. Oh, God. You stupid cow. What have you done?

'Ice-cream,' she said as brightly as she could and looked desperately for the waiter.

'I want another one.' Rory laid his spoon on the table and smiled defiantly through a beard of melted vanilla.

'Should you not . . . ?' Marg touched her own chin.

'Wipe,' said Quinn. He handed Rory a napkin. 'And you're not allowed two.' He turned to Marg. 'He's not allowed two.'

Rory glared at him and sank below the table.

'What's he doing?'

'He likes hiding under things,' said Quinn. He fiddled with his napkin and his gaze slunk to the door.

Rory reappeared at Marg's side of the table and stood up next to her. 'What's your favourite animal?'

'No idea,' she said. 'Pig?'

'Why?'

She shrugged. 'They're pink.'

'They smell,' said Rory. 'Smelly pigs.'

'No they don't, they're the cleanest animals around,' said Quinn. 'Remember on *Animal Planet*?'

Rory ignored him. 'What's your second favourite animal?'

Marg was tiring of the game. 'Aardvark,' she said.

'That's not a real one,' said Rory, with all the contempt his four years could muster.

'It is. It's a kind of anteater. From Africa.'

'It's not.' Rory shook his head.

'It is.' Marg nodded.

'No it's not.'

'It absolutely is.'

'Not!'

'When is Dad getting back?' Quinn, the peacemaker, interrupted.

Soon. Please God, soon, thought Marg. He must have heard her because her mobile started to judder on the tabletop just at that moment. She snatched it up.

'Marg. Christ, I'm sorry about this. It might be another hour or two. Look, I can give you their mum's address and you could all get in a taxi.'

There was no way she was turning up at his ex's with the ex's sons in tow. She'd pick the animal game any day. 'It's fine. I'll take them back to the flat. We can watch TV.'

'I really am so sorry. The party and now this. It's a real baptism of fire.' He tried to laugh but it sounded like it stuck in his throat.

'I'll manage,' she said.

'Can you put Quinn on?'

Quinn took the phone and listened intently. He nodded and handed the phone back.

'Dad's late,' he said to his brother. 'We're going to Marg's home.'

'To live?' asked Rory.

'No!' Quinn swatted him on the head. 'For a play.'

She hadn't anticipated that Rory would press all the buttons in the lift and they would have to stand in interminable silence as they bumped slowly through every level to reach her floor.

Neither had she anticipated that they would have assessed her TV channel options in the space of thirty seconds and found them wanting. 'No Disney?' asked Rory, with a look of such horrified pity that Marg almost laughed out loud.

And she certainly hadn't anticipated that when a four-year-old needs to go and doesn't know where the loo is, they get creative. She stood at the lounge door with the two cups of orange juice and looked at the small brown turd next to her lovely, low sofa.

'Wha—?!'

'Rory had an accident,' said Quinn. 'He . . . we didn't know where the bathroom was.' All she could see of Rory was a small tuft of hair at the sofa's other edge.

'He didn't mean to,' said Quinn defensively. 'It just sometimes happens.'

'It's okay. It's fine. Really.' Marg put the juice down and headed back to the kitchen for Dettox and kitchen roll. Not fine, actually. Getting a little out of control here. She leant on the sink, took a deep breath, then scooped up the phone and headed quickly up the hall, punching in the numbers as she went. It was picked up almost instantly.

'He's done a fucking turd next to my Heal's sofa!'

She heard Cate splutter.

'Adam got called away and I offered to sit with the boys. So I took them back to the flat. It was either that or meet the ex on my own. And now Rory. He's done a fucking turd. Right next to the sofa. The white one.'

Cate burst out laughing. 'First things first. It's not a fucking turd. It's a poo. Or maybe something else. You have to find out what they call it in their house.'

'You what? You give these things names?'

'Yup. Might be "ploppy", or "whoopsee", even. You need to ask.'

'Why?'

'So you can say, "If you need a poo, you have to use the bathroom." Anyway, you sound very echoey,' said Cate. 'Where are you?'

'In the bathroom,' said Marg. 'It's the only one with a

lock on the door. I can't get away from them. They're always wanting something. Juice. A biscuit. Better TV options. I'm just waiting for the request for a pound of flesh. Is it always like this?'

Cate couldn't speak for giggling.

'Okay, you've been a great help. Not,' said Marg. 'I'm putting the phone down now.'

'Just don't call it a turd,' said Cate. 'And especially not a fucking turd.'

Marg reappeared in her Marigolds and held her breath as she used a forest's worth of kitchen roll to lift the poo/whoopsee/ploppy – she wasn't going to ask. Rory peered furtively at her from the far side of the room. Quinn flicked idly through the channels before giving up and throwing himself back in the chair with an exasperated sigh.

Marg stood up. This was not working. 'Right,' she said, heading for the kitchen with her foul-smelling bundle. 'Coats on.'

Quinn sat up. 'Where are we going?'

'An adventure.' She opened the bin in the kitchen and deposited everything then washed her hands, twice, and grabbed her keys.

Quinn was shrugging on his jacket in the hall. 'Does Dad know?'

'I'm just going to call him,' said Marg. 'I'm taking you to my office.'

'Why?' Rory stood dutifully while Quinn zipped him into his anorak.

'It's a special day today, when children can come in.'

'Why?' asked Rory.

'It just is.' Marg shepherded them down the corridor, suddenly aware that she hadn't done her checks. No turning back now, though. How many questions would that prompt? What are you doing? Why?

She reached the lift and pressed the button, taking a deep breath as they slid towards the lobby. 'Oh, and when we get there,' she said, as the doors opened, 'if anyone asks, you're girls. Okay?'

The security guard was the first to do a double take. He nodded brightly as Marg strode through the revolving doors, trailing two small figures in her wake.

'Two visitor passes, please,' said Marg. She stood at the front desk, drumming her fingers on the shiny polished counter.

'I think you mean VIP passes,' said the guard. He winked at the boys.

'Whatever,' said Marg impatiently, anxious to be in an environment where she didn't feel so out of her depth. She bypassed the news room, horrified at the prospect of running into Rick, and found one of the smaller studios empty. She flicked on the lights and turned to Quinn.

'You like sports, right?'

He nodded, blinking in the sudden, sharp glare.

'Okay,' said Marg. She took off her coat and threw it down on the floor. 'You go and sit over there. Pretend you're doing a sports report. World Cup Final. Let's say England v Argentina. Penalty shoot-out. England are three–two down. Rooney's stepping up to the spot.'

Quinn beamed and bolted for the desk.

'What do I do?' Rory tugged at her arm.

'You're the cameraman,' said Marg. She helped him out of his anorak. 'You're going to do the filming.'

Two small voices spoke in unison. 'Cool!'

It was close to 4.30 p.m. when Adam phoned to say he was in reception. The boys charged at him when they reached the lobby.

'Dad! I got to be on film.' Quinn held up his video. 'I was in the chair where they do the sports from. Marg filmed me. I've got the tape.' He looked back at Marg shyly. 'I've got the VT, you say VT, don't you?'

She nodded.

'It means videotape,' said Quinn. 'They don't really use them any more in TV. Did you know that, Dad? But Marg got one for my bit, just so you could see.'

Adam was beaming. He lifted Rory into his arms. 'And what about you, scout? Are you famous, too?'

'I got crisps.'

'And you got to hold the camera,' Quinn reminded him.

'And I got to hold the camera.'

Adam looked up at her. She had expected the grateful smile, but she hadn't anticipated the look in his eyes. Intense and unsettling. She shrugged. 'It was take your daughter to work day, and they were getting bored so I figured . . .'

'Thank you,' he mouthed, over Rory's bobbing head.

She mouthed back, 'I should think so too,' and then she started to laugh.

'Can't take you anywhere.' Dan smiled and handed Cate his napkin. She put hers down and dabbed at the large stain of good Burgundy on her fancy bodice.

'Shouldn't you be doing this for me?' She looked over at him. He wasn't drinking and she must have had most of the bottle. She felt giggly.

He raised an eyebrow but didn't reach across.

'It's new on as well.' She dribbled some water from her glass onto the cloth and pressed it onto her chest. Trust her. Other than the spillage it had been a good night. The restaurant had the kind of downlighting that made the glasses sparkle and softened your features, and apart from another little strop about her commission money, Dan had been pretty nice. Although she hadn't got round to anything meaningful yet, and she hadn't wanted to break the mood. Maybe when they got back to the house.

He emptied the water jug into his glass and hers and stood up. 'Will you excuse me?' She watched him cross the room towards the toilets. He'd made an effort, picking out a blue shirt and a good tie. He looked beautiful. She looked down at her top, red wine on silk. What a waste. She dabbed at it again.

It wasn't the noise that attracted her, but the movement of his jacket. His phone must be going. She looked at the garment hung neatly over the back of the chair, shuddering in anticipation, pulsing with something it needed to tell. It was Saturday and late. He wore a pager for work emergencies. He wasn't on call. This must be different. She reached over instinctively and lifted the mobile from his pocket.

Text message: Read Now? I don't text, Cate, you know that.

She felt her thumb press the button and the words sprang onto the screen.

Huntrs. Now. Cn u escpe? Gll xx.

She sat completely still. It was the last two letters that had struck with the most force. xx. She steadied her other hand round the stem of her wine glass. Oh, God. Oh, God. No. She'd got it all wrong. Oh, God. No.

She looked up. No one was looking her way, at the woman with the wine stain and the phone that wasn't hers and the white, stricken face. She pressed the buttons until the message disappeared and slipped the phone back into his pocket, then lifted her glass unsteadily to her mouth.

He wove his way back across the restaurant with a blank, oblivious smile just for her, and slipped into his chair.

'If you don't mind,' she kept her voice as flat as she could, 'can we skip coffee? I don't want to be too late back for Mum.'

'No, that's fine.' He raised his hand to summon the bill.

In the car, she closed her eyes and managed to pretend that she was tired until he turned into the driveway. He switched the engine off and pulled the keys from the ignition. 'I'll run your mum home.'

'When you get back,' she said quietly, 'we need to talk'

He sighed and opened the driver's door. 'Cate, it's fine. Do what you want with your commission money. Really. I'm done going over it.'

'No.' She turned to face him, so he could see her eyes. 'We need to talk about Gill.'

37

By the time the Golf settled back in beside the Honda she
was in the kitchen, with a pot of PG Tips growing cold
on the table, the taste of Oraldene stinging her tongue and
the panic pressed deep in her chest. In the utility room,
her ruined blouse flailed around, soapily, in the washing
machine.

He must have sat behind the wheel for a moment, because
it took him longer than normal to reach the door. But not
much had been normal about Dan for months now.

He didn't speak as he came into the room, just used his
foot to pull out the chair opposite her and sat down heavily.
He had kept his jacket on. She looked up at him, hoping
he would go first, wondering if he had prepared a little
speech on the journey back from her mum's.

'Gill,' she said finally, when he stared at her expectantly.
It was a statement, not a question.

He gave a sigh. 'What about her? Cate, we've been through
this . . .'

She cut him off, horrified that he might think this was
just another awkward query. 'She sent you a text tonight.
While you were at the loo in the restaurant. I read it.'

She saw his throat convulse in an instinctive swallow.

'She was wondering if you could escape. I think that's
the word she used.' She reached for the tea and poured
herself a mug she didn't want. 'Tea?'

He shook his head, blankly.

She carried on. 'Oh, and there were two kisses at the end. Of course, if you don't text you might not know that's what a little x means. But it does. When you put an x at the end of a text, it means a kiss. Just the same as in a letter. But you do text, don't you?'

He sat back, shaking his head. 'Cate, it's just a drink. She's in the cycling group. They were going out. I couldn't go. I said I was out with you . . . it's . . .'

'Dan.'

'Cate, nothing's happened.'

'Are you sleeping with her?'

'No. God. No.' He leant across and tried to grab her hands, but she pulled them back.

'Dan, are you sleeping with her?' She stared at him, searching his face. 'Is that why you didn't, why you don't want to sleep with me?'

'Cate, no. No.' His voice cracked in anguish. 'Christ, Cate.' He dropped his head onto his arms and left it there.

'You need to tell me, Dan. What's going on?'

'Cate, I can't. I can't.'

'Can't what?' She knew her voice was rising but she couldn't stop herself. 'Can't what, Dan? Can't tell me, can't . . .'

He raised his head so quickly that she jumped. 'I can't fucking well sleep with anyone. Not you. Not anyone. Are you happy now? Is that what you wanted to hear? You're right. I can't do it, Cate. I can't fucking well do it.' He pushed his chair back, his hands pressing agitatedly on his legs. 'Do you know how that makes me feel? And you keep pushing and demanding and . . . and you know what? Gill, she doesn't want anything from me. She doesn't expect anything. She's a friend, Cate. A friend. She knows what I'm going through at work. She doesn't want me to . . . perform. You do. You want me to be everything; the perfect dad, the perfect provider, the perfect fucking husband. And I can't do it, Cate. I can't do it all.'

He looked at her, so changed, with his shorn hair and his stricken eyes. A spasm of shock and sadness gripped her and her voice faltered.

'I don't want you to perform. I don't want you to be perfect. How could you think that I . . . ?' She felt the tears hot in her eyes. 'God, Dan.'

The roar of the washing machine grew louder as it built up to its final violent spin. Dan put his head back down and closed his eyes and they sat in silence until the Hotpoint had eased into its last few faltering turns.

Cate reached across and put a hand on his arm. 'You should have said something. We should have talked earlier. I tried.'

He didn't move to touch her and she lifted her hand away, feeling a strange surge of anger. 'I've been trying everything, Dan. I've been trying to talk about it.'

'Yeah,' he said flatly. 'It's all my fault.'

'That's not what I meant,' said Cate sharply. 'Dan, don't twist my words.'

'That's what you're saying, though.' He pressed his hands flat on the table. 'It's all my fault.'

'It's no one's fault,' said Cate in exasperation. 'You've been so tied up with work . . .'

'So have you.'

She frowned. 'What?'

'Been tied up with your work.' He leant forward and pulled absently at a loose bit on the corner of one of the table-mats.

'What do you mean?'

'We earn enough, Cate,' he said. 'I'm working my arse off to earn enough.'

Cate took a sharp breath. 'What are you saying? I shouldn't work?'

He shrugged. 'I thought you liked staying home with the girls.'

'I do. I have. For more than ten years. But this is something I'm really good at, Dan, and I've been bending over backwards so it wouldn't inconvenience anyone. I thought you'd be proud of me, be interested. I'm making money. Any normal husband . . .' She realised what she had just said.

'Any normal husband?' He looked up at her.

She shook her head in frustration. 'You know what I mean. Jesus. We've got to be able to talk about this without you looking for a fight.' She suddenly remembered the lurch in her heart in the restaurant. Her voice rose. 'Hold on. An hour ago I'm reading a text from one of your lady friends and now, what, it's me? I'm the problem here? God, Dan.' She sat back and held on to the table to control her fury. 'I don't know who you are any more. Don't know what you want.'

He looked back at her with empty eyes. 'I don't know what I want,' he said.

She felt his words like a blow to the stomach and reached across instinctively for his hand, but he stood suddenly. 'Look, I think I should stay somewhere else tonight.'

'What? Where?'

'I don't know. The hospital. Guy's. Hotel.'

'Why? No. Dan, we should talk. We haven't even begun to . . .'

He shook his head and held up his hands. 'I just need some space. Okay. It's too much. It's just too much.'

She was too bewildered to respond and stood and moved over to the sink, trying to gather her thoughts, not sure what she should do. She heard his footfalls on the stairs, heard him pause outside the girls' bedrooms. Please God, let them all have slept through.

She stayed where she was until he reappeared at the door with a small rucksack. 'I'll see you tomorrow,' he said brusquely. He paused as if he was about to say something else, but then turned and headed for the front door.

She saw it shut; heard the emphatic snap of the Chubb lock, and felt the silence close around her.

Even though it was dark in the utility room she could see that the stain hadn't come out. She held the wet shirt in her hands, breathing in the fresh, familiar smell of the washing powder. Stevie's laundry basket was perched by the sink, hung about with small, discarded clothes. The top with the green mouse on the front, the trousers that were getting too short. Waiting for the wash. Waiting for the familiar routine to start all over again. Morning and Night. Mum and Dad. Everything comes up clean.

She dropped the shirt into the bin in the kitchen and took the stairs slowly. Stevie lay like an infant, one arm raised above her head in a small, fisted salute. Jo was turned towards her desk, where Hamish spun busily on his wheel. Emma was on her back, giving soft, contented snorts under the steady, brown-eyed gaze of Orlando Bloom.

In the hall Cate pressed her back into the wall. Her girls. Their girls. What if they couldn't fix this? She felt a sob rise in her throat and turned for the bedroom. When she picked up the phone it struck her that she knew the number off by heart. She managed to say, 'Hi.'

'Cate?'

She must have known instantly.

'What's wrong? Cate. Hon. What the hell's wrong?'

38

'Jesus. Men. I swear nuns have the right bloody idea.'

Cate nodded bleakly and pulled the duvet around her. It didn't stop her shivering.

'Are you okay, hon?'

'Not really,' said Cate. 'I'm just . . .' What was she? Curled, fully clothed in her bed like a sickening child. Confused, panic-stricken, angry. All and none. She didn't know. She pulled the covers tighter around her.

'I don't know what to do, Marg. I don't know what he wants.'

'Of course you don't,' said Marg. 'It's a bloody mid-life crisis. He doesn't know what he wants.'

'But he's been right about his work,' said Cate. 'I couldn't care less what was going on. I've not been to any of his dos. And I've been putting pressure on him about sex, about cycling and this Gill woman. Maybe I overreacted. Maybe I should just have let him be. I don't know.'

'Would you stop trying to blame yourself?' There was a prickle of annoyance in Marg's voice. 'You knew something was up, you've been trying to find out what. He's the one who's been holding out. God, he's a doctor, you'd think he'd have figured out there was something wrong with him.'

'Yeah, but all the stuff about impotence says communication is the key, but we can't even talk. He doesn't want to.' A sudden panic gripped her. 'Oh, God, Marg, what if he went to her? Gill. What if he went to her?' She didn't know why it hadn't occurred to her before.

'Stop it,' said Marg sharply. 'He's not gone to her. She's nothing in this. A diversion. She's like Susann I work with. Someone you talk to. But this is between you two. Okay?'

'Okay,' said Cate weakly. 'I'm just quite scared about it all now. I mean, if I'm not his friend and I'm not his lover, then what's left?'

'Don't talk like that. Okay, it's not exactly your happy ever after at the moment, but anyone who thinks they have that is deluding themselves. It's a real relationship and they can get messy. It's not the end of anything, Cate. It's out now and it's fixable. Really. And sometimes everyone and everything needs a kick up the arse. Especially a marriage.'

'But how do we sort it?'

Marg's voice softened. 'That I don't know. You and Dan need to figure it out. But you will, hon. You're a fit, the pair of you. And you've got a lot at stake, so you'll sort it. You will.'

Cate lay back against the pillow, tears sliding from her eyes. She held the receiver tight against her cheek. 'What would I have done if we hadn't got back in touch?' she said quietly.

'You'd have been fine,' said Marg. 'You'd have called that nice Irish girl, Darla. She'd have got you through.'

'Orla,' said Cate. 'But it wouldn't have been the same.'

'Sure it would,' said Marg, but her voice sounded funny. She went quiet for a moment. 'You know your mum would say it was fate that we got back together, wouldn't she? Cometh the hour, cometh the old best friend, or something like that.'

'Maybe she'd be right,' said Cate.

'You've been watching *Steel Magnolias* once too often,' said Marg gently.

Cate smiled weakly in the dark.

'You going to be okay?' asked Marg.

'I don't know,' said Cate.

'Sleep on it, hon. And call me tomorrow. Any time. Okay? I mean it. Any time.'

'I will.'

Cate laid the phone on the top of the pile of novels she'd been meaning to read since Christmas last and looked across at the other side of the bed. Flat where there should be a form, like a sleeve where there ought to be an arm. She shut her eyes against the image and willed sleep to take the emptiness away.

If it was Dan, he had snuck back in without her hearing and he badly needed a shave. Cate squinted at the large plush face grinning at her from the next pillow.

'Boo!' Stevie sprang over the top of Barty Bear and landed on Cate's side of the bed in pants, vest and one long sock.

'Boo yourself.' Cate buried her face in Stevie's shiny dark hair. She felt like hell. Must look it, too. Her eyes felt like they had been glued shut, her hair like it had been teased by a manic barber.

Stevie wriggled free and studied her. 'You were snoring, like this.' She made a sound like mud clogging in a drain. 'And you've got a mark.'

'Have I been sleeping on the buttons again?'

Stevie shook her head. She reached across and ran a small, warm finger down the side of Cate's face.

'It's a big long line. Like Scar from *The Lion King*.'

'Great.' Cate gave her a weak smile. 'I see you've got pants on.'

'I like pants now,' declared Stevie.

'That's a good thing,' said Cate.

The door swung open and Jo appeared, followed by

Emma, who didn't seem to be fully awake. They crawled across the top of the duvet and curled in beside her in an arrangement of soft cotton and long limbs.

'Where's Daaaaad?' Emma yawned.

'Cycling today,' said Cate quickly. 'Big cycle.'

'What are we doing?' asked Jo.

'What would you like to do?' Cate tried to make it sound like nothing had changed, like anything was possible.

'Can I get my hair cut?' asked Emma, studying a long, light brown strand. 'It's almost the same length as Jo's and I don't want to be a complete crone of my sister.'

'Clone,' said Cate. 'And you're not. You're very different.'

'They do ear piercing at the hairdresser's,' said Jo casually.

'Yes, they do, but no,' said Cate. 'But we could go shopping. A girls' day out. How about that?'

There was a collective 'Yeah!'

'And I want to take some flowers to Grampa today as well,' added Cate.

The girls all nodded. Everyone went quiet.

Cate turned onto her back and closed her eyes. When she opened them Dan would be there, just back from a cycle. How are my girls? he would say. Who wants a sweaty cuddle?

She would say yes and the girls would shriek in feigned horror and they would all laugh.

'There were five in the bed,' Stevie started to sing.

'There's only four,' said Emma.

'Five,' said Stevie. 'Barty's here.' She started up again. 'There were five in the bed and the little one said, "Roll over, roll over."'

'So they all rolled over . . .' sang Emma.

'And one fell out . . .' yelled Jo, barrelling over into her sisters.

Three heads turned to look expectantly at Cate.
'Can we sing something else?' she said.

Marg looked around the kitchen. Garlic press. Where the
hell would he keep a garlic press? She opened a drawer by
the sink and raked through stray cup lids, and spoons with
bright plastic handles, and half-chewed plastic straws kept
for reasons she couldn't even begin to fathom. No garlic
press. She reached for her wine instead and leant back against
the counter, listening to the faint bumps and muffled conversations drifting down from upstairs.

The boys had been ready for bed when she had arrived
at the house but had been allowed to have their supper in
the lounge while she and Adam had a drink. They'd sat like
small Victorian uncles until Rory upended his milk onto
the rug and Adam shooed them upstairs. He'd said, 'Give
me ten and bung some garlic in the cacciatore,' but he'd
been gone at least twenty minutes.

The large pot on the hob spat out a thin spray of red
sauce and Marg gave it a half-hearted stir. It smelled good
but she'd worn a white shirt. What was it with this man?
With his kids and his eternal bloody optimism and his rustic
dining options in London W9.

'Sorry about that.' Adam appeared at the door. 'They're
excited about you being here.'

'Garlic press?' said Marg.

'Don't have one.' He moved across to the counter and
slid a short, fat knife from the block. 'Should have said.
That's the thing when you split one household into two.
Someone's not going to get the garlic press.'

'Can I ask you something?' Marg watched as he slid a
clove from its oniony skin and started slicing.

'Sounds ominous.' He grinned at her.

'When you split up with Helena Christensen there,' she

gestured towards the lounge and the bank of photos on the sideboard, 'how did you know it couldn't be sorted?'

'Sorted?'

'Fixed. Mended.'

He stopped chopping and scraped the garlic into the pot. 'Why do you ask?'

'I have a friend going through something at the moment. Married, but it's gone a little bit pear-shaped.'

Adam picked up his wine and tilted it to his mouth. 'Well, there was someone else. For her part.'

'And she didn't want to give him up?'

'No, she didn't.' He put his glass down. 'But I think we were past it before then anyway. Difficult to say, really. You just realise you're headed in very different directions, too far apart to compromise.'

'Even for the kids?'

He nodded and she saw his expression change. 'Even for the kids.'

'Do you mind me asking?' said Marg.

He laughed. 'It's not exactly the kind of conversation I'd planned for this evening.'

'And what did you have pl . . . ?'

'BED!'

Marg jumped, spilling a splash of wine onto the toe of her suede sling-back. 'Shit! Pardon!'

There was the sound of stifled giggles outside in the hall then small feet thundering upstairs.

Adam swung his head round the edge of the door. 'Bed! Now.' A door slammed. It went quiet.

He turned back to look at her, saw her puzzled expression and roared with laughter. 'You thought . . . Did you think that was a come-on? Screaming "BED!" at you? I'm a little more subtle than that.'

Marg laughed, bending to rub at the wine on her shoe.

'I did wonder. But I suppose you prefer the turning-up-unannounced-on-the-doorstep kind of subtle?'

Adam shrugged and bent forward to refill her glass. 'Felt right,' he said.

She smiled back at him and said nothing. It had. It did.

It was almost 11 p.m. before they finished their dinner. Marg laid the glasses she had carried through from the dining room onto the kitchen counter and glanced down at her watch.

'I should head off. Can you call me a cab?'

He was at the bin and he turned, still holding the plateful of food scraps. 'You can stay.'

She shook her head. 'I don't think so.'

'Really. It would be okay. I'd like you to.' He put the plate down and moved over towards her. 'The boys would be fine about it. They like you.' He put his hands on her hips. 'I like you.'

She shook her head again and he laughed.

'You know, that would have been the moment for you to say, "I like you too."'

She smiled at him and took her time. 'I like you too,' she said finally. She lifted his hands away. 'But I'm not staying. Not tonight.'

He didn't press her but caught her hand and led her through to the study. 'Well, before you go, I need to show you something. I don't think he'll mind.' He bent before the computer and swivelled the screen towards her.

'Dear Faisal,' read Marg. 'My name is Quinn. I am eight. My favourite food is pizza and my favourite player is Thierry Henry. Do you like football? My favourite team is Arsenal. They're not doing so good at the moment. What's your favourite team? If you have one. Is it hot in Chad? It's raining here.'

'It's not Hemingway,' said Adam. 'But it's a start.'

'Did you ask him to do that?'

Adam shook his head. 'No. Hand on heart. It's all his own work.' He looked back at the screen. 'You know, it occurred to me someone might end up writing to your boy out there. What was his name again?'

'Amodu,' said Marg. 'And I doubt it.'

'He found help before,' said Adam. 'He'll find it again.'

'Maybe,' replied Marg. 'I'd like to think so.'

'Well, do,' he said. His voice softened. 'You're not going to find him again, Marg. So wish the best for him, even if it is against the odds.'

She realised that if someone else had said that to her, she would have cut them off with a curt what-do-you-know? But he did know, sort of, and maybe he was right. She nodded instead.

He closed the document and turned off the computer. 'Of course, Rory still thinks Faisal's going to come and live here. Oh, and talking of Rory, he asked if you would say goodnight when you left.'

'But he's asleep.' Marg looked at him, puzzled.

'Do you mind? I'd like to be able to tell him that you did.'

'Is this another strange parenting ritual? Child whispering?'

'Probably, but I'd rather say that you did than you bellowed from the bottom of the stairs.'

'Okay, okay.' She mounted the stairs behind him and went into the room, dark and still with two sleeping forms in the bunk-beds. A small foot protruded from the duvet's edge on the lower bunk.

She stepped over a collection of twigs discarded on the floor like a fallen game of pick-up-sticks. Quinn was turned away from her. Rory was facing the door. His mouth was slightly open as if he was about to speak and his glorious lashes were fanned and still on rounded cheeks.

Marg bent forward and heard the soft, steady huff of his breath. He looked almost loveable in this quiet, inert state. She lowered her voice to the barest whisper. 'Night, Rory,' she said.

39

Cate stepped into the lunge and watched herself in the wide wall of mirrors dipping unevenly towards the floor. She held the pose, wobbling with exertion, trying not to notice the small split in the crotch of her Lycra pull-ons, and the flash of dull white from her no-one's-going-to-see-them pants.

'Aaaand change.' The instructor switched legs and Cate copied him, a beat behind the rest of the Sunday afternoon class who seemed to move as one, so much faster and more focused than the weekday crowd.

She glanced at the clock. Only ten minutes to go, but she could idle over her shower and getting changed and she could chat with Tif and delay for as long as possible the moment when she had to go home or switch on her phone and know that he had or hadn't tried to reach her. She'd left the house with the girls early and had taken them to the cemetery and then for brunch and then into town before she left them at her mum's, trying to lose her thoughts in constant motion.

It had been around lunchtime that she realised she actually had no idea what she would say to him. In the warm crush of Claire's Accessories as the girls fussed over baubles and bangles, it occurred to her that had Dan appeared at that very instant she would have been at a loss as to what to say next, beyond 'What now?' It was the only thing she had been able to come up with since he had left. 'What now?'

The young woman in front of her raised her arms backwards into a shoulder stretch. Cate looked at the tangle of coloured charity bands on her slim wrist, and the small scripted tattoo above her low-slung joggers.

Maybe she was struggling with something today too. Something heavy and hurtful that belied her poise. 'You never know,' Cate's mum liked to say. 'You never know another's life.'

Cate watched the girl stretch and move, sure-footed and energetic. Or maybe her life was just fabulous, just absolutely bloody perfect, with a job and friends and a lover to meet who wanted her there.

She felt the sudden rush of anger and shame. God, shouldn't it be instinctive? Dan's physical response to her, his need for her. Shouldn't it? It always had been. She had learned very quickly what worked and what didn't. A camisole strap left fallen. Going braless in public when he knew he couldn't touch her. Her hand on his neck at a dinner party, slipped down inside his collar.

She thought back to the printout, still folded neatly in her drawer. It's not you, it had said, so often that she had worried it protested too much, a mantra for the devastated and doubting.

The instructor motioned for them to lie on their mats and curl into the first of the sit-ups. Cate lay back and pressed her hands palm down. She closed her eyes. If it really truly wasn't her, then how could she help? What could she do?

He must have parked a little way up the street because the first she knew of his presence was when she dropped her bag by the stairs and noticed the rucksack and then the flash of movement at the top.

'God, Dan. You gave me a fright.'

He came down slowly, his face impassive. 'Sorry.' He stopped on the bottom step, one hand on the balustrade. 'Where are the girls?'

'At Mum's. I'm just going to head out shortly to pick them up.'

'Did you . . . ?' He couldn't finish the sentence.

'Tell her anything?' Cate shook her head. 'No.' Even if she had wanted to she would have had no idea what to say. Dan's impotent, he's got a new friend and I don't know if he wants to be my husband any more. She suddenly wanted to add, but I told Marg and she says you're a walking bloody cliché for having a mid-life crisis. The thought made her feel a little stronger.

'I came back late morning,' he said. 'But no one was here.'

'We went to see Ed.' It had been the best thing she could have done. She hadn't been able to say much beyond 'we miss you', because the girls were there. But she had kissed the cold stone and knew the hurt he would have been feeling for her if he had known, the warm words of constancy and reassurance he would have offered.

Dan nodded. 'Your hair's wet.'

'Gym,' she said, wincing at the awkwardness between them. She took a breath. 'How are you doing?'

He gave a little shrug and moved past her towards the kitchen. 'Do you want some tea?' He spoke over his shoulder. 'I'm just boiling the kettle.'

She stayed where she was, trying to hold her breath steady. 'I'd rather know how you are.'

She heard his sigh above the click of the appliance. He didn't reply and she followed him into the kitchen and stood a little way off as he lifted two mugs from the rack.

'Dan.'

'What?' He turned and her heart sank at his tight, pained expression.

'How are you doing? Are you ready to talk?'

He sighed again, a long, slow exhalation, then turned back to the kettle. 'Can we not just have a cup of tea?'

He sounded so flippant, so bloody petulant that she had to bite her lip to stop herself snapping back at him. She moved to the cupboard and found a pack of digestives.

'We do need to talk,' she said, trying to keep her voice light.

'Cate.' He turned to face her again and raised one hand like a lollipop man.

'What?' She leant back against the hob and looked at him, crossing her own arms instinctively.

'Leave it be. Really. Leave it be. Just now. Right?'

She couldn't. 'We need help with this,' she said. 'I think we should see someone. Counselling.'

He gave a snort.

'There's no shame in having to.'

'How would you know?' he said sarcastically. He poured hot water into the mugs then ran his hands through his hair. 'Look. I just wanted to come back and not have . . .'

'And not have what?' Cate's voice rose. 'Not have me bring it up? Not talk about it?'

'Cate, leave it, please. Really.'

'I can't, Dan,' she said, swallowing the rising sob in her chest.

'Fine.' He clattered his mug onto the counter and pushed past her into the hall.

'Where are you going?' This time she followed him.

'I'm advising on a septoplasty first thing, so I'll stay at the residences again.' He spoke to her as if she were an intern, coldly and clinically.

'You don't have to, Dan.'

'I know,' he said blankly. He picked up his bag.

'So that's it.' Cate felt the first flash of proper rage since the previous night. 'We're just not going to talk about it. You're just going to run off again.'

He opened the door.

'Dan!'

He said nothing but looked back at her, a brief, bleak glance, and then he was gone. She sat down shakily on the bottom stair. The pack of biscuits was still clutched in her hand and she hurled it suddenly at the burnished wood of the door and watched it explode in a spray of crumbs and shiny paper.

The mess lay untouched for several minutes as she tried to gather her frantic thoughts. She heard the cuckoo clock in her office sound out 5 p.m. and stood to go and get the dustpan and remove all traces of Dan's abrupt departure and her angry response before she got the girls. It was in Jo's room where she'd left it after sweeping up sawdust and seed shells from around Hamish's cage. Emma had given him up more than willingly when Jo had moved out and Jo had accepted him a little reluctantly, fussing over the space he occupied in her new, still freakishly tidy room.

The water bottle was less than half full so she unclipped it from the bars and carried it through to the bathroom to be refilled. She knew she was moving like an automaton. Shriek at your husband. See to the family pet.

Back in Jo's bedroom she fixed the bottle back on and opened the small wire door to drop a fresh handful of sunflower seeds into the dish. She sat down at the desk and tapped on the bars, hoping Hamish would emerge and stretch, wanting something familiar and innocent to distract her from the awful feeling in the pit of her stomach. The small shredded nest in the corner stayed still, so she reached in gently.

He must have been dead a good while because there was no hint of warmth in his body when she lifted him from his bed. The small legs with their tiny translucent claws had stiffened into an unnatural pose and his eyes were blank and glassy. She sat back on her heels and looked down at the motionless form. Such an inconsequential passing. Such a small loss in the scheme of everything, but she felt all the wretchedness and pain and hurt and anger surge unstoppably within her. She cried for a very long time.

Marg perched on the high stool and watched as the barman pressed a glass under the optic and then slid it expertly along the counter to join the others.

'Three Bloody Marys, was it?' he said over his shoulder.

'Yup,' said Marg. 'Two rum and cokes, a vodka tonic and a Laphroaig – the ten-year-old will be fine. Oh, and a packet of chicken tikka crisps.'

'Rutner special coming up,' laughed the waiter. 'I'll bring it over.'

'It's okay,' said Marg. 'I'll wait.' She was actually quite glad to be away from the group in the corner, cloistered in the same banquettes where they always sat. She watched Rick, mouth moving, hands aloft. He was wearing a pink Ralph Lauren shirt and his belly sat stoutly above his belt. She thought for a second of Adam's body, prone and asleep in her bed last Monday, and found that she was smiling.

Deep within her Mulberry tote, her phone started to ring. She scrabbled past a log-jam of pens and pulled it free. It was Cate.

'Hey,' said Marg, more brightly than she meant to. 'I've been thinking about you.'

'Hey.' Cate's voice sounded small and utterly flat.

'Are you okay?'

'Not great, actually. Not going too well.'

'Oh, hon.' Marg shifted herself fully onto the stool and

pressed her free hand in her other ear trying to drown out the tinkling and chatter all around her. 'I was going to call you later, see if you'd managed to talk some sense into him. Not happening?'

'No,' said Cate. 'Not happening. He won't talk to me, Marg. He's just gone off again. Slammed out.'

'Stupid bugger,' said Marg, and smiled weakly at the barman when he turned. 'Will he just not listen?'

'No,' said Cate. 'I think he just wants to pretend there's nothing wrong. I don't know. Maybe he doesn't know. God, I don't know.'

'You've got to ask him,' said Marg.

'I've tried. I'm trying.' There was a pause. Cate's voice cracked. 'Marg, I think I'm going to lose him. It feels really strange. Just not right. You should have seen the way he looked at me when he left.'

'Hey, hold on there.' Marg felt a rush of anger and protectiveness. 'Why the hell are you scared of losing him? He's the one who should be scared. He's the one who should be absolutely bloody terrified that his stupid fucking intransigence means he might lose you. And the girls.' She turned on the stool and lowered her voice to an agitated whisper, aware of the furtive glances from the other patrons. 'Christ, Cate, does he want to be the kind of dad who sees his kids in some Little Chef halfway up the M8? Has he thought of that? *He* should be scared.'

'I don't think he's thinking like that,' replied Cate. 'I don't think men think that way, do they?'

Marg sighed heavily. 'No,' she said. 'Which is why, hon, if you want your happy ever after it's probably going to have to be you who has to fix it.'

'But he won't talk to me.'

'Then you have to talk to him,' said Marg. 'Lay it all out. Scream at him, if need be.'

'Tried that,' said Cate. 'And throwing biscuits.'

'Did they hit him?'

'The door,' said Cate.

'Waste of good carbohydrates.' Marg nodded at the waiter, who was gesturing to the tray of drinks, and watched as he crossed the floor to Rick's table. 'I wish I was up there. Do you want me to come up? I could maybe get a day or two.'

'No, really,' said Cate. 'You're right. I need to sort this out myself. Somehow.' She sniffed loudly. 'Oh, and Hamish died. I just found him.'

'God, Cate. Are the girls gutted?'

'They don't know yet. They're at my mum's.' Cate paused again. 'There's some kind of weird *Four Weddings and a Funeral* joke in here somewhere, isn't there?' she said weakly.

'No,' said Marg. 'Just a lot of bloody heartbreak.'

There was a longish silence.

'You still there?' asked Marg.

'Mmhm.'

Marg pressed the phone tighter to her ear, struggling to hear above the ebb and flow of all the conversations around her. 'Look, let me get out of here and we'll have a proper chat.'

'No. No, really. Go and get back to your . . . Is it Adam?'

'He's taken the boys to Chessington,' said Marg. 'I'm in Popinjays with Rick. And the others,' she added quickly.

'I should go anyway,' said Cate. 'I need to get the girls.'

'Well, I'll give you a call tonight. Okay?'

'You've got work tomorrow,' said Cate.

'It's fine,' said Marg. 'I'll call. And in the meantime, Catriona Beane, you need to go and get that man sorted. He might not know what he wants, but you can tell him what he might not have if he doesn't bloody well figure it out.'

'Okay,' said Cate. Her voice was still small but for a second Marg thought she sounded like she might.

Cate sat on the rough felted chair, staring blankly at the curtains screening the door to the consulting rooms. Why did hospitals always pick fabrics in the most inappropriate of hues? Pinkish, yellow, beige and grey, the colours of flesh and gristle. She would have chosen something vibrant, rich and life-affirming, something with a texture and a sheen. It seemed surreal, waiting for an appointment to see her husband. But he hadn't answered his mobile all last night and when she'd phoned his secretary after dropping the girls at school she said he had a gap at 10.55 a.m., so she could nip in then. 'Is it urgent?' she'd asked, ever so nice, a little perplexed. 'I could page him if you want.' And Cate had said no, even though it was urgent, because she couldn't give the reasons.

She had tried to rehearse a little speech. Once the girls were in bed, once Hamish was buried, with a few tears and much ceremony, in a little padded envelope for want of a small enough box. But every time she had tried to call and found his voicemail, the anger and the hurt grew until she couldn't think straight and she drank too much Pinot Noir from an already-opened bottle and talked to Marg again who said, 'Go get him.'

The door to the consultation area opened and a woman appeared with a small boy, dressed for school, with a small curved hearing-aid in his right ear. The woman stopped at the reception desk and bent over some forms and the boy leant over the nearest chair and swung his legs high behind him. He looked over at Cate and she gave him a grin. He grinned back then pulled a face and Cate did likewise, pushing her nose up with one index finger and pulling her lower eyelids down, enjoying the look of delighted surprise that he had lucked upon a willing adult in the waiting room of the place he can't have wanted to be.

'Cate?'

She swivelled suddenly. Dan must have followed the woman and the boy in. She stood up quickly, all plans for a haughty entrance shot to hell.

'Hi.'

He took her elbow and led her through the fleshy-curtained doorway. 'Is everything all right?'

She almost laughed out loud, but said nothing, and waited until they were in his room with its flat grey desk and moulded models of the inner ear; the delicate sculptures of the cochlea and Eustachian tubes that so fascinated the girls when they came to visit.

'No,' she said, when he had shut the door.

'No what?' He looked confused and very tired and he crossed his arms defensively and stayed standing as she perched on the edge of his desk.

'No, everything's not all right.'

'Cate.'

She cut him off.

'Dan, please let me finish.'

He rubbed his hands across his face. 'Can't this wait till I get home?'

'I didn't know you would be home,' she said sharply and felt a ridiculous surge of relief at his look of surprise. 'And I wanted somewhere where you couldn't run away from me again.' She dropped her voice. 'Dan, I don't want to fight and I know you don't want to talk, but if we just leave this be then I think that's a huge mistake. And I don't know where we'll end up. Something's not right. Really not right. Not just the physical thing. Us. We need counselling, we need help with this, if we're going to sort it.' She realised her gaze had dropped to the tabletop and looked back up at his face. 'We need help. And I want to fix it and I don't know if you do. I don't know if you know what that means.'

He started to speak but she ploughed on.

'And I'm going to keep doing my interiors. Maybe you don't like it, but I'm good at it and it's something I need to do for me. For us, frankly.' She took another gulping breath. 'And if you do decide you want to fix it, it can't just be for the girls. If you're doing it only for the girls. I couldn't live like that. If it was just for them. It has to be for us. For me.'

She knew it had come out in a disjointed rush, but she'd said her piece and he hadn't bolted and no biscuits had been hurled. She looked at him. He was staring at her and his face was pale.

'Cate . . .'

The intercom crackled viciously into life and Cate jumped. Jesus. Two minutes. Two minutes to save my marriage. Is that too much to ask?

'Answer it,' she said blankly.

He pressed the button and she listened to the apologetic tones of the receptionist.

'Uh-huh. Yeah. Okay.' He spoke automatically and lifted his finger from the console.

She stood up. 'I'll go. I need to. You think about it and we'll . . . we'll see you when we see you.'

He leant forward and caught her arm. His face was still pale but the tightness had gone. 'Cate.'

'No, really.' She pulled her arm away. 'You've got work. I just needed to say that. Okay? And I'm going.'

He pulled her back and into an awkward hug. He spoke somewhere near the crown of her head. 'I'm sorry, Cate. I'm sorry.'

She wasn't sure what kind of sorry it was, but she relaxed a little against him, thinking it almost didn't matter.

'Tonight,' he said. 'When the girls are down. We'll talk. Okay? We'll talk. When I'm home.'

She nodded into the stiff white cotton of his coat and stepped past him and out of the door. The boy and his mother had gone and the receptionist was busy with an elderly man. She pushed through the double doors and set out along the endless corridor. If this was make-believe, she thought, he would reach her at the revolving doors, where he would press his hands through the swirling glass and mouth his love and his regret. But it wasn't and he had glands to feel and tubes to check and she had to get to the gym and they were out of toilet paper and she'd promised she'd stop at the pet shop and research rabbits.

She felt her pace quicken with purpose. We'll talk. When I'm home. It might not be her happy ever after but she could live with that for now. And she could make it work.

40

Marg stood by the sinks and studied herself in the broad, darkly silvered mirror. It had been a bit of a rush that morning, what with Adam staying over again, and her straighteners had not been properly hot. She pulled at the small curl curving around her right ear and remembered the touch of a hand on her face. On the night she had first asked him to stay, on the day it had all started to happen.

The noise from the cubicle died away and Susann emerged and moved to the glass where she flicked distractedly at her perfect, unmoving hair. She was on edge. It was the awards dinner tonight and if she didn't get Best Anchor the following week would be hell, five days of pursed-lip pique. Marg was glad she was going to Heiligendamm for the G8 on Monday. Although, if she was being honest, she was nervous about tonight too. Adam had been surprisingly unfazed at being asked, obviously not realising just how momentous it was for her to consider bringing someone to a work event. But he had switched weekends with his ex so he could come, and he had promised that he wouldn't wear a kilt.

'So.' Susann sluiced her hands under the cold tap and continued the conversation they'd been having before she started hollering in cubicle three. 'How's Rick feel about you bringing Richard Gere?'

Marg turned to look at her and gave a little shrug. 'Dunno. I assume he'll be fine about it.'

'You've not told him?'

'Rick and I are not together,' said Marg. 'We never have been. And anyway, he'll have someone suitably bland and glam all lined up. He's been dating the arts correspondent again. I swear the girl has gone and had a nose job. Either that or the monitors are wonky.' She peered closer into the glass and pressed her fingers lightly under her eyes. Bags. Late night, loved-up bags.

'Probably.' Susann laughed. 'So, this guy. Does he look like Richard Gere? Or just act like him?'

Marg walked to the door and held it open. 'Actually, he looks more like Tintin.'

'The little French cartoon guy?'

Marg laughed. 'That doesn't really do him justice.'

'Well, what's he like?' Susann linked a bony arm in hers as they walked up the hall. She smelled of powder and hair-spray.

'Pretty normal,' said Marg. 'Nice.'

It was only as she took her seat and turned to face the battery of manically flickering screens that she realised what she had just said.

The world hadn't ended by 9 a.m., but Rick had come to find her. He was perched on the edge of her desk when she got back from the studio, flicking idly through a TV guide.

'You planning a night in?' Marg dropped her papers on the desk and sank into her seat, swivelling to face him.

'Never.' He grinned at her. 'I'm taking my favourite girl out on the town tonight. Fabulous media do.'

'You don't have a date, do you?' She was a little surprised. For events such as this he often had two.

He pretended to look shocked.

'Well I do,' said Marg.

'Your schoolboy?'

'He's not a boy.' She reached across and fastened the one undone button on his best Ozwald Boateng then gave his tummy a little pat and scooted her chair back. 'You'll realise that tonight.'

He leant forward and lowered his voice. 'Well, maybe after, you know, once he's gone home, you could . . . ?'

She shook her head firmly. 'No, Rick.'

'No?' He arched his best Roger Moore eyebrow. 'Not with this one?'

'No. Not with this one.'

He sat back and folded his arms, studying her closely. 'I think,' he said finally, 'I'm being discarded.'

She laughed at him, but gently. 'Not discarded, Rick. Relinquished. Reluctantly.'

He tried out the words. 'Reluctantly relinquished. Don't put that in a bulletin.'

'I won't.'

'Well, good luck to you, babe.' He bent and kissed her warmly on the cheek. 'But if you change your mind . . .'

She laughed again as he stood and stretched, gazing around the room. His eyes stopped at the arts desk. He gave Marg a last, regretful smile, and was gone.

She looked down at her own desk. So much to do before she could head home. Germany next week. Interviews to confirm. Contacts to call. Roy to meet. Outfit to pick. Where to start?

She reached across for a pen from the desk tray and her hand brushed the small well of paper-clips. She paused, then fished around among them and picked up a handful, stringing them and holding them up so they swung before her in a short silver line.

Adam was right. They joined together really rather well.

★

Cate bent over the newspaper and read the story again.

> *Conservationists have cried foul after planners yesterday*
> *narrowly approved the demolition of Abbeyhill High, despite a*
> *high-profile campaign to save the distinctive comprehensive.*
> *The building, once described by the Prince of Wales as 'a wart*
> *on Edinburgh's royal rump', will make way for ancillary offices*
> *for the Scottish parliament.*

It was Orla who had spotted the piece and had told her about in the café beside Tif's. Orla who had asked, as she always did, 'How's the lovely Danny?' And had accepted Cate's 'fine' without remark.

She had felt a little guilty that Orla knew nothing of what had happened. She was a good friend and she might have been able to help. Though not in the way that Marg had. How could it be that, after such a long absence, someone could become so integral to your life? People used the term inseparable to define closeness, but that wasn't right. Because you could be separated, time and distance between you, but keep a connection that was never lost. But she had been right in what she had told Orla. Dan was fine, more or less. He would be home soon and they would all have tea and then Cate and he would head out for another session with the couples' counsellor while her mum babysat the girls.

There had been a six-month waiting list for marriage guidance, something that had made Cate feel better when she knew it shouldn't. And it had only seemed right that she should use the money from her commission to go private. Dan hadn't baulked at the cost. So he must have realised they needed it right now, or thought they were worth it. She hoped it was the latter. She knew it was too soon to tell.

He had been to the doctor, too, who had ruled out any underlying physical cause and had prescribed Viagra, which was still on the shelf in the bathroom, wrapped tight in the pharmacy's paper bag. And as curious as she was to see how it worked, she hadn't pushed him, knowing the first move had to come from him.

The door opened and Cate's mum poked her head round it. The voices of the girls drifted in past her.

'Darling, it's almost five, do you want me to get the pasta on?'

'Would you mind? I've just got a couple of quick calls to make.' Cate smiled at her warmly. She had been such a rock when Cate had explained about the counselling, offering to babysit whenever they needed it. Though not next week when she was off to Playa Del Mar with two friends from the Ladies' League. 'I think I might take a little trip,' she had said, and Cate had hugged her.

The door closed and Cate looked back at the article.

It's thought the bulldozers could move on site within a matter of weeks. The school had begun to show cracks on its frontage . . .

Well, who doesn't have a few cracks on their frontage when you get to this age? She picked up the phone.

'Marg Holland.' The voice was brusque, a little impatient.

'Do you know, I've almost got used to you with that name,' said Cate.

'And I'm almost used to you being a Beane,' said Marg. There was a faint rustle of plastic.

'Am I interrupting?' asked Cate.

'No. You can help me decide: Ben de Lisi red silk, or pale grey Amanda Wakeley?'

Cate thought for a moment. 'Amanda Wakeley,' she said. 'It's a news do, isn't it? You want to be sleek and subdued.'

'And there's less chance of it clashing with Adam's kilt,' added Marg.

'Is he wearing one?'

'He's promised he won't but I have a sneaking suspicion he might,' laughed Marg.

'I thought you said he had good legs?'

'He does, but that doesn't mean we all have to see them.'

'I was telling my mum about him yesterday,' said Cate. 'She thinks you've found your lid. Have you found your lid?'

'Was there a reason for your call?' said Marg, archly.

Cate laughed. 'There was, actually. The school's gone. Well, going. Planners have approved demolition. There's a piece in the paper today.'

'Boo fucking hoo,' said Marg.

'Not even a little bit sad?'

'Not at all,' said Marg. 'If they hadn't been going to knock the bloody thing down, you'd never have got in touch. We wouldn't be talking right now.'

Cate thought for a moment. 'You wouldn't have met Adam. You'd be going to this thing tonight with Rick. And I'd probably be sitting here still trying to finish my dissertation.'

They both fell quiet.

'Pretty damn effective Wrecker's Ball,' said Marg finally.

'Yeah,' said Cate. 'Pretty damn effective.' She glanced up at the clock. 'Anyway, that was all. I gotta go. Got another call to make before five o'clock. You know, mover and shaker and all that.'

'Did you call that designers' website I told you about?' asked Marg. 'The one with the free ad space?'

'I'm just about to,' said Cate. 'I just wanted to let you know about the school. Phone me tomorrow, though? Let me know how your night went?'

'I will,' said Marg. She sounded like she was still lost in thought. 'But I'm thinking of going with the Ben de Lisi.'

'Why?'

'Because, hon,' replied Marg, and the rustling intensified. 'It's a red letter day and I feel like making a statement.'

Cate put down the phone then lifted it again immediately and dialled the number scribbled on the pad in front of her. Her eyes slipped to the fat box of business cards she had picked up yesterday, the ones that said Catriona Wishart Interiors in a beautiful glossy script.

The girl who answered was brisk and efficient and Cate gave her details and discussed what she needed to do to have her name included in the listings.

'Can I ask how you heard about us?' asked the girl finally, the distant tapping of keys spelling out Cate's new identity and purpose. 'Was it newspaper, magazine, Internet or other?'

'Other,' said Cate and she smiled as she spoke. 'It was my best friend.'

Epilogue

Cate eased the g-string gingerly over her thighs and winced as she pulled it into place. Jesus Christ, Marg. What were you thinking?

She looked at herself in the long mirror on the back of the hotel bathroom door and started to giggle.

'What's going on in there?' Dan's bemused voice drifted through from the bedroom.

'Just be a minute,' she shouted back. A hiccup rose in her throat and she reached for the glass of champagne on the edge of the broad marble sink. It felt like she'd been drinking since they'd arrived, although it was a celebratory weekend after all. Her diploma done and hanging on the wall, a new commission just about to start and the counselling still going well.

And Dan had booked it himself, and even agreed to the buzzards, which turned out to be sparrowhawks – beautiful ones that rose obediently into the air from their outstretched arms.

She took another look in the mirror. What to wear with a sweetie g-string? Nothing too clingy because the VPL would be hell. She reached for the fluffy white bathrobe. Dan was already in his, on the other side, waiting for her. Her shoes were by the bath, soft suede, high-heeled, but too chic to be fuck-me-now. More, I might be available. If you ask nicely. She stepped into them, took a deep breath, moistened her lips, and opened the door.

'What on earth were you doing in there?' He held out a fresh glass of something fizzy.

'A surprise,' she said. The bubbles rose into her nose.

'Well?' He looked at her expectantly. She took a deep draught of the champagne and handed him back the glass, unknotted the robe as seductively as she could and threw it open.

It was the clasp of her watch. The loose bit she'd been meaning to get fixed for ages. It caught on the elastic and snagged it and a handful of small pastel-coloured sweets pinged off and landed noiselessly on the thick pile of the carpet.

'What the . . .' Dan put down his own drink. He looked at her and her dangling, damaged g-string, then down at the floor.

'Is that sweets?'

She nodded miserably as he burst out laughing. 'Cate, you crack me up.'

She dropped to her knees and scrabbled for the fallen candy, feeling the tears sting in her eyes. Not tonight. He wasn't supposed to make fun of her tonight.

'Hey. Come here.'

She looked up, sniffing loudly. He was sitting on the edge of the bed.

'Come here.'

He held out his hand. She got slowly to her feet, little pieces of candy continuing to fall from her broken briefs. He was still smiling, trying not to laugh, but there was something else apart from amusement in his eyes. She wasn't sure, as she went to him, but it maybe looked a little bit like lust.

'Who decided that ducks like bread anyway?' Marg held up the half bag of Hovis Granary slices and waved them in front of Adam's face.

He laughed. 'No one decided. It's just something you do. Ducks. Pond. You throw them bread. Didn't you feed ducks when you were a kid?'

Ahead of them the boys chased across a wide expanse of grass, Quinn rather expertly dribbling his football, commentating as he went, Rory holding aloft a large branch he had found in a flower-bed.

'He's going to have someone's eye out with that,' said Marg.

Adam grinned and caught her hand. 'You're really getting the hang of this, you know.'

She made a face at him, but she knew he was right. In days past she wouldn't have given two small boys with a ball and a stick a second glance. She might have run right past them on one of her sessions with Roy.

So many changes. Finding Cate again, meeting Adam. And now Susann leaving, poached by NBC in New York, and Rick all lined up to take her place as anchorman. Time to try something new, he had said, and Marg had understood. She glanced across at Adam. Three days ago he had asked her to move in. She wasn't sure and had asked for more time to think about it. He'd cleared it with the boys, of course, and said they were fine about it. More than fine, in fact. Pleased.

The boys reached the edge of the grass before the pond and stopped to wait for them. Rory held out his hand for the bread. They stood and watched as the handfuls of Hovis went into the water and the ducks mobbed towards the edge.

Adam passed Marg a piece. She held it like a skimming stone and hurled it high in the air. It landed squarely on the back of a small mallard that rose in an indignant flutter.

'You're supposed to feed them, not pelt them,' laughed Adam.

'What happened?' Quinn and Rory turned.

'Marg threw the bread *at* the ducks,' said Adam. 'You'll need to show her how it's done.'

Quinn smirked and turned for another throw. Rory leapt up and down at Marg's feet. 'I want to see. Up, up.' He lifted his arms, not to his dad, but to her. She looked at him. 'Up!'

She reached down. It was an awkward hoist. A small hand snaked round her neck, knees dug into her, an elbow jabbed her ear.

'Where?' Rory scanned the water and Marg stretched out her free hand and pointed to the mallard, still sporting its scrap of granary.

Rory laughed and threw another piece in its direction. And Marg laughed too. Not at the duck with the bread on its back, but at the unfamiliar sensation of small limbs clutched around her. And at the picture that everyone else must be seeing if they cared to look. There, at the edge of the pond. Standing still and smiling. The person she had vowed she would never be. The woman with a child in her arms.